REDCOATS FOR THE RAJ

(TALES FROM A VICTORIAN BARRACKROOM)

To my friends
Roger and Jill,
Who have been bored
by hearing of this
book for the past ten
years!
Donald Featherstone

REDCOATS FOR THE RAJ

(TALES FROM A VICTORIAN BARRACKROOM)

by

Donald Featherstone

VALDA Publishing

Published by Valda Publishing

4, Abbey Walk,
Church Street,
Romsey,
Hampshire,
England,
SO51 8BU

FIRST EDITION

A CIP catalogue record for this book is available from the British Library

ISBN 0 9526861 0 4

Typeset by Amanda Jane Hill at Coup de Plume, Southampton
Printed by Antony Rowe, Chippenham, Wiltshire

"And what have kings that privates have not too,
Save ceremony, - save general ceremony?"

Shakespeare: *King Henry V., Act IV, Sc.I*

AUTHOR'S NOTE

India was the 'Jewel in the Crown' but - in the period of this story - it was a gem in a sordid setting, compounded by harsh social and racial conditions. These were the standards and customs of that time and, when reading this book, should be accepted with an historical awareness separate from that which hindsight and current belief systems afford us.

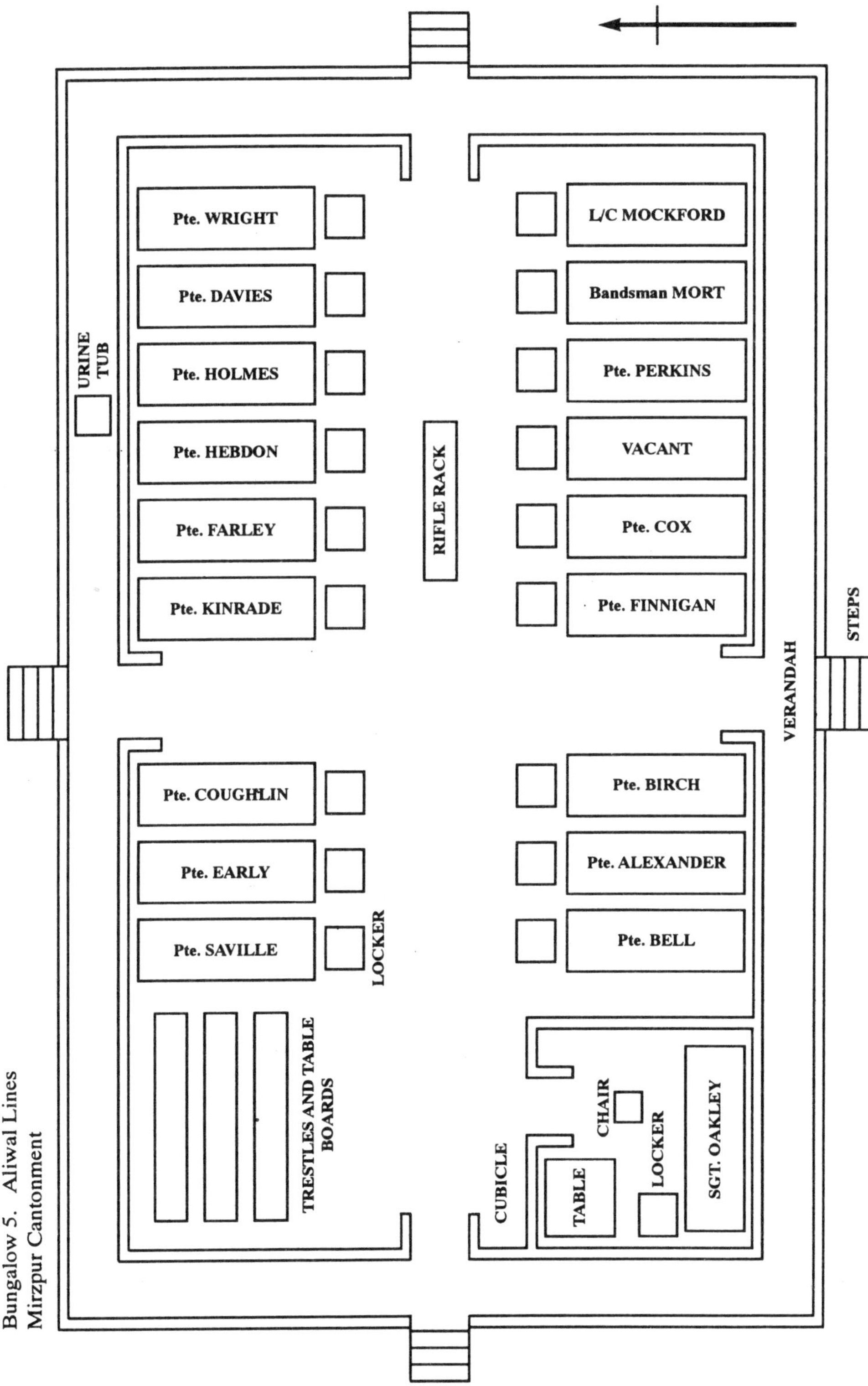

Bungalow 5. Aliwal Lines
Mirzpur Cantonment

I

The Hot Season on the Great Plain was like a mighty celestial crucible, spilling molten metal in an incandescent blanket onto the arid earth below. Natives ventured forth only in the cool of early morning and evening, but the incredible British Army drilled at dawn before shutting its soldiers in their bungalows from eight in the morning until five at night - except on Sundays when everyone paraded for church. Nothing moved on the vast, tan-coloured expanse save the dust-haloed bullock-cart, ponderously creaking along the sandy track. Sitting cross-legged under the sparse shade of the cart's mat canopy the soldier narrowed his eyes and peered through the heat-haze: beyond the undulating rumps of the plodding bullocks he could just see the shimmering outlines of distant buildings. Stiffly he stretched out a leg until his toe touched the dozing native driver who awoke with a start. The soldier nodded towards a roadside tope of mango and tamarind trees clustered around a masonry enclosed tank. The cart pulled off the track and halted in the merciful shade.

Pitching out his bedroll and pack, the soldier lowered himself to the ground and stretched, peeling off the clothing that stuck to his skin with a paste of sweat and dust. He slowly unfastened the wooden water-canteen and took a brief swig, grimacing wryly as the hot, brackish water rinsed round his dry mouth. It was spat on to the sand where it immediately vanished. Off came the white, cloth-covered forage-cap, his fingers wiping the sweat-beaded forehead, seamed by an angry red welt from the cap's hard edge: he ran a hand through his short stubble of tawny hair. With slow, economic movements, the soldier unbuckled the webbing straps. As the bed-roll opened some carefully folded white drill trousers and a red tunic were revealed. On the tunic's sleeve lay the sun-bleached sergeant's stripes and, suspended from a scarlet and white striped ribbon, a single medal bearing the young Victoria's diademed head. From the pack he ferreted out a boot brush, button stick, boot polish and some brass cleaning paste - all neatly wrapped in a grimy cloth. Easing himself down onto a rug which the driver had lain in the shade, the sergeant began by putting a shine on his buttons and regimental numbers; then the brass belt-buckle and the numerals '131' on the front of his forage-cap. Finally he rubbed at the silver medal and its two slim bars bearing the honours 'LUCKNOW' and 'CENTRAL INDIA'. The performance of these practised movements allowed his thoughts to remain far away and his blue eyes, set deep in the bronzed face, stared forward but unseeing. With unconscious diligence the tip of his tongue ran constantly across the ragged end of a heavy moustache that curved down at the corners of his mouth.

When the task was completed the sergeant rose to his feet and stripped off his sweat-blotched khaki drill-tunic and trousers, exposing his damp, clinging, cotton drawers and a white issue-shirt, ragged with rough edges where the sleeves had been torn out. The bronzed face and hands contrasted starkly with the pasty white shoulders, arms and legs, but to bare the body to the sun was an offence against good order and military discipline. And sunburn constituted a self-inflicted wound subject to punishment by court-martial. The well-muscled shoulders, flat belly and heavy, tapering thighs belied an official Army height of five feet nine inches - a sore point as he had always felt that senior NCO's should be tall and impressive.

Unlacing his dust covered, iron-tipped and studded ammunition boots, the sergeant set them to one side and opened a tin of black polish. Briskly knocking off the dust, he applied the polish and conjured up a little saliva from his dry mouth, rubbing with his finger-tips inside the polishing cloth until the scuffed boots had acquired an unbelievable shine. Then, with the boots standing sentinel on the rug, the stiff and stained grey worsted socks were laboriously removed from flaking feet and the toes were contracted and relaxed in delightful freedom. From his pack the sergeant pulled-out a harsh, frayed towel, folded to contain a sliver of yellow soap, a stubby brush and a cut-throat razor.

There was little pleasurc to be found in ablutions in the warm scummy water of the tank and soon the sergeant was rummaging in his pack for the drawers and issue shirt laundered by the dhobi-wallah at the last bullock-dak. He savoured the momentary freshness of clean linen on a washed body, aware that within minutes both he and the clothing would be sweat-soaked. With care, he slid on the spotless white trousers and red tunic, buttoning it up to the neck with a grimace of distaste. He put on a white waist-belt bearing a bayonet-frog and a sidearm on his left hip. Holding the forage-cap in both hands, he studied it thoughtfully before reluctantly removing the grubby puggaree from around its white cloth cover. The unofficial native drawers and wilfully damaged Army issue shirt would be out of sight, but he had no way of knowing whether protective neck coverings were currently authorised, and he could not return to his regiment improperly dressed.

With discarded clothing bundled into the pack and boots carefully eased on, the sergeant stood upright on the rug and, without glancing towards the native driver curled in sleep on the dusty ground, he called loudly. Instantly the native awoke and scrambled over to the rug knowing he was required to carry the sergeant on his scrawny back to the cart, the shiny boots could not be sullied. The native then rolled the bedding into the rug, placed it with the pack in the cart, and scrambled aboard for the last silent mile of the six hundred or so they had already travelled. Within a few hundred yards the red-tunic was sweat-blackened at spine and armpits; the polished boots and brasses quickly dulled with the dust's sempiternal patina.

Approaching the gates, the sergeant reflected that he felt a bloody sight better now than when last he came through them. Staring at the familiar scene he considered how nothing altered while everything was changing - it all looked the same. There was the heat-cracked and faded notice announcing to an uncaring world that this was Mirzapur Cantonment, home of Her Majesty's 131st Regiment of Foot. In the thatched matting shelter that had protected generations of British soldiers from searing sun, hard, sand-laden winds and the chill of night, the perennial sentry leaned motionless on his bayonet-fixed rifle. Coming closer, the sergeant peered into the shelter's dim interior, observing that the soldier was wearing a puggaree around his cap - sod it, then they were regulation. With a start the sergeant's voice fractured the still air, sharp and compelling as though to reassert neglected authority. 'Not asleep, are you lad?'

Shaking himself, the sentry peered out at the newcomer whose looming presence blocked out the mid-morning glare.

'No. Sarn't!'

'Supposed to challenge me, aren't you?'

'Yes ... but ... well, I could see you were ... a soldier, Sarn't ... an' I thought...'

'You're not paid to have thoughts, lad. You challenge ANYONE who comes near your post ... you understand?'

'Yes Sarn't.'

'Right, then ... make sure you do it!'

Roused by the novelty of the noise at that time of day, the Guard Commander came out on to the verandah, his heavy boots raising echoes from the polished wood floor. He screwed up his eyes against the sudden blinding glare.

'What's all this, then? What's going on?'

'Morning, Sarn't ... One three O three ... Sarn't Oakley reporting for duty!'

The Guard Commander's eyes focused on the new arrival, recognising him. 'Oh yeh ... Ben Oakley ain't it? Yer back then ... where yer bin?'

'Taking me kids to the Lawrence Asylum at Sabathu.'

'Oh yeah, heard about that ... it's a bloody long way, ain't it ... near Kussoulie ... how long yer bin gone?'

'Marched out with the Reg'ment on the cholera dodging route.'

'That were ... two ... three months ago ... bin on the go all the time, have yer?'

Sergeant Oakley nodded, weary of standing out in the sun he climbed the steps onto the verandah. 'Yep ... an' I'm sick an' tired of dak bungalows and cooter-goosht ... be a change to get back to a bit of soldiering.'

'Won't get much 'ere mate ... in the 'Ot season ... shut up in bleedin' bungalows from morn 'til night. Come inside ... there's some orders for yer on the spike.' Automatically, the Guard Sergeant put his boot into the ribs of the punkah-wallah, hunched on the boards of the verandah, pulling on the rope that rhythmically moved the matting-fans inside the stifling guardroom, he snarled, 'Cinch, you black sod ... don't go ter bleeding sleep!'

The creaking punkah and water-soaked tatties over the barred windows fought a losing battle against the heat. The whitewashed, thatched-roof building was a sombre oven, redolent with the odours of unwashed feet and bodies of the Main-Gate guard, adorned in full uniform and equipment and laying in restless repose on their charpoys awaiting their next two-hour 'stag' of the twenty-four hours duty. The Guard Commander reached for the wad of creased paper-chits impaled on the wooden-based spike. 'Ere we are ... 1303 Sarn't Oakley B ... posted ter 'C' Company ... left 'alf ... third section ... fifth sub-section. Yer takin' over Bungalow Five in Aliwal Lines. You ain't lived in a barrackroom for a while 'ave yer. In Married Quarters, weren't yer?'

Sergeant Oakley slowly shook his head, pursing his lips thoughtfully. 'C' Company eh? Done most o' me soldierin' in 'H' Company ... d'ye know what happened to the bloke I'm takin' over from?'

'Dunno ... I'm 'A' ... dunno much wot goes on in other companies ... might have been fever ... ain't 'ad no cholera since we marched out ... could be sunstroke ... or a hot-weather shooting ... take yer choice!' The Guard Sergeant kicked the nearest charpoy. 'Blake! Get yer arse off that wankin'-pit and take Sarn't Oakley 'cross ter Aliwal Lines!'

Reluctantly, the soldier slowly levered himself up, fastened his belt-buckle and collar hooks, settled a shako on his cropped head and clattered out on to the verandah. The Sergeant impatiently led off down the steps into an angry, aggressive heat that scorched the head while muddling and confusing the brain within. Hard, bright light battered their eyes into narrow slits and even the thick-soled boots could not protect feet from the heat rising from out of the ground beneath; both men felt sweat starting from every pore and prickling discomfort took over the body. The Sergeant signalled to the bullock-wallah to follow, and set off at regulation pace towards the near corner of the parade-ground, stretching baked and bare before them. He glanced sideways at the private, half a pace to the rear. 'Pick up the step, man! Lef' ... right ... lef'...'

The bullock cart trundled straight forward, towards far lines of whitewashed buildings, reflecting the sun that hurt the eyes.

'Hi, you black soor!' cried the Sergeant, 'Follow us! You never cross the parade grounds ... you always go round 'em!'

'Bloody 'ot ain't it, Sarn't? Saw a dog yesterday wiv wounds like sabre-cuts ... caused by the sun ... poor bugger wasn't half 'owling!'

A recent lack of communication with fellow-countrymen caused the Sergeant to overlook the private's informality, he nodded. 'I remember ... ten years ago ... back in '58 with General Rose chasing the Ranee of Jhansi in Central India ... elephants as couldn't walk with the soles o' feet all raw. Couldn't fire our Enfields 'cos metal swelled in the heat ... an' one day during a battle Sir Hugh himself fell off his horse three times with sunstroke!'

The private shook his head wonderingly at such thoughts.

Company lines lay before them - eight ordered rows of single-storey bungalows, facing West to best cope with the morning sun. High and long, built of light coloured stone and lime-washed annually. Standing on two-feet high brick pillars their thatched roofs extended over the surrounding verandahs. All were identical with a line of glassless windows about ten-feet up, under the eaves. There were four doorways, one on each side, covered by woven grass tatty-curtains. Ground was plentiful in India, so they were spaced well apart; in chronological order from the front, Lines were named after a battle of first or second Sikh Wars.

Thus, eight sub-sections of 'A' Company lived in bungalows in the first row of MOODKI Lines; 'B' Company in FEROZESHUR Lines; 'C' Company was in ALIWAL Lines - the Sergeant's 5th sub-section of the left-half of Company was in bungalow No. 5. The remaining Company's were - 'D' in SOBRAON Lines; 'E' in MOOLTAN Lines; 'F' in RAMNUGGUR; 'G' in CHILLIANWALLAH; and 'H' in GOOJERAT Lines. The Lines themselves, the space between each row of bungalows, were wide enough to allow a whole company of about 135 officers and other ranks to form-up on parade. Centrally situated behind the bungalows they served were pairs of low huts housing ablutions and latrines.

In the entire cantonment, the only living things seemed to be two marching soldiers and the plodding bullock-cart. A torrid brooding silence blanketed and denied the very existence of the other thousand odd men incarcerated in this symmetrical collection of bungalows. Taking a long route so that the bullock-cart could follow, the Sergeant and the private rounded the ends of 'A' and 'B' Company Lines and turned into Aliwal Lines, halting outside the fourth hut down.

'Here you are, Sarn't.'

The Sergeant fixed his eyes on bungalow 5. Private Blake drew himself up to attention, perfunctorily turned-about and, at a noticeably slower pace, retraced his steps back to the Main Guardroom. Unloading the pack and bedroll onto the verandah, the bullock-wallah dexterously caught a handful of small coins tossed at him. His mouth, opened to complain, was closed by the Sergeant's uncompromising glare, he salaamed his palms together and the cart trundled off.

Diffidently the Sergeant slowly mounted the wooden steps up to the verandah. A native boy, sprawling on the wooden boards and languidly pulling on a punkah-rope, turned his incurious eyes upon the unknown sergeant standing at the tatty-curtain. Beyond it, above the eternal hum of insects, came a monotone of male voices, broken occasionally by bursts of raucous laughter that stimulated the Sergeant's long-evaded realisation of re-birth. He was embarking upon a new style of life in a world bound by bungalow walls; a rough, sweaty community of unmarried men where all conversation was shouted and besprinkled with oaths and crude expressions. Through no personal fault or wish, he was again condemned to this hell from which he had escaped eight years before, returned to an existence where perversity, selfishness, greed, hate and ambition were incongruously balanced by rough kindness and comradeship.

Temporarily overcome by self-pity, the Sergeant quietly stepped from the verandah and went to the back of the bungalow. A cacophonous hum from black clouds of flies allied itself to the sweet stench of corruption, indicating the site of the latrine - a square hut with a thatched roof supported on four corner poles, matting walls leaving two-foot gaps between the baked earth below and a roof above. Although passing through the doorless opening was a welcome transition from pitiless heat to shade, the interior nurtured a noisome miasma, so thick as to be almost tangible, causing the Sergeant to involuntarily gag and break step. It was a ten-holer, a long wooden box occupying the far side of the hut, patterned with half-a-score of round holes over metal pails, removed by the Sweepers from outside and emptied daily. Seeking a hole that might be cleaner than others, the Sergeant saw that this had not yet been done and the acrid stench of accumulated night-soil made his eyes water, bringing him near to retching. All the holes had their own deep mahogany coloured collar, over fifty years polished to a shiny veneer by soft flesh rubbing into the wood a compound of excrement, urine and vomit. Lowering his trousers the Sergeant settled his buttocks into the hole nearest the doorway, facing the urinal trough that slanted down to the pipe and waste-bucket below. His insteps gripped the foot pole and his back rested against a smoothed plank that stretched across the hut above the box. As he knew it would, the security of forgetfulness was banished by inactivity. His mind immediately began to play out the haunting charade he seemed destined perpetually to re-enact. Effortlessly, his wife, Amy, and his children pushed aside that dogged barrier of revulsion that inevitably assailed him whenever thinking of them in such places as the foul smelling jakes. There was nothing he could do about it, he thought about them everywhere, all the time.

Memory ran its course with familiar and tragic inevitability, beginning so normally at the dawn of that unforgettable day when he and Amy stood outside the bedroom door charmed by their children's piping voices as they lay in bed, singing hymns. Later, all fresh and clean, hearty and well, the three children and their parents sat around the breakfast table saying Grace. The thanksgiving to God ended abruptly when their youngest, three-year old Timmy, cried out and doubled-up with pain. The Sergeant recalled how he had lifted the child onto his knee to catch the vomit in a napkin. White-faced, Amy rose only to sink back into her chair with identical symptoms. He remembered how the sun's heat retreated before the chill winds generated by the Angel of Death. He had seen cholera often enough to recognise it now, unaware that twenty-seven of his comrades had already died overnight from the fearful disease.

Ignoring personal danger, the Sergeant had sat in the hospital cholera ward between the cots that bore his wife and child. He had watched them suffer cruelly, had prayed to take upon his own body their sickness, intestinal pains and dysentery. Despite frequent drinks to relieve their unremitting thirst, mother and child dehydrated and shrivelled up before his eyes, turning from beloved living people into wasted bags of skin and bone. By mid-morning he had lost them both, and before the midday sun had reached its zenith, Amy and little Timmy were laid in a common grave, wrapped only in sheets, the numbers of dead having outstripped the supply of coffins. In twenty-four hours the Regiment lost four officers, a colour-sergeant, two drummers, eighty-seven rank-and-file, five wives and eleven children. The Sergeant, who would have thanked God to be among them, remained unscathed.

When his first fierce grief had abated, he understandingly recalled a fellow-sergeant in a past epidemic, losing his wife and all four children. The distraught man had gone to the cemetery in the dead of night and dug down to his poor wife for a last kiss. It was a fatal embrace and at daybreak he was laid alongside those he had loved too well. The Sergeant knew he would never do that.

In care of the sergeant-major's wife in the next bungalow, the Sergeant's children - five years old Clara and seven years old Danny - were an immediate worry as a way of caring for them had to be found. Later that day the Colonel's Lady solved the problem when in kindly, but authoritative manner, she outlined to the numbed Sergeant a plan devised by her harassed husband and the Adjutant. She explained that now he was officially unmarried he could not continue to occupy a Married Quarter and would have to live in a barrackroom; this meant that his children could not receive necessary care and attention. At nightfall, the Regiment, together with all the wives and children 'on strength', were packing-up and moving out on a cholera-dodging march. The Sergeant and his motherless children were to go with them until a point was reached where it was considered that the epidemic had been outstripped. Then the Colonel had kindly authorised the Sergeant to take his children in a bullock-cart to Sabathu, to the Lawrence Asylum for orphaned children of Other Ranks. Leaving them there, he would rejoin the Regiment as quickly as possible. Of course, if later on the Sergeant re-married, some means could be found of fetching the children from the Asylum and his family would be re-united.

In the painfully silent bungalow the Sergeant had gathered together some clothing and necessaries for the children. He pocketed a few of Amy's trinkets, brokenly glanced around, then marched without backward glance from the happiest phase in the thirty-one years of his life. At midnight, after seeing his children settled in a bullock-cart with another family, the Sergeant paraded with 'H' Company and the regiment marched out. At the head of the column the Band played them on their way with the Regimental March - The Dandy 'O'

For nine days they marched into the wind before the cholera burned itself out, pitching camp after each day's route and continuing the next morning if anyone had fallen sick during the night. Before turning back, the Regiment lost another two officers and thirty-six men, two more wives and nine children.

Devoid of fatigue or any other physical reaction, the Sergeant automatically plodded through mile after mile of dusty track with all the time in the world to ruminate and brood. In the march's early stages he was consumed with fear that his children would be ill or dead when he rushed to see them at the new camp-site - they did not even have the dubious medicine of the man-in-the-ranks tot of rum.

Then came the day when he handed his Snider rifle into the QM's wagon, pitched his bedroll, pack, and the children's few belongings into the bullock-cart, clambered aboard and instructed the native to head towards the hills. The Regiment, and a straggling tail of native followers stretching over two miles of road, set off in the opposite direction, retracing the steps of their journey to nowhere.

As far as was possible, the Sergeant enjoyed the next thirty days, by far the longest period free of Army routine since he enlisted fifteen years before. Changing bullocks every ten miles allowed a leisurely twenty miles a day, stopping for the night at dak-bungalows. He discovered unknown facets of his children, enjoyed them and their spontaneous pleasure at the monkeys, birds, fakirs, dancers and the whole colourful panorama of India. At last the morning arrived when their seemingly timeless progression was overtaken by reality. The protective cloak of escapism dropped from his shoulders on the day he left his children with strangers, perhaps never to see them again.

For nearly half an hour the Sergeant sat hunched on the wooden latrine-box, his forearms resting on bare thighs; then, shaking his head, he looked around as a man waking from sleep. He did not feel so bad now about thinking of them in this stinking place, after all, every soldier knew that the shit-house was the only place in the Army where a man could be alone to sit and think. Resolutely he stood up, tore a piece of newspaper from the nail in the plank behind him, pulled up his drawers, tucked-in his shirt, tugged down the tunic and straightened the cap on his head, cropped by native barber at the last dak. He rubbed the dust from his boots with a pad of newspaper. Straightening up to full height he pulled back his shoulders, drew the chin in and eyes in an expressionless face stared directly to the front. The Sergeant marched out of the latrine like a Marker taking position on the Ground for Commanding Officer's Parade.

II

There exists in the rank-and-file an habitual apprehension immediately aroused by any unexpected, and subsequently threatening, sight or sound so the Sergeant's clarion clatter up the wooden steps and across the verandah boards triggered off an instantaneous reaction, producing a hushed black void beyond the damp khas-khas grass tatty-covered doorway.

His immediate impression was of overpowering heat and stuffiness and a blend of odours. Dirty sweating bodies and feet, stale food, rifle oil, unwashed blankets and stale straw palliasses, all combining to form an almost forgotten barrack-room smell. Only the rhythmic creak, creak of the punkahs hung in the air. As at sea where the rise and fall of the ship puts the ears under continual assault by creaking timbers and metal so during the Hot Season the bungalow was never free for a single moment from the noise of moving punkahs. Nothing spurred men into action more quickly than a punkah-wallah ceasing to pull on his rope, causing them to leap passionately from their charpoys, kick out ferociously and howl the time-honoured formula, "Cinch ... you black bastard ... cinch!"

The dramatic transition from bright sunlight to semi-darkness momentarily disconcerted the Sergeant and he took only three paces into the room before his moving foot completed its pace and the rear foot came up into line, bringing him to a crashing halt that echoed from high walls. Standing erect and motionless and fighting off the urge to blink his eyes - which might possibly be taken for nervousness - he sought desperately to adjust his vision to the gloom. White, blurred faces in twin lines stretching along both sides of the room swam into focus, gradually taking on aspects of individuality and becoming startled, resentful or expressionless. Some were bearded, moustachioed or clean shaven. Some were balding but most had hair, of various hues but all uniform in being close-cropped. It became apparent that each face topped a body, in various stages of undress, recumbent upon matching lines of low charpoys placed regularly along the side-walls. Stretching like stepping-stones into the dim and distant confines of the barrack-room a black metal locker stood at the foot of each bed, solidly anchored in the centre-space between the lines of beds. Their apprehension was justified when the invader ruptured the still air.

'Fifth Sub-section! Come on ... let's be having you! Stand to your beds ... come on ... come on ... look lively!'

Reluctantly, men levered themselves slowly up, dropped their bootless feet onto the dusty flagstone floor and formed-up in ragged semblance of military stance at the foot of their beds. Noting for future reference that a tall, lean, dark soldier, about halfway up the room on the left-hand side, moved with such studied indifference as to be last into position, the Sergeant paced slowly up the room, timing words to steps. 'My name is Sergeant Oakley ... Benjamin Oakley ... I am 5th sub-section sergeant ... and in future I will expect you to move a bloody sight sharper than that! Who's the room NCO?'

In stockinged silence a figure marched out of the shadows to halt a yard away, brought heels together and drew himself up. 'Lance Corporal Mockford, Sarn't.' He was an old soldier, plump and balding, with a grey-flecked beard. Despite the heat the buttons of his sweat-stained grey-flannel shirt were done up to the neck in regulation fashion.

'My kit's on the verandah ... have it brought in, Corporal.'

'Sarn't! ... Saville, Birch ... bring the Sergeant's kit into his cubicle!'

In nervous haste, two men standing by their beds near the door noiselessly clicked their boot-free heels together and doubled out, returning to dump the pack and bedroll in the corner cubicle: a relatively private area partitioned off by matting stretched upwards from the floor half-way towards the beamed ceiling above.

It was a high room, forty-four feet long by eighteen feet wide. Walls were fifteen feet high with thirty-two small glassless window apertures set high under the roof beams and there were four doorways, one at either end and in the middle of the side walls. The doors fastened back and the spaces were covered by tatty-curtains. Along each side-wall, exactly twelve inches apart, were positioned nine charpoys - native beds - six feet long by two feet six inches wide. Made up of four low wooden posts supporting a rectangular bamboo frame and bearing a knotted string mesh, each charpoy was covered with a lumpy straw palliasse and a rug or blanket. Boots wrapped in a towel served as a pillow. Each bed-space was identical to its neighbour. Scrubbed and whitened webbing-straps and equipment hung on wall-hooks in a regulation pattern; mess-tins, mugs and water bottles sat on small shelves high above the beds; men's issue-clothing and a few personal belongings, together with a rifle-bolt and bayonet, were kept in the black tin-box squared-up at the foot of each charpoy. To prevent militant tribesmen arming themselves with stolen rifles the weapons were kept together in a strong rack, weighing five or six hundredweight and bolted to the floor. A heavy lid dropped to lock over the muzzles and strong chains passed through the trigger-guards to a padlock at the end of the rack. The bottom end of the bungalow was taken up by the room NCO's cubicle, ten feet long by six wide, fashioned by four posts supporting the matting screens and a gap left as a doorway. Opposite was an open area used for stacking table-boards and trestles when not erected for meals.

The Sergeant's gaze travelled slowly from man to man; some met his eyes, others, without moving their heads, looked away. The lance-corporal remained steady, looking at nothing in particular.

'Room! Fall-out ...dismiss!'

All turned raggedly to their right, briefly paused and then dispersed, resuming lolling postures on their charpoys; some muttered to neighbours but most lay back in reflective silence. Turning on his heels and followed by Lance-Corporal Mockford, the Sergeant moved into his cubicle. Primitively furnished, it included such privileges of rank as a rush mat, bamboo table and a string-seated chair. The Sergeant gazed quizzically at the charpoy, sagging miserably. Knowing that his arse would touch the ground he turned to the lance-corporal. 'Get that restrung ... and I want some dhobi-ing done ... want 'em back by tonight.'

'Sarn't Digges were a heavy man ... bigger'n you, Sergeant.'

'What happened to him?' Following the Corporal's upraised eyes, the Sergeant studied the beam above, marked by a large stain that a hasty lime-wash had not obliterated,

'Hot-weather shooting?'

'Sarn't Digges put the muzzle of the Snider in his mouth an' blew orf the top of his head.'

'Why?'

'Dunno ... really ... none o' my business ... 'e let things upset 'im.'

'It's part of your job not to let things upset your Sergeant ... I'll expect more than you apparently gave Sarn't Digges!'

The lance-corporal opened his mouth and closed it without saying anything. Dismissed, he turned-about and left. In due course natives sidled in for the charpoy and dirty washing. The Sergeant transferred the few remaining items from his pack to the tin-box, reflecting that the less you owned, the less you had to worry about. He got out of his number ones, hung them up to dry and put on khaki-drill fatigue, trousers and a grey flannel shirt. He removed the dust from his boots and put a shine on them, likewise with the brasses on the red tunic, belt-buckle and cap and looked at his watch, still only eleven o'clock, another hour to dinner.

Eight years absence had undoubtedly dimmed the memories of barrack-room life, but the old rule 'in bed or out of barracks' still prevailed; as the long hours slowly droned themselves away, save for periodic visits to the urinal tub on the verandah not a man stirred from his charpoy. The tempo suddenly changed at noon as men pattered up to collect table-boards and trestles from the pile outside the cubicle, setting them up in the aisle between the beds. The last board was barely in place when a ragged cheer heralded the entry of four natives bearing smoke-blackened dixies which they set down on the middle table, despite curses from a man sitting up on his bed.

'Not that board again, you black soors ... I scrubbed it yesterday! ...why does it always have to be on my bleedin' table?'

'Shut your gob, Hebdon! You want your fucking scran don't you?'

Picking up a tin plate, the Sergeant walked out to where the Lance-Corporal was serving food from the dixies, fishing from the soot-encrusted pot a large lump of steaming grey meat dripping with grease-gobbetted gravy.

'What are we eating?'

'Today's Wednesday, it'll be red mutton Sarn't. The stringiest salt beef you ever ate ... tomorrow it's mutton ... might be chops ... but it's bloody goat anyway ... not sheep. We gets stopped over three annas a day for muck that ain't worth a bleedin' light even afore them native cooks get at it.'

The crowd around the table nodded in morose agreement. Hearing murmured complaints about dinner-ale not being ordered although there was a senior NCO in the barrack-room, the Sergeant told Lance-corporal Mockford to take names and money for the next day, and he'd get a chit from the company sergeant-major to show the canteen sergeant.

His tin plate heavy with a slab of meat, boiled potatoes and bullet-hard peas and a wedge of grey suet pudding and a hunk of wheat flour bread on his other plate, the Sergeant moved away as Lance-Corporal Mockford cried out, 'Are you all ready for me to bob-out the who-shall?'

'Hurry up, we're bleedin' starving!' Was the response.

The Sergeant turned. 'Bobbing-out? I haven't seen that done in years ... thought it had died out.'

'It has really, Sarn't ... but we though it'd be a bit o' fun ... makes bloody awful scoff a bit more interesting!'

Hacking at the tough meat, Mockford dumped a lump on each of the tin plates laid on the table. When all were filled he tapped a plate with knife-handle as the man on the right turned his back.

'Who shall have this?'

'I will!' The man turned and grabbed the plate. 'Come on, give me plenty of gyppo,' he shouted, helping himself to peas and potatoes.

The repetitive formality tediously unrolled itself, the majority accepting the tapped plate but objectors being cursed and reviled. Conforming to established custom, every one moaned about his portion, exhibiting it as being all bones, fat and gristle, which it was. Finally all were settled, silently shovelling down the food as if haste would disguise unpalatability. Although the tables stretched the length of the room it was difficult to use them, the low tin-boxes on which men sat only allowed heads and shoulders to project above the scrubbed boards so most men balanced their plates on knees. Intermittently, Private Hebdon swore about his tabletop, swimming in gravy and gobs of fat purposely spilt by the server in the hope of stirring up a row that would relieve the boredom.

Tables and trestles noisily dismantled and packed away, pots removed by chivvied natives, vitality sapped by heat and the heavy meal, men resumed their recumbent postures and for three hours a torpid blanket hung over the room, broken only by snores, wheezes, belches, farts and drowsy mumbling. The struggle back from languid depths was heralded at half past four by another clatter of trestles and boards. A single table was set up to hold bread and coffee, the last official meal of the day, eaten standing as though men, satiated by rest, were impatient to cross a start-line and be off on a race to nowhere. Strangely contrasting with the inactivity of past hours, everyone now moved purposefully, carefully unfolding charpoy rugs to reveal clean khaki-drill, creased and pressed throughout the long day by the warm weight of bodies. Next, brasses - crested buttons, belt-clasps, badges, buckles and numerals - were isolated in button-sticks and vigorously polished with paste-coloured rags. Almost caressingly, dust was removed from the gleaming toe-caps of 'best' boots, kept for parades and off-duty wear, before they were subjected to a ritualistic circular rubbing with a rag-covered forefinger coated in boot polish and supplemented by regular drivels of saliva.

The Sergeant, gazing upon the activity from his cubicle doorway, recalled the days, weeks, months, and years when he too had been an ant in such stirred ant-hills. Then, realising that once more the role had been thrust upon him, he hastily became one with his sub-section in turning himself out in a smart and soldierly manner, as though for an evening in Aldershot, or some other English garrison-town.

Sharp at five came the signal that started the feverish off-duty race, and ended the monotonous, inactive nine hour Hot-Weather blanket-drill, officially recognised as a 'Parade'. Dotted around the cantonment, buglers manfully blew thin lilting notes that forced a way through the heavy sultry air, musical keys to open bungalow doors and release blinking heavy-eyed other ranks like boys from school.

Ablution tanks and troughs became muddy morasses as men jostled and pushed, dabbling their finger tips in turgid brown water so as to moisten sleep encrusted eyes or sweat-salted brows. Perfunctory as washing was, shaving was a hazardous enterprise that put noses, ears, lips and throats at considerable risk. Men, shoulder to shoulder and cheek by jowl, sightlessly wielded open razors that were far sharper than their bayonets and remorselessly scraped away at their faces to attain a smoothness of face, essential for both evening activities and parades on the following day.

Rank gave the Sergeant the privilege of carrying out ablutions within his cubicle, washing from a tin basin and shaving with the aid of a sliver of mirror on the wall. From freshly laundered clothing laid out on the re-strung charpoy, he selected khaki-drill tunic and trousers and fitted a clean cloth-cover to his forage-cap.

The Sergeant had already checked that none of the utensils - broom, bucket, etc., - on charge to the bungalow were missing. Before going to the Mess he did a tour of inspection of the hut's surrounds, as they were his responsibility. With his boots maintaining a staccato rhythm on the bare boards, he marched around the verandah, arriving at the site of the urinal-tub as it was being removed by the sweepers, carried by a stout bamboo-pole through its rope handles. Heavy with urine accumulated since the previous day, the large wooden tub was so awkwardly lifted by the two scrawny natives that its contents slopped over the side. This daily performance had transformed a large area of verandah floor into a foul smelling, mouldy, fly-infested patch. Regulations ensured that the tub was always sited on the northern side of each hut, mid-way between middle and top doorways, three yards from each, and exactly in the middle of the verandah. Long ropes were extended up, down and across the lines, each bisecting the urine tubs on their respective verandahs and so forming an exact chess-board pattern. The time taken walking around the verandah and cursing the sweepers allowed the barrackroom to clear. Men freshly-shaven and immaculate in their clean, pressed khaki-drill, hurried off to the canteen, the 'Rag' or the bazaar. Guarding the rifles padlocked in their racks, a solitary soldier lay reading on the charpoy opposite the cubicle. As the Sergeant approached he jumped to his feet, coming up to attention, eyes fixed on an invisible point above the Sergeant's head.

'Three seven six eight Private Saville, Sarn't!'

'Stand easy ... what are you reading?'

'Chaucer's 'Canterbury Tales', Sarn't.'

The Sergeant nodded. It did not mean anything to him, but then, you saw very few men reading books in barrack-rooms, although this lad's voice was educated. The Sergeant studied him - young, perhaps 21, soft-brown eyes in a fresh sensitive face far removed from the usual pinched and furtive features of youthful other-ranks. The fair down of a potential moustache shaded his upper lip. The Sergeant surmised that he might well be having a rough time in the ranks, probably get a few of the older men after him too.

That evening in the Sergeant's Mess confirmed the reality of Sergeant Oakley's return to Regimental Duty, although he found a certain comfort in the fellowship of boisterous senior NCO's industriously engaged in their nightly routine of drinking away boredom. The quantities of brandy, grog, arrack, gin, port-wine and ale consumed in the Mess were notorious. The Sergeant, living in Married Quarters, had never been a great one for boozing and was an infrequent visitor, a fact that had not escaped the notice of the Mess President, Sergeant-Major Robinson.

One of the earliest winners of the Victoria Cross, at the Alma, first battle of the Crimean War, in September 1854, 'Robbo' Robinson was now middle-aged and had gone to seed through heavy drinking. He was still a very large and impressive character whose sheer bulk and presence dominated NCO's, lower ranks, and even many officers. Running the Regiment with an iron hand, he was quick to detect and stamp on anything that might disturb the uneventful progress of other-rank existence - such as a bereaved young Sergeant, softened by years of married-quarters, harshly exposed to barrack-room bachelordom.

Throughout the aimless evening the Sergeant, aware of his ruminative almost baleful scrutiny, had expected to be summonsed to the Sergeant-Major's presence. Eventually, when the last of the great man's cronies had departed, he was called to the Sergeant-Major, sitting at his small wooden table and was curtly motioned to sit. In drink but far from drunk, his low-pitched unemotional voice, far removed from habitual fearsome parade-ground bellow, had a menacing edge not lost on the Sergeant. He was keeping an eye on him ... he had to remember that barrackrooms were far-removed from Quarters ... the Hot Weather routine made him captain of the ship for two-thirds of the day ... alone, like God ... in sole charge ... a lonely existence sitting in the cubicle ... that didn't mean he could mix with lower-ranks ... it was easy to relax and impair discipline ... they were a bleedin' bad lot in his bungalow who had got out of control without a proper room NCO ... Sarn't Digges wasn't a good disciplinarian ... couldn't hold his drink ... I want to see you in the Mess, being sociable with fellow sergeants ... you need 'em 'cos no man can carry on alone ... or you'll end up like Joe Digges ... with a Snider muzzle in your mouth.'

The Sergeant listened, nothing he could say, he wasn't expected to say anything. The Sergeant-Major was more or less right, there was an accepted pattern of life and everyone had to conform to it; one could not defend men whose names had yet to be learnt, and they seemed to be about the same as any sub-section. Walking through the sweltering night the Sergeant realised that this identification with his men was about the only reassuring feature of the day.

Lights-out was 9.30 and, with twenty minutes to go, about half of the sub-section had returned. Some happy and talkative, others sullen and withdrawn, faces wearing the many masks adopted by bored men drinking for what it did to them rather than because they liked it. When the Canteen doors opened at 5.30, a parched avalanche poured into the bar; the same men, their thirst still unassuaged by warm ale, reluctantly stumbled out into the warm darkness when stop-tap was called at nine o'clock. For three and a half hours they had been purposefully swilling down local beer at sixpence a quart, grog (Bengal rum), or native arrack, watered down earlier in the day by the Canteen Committee in the presence of the orderly officer. The Canteen had to accumulate a cash reserve, spent on soldier's comforts and new cap covers, and used as a fund for soldiers' widows, or as gratuity for men and their families returning to England. To enable this to be achieved, a blind eye was turned to the general order that a man could only buy one dram of grog at opening time, a pint of beer between six and seven, another grog between seven and eight, and a final pint of beer to last him until stop-tap.

Not everyone patronised the Canteen. Some men went to the bazaar to dig an early grave by drinking darro, a native firewater stronger than brandy at two-pence a bottle, or Billy-Stink made from wood alcohol. Those men who, through boredom or sheer stupidity, persisted in these habits, usually achieved their aim of getting out of the Service, through blindness, pain, loss of consciousness and finally death. A boozing expedition into the bazaar almost inevitably included having a woman, with equally unpleasant results through diseased native prostitutes, or, worst of all, up against the wall in an alley with a Sand Rat - a woman so diseased that she had been thrown out of even the sleaziest native brothel. Periodically, most men had to make the unenviable choice of going to the canteen for a wet, or visiting the Regimental Brothel, the Rag, where large numbers of customers and the few clean and supervised girls made for such lengthy queuing that a man could not reckon on getting a drink as well. It was generally accepted as good for the health to regularly get dirty water off your chest, and most men paid weekly visits to the Rag.

The Sergeant knew that any soldier asked as to why he drank away his off duty hours would, after scorning such a stupid question, say the only way of coping with the heat and insects and thereby avoiding a sleepless night, was to go to bed drunk. Gazing down the room from the doorway of his cubicle the Sergeant noted that the men in beds at the far end already had their heads down; old soldiers, if left to themselves, would come quietly into the barracks, steal into bed and remain there until reveille.

With lights-out only minutes away a soldier pushed through the tatty-curtain at the top doorway. His cap gone, tunic blood-spattered and torn, red faced and dripping sweat he weaved unsteadily down the room until he reached a man lying fully dressed on a charpoy, eyes closed and breathing heavily through an open mouth. The drunk halted and stared down at the humped figure. 'Why! It's ole Taffy! 'Allo mate ... it's Hebby, your ole pal ... 'ere Taff ... wake up ... I wanna talk to yer!'

Leaning forward to shake the sleeper, Hebdon lost his balance and fell sprawling across the charpoy and its occupant. Startled by the sudden attack, the man convulsively sat up and hit out at the invader who now found himself involved in a desperate struggle. The charpoy collapsed and the two men rolled about on the floor, grappling, gouging and punching, furiously bellowing.

'Fuckin' Hebdon ... I'll kill you ... wakin' me up!'

'You, you stupid ole cunt ... bleedin' Welsh git ... you're too old ter kill pussy!'

From all parts of the room men drifted up to see the fun, surrounding the fighters and shouting encouragement, pushing them back into contact when they rolled apart. The Sergeant came to the door of the cubicle. 'Shuddup! It's bloody lights out! Room! Attention!' He advanced to the fringe of the fracas. Like a bucket of cold water, the voice of authority poured over them, catalysing with training and habit to produce silence and immobility. Taffy, suddenly free, pitched across the floor and laboriously struggled to his feet, gasping for breath and glaring around like a baited bull seeking the enemy. He was middle-aged and balding, his heavy, black beard matted with blood from his nose. Bloodshot eyes peered out from his lowered head and focused unsteadily as he lurched toward the nearest man, fists raised.

'Taffy! It's the Sarn't!'

The sharp call penetrated his befuddled mind and Taffy halted. He slowly lowered his arms and painstakingly drew himself up to attention.

'Sorry, Sarn't ... 4375 Private Davies reporting for duty.'

Curtly ordering all to bed, the Sergeant went round the bungalow turning down the oil lamps that dimly lit the stuffy insect-ridden room. He was relieved that the old soldier had regained his sense of discipline. Striking a superior officer was one of the most serious offences a soldier could commit, possibly carrying a death sentence if confirmed by the Commander-in-Chief; when there had been a number of recent cases it was considered a deterrent.

A threadbare blanket protecting his naked body from voracious insects, the Sergeant composed himself for the torturing nostalgia that invariably preceded an uneasy sleep. His emotions were tinged with guilt at not having thought of Amy and the children since mid-morning; even now they were not coming through as clearly as usual, their sweet faces revoltingly taking on images of the Sergeant-Major and the men of the barrackroom.

Night came as a remission rather than a reprieve. Although there was no sun to burn, the air was hot and heavy and resounded with insects whose ministrations could drive a man nearly mad. Overriding their humming was the continuous night noise of restless men - snores, coughs, incoherent mumbling and sudden startling outbursts of crying or shouting, as itching bodies, bathed in sweat, tossed and turned, joylessly consuming the few short hours when a soldier was allowed to command himself.

III

It was still dark at 4.30 am when from all corners of the Cantonment, drowsy, unwashed boy-buglers, eyes puffy from restless sleep, split the still air with the reveille call - "Rise soldiers, rise, and put your armour on!" Through the discomforts of the night, none arose with alacrity. Presently the shirt-sleeved sergeant emerged to aid Lance-Corporal Mockford in getting the room to its feet.

'Let's be 'avin' you! Ek dum!'

'Rise and shine! The sun's scorching yer eyes out! Come on ... get outa them pits!'

In his time the Sergeant had known many room NCO's who unceremoniously tipped beds over, shattering the air by banging on table-tops with staves. He hoped that this lot would never provoke him to so brutally return them to their harrowing daily cxistence.

To be on parade at 5 o'clock meant that a man had time only to throw on fatigue dress, make up his bed and tidy the area around it, pull through and rub an oily rag over his rifle. With luck he might get into the latrine without queuing too long, a blind eye usually being turned to men who used the night urinal tub in daytime. Few men washed, shaving had been done on the previous night and, unless bread had been saved, no man ate until breakfast at 8.30.

At 5 am, with the fast rising golden orb of sun bathing the Cantonment in an illusory mellowness, the bugler sounded 'Assembly' and signalled the start of the daily Regimental business. From sixty-four symmetrically spaced bungalows men poured out into the dusty Lines, like torrents of water finding their own level they formed their sub-sections in two ranks at close order; files nearly touching, tallest on the right, shortest on the left. They fell-in with arms at the order, rifles held upright at the right side with the butt on the ground in line with the toes of the right foot. The right arm bent slightly, holding the rifle below its muzzle with the backs of hand to the right, fingers together and slanting towards the ground, thumb against thigh. After taking position and checking that dressing was by the right, each soldier automatically stood himself at ease, keeping his legs straight and carrying the left foot twelve inches to the left so that body weight was rested equally on both feet. At the same time the rifle muzzle was inclined slightly to the front with the right hand arm close to one side and the left arm remaining in the position of Attention.

The repetition of the years ensured that assembly was completed almost simultaneously by all sub-sections, who were then brought up to Attention by their sergeants and ordered to dress their ranks. The tallest file on the right flank of each group stood firm as every head swivelled sharply and right arms jerked upwards so that fingertips touched the shoulder of the next man. This sudden revision of spacing, with the need to get into line set up much foot shuffling, accentuated by loud verbal directions from the lance-corporals positioned on the right flank to ensure that each line was unwaveringly straight. When deemed satisfactory, sergeants ordered "eyes front", and heads resumed their normal positions and arms dropped to the sides. Next, sub-section commanders moved slowly down the ranks from right to left, inspecting their men to ensure that all were fit to face the scrutiny of more senior eyes. Faults in tidiness, cleanliness or length of hair and lack of shaving caused the offenders name to be 'lost' - written in a notebook as a prelude to punishment.

Inspecting the 5th sub-section the Sergeant surveyed each man from head to foot, then asked his name. Birch, tall, thin, fair, heavy moustache. Saville, a very young man, slim sensitive features, perhaps a disgraced younger son or gentleman-ranker. Kinrade - the man who moved slowly yesterday - dark, saturnine, deep-set eyes carrying a trace of mockery. Alexander who made three stuttering attempts to give his name was the most unsoldierly man in the group, short but gross with a flabby acne-ridden face, loose wet lips, half-closed piggy eyes, probably mid-twenties. Hebdon, last night's fighting drunk, bore a young open face with a natural comical expression and giving the appearance of perpetual amusement, he claimed to be growing a moustache when accused of not shaving. Next came the short, plump Lance-Corporal Mockford, epitome of an old soldier with a short grey-flecked beard, neatly trimmed, spotless turn-out. Perkins, a small, perky man with a round face and thinning hair; Wright, short, middle-aged, heavily bearded, a lugubrious face bearing all the shrewdness of a veteran. Davies, another bearded old soldier, showed signs of tiredness after last night's violent awakening. Cox - ginger hair and moustache, round freckled face, short and stocky; Bell - thin, harassed face, medium height, slight build; Finnigan - raw carved face and snub nose of Irish peasant, lips drawn back from his stained teeth and cropped hair that revealed his boil-scarred scalp. Early was a slim balanced man who gave an impression of suppressed energy; a long, thin nose and intelligent eyes sat in a face made older by the dark moustache drooping over mouth corners. And finally, Coughlin, middle-aged with a neat spade beard, tall but stooped.

Rounding the end of the second rank the Sergeant strode over to the third, or super-numerary rank, formed of two soldiers taking dressing from the men at each end of the second line. Looking the boy among men that he was, Bob Farley was small for his fourteen years. A chunky five feet nothing who instead of a rifle carried a slung drum that was half as big as himself. The Sergeant studied the spotty faced youth, finding nothing to complain of in his turn-out. More than some of the men in the squad the lad bore himself with the cockiness of one who had known his military destiny from the moment he could imitate his father's marching steps. The Sergeant finally came to Private Holmes, Regimental Carpenter in Pioneer Section, parading with the sub-section in whose bungalow he lived when his specialist group was not assembled. In his mid-thirties, the open guileless visage and the clear blue eyes of a countryman classified him as the village carpenter he would have been had Fate not decreed otherwise.

Returning to the front of the formation, the Sergeant felt a fleeting affinity with these men, sensing in them certain individual qualities that had survived the deadly boredom and soulless routines of the Army. He fancied a third of them were Irish - half the bloody British Army were fugitives from poverty and potato famines, the march of the Empire was milestoned by graves bearing Irish names. His eyes counted the men with Lance-Corporal Mockford confirming that the missing man was Bandsman Mort. He was on parade with the Regimental Band although they performed only on Saturday's Commanding

Officer's Parade.

At half past five, Parade was taken over by the Company Sergeant-Major. Assured by each sergeant that their sub-sections were present and ready for duty, the Sergeant-Major tried them out with a flurry of repeated commands; standing at ease, to attention and at the slope arms. He then ordered the Half-Company Markers to take position. Following the measured beat of a single drum, the two senior half-company sergeants marched ten yards out from the ranks and halted, one at each end of the parade. They turned to face the imaginary line upon which the two half-companies were to form up. The command 'Fall in on markers' signalled a strangely organised chaos as 130 men, with rifles at the slope, marched in all directions at the regulation quick-time pace of thirty inches. As the men approached, each sergeant held out his inner arm, fist clenched, at right angles to his body, dropping it back to his side after the tallest soldier had marched up to it and halted. Now, instead of the tallest men on the right and the shortest on the left, the half-companies were sized from flanks to centre, front and rear men nearly the same size so that the tallest men were at both ends of the full company with the line dipping down to the smallest men in the centre. Officially sized, everyone had to remember his relative height and always fall-in in the proper place - two ranks at close-order, files nearly touching.

The Sergeant-Major now handed over the Parade to the Right and Left Half Company commanders, lieutenants with drawn swords who ordered their formations to fix bayonets and, accompanied by a notebook-bearing senior sergeant, walked slowly along the ranks closely inspecting the men. With this protracted business completed, each officer marched to the front of the parade and ordered bayonets to be unfixed and arms to be ported for inspection. Once more lieutenants and sergeants progressed haltingly along the ranks, checking each man's rifle for cleanliness and freedom from rust and a spotless breech-action with sights set at zero and no parts loose or damaged. Finally, with the soldier's right thumbnail in the open breech to reflect light into the barrel, the officers looked down the muzzle-bore to see that it was cleaned, oiled and free from obstruction. Then, with no word of command, the soldier rolled the breech closed, ordered arms and stood at ease.

Back in front of their commands, the lieutenants brought them up to attention and reported their half-companies to the Company Commander as being all present and ready for inspection. Taking over the Parade, Captain Fagan sharpened the men up with a routine of repetitive commands. Placed at the head of an entourage consisting of the Company Sergeant-Major, the half-company commander, the senior sergeant and the sergeants of sub-sections being inspected he set off along the ranks. Many names were 'lost', some for the third time that morning, and the Company Commander returned to face the Parade.

The officers, the sergeant-major and the sergeants formed a third super-numerary rank behind the formation, preparatory to Captain Fagan 'proving' the Company by numbering them off from right to left, telling them off into two half-companies and then four sections. He volleyed commands in rapid succession.

'Right-half Company ... Trail ... arms! Left-half Company ... Trail ... arms! Outer Sections ... Order ... arms! Inner Sections ... Order ... arms! Fours ... deep ... Front! Fours ... Right ... Front! Fours ... Left ... Front! Fours ... About ... Front!'

Breathing hard and bathed in sweat, the Company re-formed two deep, each man knowing exactly what would happen next. The Captain always proved them the same way then practised repelling cavalry, despite the fact that there were few, if any, recorded instances since Waterloo, fifty-three years before, of British infantry having to form square against horsemen. It was generally believed that the Captain's mother, when carrying him, had been frightened by a horse. Nevertheless, their commander's whim was not unwelcome, being the first and only break from the rigid and formal drill movements. Movements that entailed carrying a Snider-Enfield rifle, weighing 8lb.14½oz, for one and a half hours under a remorselessly rising Indian sun. With the passing of time the Sergeant realised that his Company Commander was shrewd, rather than eccentric.

The Captain ordered the lieutenants who commanded the two halves of the Company to double to the far ends of the Lines and stand with drawn swords. The Parade, awaiting the familiar caution, poised themselves for movement.

'Prepare for Cavalry! Form Rallying Squares!'

In a jostling flood-tide, revelling in a short-lived freedom, everyone doubled up towards their respective half-company commanders. Holding his sword up and pointing it towards the imaginary enemy the men formed-up, without crowding, into a two deep oblong around the commander. Each man took up his position, ordered arms, fixed bayonet and turned outwards, the front rank kneeled and presented a bristling fence in all directions. There then followed swirling manoeuvres as the Captain, in the middle of the Lines, ordered the squares to move.

'The square will advance ... will retire ... will move to the right ... will move to the left.'

Each of Captain Fagan's 'cautions' were repeated by the officers on whom the squares were formed and followed by.

'Inwards ... turn! Quick ... march!'

On the word 'turn' everyone turned in the direction named, on 'march' the square stepped-off, marching by the left of the leading face if advancing or moving to the right, by the right if retiring or moving left. The delights of free movement were eventually curtailed when the Captain halted the square and cautioned. 'Company will re-form.' Bayonets were unfixed and the left marker moved out to denote where the left flank of the Company was to rest, facing the supposed enemy.

'Re-form Company ... Quick March!'

As men formed-up on the Marker and the officers fell-out to the Mess for breakfast, 'C' Company once again became the Sergeant-Major's property.

Visibly wilting in the already blazing sun, in the manner of mindless automata, the men plodded through the monotonous, rhythmic reprise of Company Drill. Their mouths were dry, their eyes squinted in the strong light and their faces were plastered with a paste of dust and sweat. No matter. They marched to Front and Rear, wheeled, or formed from Line into Column and Column into Line ... from the Halt and on the March. They changed Front as the Base Company of a Line Formation, they File Marched and Wheeled in Files; formed in fours closing on a rank, or on the centre, and re-formed two deep. They diminished and increased Front by breaking into ... or breaking off ... Files or Fours ... brought to the Front ... re-form the Company. Although inured, most men were nearing their physical limits when the welcome bugles sounded 'Dismiss' at half past seven.

IV

Trailing wearily back into the bungalow the men removed their caps and wiped their streaming brows with the backs of their hands. Some sank down on beds and closed their eyes, others dashed off to the latrine and a few lay squirming, waiting for the first rush to die down. Rifles were secured in the rack and, possessing the only key, the Sergeant ensured that the chain was through each trigger-guard before he padlocked it to the sturdy staples. Tidy bed spaces became littered with boots, caps and tunics and the room rapidly assumed its habitual daily resemblance to a working man's lodging house. Despite their exhaustion everyone managed to visit the jakes and be in shirt-sleeve order, without boots, when the bugles sounded the breakfast call, a sonorous commencement to the day's incarceration.

Boards and trestles were set up and natives brought in the bread and coffee. They returned later to clean up the mess of crumbs, crusts and puddles of coffee before the tables were dismantled and stacked in the corner. Then the room lapsed into its daily life-wasting routine. Men settled themselves down, wriggling their half-clothed, sweat-damp and itching bodies in search of comfortable positions on hot rugs and straw palliasses. Those who had taken drink on the previous night closed their eyes and dozed; others looked around seeking openings for arguments or piss-taking that would, perhaps by precipitating bad-feeling or even a fight, relieve their boredom.

Every word bounced like a tennis ball over the low matting partition that separated the Sergeant from his sub-section. With the passing of time he developed the sub-conscious ability to blanket off these extraneous sounds, transforming them into diffused monotones allying themselves with the hum of insects and providing a perpetual background. Occasionally he failed to attune. His need for companionship caused him to sometimes remain detached but aware of what was being said outside.

On this particular morning early rounds of argument and

abusive bandinage did not achieve their end. An uneasy silence disturbed those men who, when not sleeping, required sounds to assure them that they had not been left alone in a world bereft of the Army-style close human contact, and its accompanying hubbub. Obviously seeking to remedy just such a situation, a flat, nasal, Midland accent launched into a narrative, polished and rehearsed over the years and surfacing through some chance word or reminder.

'Remember once ... in '58 it were ... we was ordered out on a General Parade to witness a rebel Rajah an' 'is son get the chop ... to be executed. It were one parade none o' the lads wanted ter miss, as it were known that these two bastards 'ad roasted white prisoners alive.'

It was a good start. The promise of violence and vengeance was calculated to secure the attention of those who could keep their eyes open. It certainly interested the Sergeant, who had been personally involved in it whilst serving with HM's 53rd Regiment at Bareilly in 1860. He well remembered the Rajah, a tall and strong old man with a long white beard and small, sharp piercing eyes. He had made a great impression on the young private soldier standing guard over him. More than once the old man, speaking good English, had declared that he and his son would not be executed but would be exiled overseas. However, after a trial lasting nine days, both were found guilty of murder and rebellion and sentenced to be executed. Although not something the Sergeant chose to think of, the scene was recalled.

The Regiments were formed up on three sides of the parade-ground. Two artillery pieces - six-pounders loaded with two-pound service-charges of gunpowder - stood with their lowered muzzles directed towards the open face of the formation. In a calculated insult to their religion, the prisoners were conveyed to the place of execution in a dung-cart, escorted by a section of the 53rd and some armed police. The old man sat firm and erect, his face a mirror of bitter hatred and defiance; the son was not so brave, his restless movements and twitching features earning a contemptuous glance from the father. They stood passive while the sentence of the court was read to them. The Rajah's snow white hair and beard earned some sympathy as he walked firmly across to the gun but the son struggled violently against the policemen holding his arms. He shrank from the gun and had to be forcibly held with his back against the muzzle while he was lashed to the wheels. The old man waved the police away and positioned himself, settling the small of his back firmly against the muzzle and standing calm while the lashings were made fast. Everyone moved away, leaving them alone - the old man standing firm, the younger one struggling and arching his back as though to lessen the effects of the charge that was about to blow him away.

Every detail of the grim scene was indelibly printed on the Sergeant's memory, nor had it been forgotten by the tale-teller beyond the matting wall.

'It were so quiet you could 'ear a man breathe ... then we nearly jumped out of our skins when the father began crying out, the same sentence over and over again, ringing and echoing round the ground, his old high-pitched voice sent a chill up the spine. Later we heard that he was cursing us, praying that his surviving children would be spared to burn all of us, like they had burned their other prisoners. At last, the old man's cries were drowned by the orders of the artillery Commander, "Division! Ready! Fire!" We knew when we marched-on that we were going to see two human beings blown to pieces before our eyes, but none of us was prepared for what happened. The still air was shattered by the two explosions that sounded as one, sending out a great billowing cloud of greasy smoke that hung motionless in the air as though trying to hide what was going on.

It was like a bloody dust-storm, the torn and shattered remains of the old man came out in a cloud made of shreds of clothing, burning and smouldering flesh and muscle, frizzing fat and great gouts of blood. It scattered all over the parade-ground. Being tied to the gun, the arms and legs fell close to the cannon mouth, the head and upper part of the body were blown about fifty yards, the face was quite untouched and still had the proud defiant look.

Writhing and struggling in his ropes, the younger man slipped from them just as the order was given to fire, only to hang suspended just below the muzzle. When the gun fired his shoulder was blown away and his arm set on fire. An officer ran forward to present his pistol at the man's head but it misfired three times, at each snap the poor sod shrank away from the expected shot. The officer stood back and ordered a man out from the ranks, one of me mates doubled forward and fired into the back of the man's head. He hung in the ropes with blood pouring out of his nose and mouth like water from a briskly handled pump. It was the most horrible sight I ever saw in my life. I seen death in many forms but nothing to equal that.'

A new voice, nearer the cubicle, took up the theme.

'Saw a shooting in Barrackpore when the Pandy's whole body went skyward in a red cloud, his head must have gone thirty feet up. It were the first they'd done so didn't know about backboards to protect the gunners, when the body burst like a goatskin the gun's blast sucked back the blood, guts and gobbets of smoking flesh and covered the gunners from head to foot.'

'Weren't it in Barrackpore where a couple of widows of officers murdered by the Pandies, dressed all in white and mounted on Arab greys, spurred deliberately forward into the line of fire, riding away dressed in scarlet ... on red 'orses?'

'Yes, that's true ... didn't see it myself but some of me mates told me about it.'

In strange contrast, an educated voice spoke, the Sergeant recognised it as belonging to Private Saville, the Gentleman-Ranker they called 'Captain'. 'It's not civilised ... why did they have to do it that way? Why couldn't they hang the poor buggers?'

'It's a quick death, they feel no pain, takes the heart away in one go.'

'No, that ain't why they did it,' interrupted another man, ' ... the prime reason is that it's about the only death that frightens the bleedin' native. If he's hung or shot he knows friends or relatives will claim his body and give him the funeral rites of his religion. If he's sentenced to death by being blown out of a gun he knows his body will be in so many bits they won't be able to pick 'em all up, and he can't bear the thought that perhaps a hand or foot of some other bloke of a different religion will be burned or buried along with his bits, 'cos that's contrary to his religion.'

The reflective silence was broken up by a high-pitched Irish voice.

'I'd like to blow that black bastard Babu in the Q.M's stores from the biggest gun I could lay my hands on. D'ye know, yesdiddy I tried to get a shirt replaced ... it was just a lot of ragged holes hanging together ... he said it had been wilfully damaged and the bloody quartermaster agreed with him!'

'Well, 'e would, wouldn't 'e? The Babu slips him bottles of rot-gut and fixes him up with women, don't 'e? Got to support his own staff, ain't 'e?'

'It'd be champion if we could frighten the bleeder ... make him think we're going to blow him out of a bloody gun ... wonder how we could do it?'

'Be easy if we was Top Khana ... could always borrow a gun for the afternoon. Don't know where we could get hold of one ... ain't never seen a gun around these cantonments.'

'How about making one? Not a real gun ... but one out of wood, with wheels ... that looked like a real gun.'

'Christ! It'd take ages ... even if we could lay our hands on the wood and stuff.'

'Yes, but we've got ages, ain't we? What pressing jobs have you got in your off-duty hours, Private Cox, that wouldn't allow you to give your mates a hand in making a gun?'

Private Richard Kinrade, sardonically articulate and acknowledged leader of the Pope's Boys, the Catholic faction in the bungalow, sensed a great opportunity to utilise his undoubted ability to 'stir it up', beside shaving a tilt at authority. 'Will ye listen for a moment, me lads? Private Finnigan ... may the Saints bless him ... has come up with an idea that'll not only fix the Babu's duff, but'll keep us occupied an' out of trouble. It's gotta be organised ... we musn't go off half-cock ... must do it right ... d'ye all agree? Good! Now, in this room we got the very man who can advise us ... Private Holy Holmes, the Reg'mental Carpenter no less! Holy, me boy ... tell the gentlemen if ye reckon we can make a reasonable looking gun?'

Overcoming the surprise at suddenly finding all eyes upon him, Holmes considered aloud. 'Well ... it could be done, I s'pose ... ye'd need timber fer the carriage ... the barrel needn't be iron or brass ... could be shaped outta wood an' painted or boot-polished ... it's the wheels I'll have trouble with ... I couldn't make no wheels ... not them big iron bound gun wheels.'

'It don't have to be too good ... it ain't got to fire and the bloody Babu will be far too fuckin' frightened to notice the barrel's made of wood!'

Kinrade nodded approvingly. 'That's right, Paddy. So we're agreed, we'll make a gun and pay off old scores with the Babu? Good! Now, we'll have to do this right ... have a properly constituted committee, with a president ... and a duty-roster so's no-one shirks his whack. I don't want to be president ... Private Finnigan thought it up so I propose him for the position ... alright Paddy?'

'Trust you Kinrade, to push the job onto someone else.'

'Well me boy, I'll give you all the support and assistance. Now, who else is on the committee with Paddy and me? How about you, Pat ... and Cocksy?'

A sour voice of dissent broke in. 'Why does it always 'ave to be Pope's Boys?.. there's decent Christians 'ere too can 'elp! Like ... er Din Dong Bell ... 'ow abart 'im? An' what abart Big Sanny ... 'e'll be useful fer fetching an' carryin' '

Hearing his name, the lumpish Scotsman jerked upright. 'Yeah, yeah! I'd like that ... I'm big an' strong ... but I got to have Ding Dong ... he'll tell me what to do!'

Kinrade rapidly reasoned that this new project was more important than a run-of-the-mill religious argument: 'Alright, alright! Then the bleedin' committee will be Private Finnigan as President, Cocksy Cox, Ding Dong Bell, Big Sanny ... an' me. Oh yes, an' Holy Holmes as Technical Adviser!'

Out of sight behind the matting walls, the Sergeant slowly shook his head. That bastard Kinrade! Well knowing that every word could be heard he was chancing his arm, testing his authority to see how much he'd take, and they could get away with; he'd keep eyes and ears open on this one. Rising to his feet, he stretched, then strolled out into the room. Coming among them brought an end to the conversation and all eyes were turned warily towards him. He walked slowly up the centre aisle and on reaching the rifle rack a man laying on the last bed at the top of the room, respectfully attempted to disarm him.

'Sarn't! Wasn't that the Mutiny Medal I see' you a'wearin' ?'

It was the man who had told of the executions - an old soldier, forty or so, lean and cadaverous with a thin pointed face and deep-set, dark eyes framed by cropped black hair and a full beard.

The Sergeant halted and faced the speaker. 'I was in the 53rd ...1st Battalion the Brickdusts ... the old five an' three pennies ...

an' I was on that shooting parade you talked of ...'

Turning, the Sergeant re-traced his steps. As he came level with the charpoy by the eastern door, the man lying on it said. 'I 'member seeing the 53rd ... got yellow facings ain't they ... at the Second Relief o' Lucknow.'

The Sergeant nodded and carried on to his cubicle, leaving Cockney accents in the air.

'Me an' Coughlin were there ... wiv the 1st Bengal European Reg'ment inna 5th Brigade o' Walpole's 3rd Division ... we was fusiliers in ole John Company's Army. Sarn't, did'ja see the Treasure Room inna Palace? It were full o' boxes o' jewels an' gold ... nearly all gone when me and Coughlin got there. I gotta pair o' pistols wiv jewels inna butts ... too heavy ter carry ... sold 'em to an orficer fer ten sov'rins. Sarn't, d'ye know, Coughlin found a little leather bag filled wiv diamonds, didn't ye Pat? An' he never gave me none an' he's got 'em 'idden, ain't you Pat?'

'Birchy! Fer Gawd's sake don't be going over that ole tale again! I ain't got no diamonds an' never 'ad none!'

'Oh yes you did, Pat! An' if you was a real mate ... a real file ... you'd share it wiv the bloke wot saved yer life when a bleedin' Pandy was going ter stick yer in the back. Never mind, I'll find 'em one day 'an do me own sharing out!'

'Birchy .,.. if I catches yer ferretin' around me kit ... I'll kill yer!'

'Yer ain't got the guts!'

The Irishman reached up to the equipment hanging on the wall behind the bed, to the bayonet still in its scabbard from morning parade. He then padded across the room to stand over the recumbent Birch, the dully gleaming blade poised threateningly. Rigid, hands clasped behind his head, Birch blinked up at the seventeen inch equi-angular hollow-ground Snider bayonet. Then, reassured by the metallic hiss of bayonets being withdrawn from sheaths in other quarters of the room, he smiled shakily in the knowledge that his C. of E. mates would not allow the Pope's Boys to have it all their own way.

The Sergeant, who had remained standing inside the cubicle doorway, stepped out and glared down the long room. 'What the hell's going on? Put them bleedin bayonets away before I crime the bloody lot of you! Corp'l Mockford! If you can't keep an eye on these wild men then I'll get me an NCO who can!'

The menacing atmosphere grudgingly dissolved into habitual languor. The Sergeant returned to his charpoy, aware that he had been unfair to Mockford, whose bed, far away at the top of the room prevented him intervening, even if he had been inclined. He wondered if the whole incident had been staged to try him out, if so then he had not handled it very well. He could have ... should have charged Coughlin, showed them he meant business right from the start. Difficult getting witnesses from among his mates though, they would all stick together. Anyway, he didn't fancy criming anyone on his first full day in barracks. All the routine of ordering the lance-corporal and two men to dress, with sidearms, to march the Irishman over to the guardroom ... in this heat. Then there would be the timeless ordered formality of Company Commander's Orders, giving evidence ... all repeated later in the day when the case was probably remanded for Commanding Officer's Orders ... or even court martial. No, that was not the way to win the confidence of the sub-section, and certainly not how he wanted to return to Regimental soldiering.

V

The Sergeant dreaded the dragging hours, marooned in the cubicle within hearing of all that went on beyond its matting walls, yet his rank not allowing him to be part of that world. Already he was sickened by the constant raucous exchanges of obscenities, cold between-the-teeth swearing, coarse personal allusions and re-iterated crudities continually echoing around the lofty room. He wondered if he had behaved similarly when a young soldier in barracks, a lifetime ago.

Hours of enforced listening taught the Sergeant to put a name to a voice. From some of them he learned to expect nothing but repulsive swearing and, at times of particularly unbearable clamour he would clap his hands despairingly over his ears. Not all were banal gutter sounds. On occasions he felt inclined to stroll from his cell and talk, perhaps with the Gentleman-Ranker, Private Saville, who, although young was intelligent and well-educated, his sharp, dry wit invariably beyond most of his comrades and thus misunderstood. The American, Private Early, was grazing in strange pastures and could have felt solitary in an alien world yet, without ever descending to abuse or bad language, he seemed perfectly at home in the kinship of professional soldiers from another nation. Some of the older men chose to take his occasional mentions of Antietam, Gettysburg and other battles of the American Civil War as slurs on the British Army with whom he now served. But the American's caustic tongue and iron fists had long ago moulded their objections into mumbled growls.

The veterans all had colourful tales to tell. Personal experiences that were invariably nostalgic and underlining former comrades who were larger than any life could be. These gruff and untutored recitals were always received with a respectful silence. The Sergeant knew if they could be cajoled into regularly talking these inarticulate veterans could teach younger comrades much about soldiering, facts that could save lives up at the Frontier. In any event, tale-telling sessions could never be worse than the bickering, swearing and fighting that made nightmares of daily Hot Weather Bungalow Parades.

At times, the Sergeant deeply resented the noise from without encroaching upon his private thoughts and memories of his wife and children. On other occasions he found himself hoping that something would return him to reality and banish the obsessive grief and morbid daydreams. When sweating in restive boredom on his charpoy the Sergeant was often hard pushed to tell whether he was asleep or awake. In a limbo beyond the confines of the bungalow ... the cantonment ... even of human existence, now and then he thought of God. Of God gazing down on those whom he had created, looking with disfavour no doubt and being disappointed to see what a collection of bastards he had turned out. Noting the nocuous cruelties, injustices and evil deeds, bet He sometimes wondered why He'd made us, and got so upset that He could stand it no longer and came down to inflict punishment ... stir up an earthquake ... kill the crops and cause a famine ... innocence suffered along with guilt ... just like in the Army. Bit like a sergeant-major was God! In a way he ... Sergeant Oakley ... was God ... for nine hours a day ... and only in the Hot Season ... he had to quieten that sod Kinrade, stirring up his Pope's Boys against the C. of E's ... had to crime someone for dirty boots or not shaving ... sometimes he had to lean heavy on someone ... maybe not the real offender ... unlike God he took the line of least resistance by criming a lad who he knew wouldn't be as awkward as an old soldier ... or wouldn't argue his case so well on Company Commander's Orders. The Sergeant felt bad about that ... he apologised to God ... explained that he was only an ordinary man who'd had his share of troubles ... he'd try and do better in future. He wondered of other blokes in huts all over India were having conversations like this with God ... how did He handle them all at once, listen to everyone and give answers and rulings?

Yes, God was just like a sergeant in the Hot Season ... or rather sergeants were like God ... they were lonely, like God was lonely, because they could not mix with lower ranks ... and God was the highest rank of all ... no-one to talk to ... no Sergeant's Mess to be President of ... to go to in the evenings and talk to other sergeant-majors, all friendly over a pint of ale or a dram of grog.

The Sergeant looked up at the high white-washed beams at the brown stain that was the only mark Sergeant Digges had left on Bungalow No.5 Despite the heat he shivered. He wouldn't have the guts to put a Snider muzzle in his mouth, no matter what happened. Was that God coming down on one of his punitive raids? Like when the Army went out and burned a native village on the Frontier ... that was the end of their little world too ... but they were tough ... always bounced back ... probably blamed it all on their God who wasn't the same bloke that we come under. Suppose their God was black. The Sergeant always thought of God as a benevolent old man who could be really strict when necessary ... a bit like his old Grandad ... everyone was frightened of him, even when he was really old and sat all day in his high-backed chair in front of the fire ... probably never have joined the Army if it hadn't been for Grandad and his tales of the Light Division in the Peninsular, of Wellington and Black Bob Crauford ... of the 95th Rifles in the sand-pit near the farm of La Haye Sainte at Waterloo. The old chap had never forgiven him for joining the 53rd instead of the 95th, but he had to vanish quickly into the Army at the time and he could only find a recruiting sergeant for the old Brickdusts. Silly things you do when you're young ... he could have swung for that lark, punching a Peeler who fell heavy and hit his head on the kerb ... he'd never been stupid-drunk since ... most of the trouble men - particularly soldiers - get into happens when they're over the mark.

It was mid-afternoon when the Sergeant was dragged up from a deep pit of unconsciousness reverie as a swimmer fights his way back to the surface. He had been revived not by any sudden noise or shock, but by the far greater alarm of utter silence from outside the cubicle. Barrackrooms were never completely silent, even in the night men grunted and farted, coughed and called out to the ghosts of their night. No noise at all meant that far from being asleep everyone was wide awake, their attention riveted by some compelling sight. Easing himself from his charpoy the Sergeant slid silently out into the main barrackroom where he became part of a strained tableau with its fuse burning short.

Every man in the room was wide awake. Stiff on their charpoys and fearing to move in case they missed one moment of the unfolding drama in the bed space where Private Birch lay, on his back with hands clasped across his chest. He seemed quite oblivious of the tall figure standing over him, hands wrapped dagger-fashion around a threateningly poised Snider-Enfield bayonet, its slim blade glinting in the half-light.

'Coughlin!'

As a starter's pistol galvanises athletes into action, so the Sergeant's bark broke the spell. Men breathed again, shifted and stretched, Coughlin jumped violently and lowered the bayonet. On the bed beneath, Birch jerked upright and unclenched his fingers, releasing a bright metal object that dropped to the stone floor with a light metallic tinkle.

'Coughlin, were you attacking Private Birch?'

'No, Sergeant, not at all! I came over to get a closer look at what he were holding ... he's got my sovereign purse ... look, here it is.' Bending down, the soldier picked from the floor a small nickel-plated cylinder and held it out for the Sergeant to see. 'Ain't got no sovereigns in it ... I wouldn't have used me lunger ... I only brought it to hold him off ... he's younger'n me ...'

The Irish voice tailed off and Kinrade's edged voice cut in. 'That's the truth an' all, Sergeant ... Roomy there is always a'searchin' Pat's kit for diamonds ... when he see's something what takes his fancy he's like a bleeding magpie ... ole Pat always takes his lunger when he's tackling Birchy.' Private Kinrade looked round the room, getting the confirmatory nods he sought.

'What you got to say, Private Birch ... did you take Private Coughlin's property? Come on, stand up, man ... stand to attention when you address an NCO!'

The tall gangling Birch drew himself up before the Sergeant, eyes downcast, justifying himself in whining nasal Cockney tones. 'Sarn't ... he's got them diamonds an' I gotta right to a share ... I weren't out on the nick ... I ain't a tea-leaf ... it were shiny an' nice to hold ...'

'That's as may be ... but the rest of the room ain't going to feel very happy knowing their belongings aren't safe, are they?'

Shrewdly assessing the Sergeant's indecision, Private Kinrade, in sweat-stained grey flannel shirt, wrinkled trousers and holed worsted socks drew himself up in a ludicrous parade-ground posture. 'Permission to speak, Sergeant!' The Sergeant nodded. 'Sergeant! From the evidence, Private Birch is guilty of stealing from a comrade ... the worst o' barrackroom crimes. Won't be good for the section, for Birch ... or, begging pardon, for the Sergeant ... if he comes up afore the Company

Commander and maybe gets remanded for the CO an' a court-martial.'

The Sergeant pondered. Birch was not a thief in the strict sense of the word, but military law made him one; if charged he would undoubtedly be found guilty and sentenced to a cruel number of days in the Mirzapur Cantonment Military Gaol, a corrugated-iron roofed oven. More likely, he'd get fifty or a hundred lashes; and they'd all have to parade to watch a strong-armed drummer lay into him with a cat and lacerate his back to a bloody pulp. By the same token, Coughlin's antics with the bayonet would be revealed in evidence and he'd be charged too. There'd be Company and CO's Orders, Summary of Evidence to be taken, witnesses to be organised. An unwilling and not too efficient officer would be detailed as Soldiers Friend, unlikely to vigorously defend the prisoner for fear of crossing the Adjutant, who would be prosecuting. The sub-section would be disrupted and its spirit affected just when he was beginning to straighten them up. And Robbo ... the Sergeant-Major was looking for something like this, he'd use Birch's petty failing as a charge that Sergeant Oakley was falling down on his job.

'You're suggesting barrackroom justice?'

Kinrade nodded.

'Well, it'll have to be a cobbing ... an' nothing that'll make him unfit for duty. Get it over with! Corp'l Mockford! Come with me!'

Non-commissioned officers could not become involved in barrackroom justice in case the victim fought, when he might make himself liable to severe charges of striking an NCO. Nevertheless, the Sergeant was far from happy with the situation, conscious that he was shirking responsibility, and that Private Kinrade knew it. The lance-corporal sat stiffly on the chair, the Sergeant restlessly moved about the small cubicle. Both knew what was going on and they could hear just enough to virtually transform the thin matting partition into a window.

'No fucker's marrowing me!'

'Now come on, Roomy ... we don't want no bobbery, do we?'

The Sergeant looked at Mockford. 'Why do they call him Roomy?'

'He's a Cockney ... they got a slang ... say birch broom for room ... an' his name's Birch.'

There was no shouting or raised voices, just the scuffle of

feet, hard breathing and muttered curses. Now and then the Sergeant heard Birch's shrill, fearful tones and Kinrade's insidious cajoling. In the end the attackers put military training into practice. A frontal feint distracted Birch from the rear attack who came up behind the struggling Cockney to throw a blanket over his head and pin his arms to his side with belts. Writhing and kicking, the body of Birch was carried to a trestle and dumped across it.

With trousers around ankles, his pallid spotty buttocks became the target for a cascade of swipes from bayonet scabbards. Sweeping strokes were laid on with all the strength of the four men who jostled for the best position. Screams and cries muffled by the smothering blanket vied with scuffling feet until, as suddenly as it had begun, the beating ended. Men dispersed in all directions, leaving Birch hanging over the trestle. He heaved and sobbed at length before wearily disentangling himself to stand painfully upright and gaze around the room with lowered eyes. He saw men in every possible posture of sleep, some ostentatiously snoring, united in ignoring their victim, indicating that he could blame no man more than another.

Throughout the afternoon, face downwards on his charpoy, Birch sniffled and gulped himself into a deep slumber. At five o'clock he was tenderly woken by Pat Coughlin who pressed a dram of grog to his lips and invited him to the canteen for a pint of porter. Other men, including Kinrade, drifted across to fuss over him like an erring child being assured that he had been punished for his own good but was loved nevertheless. Just before lights-out they all staggered in drunk as rolling farts. The unconscious Birch was carried in their midst and gently lowered - stomach first - onto his charpoy. The men's kindness and solicitude persisted for the couple of days he hobbled around. On parade the Sergeant turned a blind-eye to Private Coughlin taking over as sub-section Marker, with Private Saville as his rear-rank file, so that he and Private Kinrade could support Birch with their shoulders during drill.

VI

The day had started badly for Private Coughlin. His name had gone in the book twice - for not shaving and for having a dirty rifle. Like everyone else in the barrackroom he had shaved the night before, but his beard seemed to grow quicker these days! He had cleaned his rifle too, and pulled it through - a bit quickly he owned - before rushing out on parade. Not cleaned well enough to stop Lieutenant Layden-Hill, 'C' Company Left-Half Commander, from detecting dust in the bore. Angrily, Coughlin banged the offending weapon into its place in the rack. 'Sure, an' its bloody unjust! I bloody well shaved an' bloody well pulled me bloody rifle through ... same as the rest o'ye ... an' Pat Coughlin's the onny one what gets crimed!'

Roomy Birch, always ready to have a go at his big Irish File, bawled across the six feet of floor space between them. 'Shouldn't have joined! Dear Muvver, the Army's a bugger, sell the pig an' buy me out, your loving son, Pat!'

Instinctively, every man in the room chanted the time-honoured formula, "Dear Pat, pig's sold ... soldier on!"

Ruefully, Pat Coughlin shook his head. 'Me darlin' Mother nivver owned a bloody pig ... nor me ole Da either come to that!'

Hanging his equipment, Pat thought of his parents in their low cabin, walls cut out of the living bog with an entrance so low that you had to crawl in through the mud. His nostrils wrinkled, fancying he could smell the acrid fumes of the turf fire that never went out. They'd been gone these twenty years, dying on the same day of fever, in a windowless cellar in Liverpool. Furtively, he crossed himself, wryly cursing the dire need for food, clothes and a roof over his head that had forced him, a nineteen year old orphan, to adopt the British Army as his family.

The brief exchange touched off a wave of nostalgia. Private Finnigan said to the world in general. 'We kept a pig in the corner of the cabin an' me an' me brothers an' sisters slept on the mud floor wid not a stitch on us ... din't need it, the peat fire warmed us night an' day ... I recall we were happy, we danced and sang ... an' had plenty to eat ... until the tatie crop failed in '45.'

Private Cox nodded thoughtfully. 'I were only two then, but it did for us, that an' the hanging gale. They evicted us ... an' me mother carrying, wi't me an' six others at her skirts ... so me Dadda made us a scalpeen ... for you high an' mighty English, that was a hole dug in the ground, two, three feet deep, in the ruins of a tumbled house, wi't a roof of sticks and pieces of turf . An' we existed in that burrow an' others like it throughout the hard winter of '47. Turfed out each time they found us ... landlord had the help of the military ... later I heard tell they was the 49th Foot an' whenever I meet up wi't any of 'em I settle old scores! 'Course, that's not why I j'ined, it were the magistrates idea, I were up before him for vagrancy ... an' he gave me a mighty fine choice - a spell in the 'steel' with the pleasures of the treadmill, shot-drill an' crank, or become one o' Missis Victoria's boys!'

Private Cox recalled the key grating in the lock and how, when half asleep, he nearly jumped out of his skin at the Recruiting Sergeant bellowing, 'Come on NOW! Let's be havin' YER.'

Back then, in a gloomy courtroom along with three other bemused lads pushed and jostled into line, a Testament was thrust into each uncomprehending hand. The Magistrate swept in and was crashingly saluted.

'All present and correct, Your Worship!'

His Worship nodded, staring absently through old-fashioned spectacles at the bedraggled bunch before him. Holding up his hand, he addressed the air above their heads in a dry old voice. 'Now listen to me, you men! All of you here do make Oath that you will be faithful and bear true allegiance to Her Majesty, her Heirs and Successors, Crown and Dignity, against all enemies ... observe and obey all orders of Her Majesty ... of all the Generals and Officers set over me ... so Help You God! Now kiss the Book ... take them away Sergeant.'

Cox's recital, aimed at no one in particular and heard with only half an ear, stimulated memories in at least two of the half-naked men lolling on their sweat-damp charpoy rugs. Private Kinrade only needed to cast his mind back a year to picture those bog huts, and the guilt he felt at his own comparative comfort in a windowless cabin with patches of old white-wash peeling leprously from the sagging walls. The single, earth-floored room where bleak winds and bitter cold were kept at bay by the smouldering peat-fire spilling smoke from its open hearth.

Kinrade's heart was still full of the black hate for the English that had driven him to become a Fenian, a member of the secret Irish Revolutionary Brotherhood who met and muttered interminably in closed rooms where the sour smell of damp clothing vied with the thick smoke of plug tobacco, producing an atmosphere challenging only that of barrackrooms where he now spent most of his life. Young and hot-blooded, his impatience at talking boiled over into the night when he led a gang of sullen, emaciated tenants, armed with spades - their only possible weapon - to 'reason' with Protestant Captain Dennis McMahon, the ex-cavalry officer who had recently inherited an estate where tenants, three years in arrears of rents, would neither pay nor go. They waylaid Captain McMahon as he travelled home in an open carriage from a meeting with the local relief committee. He was tired and frustrated, they were bitter and resentful. Reasoned words quickly escalated into heated arguments and sour recriminations. Eventually, in the recent tradition of the half a dozen landlords assassinated in two months, the captain was hauled from the carriage and spade-hacked to death. His driver and soldier-servant, who had ridden with his master in the charge of the Light Brigade at Balaclava, were similarly treated for fear they might recognise the Fenian murderers. The police were soon on to Richard Kinrade who managed to save his neck by enlisting at Cardiff, black and filthy after being smuggled across to Wales in an empty coal vessel returning from Cork.

Cox's mention of the magistrate rolled back more than a score of years in Private John Wright's memory and he recalled the time when he had been facing far more than a local Justice of the Peace on a petty vagrancy charge. He had done things in style at the Old Bailey, on a charge of murder. It had all been so unfair. A flood-tide had relentlessly engulfed the boy and his family and friends, only ebbing when it had washed them all into the dock at England's best known Court of Justice.

John Wright and his three brothers were brought up on a neat small-holding in a quiet village in Warwickshire where little happened that could not be handled by the part-time parish constable. Then came the caterpillar crawl of the railways, ruthlessly devastating the peaceful green fields with its earth turning trail of cuttings, embankments and bridges, built by a locust horde of navvies and their camp-followers. Situated two miles or so from the slowly lengthening scar of progress, at first the village saw it only as an exciting novelty - until the long Summer days encouraged gangs of boisterous navvies to venture further afield, seeking uncrowded inns and simple country folk to terrorise. Approaching echoes of raucous songs and shouts hanging on the still evening air drew people from their thatched cottages. Most of the village's inhabitants, curious and bewildered, had gathered in the street when the gangs appeared. As alien as invaders from another planet, a dozen brawny navvies, in strapped velveteen clothing and spotted neck-ties, swaggered down the wide village street leading to the green, duck-pond and signboarded inn. Kicking up the dust, they glanced insolently from side to side, indicating amusing sights to each other, pointing and shouting coarse jests and ribald comments at the younger women and brazenly daring anyone to challenge them for possession of the village.

These workers had plenty of money and were free spenders. The innkeeper, John Daniels, fawned nervously upon them, trying to laugh while being jostled, kicked and soaked with beer as he bustled around the dark bar-room. The more timid locals hastily gulped-up and fled, others were man-handled out and old Ambrose, made to dance jigs until he collapsed, was unceremoniously bundled into a corner. Then young Sarah Daniels foolishly showed herself in the doorway behind the counter and was plucked out into the roaring, stamping circle, being mauled and kissed into terrified hysteria. On trying to rescue his daughter, Daniels was felled with a pewter pot and left unconscious on his own bar floor, drenched in beer and urine.

The next days passed in dread anticipation and each night the cold-blooded gang's behaviour got worse. They lurched around the lanes, hammering on doors and breaking windows; they threw stones with vicious accuracy; accosted women and taunted their menfolk, poaching and pillaging like an occupying army. The parish constable, after being roughed-up and thrown into the pond, kept away. The villagers did not realise their luck that the contemptuous navvies did not even rate them as worthy of their short, heavy, sharp-edged excavating spades, capable of being wielded with all the ferocity of medieval battle axes. Worst of all was Saturday night, pay-day, when they drank the inn dry, smashed doors and windows, uprooted hedges and pushed down walls in contests of brute strength. When there was little left to smash, and with villagers cowering out of sight, they bet heavily on bloody bare-fist fights on the village green.

Next morning, the indignant country-men, their slow tempers finally aroused, glared round at the devastation, vowing that they would tolerate no more. Plans were discussed, discarded and developed until they all knew their role. That evening when the navvies roistered into the desolate village only a frightened John Daniels tended the bar at the inn, tremulously aware that he had taken more money in five days than during the whole of the previous twelve months, but that it would not take much to make them smash up the premises and help themselves to what they wanted. Their immediate thirsts satisfied, the navvies lurched off in search of amusement until only three remained, purposefully drinking at the counter.

Concealed within the familiar confines of their village, twenty men and youths armed themselves with stout wooden clubs. They were led, by men tactically sharpened by countless poaching exhibitions, to the local inn where they meant to pick off, one by one as they departed, those railway navvies who arrogantly strode the lanes, disrupting lives and destroying property. John Wright, seventeen years of age and barely above five feet in height, manfully played his part by the side of his father and brothers.

Aggressively good-humoured, the three roistering navvies unmercifully badgered the frightened innkeeper, demanding sight of his daughter, she being safely cloistered with the womenfolk in the depths of a nearby wood. The raucous baiting was cut short by the sudden appearance of grim-faced country-men carrying wooden clubs. No longer able to control their fury all had been gripped by the immediacy of the situation. A horrendous brawl broke out. The half drunk, iron-muscled navvies transformed every moveable object into a fearsome weapon. Men fell and were trampled by iron-shod boots, others reeled, dazed and bloody from the fray as pent-up insults and injuries were paid back by flailing clubs. So vigorous was the navvies resistance that the peaceable country-men were provoked into the same violence demonstrated by their persecutors. Reason was replaced by berserk vengeance and when the three navvies were finally borne to the ground, they jostled and pushed forward to flail repeated blows upon the huddled bloodied bodies. At last, breathing hard, the country men stood back, halted more by apprehension at their deeds than by the sudden clatter and jingle of an approaching troop of Yeomanry, called out by the desperate Parish Constable. Deferentially the men fell into nervous awe before the imperious magistrate and his officer, who briefly examined the inert navvies and declared two of them to be dead. Every male villager was taken into custody and escorted by the mounted soldiers to the gaol in town, where they remained for weeks.

Unfortunately for them, this defence of hearth and home was seen as a serious check to the march of progress, and, as at Tolpuddle in Dorset, an example had to be made that would discourage others. How could men build railways, essential to the prosperous upsurge of trade and commerce, if they were to be set upon and killed by ignorant countrymen who misunderstood their boisterous good spirits? For best effect, the trial was staged at the Old Bailey, the premier criminal court of England. The villagers, chill with fear, were lodged within the grim and notorious walls of Newgate Prison nearby. It did not take long and the bloodhound-jowled, be-wigged judge toyed with the traditional nosegay and sentenced all to transportation to Botany Bay; all save John Wright, youngest and smallest, whose head could barely be seen over the wall of the crowded dock. Glowering out from beneath his bushy eyebrows, the dust-dry voice of the judge grated into the air.

'I except from this well merited sentence the boy, John Wright, who, on account of his tender years was undoubtedly influenced by wicked elders. John Wright, I order that you shall be handed over to some recruiting officer who will enlist you and have you duly attested into Her Majesty's Army where you can take up arms against Her Gracious Majesty's enemies ... instead of your fellow country-men! God Save the Queen!'

Wright's personal musings were ended and his attention drawn back to the barrackroom when a shout from Private Perkins was aimed in the direction of Cox, who had set the narrative ball rolling.

'Hey Cocksy,' said Perkins, 'I were on road like thee, an' I'll tell ye summat happened that made me pray fer the sight of a Peeler to stick me in a nice safe gaol!'

Private Perkins had taken two bites of the military cherry. Enlisting in a cavalry regiment his perennial battle with a large and frightening horse had caused him to desert, taking to the roads to get as far away as possible from the Cavalry Depot at Canterbury. In the warm weather living rough was no hardship, although berries and root vegetables dug from the hard earth with his pocket knife were poor substitutes for food. Mid-morning of a very hot day in Romney Marshes, he came upon a small cottage on the outskirts of a village. In the garden a young woman was hanging washing, a little girl playing at her feet. The woman offered Perkin's a pitcher of ice-cold water from the well and a hunk of home-baked bread, with cheese and an onion. Gratefully he accepted the food and sat on a bench outside the cottage door where he sliced at the bread with a long bladed knife and talked idly with the child. Then, offering his thanks once again, he went on his way, reflecting enviously on the obvious peace and simple happiness that surrounded the humble home.

It had seemed a very hot day, but that was before he came to the Great Plain and spent eleven long years sweltering in almost unbearable temperatures; now he would think nothing of marching across Romney Marshes in the Summer. As he plodded along the flat, dusty road on that August afternoon, licking his cracked lips as he had done so often ever since, a heard a terrifying sound came from behind. Perkins never forgot that frightening, animal baying of angry men as he turned and saw a compact mob rolled relentlessly toward him, topped by a foliage of farm instruments - scythes, pitchforks, spades and sledgehammers. An alarming sight at any time but to a man on the run there could be only one quarry, so Perkins ran. He left the road for the shelter of a small wood, plunging through thorny thickets and whipping branches. Beyond the trees he crossed open fields and stumbled through bogs, hedges and ditches out on to the road again. Fighting for breath, his chest heaved and his head swam. His leaden feet wove a faltering course through dusty ruts until he stumbled and fell, spent and gasping. His pursuers massed around him, blotting out the sun and glowering as they dragged him to his feet. One distraught and bearded labourer, in an open-necked striped shirt with the sleeves rolled high on his hairy bronzed arms, was forcibly restrained from hurling himself onto the bewildered Perkins.

Amid a nightmare welter of curses, blows and threats, Perkins grasped the chilling realisation that he was accused of killing the little girl at the cottage where earlier that day he had been given food and water. Apparently she had vanished at dinner time and some time later was found in a corner of the field behind the house, her little throat cut from ear to ear. As the only stranger in the area, and carrying a large, long-bladed knife, obviously he was guilty. So cut and dried was the evidence that the soldier wildly wondered if he had committed the awful deed. Perhaps the sun had induced a turbulent brainstorm that he could remember nothing of. But surely, there would be blood on his hands, and on his clothes. Perkins could see none. Attempts to point this out were rudely cut short, and a heated discussion broke out - should they hand him over to the police or settle for him here and now?

Then Perkins saw, over the heads of the arguing mob, the tall shakoes and musket-barrels of a small party of soldiers marching towards them, their approach heralded by the staccato beat of the side-drum stimulating military precision into weary feet. The mob turned and the grip on Perkin's arms was momentarily loosened. He wrenched himself free and burst through the cordon to fling himself bodily upon the be-ribboned sergeant at the head of the Recruiting Party.

'Please help me!' he cried, 'I ...I was coming to enlist when these men accused me of ... of something I never did! I want to join the Army ... your Regiment!'

'Do you now?' said the sergeant, gazing quizzically at Perkins as he stepped forward to stand between him and the mob. Defending the fifteen shillings ' bringing money' thrust so surprisingly into his hands, the sergeant halted the mob in its tracks, splitting the still air with his loudest and most authoritative parade-ground bellow. 'What's all this now? I said ... what's all this? Who gave you the right to interfere with one of Her Majesty's soldiers?'

Cowed into silence, men looked at each other before the child's father stepped forward and vigorously told the story. With his head on one side the sergeant listened, then turned to Perkins. 'Did you kill the child?'

'No,' replied Perkins, violently shaking his head. 'She were alive and playing when I left ... we talked while I were eating me bread, cheese and onion!'

'Show me your knife!' The sergeant carefully studied the knife, sniffed the blade then thrust it beneath the father's nose. 'What d'ye smell on that blade?'

Glaring angrily, the man reluctantly sniffed. 'Why ... onions, I suppose.'

The sergeant nodded. 'Yes, onions. D'ye think it'd still smell of onions if he'd done this awful thing to your little girl and then carefully cleaned off the blood?'

Men looked at each other, baffled. The father stared first at the sergeant then at Perkins and shook his head resignedly. 'He must've done it,' he muttered. 'Who else could 'ave?'

'Wouldn't stand up in a courtroom my man!' sniffed the sergeant. 'I advise you all to go home and look around ... none'll rest easy in your village until you find the real villain! As for you,' he said to Perkins, 'Fall-in with my lads, we'll billet in Hythe tonight and enlist you at Dover tomorrow!'

The barrackroom digested the story in silence before someone voiced what everyone was wondering. 'Polly ... did you do fer the kid?'

'No I bloody didn't! What do you think I am ... a fucking murderer or something?'

'Judging by what I saw you do to some o' them Pandies in Lucknow, I ain't so sure!'

The room dissolved into an uproar of laughter, hoping for a fight to break the monotony. Lolling back in a sweat-soaked languor Polly Perkins was not to be roused. 'Bollocks! They were bleedin' murderers weren't they? An' only bloody niggers anyway!'

No-one argued. British soldiers never made much difference

between one brown skin and another and after the Mutiny they were even less inclined to discriminate. Every man in the room, in the cantonment, in the entire British Victorian Army, recognised the enemies as being men of different colours - with different habits, culture, codes and scruples. Up on the Frontier they well knew that tribesmen would torture and kill wounded men falling in to their hands, besides mutilating the dead. None felt any compunction about refusing mercy to native foes.

Deep at the far end of the room in a favoured corner bed-space that went with rank or length of service, Lance-Corporal Mockford was shaking his head. 'Them recruiting sarn'ts! He'd have taken yer even if yer knife'ud been covered in blood. They'll do anything ... bleeding anything ... to get their hands on bringing money!'

Private Kinrade, devoid of respect for rank, age or length of service, offered the opinion that most old soldiers, pensioners who guaranteed to attend ten days drill a year, would be taken on as recruiters. 'Why, they're so bleedin' bad that Regulations will only let 'em recruit single men! They hang around in taverns in the cities, baiting their hook with drink an' bounty money ... they'll sign anyone ... old lags, epileptics, pox-ridden ... they don't care so long as they gets their bloody money!'

'No,' interjected Corporal Mockford, 'I doan think many'd do wot one did ter me ... ter get me in. It were a time when they were making reg'mints up ter strength to send out 'ere, 'cos o' losses in the war agin the Sixes.'

In 1847, Samuel Mockford was eighteen years old, a stocky well-built ploughman's son. His open face, tanned and freckle-dusted beneath a stubble of sun-bleached blonde hair revealed a simple, unsophisticated upbringing. With the harvest in, on one of the few holidays of the year, he had tramped with his mates from Bere Regis to the fair at Dorchester. Unaccustomed to the noise and excitement, allied with copious flagons of cider, the boys were made ready for a lark. The Recruiting Party's compelling drum-beat and the shrill note of the fife set them dancing in a comical, ungainly fashion, bumping and falling and laughing wildly. It was so amusing and light-hearted that even the impressive Recruiting Sergeant genially encouraged them. Alongside his squad he stood rigidly erect, his head thrust forward beneath a tall shako embellished with fluttering coloured ribbons and a rosette. The fingers of his left hand strained down the seam of his white pipe-clayed trousers while his right hand clutched a short cane tucked under his arm. Tall and well-built, his big chest proudly expanded the scarlet double-breasted jacket emblazoned with a double row of glittering buttons, gold epaulettes, loops, tassels and sergeant's stripes. His well-fed, florid face was decorated with a large, evenly trimmed moustache that curled onto both cheeks. His mouth creased into what seemed to Sam Mockford a friendly, approving smile.

'Go on, my lucky lads!' chortled the sergeant. 'Dance away! Why, you're nimble amusing fellows. I'd be proud to buy you all a flagon if you'll do me the honour of drinking with an old soldier!'

Honoured to be singled out by this splendid warrior and hoping that their friends would see them, Sam Mockford and his friends sat on the wooden benches outside the inn, their humble attire and callow ways contrasting hugely with the awe-inspiring worldliness of the Recruiting Sergeant. With their senses further muddled by fear and respect, the young men listened open-mouthed to tales of military life. Tales that made drums beat stirring rhythms in their befuddled heads and bugles shrill out calls to wing their imagination up into the blue. These unsophisticated minds were easily hypnotised, and were skilfully directed along the desired path by the colourful promises of smart uniforms and spirited horses to ride, shining swords to wield and unlimited loot to make them rich for life.

'By God!' puffed the sergeant. 'I never did a better day's work than when I took the Queen's Shilling! Being a civilian don't hold a candle to the fine life of a soldier ... very little work to do an' you gets free an' plentiful rations of the finest food, lodgings with good beds and fine furniture, at least five different suits of clothing ... just like mine! And you gets plenty o' money, as much ale as you can drink, an' the girls fall over themselves to get at you! Travel too! Why, you'll get to see the world like a rich man. If you're lucky you'll get to India where every soldier has two, yes two, servants of his own to clean his kit and look after him, an' if they don't do it proper to your liking, then you can kick 'em like dogs! Promotion? Ah, now, glad you asked that 'cos you get the chance o' rising to Lieutenant or even Captain within a year or two ... could even end up Colonel of the Reg'ment! One of my mates did just that an' I could have done so meself, but I never had an education which held me back an' I only made sergeant. An' if you're unlucky an' the cards fall wrong ... which don't happen often ... you get a first class funeral with the reg'mental band playing sad tunes, an' a firing-party of your own mates, with tears rolling down their faces. Now come on my lucky lads ... how many of you are there? Five? Well ain't that a coincidence ... that's just how many vacancies we have afore the reg'ment is full! Although I got a lot of sensible fellows waiting in Weymouth an' I half promised them. Come on, make up your minds ... is it to be yes or no? Take my honest advice an' make it yes!'

Fishing deep into a pocket, the sergeant produced a handful of bright new coins, tossed them into the air and, let them fall onto the ale-sodden tabletop. 'Here it is ... the Queen's Shilling! Take it, me lucky lads, you'll never regret it!'

Alluringly, he thrust the gleaming coins under the entranced noses in a sudden movement that startled Sam Mockford who was drowsy from the hot sun, drink and talk. Reaching out he took one of the shillings, eyeing it curiously.

'There! He's taken the Queen's Shilling - one of you is a sensible fellow - don't let him make off with the best life in the world ... don't be left behind ... join your mate an' be a soldier of our Gracious Queen!'

Two more boys fell for this age-old military confidence trick, signed and sealed by a ribbon from the sergeant's cap pinned onto the coat to prove that the wearer had taken the Queen's Shilling. The sergeant, now strangely tired and bad-tempered, never let them out of his sight until handing over to the escorting NCO at Dorchester Castle.

Edward Hebdon, like Samuel Mockford, was a respectable, docile country lad. brought up by thrifty parents in a decent cottage home. 'It ain't changed, Corporal! Only three years ago they got me in just the same way ... only it were at Norwich ... at the fair ... an' there were the bounty money...!'

Twenty-three years old and very drunk when he encountered the Recruiting Sergeant, the cash dangled before Hebdon's eyes, by far the most money he had ever seen in his life and it presented an irresistible lure. When he joined the Regiment the money did not last very long, but the bewildered country lad didn't lack friends while it lasted. The money was regarded by new found comrades as a legitimate reason for carousel, everyone who came into contact with the recruit, before and after enlistment, considered himself entitled to a share. He had to 'see the Drill Sergeant a'right'. The Recruiting Sergeant expected a supper from him and he was lucky not to have been brought to the barracks by a Conducting Sergeant or he would have had to pay him the traditional present of five shillings! On his first night in the barrackroom he was 'set up for auction', one man brushing his scuffed shoes and another his coat, and the soldier in charge of the room told him that the ancient custom demanded he stood treat to his room mates. A barrel of ale was purchased, the room cleared and serious drinking begun. Men fought, accusing each other of drinking out of turn, beds were overturned in a scuffle that only ended when the Guard arrived and carried off the noisiest to the guardroom. The bounty quickly evaporated, but while it lasted comrades pestered Private Hebdon with requests for small loans; on being asked for repayment they indignantly denied the transaction and threatened violence. When it had all gone, and in no receipt of pay for some weeks, Hebdon found himself in desperate financial straits. The system put him in debt from the moment he joined and regular instalments were deducted from his pay to cover debts.

It was an old and familiar story to most men in the bungalow, but they listened sympathetically - they had nothing else to do anyway. As Hebdon's plaintive voice died away Kinrade, who invariably stressed the controversial anti-authoritarian aspects of any subject under discussion, called across the room. 'Hebby! Remember the India draft ... how you an' me tried to get away?'

Every man in the room had been on an India draft, either as replacements or when their regiment was ordered out from Britain, so this was another familiar subject, but Kinrade's pronouncements always carried sufficient 'edge' to make them worth hearing. 'Whin the notice went up an' we see'd our names on it, me an' Hebby ... an' a lot of others ... didn't fancy coming out here ... an' bloody right we've proved to be!' An appreciative guffaw rippled round the room. 'We tried all ways ... went sick, gave us a No.9 an' back to duty ... over the wall, but they'd got the barracks surrounded by police an' picquets ... then we made a rope of blankets and dropped out or the first floor window an' old Hebby hurt his foot an' I went back for him an' the guard caught us ... I'd have got clear away if I hadn't gone back, wouldn't I Hebby?'

'You didn't go back for me ... you've nivver gone back for anyone in yer life!'

'Sure I meant to ... the will was there!'

Lying on his charpoy by the cubicle at the end of the room, Private Saville reflected bitterly on the India draft. At the same Depot and on the draft with Kinrade and Hebdon, he well remembered it as they said - and more besides. To them going to India represented an end to a carefree existence of boozing, whoring and fighting around the long-suffering garrison town; to Saville it was a virtual end to living, a death sentence.

Thomas Saville had left Winchester to go up to Oxford and do medicine. At that same time gambling debts caused his father to take his life, leaving Saville and his brother Charlie with precious little in the way of an inheritance. Older by ten years, Charlie managed the estate which would support one country gentlemen but not two and, though Tom had been supported by the estate all his life he had not learned anything that would enable him to pull his weight around the place. Firmly, Charlie told him that there was insufficient money to put him through medical school and suggested that he took a commission in the army. Sick of argument and weary of aimlessly hanging around the cold empty house the youngster was impressed by the easy nonchalance of the numerous young officers in the nearby garrison town and found certain attractions in the idea. However, enquiries revealed the cost of purchasing a commission to be quite beyond them, so Charlie came up with a bright idea. Among Charlie's cronies was Captain Laidlaw, Adjutant at the Depot, who suggested that Tom enlist in the ranks as a private soldier then, as a Gentleman-Ranker, learn basic elements of soldiering before being commissioned in a few weeks.

Listening to the tales of simple country lads being guiled by devious recruiting sergeants made Private Saville realise that he too had been guileless in the face of what was but a more cunning and sophisticated pitch. He had fallen for his brother's sentence of dismissal, with the connivance of Captain Laidlaw who, on the completion of his recruit training - after weeks of absolute hell - had put Saville's name on the India draft and denied any knowledge of a promised commission from the ranks. Now here he was in India, in the lowest possible rank, with little chance of advancement. Charlie meanwhile lorded it over the estate back home, hopefully awaiting, as his next of kin, an eventual notice of regret at the death of Private Thomas Saville through action or disease.

Saville's train of thought was barely broken by the soft musical Welsh lilt of Private Owen Davies, the oldest man in the sub-section and senior in service to Bandsman Charles Mort by a mere month.

'It were lovely in the Valley, especially in summertime. ' O' course, we only saw it Sundays ... an' then we had to go to Chapel three times.'

'That's enough to make anyone join the bleedin' Army!' shouted Kinrade.

Scoring a point over the C. of E's, Kinrade looked triumphantly around at his Pope's Boys, whose spirited support aroused the hoped-for ritualistic uproar that finally petered out through sheer lack of energy. Taffy Davies patiently waited until it had died down.

'I hope when we see action again that you boyo's will fight as good as you talk! Anyway, as I were saying, on that glorious morning me Da, me two brothers an' meself walked down the village street - for the last time if we'd but known it - to go on shift at the mine ...'

On that bright sunny morning, Taffy Davies, alone of his family, survived the explosion that seared through the nether regions of the coal-mine and, perhaps indicating that he was the lucky one of the family he had also served through nine wars and campaigns without receiving a scratch. His mother died of grief, the pit closed because the owners would not spend the money on it to make it safe, and Taffy became neither the first nor the last Welshman to reluctantly walk away from Wales and seek employment in England. It was the year when the potato famine drove hordes of starving Irishmen across the sea and, willing to work for practically nothing and in the most abysmal conditions, they took any job that might have been within the capabilities of the Welsh lad. In the end, Jack Frost became recruiter and a cold hungry Taffy Davies, who had walked as far as Worcester seeking work, enlisted in HM's 29th Regiment of Foot for the statutory twenty-one year period.

'Why'd you join, Holy?' enquired a gruff voice across the room.

A carpenter in the Pioneer Section, Private James Holmes worked in wood, the sweetest of materials. A craftsman genuinely immersed in his work he was a man of few words.

'Put a piece in the family way!'

In the cubicle, the Sergeant restlessly turned, seeking a new position where, if only for a few minutes, clothing would cease to stick to his skin. Of course it was useless so he sat up, rose to his feet and stretched and eased his trousers from around his sweaty, itching crotch. He then contorted his body to raise the damp shirt that stuck glibly to his spine. Marooned from contacts, both verbal and visual, by the matting wall that ended far short of the beamed ceiling, sometimes he craved more than the involuntary eavesdropping that was the lot of non-commissioned officers in charge of barrackrooms. Now, irritated and made peevish by the whining of men who, not prepared to lie on the beds they made for themselves, lacked whatever was within them to fight their way out of the lowest ranks. He sauntered out into the shadowed room to stand in the space between the first pair of beds. He gazed thoughtfully at the tableau spread before him, where every man in the room lolled lethargically on a low charpoy. Flowing out from where he stood, heads progressively turned, men alerted each other and voices, dying in mid-conversation, were replaced by silent anticipation and curiosity. Conscious that he was transgressing the perennial pantomime of all being aware but not acknowledging that he could hear every word uttered in the barrackroom, the Sergeant spoke petulantly.

'Did none of you enlist because you wanted to?'

The awkward silence was artlessly broken by Private Birch.

'Yes, Sergeant ... I did!'

Grateful for the chance to relieve the tension and embarrassment, men scoffed and derided Birch who was sitting up on his elbows and smirking in tacit acceptance of insults he chose to interpret as slanted compliments. Despite frequently revealing the shrewdness of a true Cockney, Birch possessed a basic simplicity that sometimes aroused impulsive words and deeds, without thought or motive.

'Well, I wer a young 'un an' there were this 'ere notice on the wall o' the Mansion 'Ouse ... in Lonnon ... used to read it every time I went past ... '

Weather-beaten and peeling, throughout the Summer and Autumn of 1854 the poster had adorned the wall of the Lord Mayor of London's headquarters in the very centre of the great city. Every clerk, every office boy and every messenger from the host offices in the area passed by it two or three times a week. Some stopped to read, but certainly none as ardently so as Ellis Birch, junior clerk in the Cheapside office of Chambers, Chambers, Hampson, Duddlewhite and Bolney, Solicitors and Attorneys at Law. The bold but faded black print on the poster announced, 'The First Battalion, First or Grenadier Guards.' And continued.

'Commanded by Colonel Spencer Stanhope, an officer whose distinguished service is well known to all. Wanted for this fine Regiment, a limited number of adventurous high-spirited young patriots who yearn to tread the paths of glory. This opportunity, which may not occur again for many years, offers the privilege of enlisting into the finest - the premier - Regiment of the British Army.

Those few lucky lads who are approved as suitable to march alongside heroes shall receive a bounty of FIVE pounds, providing they are six feet in height and in prime physical condition.

This fine Regiment ranks high in the hearts of London's citizens - particularly those of the fairer sex - being seen constantly as it goes about its stirring traditional duties and ceremonies in London and at Windsor.

The kind treatment received by the men of the Queen's Guards is well known and is one of the advantages of a soldier's life, independent of the honour of serving Her Majesty the Queen. Your comforts in this Regiment - a regular hospitable table and a capacious bowl of punch - surpass the few comforts enjoyed by clerks and mechanics.

The Regiment is at present quartered in your own town, where you have luxurious standards of living worthy of brave and ambitious men - gallant lads at present eating beef, bread and potatoes (provided free of charge) in peace and comfort.

All you who are kicking your heels behind ink-stained desks, with too little wages and an oppressive master; all you with too much Wife, or perplexed by obstinate and unfeeling parents; those of address and education should make the immediate application that will ensure preferment and immediate promotion to the Adjutant, (or the Serjeant-in-Waiting) 1st Battalion Grenadier Guards, Wellington Barracks, Birdcage Walk (near Buckingham Palace) London.'

The final paragraph particularly appealed to the thin and weedy twenty year old Birch, who had been general dogsbody to his firm since he was eleven. Sleeping under the main office counter, rising at 5 a.m. to light fires and dust desks, tramping from one side of the city to the other in all weathers - sometimes not finishing before eight o'clock at night - and now elevated to the princely salary of £10 per annum. Every reproof and unfair chore he withstood solely through the knowledge that one day soon he would just walk out and join the Army, leaving them in the lurch. It would not be the Grenadier Guards, although it was their notice that stimulated him. Ellis Birch avidly followed Russell's 'Letters from the Crimea' in The Times and had read that the Grenadiers suffered severely at the Alma, Inkerman, and before Sebastopol. He had no desire to go out to snowy Russia as a reinforcement. Hating as he did, cold weather and London's stifling fogs, a prime feature of Birch's dream was to go to a country where the sun shone strongly and where it was always warm. Perhaps India.

Young Birch had been considering this fateful step since November the 18th 1852, when he set out with a package of documents for young Mr. Chambers, at the Law Courts in the Strand. London was in mourning. Shop windows and balconies were swathed in black crepe and pictures of the hook-nosed Duke of Wellington abounded. The streets were buzzing with crowds hastening to secure vantage points on the route of the Duke's funeral procession. Awed by the muted dirge of brass bands and the beat of muffled drums, Birch gazed open-mouthed at mounted Guards in gleaming cuirasses and plumed helmets. He gazed at the marching Guards with their swaying bearskins, at the scarlet Line Infantry, Lancers, Hussars, Artillery and at the whole panoply of the British Army that surrounded the massive Triumphal Car that bore the great soldier's coffin.

To Birch it was more than one of the greatest spectacles of the century and the most elaborate funeral ever held in the country. It was a colourful memory that stayed with him. He could not get out of his mind those upright, dignified soldiers in their affecting immaculate uniforms that contrasted so forcefully with his own shabby, frayed black suit. From then on, every official journey took hours as Birch went out of his way to watch Guard mountings at the Horse Guards in Whitehall and the Palaces on the Mall. He would peer through the railings around Wellington and Chelsea Barracks, watching the drilling and ceremony rehearsals; eyeing with fear and reverence - from a safe distance - the bustling Recruiting Sergeants.

On a chill foggy morning exactly two years to the day since watching the Duke's funeral, Ellis Birch was approached by a large, scarlet-jacketed Recruiting Sergeant who had been intently observing the tall, thin young man, shivering in a threadbare suit, watching the Guard change. A restless night when a thin blanket had failed to keep him warm in the unheated office, a breakfast of dried bread and margarine washed down by a lukewarm cup of weak coffee, being sent out into the dank streets, all that combined with the promise of a long, cold Winter ahead concentrated the boy's thoughts marvellously. Half listening to the genial soldier's expansive cajoling, suddenly Birch spoke. 'If I enlist can you promise I'll go to India straight away?'

Recruits were few and far between in periods when there was little unemployment. And everyone knew what a rough time the Army was having in the front of Sebastopol, so the Sergeant, loath to lose a lad whose mind was made up without him having to try very hard, immediately promised. Two hours later, with the Queen's Shilling burning in his hand and vainly trying to adjust his gait to the Sergeant's precise step, Birch ran straight into to Mr. Chambers - known as 'young' Mr. Chambers to distinguish him from his deceased father who had started the firm of solicitors. Peering through his thick glasses, the elderly gentleman recoiled in surprise.

'Bless my soul! It is young Birch, isn't it? What ever are you doing in company with this ... this soldier? Come away at once. How dare you waste the firm's time hobnobbing with soldiers ... of all people!'

Birch doffed his cap. Young Mr. Chambers had never been too unkind to him, so he didn't want to upset him. 'Sorry , sir, I can't come with you ... I've joined the Army ... I'm going to India.'

'Going to India?' Mr Chambers snapped. 'Never heard anything like it in all my life! Has this man tricked you into enlisting? My man! I'm taking this boy with me ... he's no soldier ... he's a clerk and not a very good one at that!'

The Sergeant saluted him politely. ' 'Fraid you can't have him sir ... he's taken the Queen's Shilling. At least, you can take him ... but you'll have to appear before a Magistrate within the next twenty-four hours, an' pay one pound Smart Money.'

'I'll do that ... we'll take it out of your salary, Birch!'

Aghast, Birch clutched the solicitor's sleeve. 'Oh please, sir! Don't do that ... please let me be a soldier an' go to India.'

Stepping back, Mr. Chambers shook himself free, glaring first at Birch and then at the Sergeant. 'I've known clerks to run off to sea. Lots of them steal the petty-cash, some get drunk and are locked up for disturbing the peace or assaulting a Peeler ... but Chambers, Chambers, Hampson, Duddlewhite and Bolney have never had a clerk who has done anything like this before! What a disgrace! We'll be the laughing stock of the Law Courts!'

With any geniality he possessed now vanishing, the Sergeant drew himself up. 'Beggin' your pardon, sir ... I don't see nothing disgraceful in a lad joining the Army and defending Her Majesty against her enemies. He'll see the world and be made a man of. It was his own free will, I never had to 'suade him.'

'Nothing disgraceful!' retorted the now furious solicitor. 'I beg to differ with you, sergeant! In my considered opinion that boy would be better off sentenced for a felony and on his way to transportation ... a convict is locked up or sent away where he can't do any harm, but a soldier can! Still, if he's going to India he'll be out of the way and forgotten. And a good thing too for an ungrateful wretch like you, Birch!'

Snapping his fingers in a gesture of complete rejection, Mr. Chambers swung on his heel and strode away.

After all those years Birch could still picture his body, quivering with indignation.

'The sergeant kept his word and got me on a reinforcement draft for John Company's Army ... he must have been laughing his bleedin' head orf at anyone wanting to come to India!'

When comment and derision had died away, from his charpoy far up the room, Bandsman Mort took up the line.

'Suppose I wanted to join too ... in a way. Never thought of anything else really. You don't ... do you ... when you're born and brought up in a barrackroom? Back in 1830 when I were born, the corners of every barrackroom ... ' He nodded his head in the four directions, ' ... were taken up by married soldiers an' their families, a blanket pulled at night served for a bit of privacy.'

Mockford, Davies and Wright, long enough in the service to remember this, bowed their heads in confirmation. Mort continued. 'Me dad were Corp'ral in the 50th of Foot. He an' Ma had me an' two others behind the blanket. Me Ma an' me brother an sister died of fever in '41 when I were eleven so Dad got me enlisted as a Band-Rat ... like Boy Farley over there ... an' when he was made up to sergeant he got me in his section an' I lived in his barrackroom. Then in '45 old Goughie led us out against them Sixes and the 50th took a right pasting, at Mudki we lost six orficers an' 'bout 120 men, much the same at Ferozeshah, and then at Sobraon, me Dad was killed, along with two hundred others, including twelve orficers an' the Colonel - every senior orficer down and little Lieutenant Wiley commanding the Reg'ment! Taffy, you were at Sobraon weren't yer?'

' Yes b'God, man! It were bloody terrible ... the 29th lost nearly 200 out of 500 engaged ... bloody Ferozeshah were bad too ... 250 down out of 700.'

'D'ye recall the night o' the first day?' asked Mort. 'Nivver known a longer one ... bloody Sikh guns firing on us all the time! Anyway, as I were saying, at Sobraon ... we were in Brigadier Hick's Brigade in little 'Arry Smith's Division, attacking the Sikh left ... we got up from laying down, formed and dressed under fire afore going forward. We were in the first line an' although we got broken up by deep nullahs, I kept close behind me Dad. They plastered us with grape, canister and musketry. Then we got up to their position an' found the earthworks too high to climb, an' we din't have no scaling ladders did we? Men bunked each other up ... I saw me Dad go up an' when his head rose above the top of the wall a bleedin' Sikh in a white turban took a two-handed hack at him with a long, shining tulwar ... I saw me Dad's head jump off an' bounce away like a ball on the hard ground.'

Charlie Mort shook his head sadly at the memory of his father's headless body. It had slumped heavily to the earth below, jetting dark blood over the ragged scarlet shell-jacket and the light blue cotton trousers. Mort shook himself, as though cold. 'Weren't a lucky year fer me. When the war ended an' what were left o' the Reg'mint got back to Ludhiana, the bleedin' barracks got blown down in a gale an' a couple o' hundred men, wimmin an' kids were killed an' injured ... including me wiv a broken leg!'

Reflections on Charlie Mort's ill-fortunes were dispelled by Boy Farley's youthful shrilling, jerked out in a haste bred from expectation of a rough quashing. 'Me dad were killed at the Umbeyla ... but I were too young to be there!'

In the barrackroom for four years, since he was ten years old, Boy Farley was rarely permitted to participate in the conversations of his seniors, speaking only when spoken to and then with proper respect for age and length of service. As a result he listened avidly, painstakingly storing for future use every curse and word of Army slang and crude Hindustani that was hurled around the room. Among the other Band-Rats he was a forceful and compulsive talker, always ready to take part in the illicit clay-pipe and ale sessions that would earn him a beating. Older comrades were united in discouraging the vulgarity, obscenity and bad habits in which they themselves indulged, putting them down mercilessly when revealed in a young soldier. No parent watched a boy as closely as did his mess-mates. Seeing him at all hours of the day and night they were ruthless in their demands for decency, more so from him than in themselves.

Later that day the Sergeant, indulging in one of his seemingly aimless leg-stretching promenades up and down the centre aisle, stopped before the boy-soldier's charpoy. 'You're not Bob Farley's son ... Sarn't Farley who was in 'H' Company ... are you?'

Boy Farley leapt from his bed, snapping up to attention in a manner that brought approving nods from the old soldiers.

'Yes, Sarn't ... he was my Dad.'

The Sergeant shook his head. 'I should've known ... never realised ... your father was a bloody good soldier ... a brave man ... I was by his side when he died. I hope you're proud of him.'

The weedy, spotty-faced boy tensed and stared at the Sergeant, his eyes suddenly brimming with tears.

Bob Farley's lad. He could see it now ... he'd look just like his father in a few years. The Sergeant's memory winged back five years to his fellow sergeant, recklessly exposing himself to every act of foolish bravery that would bring a dignified death, or restore love and respect in his wife's flashing but wandering eyes. Her ill-concealed affair with the Company Sergeant-Major was a Married Quarter's scandal. Even his gentle wife Amy could not forbear from criticising the pert and lively dark-haired Susie Farley.

'Your mother ... is she still in the cantonment?'

Boy Farley nodded. 'Yes Sergeant. She married Pig Parsons ... beg pardon Sergeant ... Sarn't-Major Parsons I mean.' Carried away by the unaccustomed luxury of free speech, the boy gabbled on. 'He hated me ... an' I him. Weren't no place in the quarter for us both. He signed me on as a Band-Rat as soon as I were old enough ... that were after I bit him!'

The room dissolved in an uproar at the comic aspect of a soldier biting a sergeant-major. The Sergeant waited until the noise subsided.

'Your father was a good soldier ... one of the best ... I'll talk to you about him one day, if you want.'

The boy nodded, too full for words.

Private Timothy Bell wondered how his father was, if he'd got over the shock of his son vanishing without a word. He'd had to get away quickly with no time for farewells. There was no-one to worry about Big Sanny, snoring like a pig on the next bed. Maybe that was why he'd tried to look after the big shambling loony, care for him and bring him round when he had one of his fits. Bell and Sanny had grown up together in Edinburgh where Sanny waited in doorways for Bell to come out of the sessional school. They had played together in the vennels, closes and wynds that branched off the High Street and Canongate. At dusk the lumpy, ungainly Sanny lumbered off to whatever dank cellar he'd found to shelter himself, while young Ding Dong Dell panted up rickety stairs to the eighth story of the decrepit 'land', where the Bell family lived among the city's poorest. Chimney sweeps, porters and labourers all lived under a baleful aura of poverty, dirt, overcrowding, unemployment, destitution and disease. In this gaunt slum tenement, perpetually tainted by the insanitary privy-midden, Timothy Bell lived with his parents, three brothers and two sisters, all crowded into two dark, damp rooms. He knew the rooms to be heaven compared with the temporary hovels that sheltered the half-daft orphan, Big Sanny Alexander.

Aged eighteen, Tim Bell, apprenticed to a printer, was weary of the constant companionship of Big Sanny, now living on scraps thrown to him for humping and carrying at the markets. One bitterly cold January evening, to avoid him Tim made his way home by a different route, passing through New Town where lived the better off citizens. Accosted by a gang of youths intent on deterring working class lads from defiling their streets, outnumbered by five to one and apprehensively aware of the cruelties and violence inflicted by these bored young gentry upon those such as he, Tim fled for his life. Whooping and hollering as they did when fox-hunting, the well-fed and fit youths kept close to his heels through the mazes of winding ice-slippery streets, alleys, vennels and closes, until it pleased them to corner their panting prey in a cul-de-sac off the High Street.

With his lungs heaving and gasping for breath, the terrified fugitive set his back to the wall. His leaden arms feebly warded off the slaps and punches that flickered in from his mocking tormentors. They prancing and postured before preparing to move in for the kill, when, like a vengeful apparition, Big Sanny was among them. Heads cracked sickeningly together and two boys slumped to the frost-rimed cobbles. Another, hands pressed to his crotch, sagged against the wall, retching and panting while a fourth slithered away to safety. There remained but one tormentor, glaring wildly into the darkness for an escape route that did not exist. Lumbering forward and brushing aside the panicking fists of the cornered youth, Sanny wrapped a powerful arm around his neck and squeezed. Before the abstracted Timothy Bell could persuade him to let go Sanny Alexander had broken the youth's neck.

Rising shakily to their feet and seeing the huddled body with its head askew, the two youths with cracked heads sidled from the alley, one crying as he went. 'Ye've kilt our Jamie ... we'll have the police on you!'

Tim Bell's mind raced over the situation; Big Sanny had no-one to speak up for him ... they'll hang him for this ... probably hang me too ... we're both in it together. They'd have to get away, but where could they go in the depths of Winter? Tim grabbed Big Sanny's arm and led him away into the gathering gloom, snowflakes tumbling around them. Four days later, famished and chilled to the bone in their poor-man's wet clothing, they were huddled in the doorway of the Glasgow recruiting officer when he came to open up. Despite Sanny's obvious mental deficiencies and epilepsy, both boys passed the perfunctory medical examination and by midday were soldiers of the Queen.

To directly ask a man his very personal reasons for enlisting was an affront to barrackroom etiquette although, with some men it could be done in a joshing sort of way. The American, Martin Early, being something of a private man both by rank and nature, was not of that type. He was not one of your slick, quick talking Yankees, although his mates, knowing no other American titles, had incongruously labelled the ex-Confederate soldier with that nickname and he, with a soldiers understanding backed by characteristic Virginian courtesy, had not bothered - forcibly or otherwise - to contradict them. Anyway, Early had learned a wholesome respect for the Yankee enemy he had fought for four years on many notable fields, different in so many ways to the Southerner, and both poles apart from these Limeys with whom he had thrown in his lot two years ago. Throughout the long morning he had listened to their varied reasons for becoming soldiers, and shrewdly guessed that those who had not spoken up were recalling similar stories. Unwilling soldiers all of them, so different from the eager volunteers he knew in 1861, but, fighting to defend your own patch was a bit different to being shunted out to this God-forsaken county to fight niggers who couldn't hold a candle to the Indians of the West. Well, he'd enlisted twice in different armies, both times of his own free will and with good intent, more than could be said for this lot.

'I sure 'nuff knew what I was up to when I joined your Army, an' I ain't regretted it none, no sir!'

This typically laconic statement caught the room's attention, all of the men had idly speculated on how the American came to be among their ranks. Any likelihood of finding out was dispelled by the long-awaited signal that ended the morning with the bustle of erecting trestles and boards and the arrival of steaming dixies.

VII

With breakfast eaten and tables cleared away, the room settled down to yet another interminable, soul-destroying day, routinely prefaced by a boisterous slanging match between the Catholics and Protestants. About mid-morning the Sergeant noticed it to be a day with a difference. For the past hour an almost unique barrackroom phenomena had prevailed in that only one man was talking at a time, and in civilised conventional tones without any of the usual abusive provocation. Displaying unexpected garrulity, Lance Corporal Samuel Mockford was holding the room's attention with a colourful account of how he foiled a rifle-stealing raid of native tribesmen.

Standing in his cubicle doorway the Sergeant surveyed the twin lines of charpoys and the reclining men in various stages of undress and all sweating profusely. This rare, euphoric hiatus told him that he had forgotten how soldiers were never quieter than when listening to a good yarn.Conscious of eyes turning upon him the Sergeant glanced at Private Saville. The young soldier coloured up and covered his confusion by saying, in a low voice. 'It's a bit like Chaucer's Canterbury Tales, isn't it Sergeant?'

The Sergeant's obvious lack of comprehension embarrassed Saville.

'I'm sorry, Sergeant, I though you'd know it ... the company of pilgrims going to Canterbury, meeting at the Tabard Inn at Southwark...' Saville closed his eyes and continued, '... the jolly host says:

My masters, certainly ye be to me right welcome, heartily:
For by my troth, and flattering none, say I
I have not seen so large a company at once inside my inn this year, so now
I'd gladly make you mirth if I knew how.
And of a pleasant game I'm just bethought
To cheer the journey - it shall cost you nought.

Mine host proposes that, instead of riding 'dumb as stone',

they should lighten the journey and lessen the miles by telling tales, to and from Canterbury. When they return to the Tabard Inn he who has told the best tale shall have supper at the expense of the rest of the party.'

The Sergeant pondered, it wasn't a bad idea for this lot ... anything that might shut them up for a bit was worth trying! But I'd never get 'em to do it ... can't order 'em, its got to be voluntary. Some one would have to start it off.

'D'ye think we could do it in this bungalow? How about you telling the first tale?'

'Oh, no, I couldn't!' Saville nervously responded. 'I don't know any stories about the Army ... and they'd never listen to me. You can't order me to do it Sergeant.'

'No, I can't order you ... but they'll listen to anyone who'll tell 'em a good tale. It doesn't have to be about the Army ... something about England and home, the outside world and how other people live.'

The young soldier mutely shook his head.

For days the Sergeant mulled over a way to encourage the stories. It would be better than the endless bickering, and he was sick and tired of thc coarseness and foul language. Listening to stories might bring them together a bit, restore some comradeship. Besides it would make for an easier running of the sub-section. As things stood it could only be hoped that men would forget their differences when up against it, in the way that outside interference unites a quarrelling husband and wife. To suggest the Canterbury tale-telling would be a calculated risk, a gamble that could improve the sorry existence of eighteen men, including himself but only he would be putting up the stakes. He could lose their respect for his rank and there might be a pack of trouble from the Sergeant-Major for over-familiarity with lower ranks. Every NCO had heard the RSM snarl, "If you want to mix with lower ranks, I can accommodate you!"

The Sergeant made up his mind to give it a go. It would be best on a Saturday, after the Commanding Officer's Parade, when the men returned to their bungalows lifted by the Regimental Band and all the familiar ceremonial drill. He wondered how best to get it started, he would have preferred Saville, who knew all about this Chaucer bloke, but it would have to be done with the authority of three stripes to ensure a silent hearing.

Each week of the Hot Season had five mornings of identically monotonous routine, and two - Commanding Officer's Parade on Saturday and Regimental Church Parade on Sunday - that were different but more onerous, the higher standards of turn-out required more cleaning and polishing, but they made a change and were welcomed.

That Saturday, sub-sections and sections formed up in the Lines, were inspected and fell-in as a Company when the bugler sounded 'Close'. In columns, the Companies marched out of their Lines. Eight scarlet caterpillars wheeled onto the Square and assembled as a Regiment. Directed by the Adjutant, the Company Markers had earlier taken ground at points where the directing flanks of their Companies were to rest. Bugles sounded 'Advance' and were immediately followed by the beats of the big-drum that heralded the Band's stirring march. Columns marched on Markers, took up position, ordered arms and stood at ease. Posted at the rear of the leading centre Company were the colours - Queens Colour on the right, Regimental Colour on the left - borne by officers with an escort of sergeants.

Despite grousing about the additional cleaning, polishing and general preparation, and the need to be more alert than usual if punishment was to be avoided, this weekly Parade was not disliked. Everyone enjoyed the Band which, together with the Colours being on Parade and the March-Past, stimulated the deep Regimental pride that hung firm in every soldiers breast.

In Open-Order, in turn the eight Companies were inspected by the Commanding Officer and received in ceremony by the Company Commander before leading-off the slow formal procession along rigid ranks, in strict order of seniority; Commanding Officer, Company Commander, Adjutant, Regimental Sergeant-Major, Company Sergeant-Major. When the Inspection was concluded the Company Commanders orders were rapped out.

'Close Ranks! ... Order Arms! ... Unfix Bayonets! ... Stand at Ease!'

Standing erect and motionless throughout the lengthy inspection, men looked forward to the March Past, a cherished 'perk' of the Commanding Officer, now standing solitary upon the Saluting-Base as the Adjutant savoured his personal moment of glory in taking over the Parade. Before anyone had marched onto the Square, the Sergeant-Major ceremoniously positioned at far flung points of the parade-ground, six Markers bearing small guidons. Standing unobtrusively immobile they came into their own near the conclusion of the Parade, marking the route taken by the Regiment as it marched-past to salute its Commanding Officer. Four of these Markers indicated corners of a vast rectangle with the Saluting-Base - a small wooden daïs - at the exact centre of its long sides, a Marker placed ten paces on either side. Opposite, facing right with left flanks resting on the long side, eight Companies were each formed in three lines, the third being a supernumerary rank of junior officers, sergeant-majors and sergeants. Loftily surveying the Parade from his charger, the Adjutant shouted, 'Her Majesty's One Hundred and Thirty First Regiment of Foot will march-past in slow and quick time! By the left ... slow-march!'

A thousand men stepped-off as one, upright bodies and wooden leg movements transformed them into mechanical marionettes, striding along to the Regimental Slow March, 'Johnny Reeves'.

Every left foot in the Regiment slid forward thirty inches, toes pointed and turned slightly outwards. Knees stiffened, legs moved directly from the haunches and their eyes fixed on the reddened, boil-scarred necks of the men to their front. Familiar words, handed down from old soldier to recruit, for more than a hundred years, were silently mouthed to maintain rhythm and steadiness while performing the fatiguing and unnatural balancing gait of seventy-eight paces to the minute:

Where have you gone to, Johnny Reeves?
Why is the plough lying idle?
The fire in the forge is burning low,
And Dobbin is still in his bridle.
Oh I have gone for a soldier to be,
The fire don't matter a fuck to me
And Dobbin can shit in his stable.

With shoulders exactly square to the front, the body straight with a forward inclination the weight was borne principally on the fore part of the feet. The head was erect but not thrown back and the chin slightly drawn in. Each soldier was a replica of all those around him but the touch of shoulders bestowed a warming sense of comradeship. The approach of the eight formations to the first of the four corners of the rectangle signalled a cacophony of commands that would assail the ears until the Parade's end, from 'A' Company, and in succession from others, came barked orders.

' 'A' Company! Left ... wheel!'

The left hand, or pivot-man, marked time, turning slowly with the Company to the new front, all eyes turned right to the wheeling flank, except those of the outside men who looked inwards as they stepped the usual thirty inch pace. The remainder regulated their length of pace according to their distance from the pivot-man, touching lightly towards him. Experience prevented crowding as each man yielded to the pressures coming from the pivot-flank while resisting pressure from the outer flank. The wheel completed and lines straightened ready to advance. Sergeant-majors on the extreme right of the third supernumerary line alerted the Company Commanders.

'By the left ... forward!'

Marking time without moving from the spot, feet alternately raised nine inches and smoothly slid into motion as, in unison, left feet pointed forwards to take up the regulation pace. So it went until coming level with the Marker, ten paces before the Saluting-Base, Company Commanders called to their Companies, 'Eyes ... right!'

Except those men on the extreme right of the lines nearest the Saluting-Base, every head swivelled sharply to remain rigidly looking right, the momentary imbalance comforted by the touch of shoulders. Simultaneously, synchronised with the left foot touching the ground, officers extended and raised their sword-arms to the right, bringing them to 'recover' by a circular motion that continued to the right shoulder. Then, smartly lowered to salute, the sword point steadied twelve inches from the ground in the direction of the right foot, arm remained straight and the hand just behind the thigh with the thumb flat on the sword handle. It was a graceful movement of four combined motions that allowed salutes to be completed in the same number of slow-time paces. Directed towards the saluting-base, heads turned to the front six paces beyond, as the left foot came to ground, officers coming to 'carry' on the following pace.

The Colours, carried by two junior lieutenants posted in the rear of the leading centre Company when the Regiment was in line, marched-past between 'D' and 'E' Companies. They were not cast loose or lowered at the Saluting-Point. During the second wheel, the Colour-Party changed flank so as to march-past on the side nearest to the Saluting-Base.

In solitary splendour on his dais, the Commanding Officer gravely acknowledged salutes by bringing his right hand elegantly to his shako-peak, lowering it when a Company had gone from his front and repeating the movement as each Company glided past, paying their respects.

Ten paces beyond the Saluting-Base, coming up to the second Marker, the Company Commanders ordered, "Eyes front!"

The formations wheeled left at the third corner and again at the fourth, marching down the long side of the rectangle. The Adjutant, on his charger in the centre of the Parade, signalled the Bandmaster to end the Slow March when 'A' Company reached their original position. Abruptly, the lilting tune was ended and was replaced by the measured, slithering shuffle of two thousand feet. The Adjutant cried out, 'The Regiment will break into Quick-Time! Quick ... March!'

Now came the joyous moment eagerly awaited by all when the Regiment was galvanised into a controlled and co-ordinated flurry of energy. Tightly grouped formations gaily broke into quick-time of one hundred and twenty paces to the minute, their rhythmically swinging right arms producing a proud and exaggerated swagger to the shoulders. This sudden and dramatic sense of freedom, still within the rigid bounds of ceremony and discipline, was stimulated by the Band thumping out the Regimental Quick March, 'The Dandy O!', a traditional 17th century country air embellished by lively words affectionately familiar to at least five generations of soldiers of HM's 131st Regiment of Foot.

The Dandy O ... the Dandy O,
The little man who wouldn't grow
Little arms and little paws
Bandy legs and toothless jaws
Guts were fat and plates were flat
But his chopper ... what a whopper

How it pleasured Widow Hopper
The Dandy O ... the Randy O
The Bandy Dandy Randy O.

When sensations of enjoyment are few and far between, slight pleasures become delights. Now, stimulated by lively music and anticipation of the Parade's end, breakfast and a day's blanket-drill, reinvigorated by the swinging, muscle-loosening pace, every man-jack swaggered blithely round the Square, wheeling smoothly round corners. Passing the Saluting-Base, a thousand pairs of eyes made their submission, signifying ungrudging affection and respect for the personal deity who reciprocated precious little mutual understanding, yet held their very lives in his hands.

Companies marched off the Square, dispersed to their respective Lines and were dismissed.

VIII

Charpoys creaked as men settled down for the morning. Heads raised enquiringly and shouted interchanges died away when the Sergeant walked into the middle of the room, feeling far from confident about what was to follow. 'Pay attention,' he said. 'I want to talk to you about something important ... something that could make a lot of difference to our lives!'

Faces mirrored a blend of curiosity and disinterest and the Sergeant continued.

'A long time ago there was a man named Chaucer ... '

'What Company was 'e in Sarn't?'

'No, he wasn't in the Service ... he wrote a book called Canterbury Tales, about a party of pilgrims going to Canterbury ... to the Shrine of Saint Thomas a Becket ... '

'I knew 'im!' interrupted Birch.

'Birch ...' sighed the Sergeant. 'How the hell could you know a man who's been dead about 700 years?'

'But, Sarn't, Thomas a Becket used ter keep an alehouse in Aldgate ... my old Dad used it ... 'ad 'is name over the door ... Thomas a Becket!'

Dissolving into uproar, eruptions of ribald laughter relieved the embarrassment aroused by this unusual sort of talk from a senior NCO. Men vied with each other in ridiculing the bewildered Birch ... did he think the Marquis of Granby, bald 'ead an' all, kept that pub at 'Shot? Had he ever seen a White Horse, a Gay Hussar, or a King an' Queen behind a bar serving ale? Suppressing a smile, the Sergeant let it run on, good humour would make it easier to get across to them.

'Alright ... alright! You've had your laugh ... now shuddup ... an' listen!'

He paced restlessly up and down the centre aisle, looking into men's faces, gazing upwards into the high beamed ceiling. Lowering his eyes, he stared into the rifle-rack.

'There were this bunch of pilgrims ... religious people

travelling from London to Canterbury ... where the Cavalry Depot is ... an' they made the long journey seem shorter by telling stories. Now we're shut up in this stinking bungalow sixteen hours a day ... that's a bloody long journey in my book! I've been listening to some of you telling tales ... like the other morning when you were talking on how an' why you'd enlisted ... you all listened ... an' the morning passed quickly, didn't it?'

Covertly eyeing each other, men nodded slowly, still trying hard to see what the Sergeant was getting at.

'Don't you see we could make all the mornings pass quicker if we had more tales ... if some of you told stories ... about life in the Service ... or something that happened back home ... it would make our journey easier, wouldn't it?'

The reaction was blank and discouraging.

'Come on!' cajoled the Sergeant. 'I never knew an old soldier who didn't have a tale to tell!'

The Sergeant felt he'd handled it badly. You couldn't talk to 'em like this. An order ... right or wrong ... from a sergeant had to be obeyed but ... on principle, soldiers never fell in with a suggestion or request from a superior officer. Resenting differences in social levels between themselves and senior NCO's, private soldiers jealously guarded their own few rights and wouldn't stomach an NCO blundering or trespassing beyond the call of duty. Reluctantly, he realised he had to put himself out on a limb by telling the first story himself, taking advantage of his rank to make them listen. It would not necessarily encourage anyone else to tell a tale, probably sheer bloody mindedness would make sure of that! As a senior rank, and their immediate commander, he was always expected to do the right thing and would probably lose face by being allied to a lost cause. Seeing his irresolution, bolder spirits began ostentatiously to settle down for a morning kip; then the American Private Early came to his rescue.

'Say, Sergeant ... do you'all have a tale to tell? 'Cos, sure as hell, I'll tell one if you will! Spinning yarns 'round the cracker-barrel is an ole American custom!'

The Sergeant warmed towards this man whose intelligence and experience surely merited more than the lowest rank. Surprisingly, he found himself battling with an upsurge of emotion so strong as to nearly bring tears to the eye, Early had spontaneously volunteered to help him get off the hook, he was probably regretting it already. Raising his hands to quell the subsequent outbreak of comment, the Sergeant called out loud and gruff.

'Well, that's that, then! I'll tell the first tale ... now ... and we'll fix days when Private Early here will do his stuff.'

Saville brought the cane chair from the cubicle and placed it between the tatty-covered doorways at the hut's mid-point. The Sergeant reasoned that there was a certain authority in sitting while everyone was laying and it may also be a bit cooler there. He drew a deep breath, feeling as though he had been ordered to fix bayonets and attack.

'We come into the Service with very little, many of us 'list 'cos we got nothing ... no food, nor clothing, no roof over our heads. The Reg'ment gives us them things in return for the use of our strong right arms. It don't guarantee much else, the only other thing a swaddy can be sure he'll get is a blanket and six feet of earth in some God-forsaken corner of the Empire ... mourned only by his mates an' forgotten in a day or two. If he lives out his time, he has memories ... plenty of 'em ... good 'uns, bad 'uns ... an' nightmares. Most memories are about mates. Blokes you've known in the Reg'ment, in barrackroom an' field. This is a story about two mates when I was a young soldier in the Five an' Thrup'pennies ... 53rd Shropshire Light Infantry. There were two lads in my section 'oo formed a file, been mates since 'crootie days. Drunk and sober they'd been everywhere and done everything together, including watching each other's back at Lucknow in '57. Yet they were different in everything, except both were just on five feet two ... minimum height for entry ... and at the Depot, when they saw they was the smallest in the squad, it sort of threw them together.'

The Sergeant pictured them as clearly as though they had just marched into the room. Bricky Tate, a quiet Shropshire farm lad, who spoke but little, and then in a soft country burr. He was a good natured, chunky little fellow, with a square head thatched with a stubble of brick-red hair set on a short neck that hunched into his square shoulders. He moved silently and lightly on the balls of his feet like the poacher he was. He had only enlisted because he was caught. Bricky possessed the gift bestowed upon some countrymen of loving animals and being able to do anything with them. Very different was Jockey Rix, well-proportioned on a miniature scale, he was a quick-moving London cocksparrow. As dark as Bricky was fair, he had lank black hair and a sallow pinched face with dark brooding eyes. Jockey was quick talking, a little man with a sharp tongue that invariably gave better than it received. He was very agile and could recognisably imitate a man with just a pose of his head or a twitch of his shoulders, always with a cruel 'bite' that caused comrades to be wary of him.

Inseparable, Bricky and Jockey shared everything, including friends and foes; to offend one was to make an enemy of both. Despite their size, the two of them were respected as awkward customers in a fight. Bricky was hard to hit or put down as he came in crouching with his head hunched deep into his shoulders like a surprisingly strong baby rhino. He had none of the belligerence that small men often display, and lacked Jockey's sheer malevolence and pent-up rage that, when aggrieved, turned him into a spitting, clawing, biting ball of fury. It was the only way for a small man to fight in the rookeries where Jockey was dragged up.

The bastard child of a sixteen year old dollymop, Jockey was dumped on a baby farmer who brought him up. At the age of six he was sold to a chimney sweep for training as a climbing-boy; the wide, old-fashioned flues had ledges and recesses far better cleaned by a scrambling urchin than a long, unwieldy brush. Sometimes, in later years, Jockey woke up in a cold sweat from dreams of the horrors of his breaking-in when the sweep would drive the terrified child up tight, black flues by jabbing a spike into the soles of his feet or scorching them with a burning brand. And customers had not always inconvenienced themselves by putting out the fire in time for the chimney to be cool or free from fumes. Surviving uncrippled, Jockey had acquired an astonishing agility, amply repaying the sweep's hopes that a climbing-boy's training would be ideal preparation for cat-burglary. Or as a 'snakesman' - an under-sized supple boy who could wriggle between bars or through small, unprotected windows to open an inside door for accomplices; sweeps possessed unparalleled opportunities for familiarising themselves with the inside layouts of houses. Jockey had no particular objection to co-operating, until the climbing-boy who shared his soot-sack bed - caught red-handed by the Peelers - was publicly hanged outside Newgate Gaol at eight o'clock on a fine Monday morning. Jockey had wriggled through dense crowds on Snow Hill to see his friend turned off, and being immediately reformed by the sight he determined to seek any opportunity for escape.

Sent up the high chimney stack of a sugar refinery in Lambeth, Jockey came out at the top and swarmed thirty feet down the outside bare brickwork and reached a wall angled against the stack. With his back and bare feet braced against the rough stonework, he worked his way down the wall to a window and the street below. Then, with the sweep in hot pursuit, he ran straight to Whitehall as planned, to breathlessly place himself under the protection of a recruiting sergeant and the British Army.

'I'll never forget the night it all started.' The Sergeant spoke out. ' About nine, ten years ago, not only 'cos o' what came from it, but 'cos of the fight ... never seen anything like it before or since ... wager few men have. We were at Ferozepore ... it was an ordinary night in the Canteen ... 'bout an hour 'fore stop-tap ... all were as happy as pigs in shit, laughing at Jockey doing his acrobatics an' getting sups of ale from men's mugs for his trouble. Most'd had their share ... some more'n others an' looking for trouble ... like Bully Baker of 'A' Company, although he wasn't as pissed as he made out an' well knew what he was up to when he came staggerin' over to our corner to get a rise out of 'G' Company. But none bit, getting on with their boozing peaceful like, making out they didn't hear him ... it had to be that way with Bully Baker 'cos there was no man who could stand up to him. An' we had our share o' rough an' tumblers in the 53rd in them days. Bully was the biggest man in the Reg'ment ... 'bout six foot five an' seventeen stone ... been a bare-knuckled fighter in his day ... claimed to have gone in the ring with Tom Sayers, champion of England who beat the American, John Heenan. His mates reckon he went thirty rounds at Guildford before magistrates stepped in an' stopped the fight.

Bully rabbited on while we carried on as though he wasn't there, until he got weary of it an' did what we all feared ... turned his beer mug upside down on the counter! Well, it was a direct challenge, wasn't it? Something had to be done or 'G' Company couldn't hold their heads in the Reg'ment ... but who'd take him on? Every one of us kept our eyes down an' not a man stepped for'ard. You couldn't blame us ... he were a terrible fighter who didn't just beat you ... he crippled men an' made them useless for so'jering.'

Perhaps to defuse the situation, or through sheer foolhardiness - more likely the latter - Jockey Rix had jumped down from his bench and swayed across the room in recognisable imitation of Bully, ending with an exaggerated pantomime gesture of up-turning a beer mug on the bar counter. Roars of laughter encouraged Jockey to venture dangerously close to the one man who saw no humour in it. Incredibly quickly for a big drunken man, Bully grabbed Jockey by the front of his tunic and lifted him a foot in the air and drew back a huge fist. Before the blow could be delivered, Bricky Tate hurtled across the room and ferociously kicked Bully in the groin. Doubled up with pain, the big man's grip relaxed, allowing Jockey to scuttle away and nimbly line up alongside his mate.

'You little bastards,' roared Bully. 'I'll kill you both!'

Keeping out of reach, Jockey said, 'We'll give you the chance ... you wanna fight a 'G' Company man? Well take us both on ... official like ... you're bigger 'n me an' Bricky put together ... we'll put up the dooks with yer!'

Bully looked from one to the other of the little men, eyes gleaming, fists clenching and unclenching; grimly he nodded. 'Free-for-all ... no Marquis o' bloody Queensbury rules?'

'Anything you like, you great fat pillock!'

'You're fuckin' asking fer it ... an' yer goin' to get it ... I can eat the bleedin' pair of yer ... an' shit yer aht wivout fartin'!'

The Sergeant's first contact with Private 'Bully' Baker had been back at the Depot in England, when he was a young soldier on his very first Main-Gate Guard. Bully, roaring drunk, stood outside, challenging the Guard to fetch him into Barracks; the Guard Sergeant told-off eight men and warned them that they were not hit but only to restrain him. Reluctantly, the unhappy Guard clattered out into the cold, wet night, keeping a cautious distance from the huge figure who rocked unsteadily on his splayed legs, his arms hanging loosely and his ham-like fists clenched. His shako-less, cropped head was thrust threateningly forward, and a scarred face and flattened nose glistened with rain. His tunic was gone and a torn and wet grey issue shirt hung open to the waist. Flurries of snow had turned to rain and laid a patina of slush on the cobbles which caused the iron-tipped boots to slip and slither as the Guard sidled warily towards the big man who, in the wind-blown lamplight, seemed formidably allied to a huge posturing shadow.

Resembling a grotesque Satanic ballet, played out on an ill-lit stage, the melee sprawled back and forth. The drink-maddened Baker lashed out savagely with his fists and boots, impeded only by numbers of the guards and disarmed by their role of restraint. Swearing and shrieking like a maniac, the big man flung himself on the wet ground, dragging men with him to roll and struggle in the slush. The uproar attracted a growing group of civilian onlookers who provided a background chorus of support for this amazingly valiant man who, having taken just a drop too much, was bravely fighting single-handed against eight sober soldiers. When three men lay motionless in huddled muddied heaps the Guard Sergeant sent out another half-dozen men and finally, after desperate battling, the sheer weight of numbers enabled them to get the 'drunkards grip' on Bully - face down with two men to each arm and leg. Closely pressed by a jeering crowd, the writhing group struggled into the Guardroom where eight men employed all their strength and weight to keep the near-naked, muddied, muscular body on the wooden floor. The crazed soldier dragged them all upright, breaking away to charge headlong into the brick wall. For Baker's own safety the Guard Sergeant ordered his wrists to be handcuffed and his legs lashed together before, still thrashing and roaring, he was thrown into a cell.

Spattered with mud and blood, the floor and walls had to be cleaned-up and the overturned furniture reassembled. Despite spending forty minutes on this, a dissatisfied Crderly Officer put the Guard Commander on a charge for failing to maintain a tidy Guardroom. Young Private Oakley nursed bruises, a swollen face and a black eye for days after. This then, was the ageing but still formidable behemoth to be tackled, for the honour of the Company, by its two smallest men.

As though the Canteen had suddenly burst into flames, leaving behind only those who had passed out, everyone jostled and fought their way out into the cool night. It gets cold in the

Punjab in Winter but all, particularly the three combatants, were warmed by the heat of battle. A seething circle formed around the fighters; Bricky, knowing they'd need all the room they could get, told mates to pass the word round not to crowd them. As there were no rules, no time was taken selecting a referee, seconds or time-keeper. The two little men hastily pulled off their belts, wrapping them around their hands with the metal clasps over the knuckles. Bricky muttered. 'Well, we've got three o' the four 'B's.'

'Bricky, old mate,' said Jockey. 'You go at 'im from the front ... an' I'll make a diversion'ry flank attack.'

Like a berserk bull, the huge man hurled himself upon them. Nimbly, the smaller men skipped aside allowing the wild rush to be absorbed by the packed ranks of spectators, some taking their chance to pay off old scores by kicking or punching Bully. In this manner, the brawl ebbed and flowed as the big man, like a bull in a bull-ring plagued by pics and bandilleros, was steadily slowed down. Then the diminutive pair went on the offensive; Jockey launched himself at Bully's right rear, momentarily diverting his attention to allow the crouching Bricky to wade in, fists pumping like pistons into the big man's guts while the knuckles of Bully's right hand broke themselves on his brick-red cropped head. Jockey, like a rampant octopus, had his legs tightly twined about Bully's waist, his fingers clasped together in an arm lock around his neck, forcing his head back and causing him to choke. Sheer strength prevailed and, shaking himself like a bear baited by dogs, Bully flung Jockey from him to land ten feet away on the dusty ground. In the same movement, the big man lurched at Bricky who, retreating rapidly, was caught when the crowd behind him did not give way. A crunching blow on the side of the head and another in the chest lifted the small man from his feet, but the packed ranks closing swiftly, kept Bully off him. Frustrated, the big man's bloodshot eyes, flickering wildly round in the half light, picked out Jockey, painfully rising from the ground. Roaring, Bully bent over the little man and clasped him round the chest and thighs. The milling mob parted like waves before a prow, as he lurched forward towards the brick wall of the Canteen, bearing Jockey's helpless frame in the manner of a battering ram assaulting castle gates. The sickening crunch of the little man's defenceless head against the unyielding wall brought a sudden, horror-stricken, indrawing of breath from the crowd of onlookers.

Drooping the inert Jockey like a spent match, Bully glowered around the seething circle, peering into shadowy faces and seeking the elusive Bricky who was stealthily circling through massed ranks, keeping out of sight and desperately wondering how to emerge with honour and least personal damage. The crowd rippled as men moved aside to let the little man slither his way through. Encouraged by whispers, pats and squeezes to his arms and shoulders, Bricky moved in concert with Bully, maintaining position to his rear and never taking his eyes from the glowering shambling shape. Suddenly, an unknown practical benefactor pressed a heavy chunk of rock into Bricky's hand and his fingers gratefully moulded themselves round its rough surface, his heart sang within him. He ceased circling, braced himself and called, 'Here I am you murderin' bastard!'

Bully swung round, staring urgently into the shadows to pick out the unmistakable red head. Ferocious anticipation lit up his great craggy face and, growling like an animal, he lumbered forward, brushing aside those that came between him and his prey. Nimbly side-stepping so that the rampaging bear surged past him, Bricky put every ounce of his nine and a half stone into hammering the rock at Bully's right temple. Awed men fell back before the giant who lurched forward on a wave of momentum and slowly crumpled onto his hands and knees. With the speed of a mongoose attacking a snake, Bricky was on his back, pulling the head back with his left forearm while his right hand repeatedly smashed the rock into the bloody, rapidly pulping, face. Teeth strewed the sand like yellow pebbles before startled men collected themselves and dragged him off.

'Fer Christ's sake, Bricky! Ye'll set yerself up fer a hanging job!'

Bricky, allowed himself to be pulled away and stood panting above the hulk at his feet. He tossed the rock away. 'He'll soldier no more ... he ain't got no teeth to bite cartridges!'

Gathering himself, Bricky pushed through the crowd who were looking down at his mate and sat cradling Jockey's head in his lap. Jockey was unconscious, his breathing shallow and irregular. 'Never mind, Jock old mate ... we done 'im ... he'll give us no more trouble.'

The injured men were looked after by their mates - to go sick might have resulted in charges being pressed. They worked on Jockey for two hours before he came round, vomited weakly and complained of a violent headache and not being able to see properly. Next morning, he struggled onto Parade and with help got through it as after a heavy jag. Recalling nothing of the fight or what led up to it, he was out for the rest of the day on his charpoy; nor could he down his share as a conquering hero in the canteen that night. In the days that followed Jockey was far from being himself, irritably cursing all who asked how he felt. His head permanently ached, he was always dizzy and giddy, and double vision persisted until the passing of time carried away his symptoms. But it was a different Jockey. His perky insolence was replaced by furtiveness and an inability to look eye-to-eye; his rapid edged patter was replaced by indecisive speech that lapsed into mumbling. He could carry out drills and duties, and his tumbling and miming seemed unimpaired, but he was not the clean soldier he had been, taking less care with his off-duty appearance and his tunic was invariably decorated with canteen medals.

Noticeably 'fanti' after the fight, Bully Baker soon left the Regiment. The bazaar gup said that he had taken his discharge in India and was tramping from one cantonment to another ... he had been knifed in a bazaar brothel ... was working on the railway ... had married a half caste bibi ... been trooped home.

It never dawned on either of the men that their partnership was no longer equal. Although still inseparable, doing everything and going everywhere together, now Bricky, in a gently paternal and diplomatic manner, led a not always compliant Jockey. In the timeless fashion of Army friendships, it might have stayed like that had Toby not come into their lives one night in the Canteen, when Bricky was fascinated by a small and scruffy monkey dressed in ill-fitting khaki-drill tunic and trousers. Toby belonged to a swaddy on the next table who boasted that the animal could go through the Drill manual, but the monkey stubbornly refused to perform. His master, having been on the shunt all night, began to crack and blind, threatening to marrow the animal. Bricky, confident of his ability to handle animals, eyed the monkey. 'Reckon I could teach the little devil all the recruit drill in the Manual.'

Ready cash, plus his reputation as the man who put out Bully Baker, persuaded the monkey-wallah to sell. Next day, Bricky took Toby to the bazaar where a native tailor, accustomed to the whims of the Feringhees, made him a smart red tunic, blue trousers with red stripes and a shako, held on the little head by a chin-strap. A countryman, Bricky undoubtedly had a way with animals and was determined to train Toby to smartly carry out the Rifle Exercises detailed in Part Three of the manual, 'Field Exercises and Evolutions of Infantry'. He went about it methodically, first personally demonstrating with his Enfield long rifle, then showing the animal the pictures in the manual.

'Now, Toby ... look 'ere ... Plate XI ... that's 'leven ... on page 110 ... shows yer 'ow to do the Shoulder ... the Secure ... the Order ... the Present ... Port and Charge ... 'ere's some more on page 126 ... the Advance ... Support ... Slope ... Trail ... an' Stand at Ease.'

Day after day, week after week, off-duty hours were devoted to training Toby, until everyone in the barrackroom was sick and tired of it - and fed up with the monkey's nocturnal antics. At night Toby, a collar round his neck and a long chain fastened to the bungalow railings, was settled at the foot of Bricky's charpoy, but he never stayed there. Instead he kept men awake by climbing over them and chattering in their ears - he took a fiendish delight in tormenting Jockey.

When Toby first came on the scene, Jockey assumed that he would help train the monkey, but Bricky intended Toby to work only for one master. Toby sensed that the mercurial Jockey was annoyed and with worthy wiles he played one man off against the other until Jockey was consumed with blind, unreasoning jealousy. The obsessed Bricky never saw this, and tried to maintain an equal relationship with both his old friend and the little animal, although secretly he had to admit to himself that Jockey was a little hard to get on with these days.

Night after night the three of them went to the canteen, but the monkey had every dram buckshee, mucking in but never buying a round, because monkeys - even those that could do small arms drill - don't have a pice to their name. This meant that much less for the two men, who were always skint long before stop-tap. As in the past, Jockey did his acrobatics - tumbling, somersaults, cartwheels, handstands and everything else - in return for sups of ale tipped into the communal bowl the three shared. Jockey, bitterly resented raising a sweat to give the bloody monkey a sup of ale and always swore that the animal drunk more than his share. He further upset Bricky by calling Toby a Canteen Rat. The little beast certainly could knock it back, drink for drink with Bricky and Jockey and night after night all three went to bed hokee-mut.

One night in the Canteen, just before pay-day with everyone quiet, Jockey returned sweating to the table with an empty bowl. Toby, unable to believe there was nothing for him, turned the bowl upside down, chattering and snarling at Jockey, who lunged at him. The agile monkey easily dodged and leapt onto the bar counter to go through Jockey's acrobatic routine, in the right order and imitating his little mannerisms. Men cheered and clapped, offered sups and some even sent over full pots of ale.

The three had thick heads next morning. Toby refused to get up at reveille and slept under the verandah all day. That night, the canteen was crowded when Jockey went through his tumbling performance; to stir it a bit and cause a bobbery, no-one gave him a drop! He went right round, then stood looking at them with the empty bowl in his hand, letting loose, cracking and blinding, setting them all laughing and shouting. Then Toby performed Jockey's acrobatics and, like the night before, sups of ale came from all sides. The three supped it up, Jockey very quiet and looking daggers at the monkey. Then, with the ale gone, suddenly Jockey jumped up and swiped at Toby, calling him every name he could lay his tongue to. The frightened monkey hid under a table but Jockey chased him round the Canteen, among legs, benches and tables. Men laughed their heads off, tripped the angry Jockey and hid Toby.

It went that way for some nights, the lads trying to get Jockey going so's he chased Toby before they'd drunk all the ale. But as with all others forms of entertainment they soon tired of this, then came the night that no-one bothered. Jockey did not understand at first and began to muck about, laying it on thick, tripping himself up and making himself look silly, he embarrassed the men so much that they ignored him. That night the three got sweet Fanny Adams and were stone sober when they got their heads down.

Bricky changed tactics. After months of instruction in small-arms drill Toby was now good at it, marching up and down, going through drills with the little wooden bundook Bricky made for him. All day, behind the jakes, Bricky had the monkey going at it, like a bloke on the sheet doing pack-drill. Come night-time, it took two hours ale-supping to revive the little devil. Then, about forty minutes before stop-tap, Bricky stood on a bench and, like the Chairman at the old Tivoli, announced that Toby would go through Manual Exercises by Numbers, with the Enfield Long Rifle. The bar counter was cleared and wiped down, then smart in his red tunic and striped trousers, shako-badge and buttons well polished, Toby fell-in, rifle in left-hand, resting against the hollow of the left shoulder, fore-part of the butt even with the front of his thigh and his straight right arm - with paws - stretched down the trouser stripes. Bricky drew himself up and faced the monkey. 'Toby! Order ... arms!'

Toby seized the rifle, right paw close above lower band, keeping his elbow as close to the body as possible. His little face was lined with concentration.

'Two!'

The rifle was brought down to the right side, butt placed on the counter top, its toe in line with the toes of the monkey's right foot.

'Three!'

Toby placed his right paw on the outside of the stock, thumb on sling, and pressed the rifle to the hollow of his shoulder, standing erect and soldierly in familiar posture. This raised an outburst of clapping and cheering, momentarily it seemed that Toby was going to acknowledge this. Glaring at him Bricky screamed, 'Toby! Stand Firm! Order please, gentlemen ... let the dog see the rabbit!'

The impressed audience went quiet, Bricky put Toby through the Manual - the monkey responding to orders and numbers - Secure Arms! ... Shoulder Arms! ... Shoulder from the present ... Port-Arms! ... Charge! and back to Shoulder-Arms! ... advance-Arms! ... Trail-Arms! ... and so on, right through in good and soldierly fashion, ending with 'Ground Arms!' Toby, on the word 'ground' grasped the little wooden rifle as in the first motion of 'The Trail', then, on the word ' ... Arms', turned rifle on heel, lock to rear, raised it off the counter, lock up, muzzle inclined to right front, the stock in line with heels; rising to return to the position of attention.

It was uncannily lifelike and for a moment all were silent with admiration, then everyone cheered and clapped. Men jostled them and patted their backs and Bricky and his monkey were overwhelmed with sups of ale. Of course, there was no place for Jockey in all this, he stood on the fringe, his face working speechless with fury. It was more than he could take. Suddenly the little man clambered onto the bar counter, seized Toby's small wooden bundook and, calling his own orders and numbers, went through the Manual, imitating the monkey.

At first, it quietened them, then, seeing how daft it was, wooden bundook and all, men began to laugh and call out.

'I ain't never seen a man mimic a monkey afore!'

'Hey, Jockey! You ain't drillin' as good as the monkey!'

'Why don' yer git Toby to go on parade for you tomorrow, Jockey? E's better at it'n you!'

Jockey gave up before concluding the drills and jumped down from the counter to glare wildly at Toby, supping steadily with head back and bowl to lips. Jockey lunged out and hit the bowl so that ale poured all over the monkey's face and tunic. Indignantly, Toby ground his teeth at the assault, then, realising his danger, scampered out of the Canteen with Jockey hot on his heels.

'Ain'cher going to look after Toby, Bricky?'

'No! E'll be orlright ... 'e can move faster'n ole Jockey!'

Jockey came into the barrackroom just before lights out. Bricky, laying on his charpoy, hands behind his head, looked around for Toby: 'Where's ole Toby then?'

Jockey did not meet his eyes.

'You ain't done nothin' to 'im 'ave yer, Jockey?'

'Couldn't catch the little sod.'

Bricky settled down, knowing his pet would be back before morning. About an hour after lights-out there was a light scampering over beds, a scratching and a chattering, particularly around Jockey's bed, causing him to loudly curse and throw boots. At last, Bricky got up to quieten the monkey, stumbling around in the darkness, calling him, but Toby lay quiet, hiding somewhere or asleep. No more was heard of him that night. On his charpoy, Jockey drifted into sleep, thinking how he had enjoyed the night, doing for Toby, then scampering around the barrackroom, scratching and chattering, imitating the monkey. He smiled smugly into the night, relishing the moment behind the Canteen when he had caught Toby, slowed up by the ale, and held him by the ankles to beat his head to a bloody pulp against the brick wall. The little body was now under a foot of sand in a nullah on the far side of the camp. From tomorrow everything would be like it used to be with him and Bricky, just the two of them. Together, they searched high and low for days, with Jockey applying himself devotedly, constantly thinking of new places to look, it was like old times, just the pair of them working together. He felt sad to see old Bricky so cut up and wanted to cheer him up so he sought out the Monkey-Wallah, who took him to a stinking, gut-choking yard where monkeys of all breeds and sizes were cramped in wooden cages. Carefully, inspecting each one and ignoring the plentiful advice offered by the Monkey-Wallah, Jockey selected the most depressingly drab, lifeless and stupid of them all. Trudging back to barracks with the monkey perched dis-interestedly on his shoulder, Jockey comfortingly reasoned that if Bricky did not get fed up with it, then he would do for this one just like he did for Toby.

IX

The eternal hum of insects duelling with the creak of punkahs filled the vacuum as the Sergeants voice died away. The end of the tale had come suddenly for some and it took a time for thoughts to gather. The Sergeant had seen none sleeping and he'd been talking for ... he looked at his watch ... nigh on two hours. Then they began commenting, mostly two or three men at once, some loudly to over-ride others.

'That were a good fight ... an' you see'd it, Sergeant?'

'Yes, I saw it ... an' it were better'n I can tell you ...'

'Reminded me of a li'l fellow we 'ad inna section back in ... in '55 ... '

'That Tom Sayers ... 'e were a good little 'un ... that there Heenan oo 'e beat ... 'e were 'bout six inches taller ... three stone heavier ... 'an eight years younger ... Sergeant, did that Bully bloke really go in the ring wiv Sayers?'

'Said he did ... an' his mates backed it ... mark you, when I'm talking about ... he'd bin through the mill .... had many a bottle smashed on his nob ... he was a bit puggled ... but he was still a hard nut ... an' a big'n at that!'

Soon the room was in full flight, some men recalled memorable fights, others elaborated on monkeys and assorted pets they had known. Quietly, the Sergeant went back to his cubicle and the conversation carried on. He felt strangely drained, yet glowing and more at peace with himself than he had been for weeks. He smiled - an infrequent exercise - thinking that Amy would have been onto him for what he had made of little Jockey Rix, but Jockey, rotting in a shallow grave up on the Umbeyla Pass, would understand.

Private Saville was standing in the doorway.

'What can I do for you, lad?'

'Sergeant ... I just wanted to say that it was very good ... that you're a born storyteller ... 'fraid mine'll not be up to it.'

'Thankee.' replied the Sergeant. 'It came easy once I'd got started ... lookin' forward to your's, an' Private Early's ... bet he's got a tale to tell ... none of us have fought in a war as big as his.'

'Sergeant, do you know he told me that he actually talked to Robert E. Lee ... and Stonewall Jackson!'

'Well, they're names to think on, aren't they ... recall Sir Hugh Rose gave me an order once at Jhansi ... I saw a lot of him when we was seeking the Rhanee.'

'Sergeant, I saw you look at your watch, you are the only one in the barrackroom who knows the time ... no-one else has got a watch.'

'Don't really need it ... meals come, you hear bugle calls ... tells what time it is.'

'I suppose so. I had a watch when I joined up, my father gave it to me.'

'What happened to it ... get it nicked?'

Saville nodded. 'Yes, in a way. I was foolish ... and trusting ... don't think it would happen in this room though.'

'What happened?'

'Well, at the Depot ... I was a recruit in the barrackroom with a lot of old soldiers, real old soldiers ... been in the Crimea some of them. One night they were talking about how we had to trust ... how we had to have faith in each other. They said I had to test it by leaving my watch and chain on the bed and go for a walk and it would still be there when I got back. '

'And it wasn't, was it?'

'No. And no-one knew anything about it. They all denied I'd ever had a watch ... and when ... when I tried to find it ... one of them hit me for touching his kit.'

Saville blinked at the recollection, even after two years his eyes easily filled when thinking of his father's watch. The Sergeant looked away, it was an old story that made him feel a bit sick with hate for the fellow professionals who had drunk for days on Saville's watch.

'You learn lessons the hard way in the Army. You're probably right when you say it wouldn't happen in this room ... no, I don't think it would.'

Private Thomas Saville's birth and breeding ill-fitted him for coping with the callous and cynical attitudes of men who had plunged through Sikh grape and cannister, frozen before Sebastopol, exacted bloody vengeance from mutinous sepoys and tackled remorseless tribesmen on their own mountainous terrain.

Compared with fourteen year old Boy Farley, born and bred in barrackrooms, it was inevitable that Saville was a military child who would be a fish out of water, lonely and wretched. Knowing it would be neither kind nor helpful to encourage familiarity, the Sergeant turned his back in dismissal.

Little occurred in such military encampments as Mirzapur Cantonment that escaped those who, in the interests of military discipline and good order, desired to be intimately acquainted with the minutiae of barrackroom life, so the Sergeant was not really surprised at being summoned to Robbo's office that evening. The Sergeant-Major was sitting at his table, its dusty blanket-covered surface bare but for a precisely centred small blue-covered book, embellished with gold lettering, REGIMENTAL STANDING ORDERS OF HM'S 131ST REGIMENT OF FOOT. With his heels snapping together, the Sergeant came smartly to attention.

'Sir?'

Without a word, Sergeant-Major picked up the book and held it across the table, the Sergeant took it from his hand.

'Read ... aloud ... Section Seventeen.'

The Sergeant turned the pages, well knowing exactly what he was going to see.

'Section Seventeen ... Dealings with Private Soldiers. Non-Commissioned Officers of the rank of Corporal and above will never walk-out, nor socially fraternise with private soldiers; nor will they appear in their company at such functions as sports, smoking-concerts etc. Enclosures and private seating are usually allotted for members of Sergeant's and Corporal's Messes, and NCO's will always make use of them.'

'Sir?'

'Don't bandy words with me, Sergeant! You know as well as I bloody do that you spent most o' this morning sitting on a chair in the middle of the barrackroom, laughing and joking with private soldiers of your Sub-Section!'

How the hell did he know that ... already? Who could have told him? 'Sir, with respect. I wasn't laughing and joking ... I was telling them a tale about when I was in the 53rd of Foot.'

'Telling tales ... laughing ... joking ... what's the difference? You were socially fraternising with lower ranks ... in direct contravention of Regimental Standing Orders, to say nothing of customs and usages of the British Army for the past two hundred years! What have you got to say?'

This was no Sergeant's Mess chat over a jar of ale, sitting across a table, using first or nicknames. No-one ever called the Sergeant-Major 'Walter', except perhaps his wife; even at the heights of conviviality it was always 'Sarn't-Major'. Now, it was 'Sir', and one stood stiffly to Attention before him, eyes fixing on an invisible point two feet above his head. Seated, the gigantic Robbo was as tall as most men standing before him.

In this fashion, the Sergeant told formally of Chaucer and his 'Canterbury Tales' ... of making the journey less onerous ... of relieving stultifying barrackroom boredom and raising morale ... of personally involving men and encouraging them to express themselves ... how, to launch the scheme, he had to tell the first tale himself, backed by the authority of his position ... his tale had been of a military nature.

'I know, I know ... about two mates and a fight over a bloody monkey!'

He knew it all then! Give him his due, he's given me a hearing, thought the Sergeant, though he did look a bit puzzled over some of it!

'Now you listen to me Sergeant Oakley! I can see you mean well, but you're out of touch ... been too long away from Reg'mental soldiering ... so's you're going off half-cock ... it isn't up to you to try to change things ... things that have gone on for centuries. Don't you know ... you ought to at your rank ... that you can't buck the Army, you can't beat the system. The Army has its own ways, tried and tested in many fierce fires, and no man ... let alone one bloody tin-pot sergeant, can be permitted to interfere with those ways! Where would discipline and good order be if sergeants ... or higher ranks ... all took it into their heads to do things different? Christ! Everyone would be thinking for themselves in their own sweet bloody way, taking no notice of orders given by them who are trained by birth and breeding to give orders to those who ain't so fortunate!'

Pausing for breath, Robbo studied the erect figure before him. noting with certain misgiving that the face registered traces of personal feeling, in direct contrast to the usual impassive, suppressed visages of those he confronted.

'This will have to stop, Sergeant Oakley, and straight away! If your men want to tell each other stories then its up to them ... ain't no regulation against it, unless what they're saying is seditious, treasonous or liable to incite men to break the rules. But you'll take no part in it, although no-one can stop you, in the cubicle, hearing all their bloody silly gup! But remember, no more fraternising or social contacts with lower ranks. If you really want to mix with private soldiers then I can easily fix it for you!'

At this abrupt gesture of dismissal, the Sergeant turned sharply on his heels and marched out. The Sergeant-Major rested his elbows on the table-top and put his fingertips together, gazing thoughtfully at them. He's a smart soldier, he thought, a good soldier ... both in barracks and in the field. NCO's like him are worth their weight in gold to a Regiment, efficient at peace and brave in war, why in God's name does he have to persist in identifying himself with his men? I'll have to break him of it ... and when I do he'll sit in this chair one day!

Through the fog of years the Sergeant-Major could vaguely see what the Sergeant was trying to do and felt a certain sympathy for him, while despising the soft, unmilitary manner he was going about things. There'd been days long ago when he'd worried over the conditions of other ranks lives, but you couldn't do anything about it. Now he was too old and past that sort of worry, all he could do was ensure that this particular regiment ran smoothly, without any trouble to the Commanding Officer, or himself.

Beyond the office tatty-curtain, the Sergeant relaxed as he marched along the passage. His boots sharply echoed from the walls and stimulated into renewed activity punkah-wallahs who, while knowing it was not the Sergeant-Major, could, as a matter of course, expect a boot from any sergeant who passed. Pensively the Sergeant stared straight ahead. It had been no worse than he had expected, in fact it was a darned sight better. He had a sneaking feeling that old Robbo had partly left the door open - he hadn't forbidden tale telling completely. Of course the Sergeant-Major was as blind as the rest of them, as blind as he himself had been until the force of circumstance drove him back into barracks and the stark forgotten realisation of the wretched lives men led in them. But did men realise it, or were they so conditioned and broken into apathy that it was accepted as perfectly normal?

Well, he could only try to improve things, although he had to be frank and admit that whatever he was doing was more for himself than for them. He owed nothing to Saville, Early, Kinrade, Bell, Alexander, Boy Farley and the rest. And, if it came to a head, they'd not thank him nor stand by him, but, if he was to carry on with this existence - and he could think of no other course except those taken by Sergeant Digges or Bob Farley - then life had to be made more bearable, until the Hot Season ended.

The Sergeant wondered how Robbo knew so much about goings-on in Bungalow Five, Aliwal Lines, although he seemed to know just as much about every other bungalow.It was as though he had a well organised network of informers throughout the Cantonment. Whom would he employ in bungalow five? The Sergeant considered individually each man in the Sub-Section, weighing up what might make a man spy on his mates. His mind lingered on Private Kinrade, a cunning trouble-maker who stirred up most of the trouble in the room. No, he was his own man, too resentful of authority ever to co-operate with a senior NCO; too deeply involved in the gun-making plot and wary of interference with his gang of Pope's Boys. Anyway, what would a man get out of working for the Sergeant-Major? He could not think of a single advantage or favour that would not stick out like a sore thumb in barrackrooms, and throw immediate suspicion on the spy. And if Robbo's system was widespread then surely, in one of the sixty four bungalows he would have been discovered and details leaked through-out the rest.

Reaching the Mess, Sergeant Oakley gave up the subject and sought solace in a few jars of ale with fellow sergeants. That night in bed, fighting a desperate rearguard action against voracious insects, he considered his position in the tale-telling situation and decided to continue actively encouraging the men to relate their stories. The hardest part - getting it started - had been done, and it would seem normal, besides freeing both talkers and listeners from restraint, if for future tales he remained within his cubicle, where he could listen without infringing on the Sergeant-Major's ruling.

X

Undoubtedly the most contented soldier in the 5th Sub-Section was the American, Martin Early who, despite the irksome discipline, was well aware that he and his eternally grousing British comrades were far better off than he had ever been in the Confederate Army during the War between the States. Then, hunger had been ever-present and the most universally desired comfort of the Southern soldier was something to eat, no effort or subterfuge being spared to obtain it. Men became resourceful in preparing scanty rations, generally worm eaten peas, sour or rancid pork, unboiled cornmeal, a pinch of flour, a little coffee - with a rare issue of sugar - and sinkers, hardtack biscuits sometimes made into a 'luxury' dish, called 'Lobscouse' by being broken in water and soaked overnight, then fried in bacon-fat. There was slap-jacks and black-strap, sow-belly and anything that could be raided from hen-roosts, farmyards and orchards, all washed down with watery java. Men bent over small twig fires, balanced battered tin-cups to heat coffee and fried scraps of fat bacon in mess tin lids; there may also be a pone of cornbread sliced with a large pocket knife that had been used for more than cooking.

In the Queen's Army food, although monotonous, was filling and you got sufficient. It was cooked for you and was more or less hot when you got it. On the march and in the field, you carried several days rations and supply wagons usually managed to get up to you so there was no need to wear yourself out foraging. The Confederacy was never able to furnish adequate food and supplies so men had to rely on their own energies and ingenuity. Regiments marching in tight columns suddenly broke ranks without being ordered and scattered over the fields picking apples and berries, only returning to their ranks when their hats were filled with booty gleaned from the land.

Lying on a rope charpoy Private Early could still evoke the nostalgic pleasure of being hungry then eating, tired and then resting, thirsty and drunk, cold and wet and then sitting by a roaring fire and drying out in comfort. The passing of time blurred the memories of mud, cold, snow, hail and wind. Rain was the greatest discomfort of all. Worse even than the severest cold there could be no comfort when it rained. Clothes, shoes, blankets meat and bread were all wet and soggy, wood too damp to burn, muskets liable to mis-fire, the ground was unpleasant to sleep on and marching was made difficult by mud and swollen creeks.

The Confederate soldier excused his ragged attire by saying: "We'uns don't put on our best suits to go killing hogs!" His wardrobe was a wide-brimmed hat, a jacket, shirt and a pair of pants in varying shades of brown - some acquired sky-blue trousers from dead Yankees - a pair of drawers and socks, and rough over-sized brogans - his feet were always bruised and inflamed. Like everyone else, he wore no socks after the first issue pair wore out and, on the march, took off his shoes and carried them over his shoulder. Early was well pleased with the stout ammunition boots issued to the British soldier.

In Calcutta, Private Early had been issued with two suits of dust-coloured linen called kharkee, with five white and two check shirts, innumerable other items of clothing and necessaries and all paid for by pay deductions. A tunic and shell-jacket were issued in alternate years, in the non-issue year the soldier had to pay the difference in value of the two articles, the sum being spent at the Commanding Officer's discretion on any articles to suit the climate of the station.

For four years Yank Early had trudged up and down Virginia with his few private belongings and a spare shirt in a rolled blanket - known as a horse-collar - wrapped around the body. Slung over his shoulder was a beehive containing smoking tobacco and a pipe, a small piece of soap and such temporary items as apples and berries picked up on the march. Now, hanging on the wall overhead, in part of a made-up set of equipment - straps, crossbelts, pouches, knapsack, bayonet-frog and bayonet - was a haversack containing a 'small-kit' of towel, soap, razor, spare boots, blacking and brushes, two shirts and two pairs of socks. With a blanket, an overcoat, ammunition and seven days rations, the British soldier was burdened with a load of about 60lbs.

With less to encumber them, the Southern soldier, proud to be known as Jackson's Foot Cavalry, had marched faster and further than any before them. Generally for the first hour of the march they were orderly, men keeping their places in the solid columns, then, a song, joke or humorous remark would convulse the ranks with laughter so that they lost step and cohesion and route-step replaced order. But still they marched rapidly forward. It looked unmilitary but everyone got there in the end, as quickly as any other army had ever done.

To lighten their load, Confederate soldiers often threw away their most valuable possessions - blankets, overcoats, shoes - but what was discarded by one man was urgently picked up by another, so on balance nothing much was lost in the end. In the British Army, with everything listed and signed for, it was a foolish man who disposed of clothing and kit in this manner; nor did they throw away bayonets and scabbards like both armies in the Civil War. But then, reflected Martin, the British soldier was trained to use the old lunger, he thanked God the Yanks weren't.

In both his armies, comradeship was equally strong, though of a different type, perhaps because Americans were usually volunteers believing they fought for a just cause, whereas this lot were mostly unemployed and joined for food, clothing and a roof over their heads. It was harsh discipline and regimental pride that held the British Army together; in the C.S.A. discipline pushed too hard would probably have deprived it of its very backbone of life and power. Like every other Southern soldier, Martin Early was always ready to fight but never willing to submit to the routine duties and disciplines of camp, barracks or the march. Each man was determined to be a soldier in his own image and do his duty as he thought best, for the love of it. Not submitting to the discomforts arising from discipline but cheerfully enduring any necessary hardships. Every privation was met with the utmost courage and devotion, the very intensity of suffering becoming a matter for humour, so that instead of grumbling or deserting, men laughed - at bare feet, ragged clothes and pinched faces. They marched cheerfully onward without hope, reward or rest; weak, hungry, cold and wet and tormented by voracious vermin. And they met the well-fed and warmly clad superior numbers of their Northern enemy.

They had discipline, but it was of a different sort. Martin

remembered troublesome regiments having guns trained on them, men having their combs cut and others going, with ears drooping like a wet mule, to an appointment with Captain Hemp. Such misdemeanours as straggling on the march column, punishable in the British Army, were handled by the men themselves. When a coffee-cooler sat by the roadside after falling-out from a marching column, striding-by, his company would call him by name; "Hello Jake Billings! Why ... there's ole Jake Billings!" Hearing this, the next company in the column repeated his name, so that it rippled along the ranks until every passing regiment had chanted the fellow's name. After an hour of being derisively recognised by the whole division, the average coffee-cooler, as mad as a stump-tailed bull at fly time, would struggle to his feet, fall-in with the nearest file-closers, and try to rejoin his outfit.

Hair and beards went uncut for months, faces were tanned dark-brown and with their hands nearly black the Confederate soldier had the fierce unkempt appearance of primitive warriors. Now, it was very different. Martin shaved every day, had his head cropped twice weekly, burnished, pressed and polished his dress and equipment to become the perfect replica of every man around him on parade. It was the very opposite of the fiercely achieved individuality of Johnny Reb. When first in India, wondering whether it was beyond his powers to change, he was helped by his old father's maxim, 'If you can't stand the heat ... get out of the kitchen.' Stubbornly he got his head down and, being a natural soldier capable of slipping comfortably into any army in history, he did all that was asked of him with smooth, unquestioning efficiency. Mates and superiors marked him as a man likely to reach non-commissioned rank if spared the bullet from an Afridi jezail, cholera, dysentery, enteric fever or some other lethal complication.

Battle had always stimulated Martin as being refreshingly different from the aimless boring days in camp and bivouac. He was not surprised to find his new comrades also looked forward to active service; anything was preferable to drowning in your own sweat on barrackroom beds and dusty parade grounds. When, after nine irksome months at Mirzapur, he had marched out on a punitive Frontier expedition, his excitement was almost uncontrollable as the thought of once again hearing balls from smooth-bore muskets 'whush' past; of spent bullets humming like nails whirling in the air and the ominous silence as a missile buried itself in a human body. He wondered if, in his excitement, he might peddle lead, catch shell fever, or even skedaddle but he re-assure himself by remembering his brother Wilbur saying, "I'd rather be found lying with my face to the moon than have any man call me a coward."

He had been intensely curious to see how the fighting styles of the two armies compared. Obviously it would be different, with the British displaying much more formality and discipline, but did that make them better fighters? Not being up against formed armies there would be no large scale operations, although he understood the Umbeyla affair of '63 had been a humdinger. Certainly there would be no twelve pounder Napoleons, like massive sawn-off shotguns, firing canister at short range. Listening to the tales of the Sikh War veterans - Lance-Corporal Mockford, Pat Coughlin, Taffy Davies, Mister Wright and Charlie Mort - revealed their Order of Battle to be a relic of the Napoleonic Wars, with units in close line or column, cavalry on the flanks and artillery in the intervals. He hoped things had changed. They started at Bull Run in '61 like that, but necessity soon altered things and Martin Early remembered it a mite different.

Confederate soldiers went into action like a bunch of friends out shooting game. Some six to twelve feet apart, skirmishers steadily moved forward, laughing, shouting, cheering and calling to each other. Reaching a good position, each man sheltered behind a tree or rock. They loaded and fired with great deliberation and precision, waited for their units to join them and meanwhile tried to drive the enemy skirmishers in on their line-of-battle. To their rear the head of the brigade came into line. On being ordered to load, men rattled their ramrods and went through practised motions, then the command 'Forward!' was given and the brigade moved off, canteens rattling, officers constantly calling: "Close-up, men! Close-up! Guide centre!" In a turmoil of crackling bushes, snapping twigs, neighing horses and harsh commands, they pressed forward through the woods. The skirmish-line sent up a hoarse cheer as the front line broke from the trees into full view. Up to now, unable to advance or retire without exposing themselves to the rain of fire passing overhead, the skirmishers had been laying prone behind trees, but as their comrades came up level, they leapt up and pressed forward; the battle of musketry increased.

Well, it could not be that way on the harsh Frontier, with rocky tracks and narrow gorges, more like work for sections and companies at the most. He imagined it would be like the Indian fighting he had done when crossing the Plains to the West Coast. When the time came, the native tribesmen sniping from concealed positions behind rocks, showed far less courage than the proud Apache, Cheyenne and Pawnee.

Martin Early had no regrets at volunteering to tell a story, he'd done it for the Sergeant who was a hunky boy and deserved all the help they could give him. He knew any number of good tales - Jed Willis and the widow's pig ... Moses Affleck and Luke Swann's rifle duel ... or how they got rid of Captain 'Turtle' Pollock, it was a question of which to choose. Turning them over in his mind, slowly it came upon him that he was being given a chance not just to tell a tale that might amuse and interest, but a tale that would stand up for his country. A wave of the Confederacy's 'Stars and Bars' flag in this God-forsaken, far-flung Indian Continent.

Breakfast was cleared away and the room settled down for the Yank's story. Seemingly in no hurry to begin, the American stretched, rose from his charpoy and slowly padded up the room, halting at the rifle-rack to rest against its corner in his characteristic cat-like fashion, ready to spring when danger threatened. With every eye on him, his gaze slowly travelled around the room. The drawling nasal voice rode high over the buzz of insects and the punkah's creak.

'Can any o' you 'uns say when Britain last lost a war?'

He looked about him enquiringly, the Sub-Section sought vainly amongst themselves for an answer. The usually knowing fellows like Kinrade and Wright had nothing to say so gradually all eyes turned down the room to rest on Private Thomas Saville, the best educated of them all. Shocked at the invasion of his secluded corner-bed, the 'Captain' blushed and became confused. 'No ... no ... I ... I can't recall one ...'

Yank Early nodded understandingly. 'O.K. ...I'll tell ya'. We Amurricans licked yer in 1812 when ole Andy Jackson, the Frenchman Lafayette and the pirate Lafitte tanned your hides at

New Orleans.'

Stiffly, 'Mister' Wright called out. 'That right, Captain?'

Saville coughed apologetically. 'Yes. I'm afraid so. The British commander ... Packenham ... was killed ...'

The American nodded. 'Dunno about that Packenham but we licked yer alright ...'

Greatly daring, Saville interrupted. 'Excuse me ... but it was only a small war ... we, Wellington that is ... were rather busy beating Napoleon and the French in the Peninsular at the time!'

Growls of relief arose on all sides, voices complimented the 'Captains' brave defence of his country. Martin Early smiled. 'O.K. ... I give it to yer ... but that aint the point I'm a-makin' ackterly ... I'm a'gettin' at the fact that none o' ye ... not a single man serving in the whole goddamned British Army today has ever bin on the losin' side inna war ... not even in a danged battle. None o' ye know what its like ... but I do. An' I wanna tell yer jist what its all about ... in case it ever 'appens to you ... not that I think it will!'

Now that they knew the Yank wasn't trying to take the piss, men climbed down off their high horses and bent an ear to his words.

'I was seventeen years old when Virginia seceded from the Union in April '61 ... me two brothers went off to enlist and after a lot of hassle, took me along with them ... for most o' the war we served in the 13th Virginia Regiment in first Pegram's, then Walker's Brigade of Gordon's Division. We were at most o' the big fights, 'cludin' Antietam ... came April '65 and we wuz with Lee, movin' south a-tryin' to join up with Joe Johnston ... a-headin' fer a place called Amelia Courthouse to pick up the Danville an' Richmond Railroad ... Grant was after us an' Sheridan's cavalry hot on our tails ...'

The last days of the Confederate Army on its march to Appomattox were an exhausting day and night progression of marching. Few could recall with any accuracy the names of places and when they were there. Irregular times of sleeping and meals taken whenever and wherever possible turned night into day and day into night. Aroused from deep sleep while it was still dark, men struggled to their feet, forgetting their empty stomachs and sustained only by brave hearts. They would form-up into their line-of-march and stumble off in a formless column, bumping into each other and sleeping as they marched. The column frequently ground to a halt when men dropped to the ground and fell asleep under hedges and trees; those who could keep awake divided the few rations that remained or had been foraged. When the column started to move again, rough orders woke some while others were rudely disturbed by comrades stumbling over them until the whole formation was again a shambling procession, encouraged by never ending cries of "Close-up, men ... close-up!"

It seemed to go on forever, like a prison sentence without remission, long weary days and nights with little chance of rest until even the most determined men faltered. All loose equipment was discarded, leaving behind the column an untidy wake that resembled a military jumble-sale. Few men carried cartridge or cap boxes, wore belts, straps or haversacks. Ammunition was carried in pockets along with pipes and tobacco, crumbs of corn and salt. Rations were at a premium and a couple of ears of corn on the cob, intended for horse fodder, was issued to each man, parched by smoky campfires and mixed with salt. It was a hard unpalatable diet, making jaws, gums and teeth ache until chewing became virtually impossible.

Martin Early's Company held off Sheridan's hovering cavalry when Walker's Division remained behind to cover the retreat at Amelia Courthouse, while the column moved towards Deatonsville on a short but tiring march. The main roads were crowded with other retreating troops, so the column and its few remaining wagons had to plough fumblingly along in pitch darkness, through the deep dust of pot-holed and rutted plantation roads. When morning dawned they had only covered six miles. Lurching into Deatonsville, with half the regiment straggling miles behind, the 13th thankfully fell out and began to cook a meal but, before the sparse rations were even warm, they got the order to get going. Dust was kicked over fires and weary legs forced themselves one before the other as again they took to the road.

Early's company of the 13th Virginia were ordered to stay back and delay the oncoming enemy. Spaced out they settled down behind natural cover to await the first sight of blue uniforms. At last they came. A scattered line of skirmishers gazing vigilantly around with rifles at the ready. When within range of Confederate Springfield rifled muskets, each man picked a target and fired. As skirmishers do under such circumstances, they immediately went to ground and a hot fire-fight broke out, men aiming, firing and loading with great deliberation. It was an uneven contest but the Southerners, greatly outnumbered and pressed from front and flanks, held their own until the enemy's line of battle crested the ridge and advanced, firing volleys as they came. Thankfully, the Federal skirmishers were absorbed by their main body and the 13th began to fall back, stubbornly contesting the ground as they retired, pace by pace, into the woods behind them.

Vanishing into the trees and undergrowth fringing the wood, the small band positioned themselves behind trees. Foraging in their pockets to sift caps and cartridges from a mixture of corn and salt, they loaded and stood waiting, determined not to run. The enemy threw out another skirmish-line which advanced confidently in free and easy style until driven to ground by the sudden volley flashing out from the wood. Leaving a few huddled bodies behind them, the line picked itself up and came forward in a more cautious manner, only to be halted by further fire. The line-of-battle came up again and added their fire to that of the skirmishers, bullets clipped the leaves from the trees and gouged chips of wood from the trunks and branches. Despite overwhelming numbers, the enemy battalions were stoutly resisted by the scattering of Confederate skirmishers that dodged from tree to tree, picking men off with the deliberation of huntsmen and each telling shot arousing a low cheer from the marksmen. Some men became so enthusiastic that they pushed forward ahead of the defence line to settle themselves down behind cover, loading and firing as deliberately as though at practice.

It could not last long. Eventually the enemy, still pushing hard to the front, began to infiltrate on both flanks. The Captain shouted loud and clear. "Boys! Take care of ye'selves!" He then stepped out of cover to stand blazing away until his pistol was empty before he turned and scuttled away downhill to the creek below. There he met up with Early and a group of a dozen men. Ashamed of retreating, the Captain suggested they made a stand here, everyone agreed and they lined the roadside ditch that faced the gentle slope down which they had just run. Almost at once enemy skirmishers came into view, breaking from the woods and waving to those behind to come up. Then, in beautiful order, their line-of-battle stepped out of the woods with Colours flying in the centre of the front rank. It was a tempting target and the ragged volley that split the air brought down the Colour bearer, the bright silk flag dragging in the dust, and the colour guards on both sides went down too. The battle-line momentarily wavered then broke into a fury of disorder as men swarmed down the hill, yelling and cursing as they blazed away.

The little band took to their heels, plunging through the creek and running for their lives up the long open hillside beyond. It was heavy going over the broken ground, under fire at every step, and before they reached the crest a gun unlimbered and poured fruitless showers of canister after them. They ran, staggering and stumbling, drawing in great gulps of air like hunted animals. Weakened by the continuous marching, hunger, thirst and lack of sleep, the race for life was the hardest thing Martin Early had ever done in his life, and the most distressing.

It was after nightfall when they reached the road where the Division was assembling, sergeants called out regimental names and numbers to aid the muster. They found the hundred or so men remaining of the 13th Virginia and rejoined their comrades, pleased to have avoided capture and accusations of desertion. Black with powder and with deep circles round their mouths from biting cartridges the faces were patterned with channels of sweat running down from the brow, concealing the ravages of despair of defeat, hunger, thirst and a fearful tiredness. Being back with their regiment gave them renewed strength and spirits, but soon they were struggling again, dropping off to sleep whenever the column halted.

Daylight saw Sheridan's eager cavalry on the line of march, following close to the flanks of the shambling column, swooping down whenever an opportunity occurred. Men halted to face them, driving the horsemen away. At intervals they came upon ominous signs of disaster - whole wagon trains standing abandoned, guns with wheels and trails hacked and burned, all this blocked the road and had to be manhandled away. Ditches were dumping places for wagon loads of ammunition, and muskets lay around on all sides, dropped by those scuttling away like rats from a sinking ship.

The coming of night brought relief, although sporadic firing continued throughout. At daybreak on Saturday 8th April, the march was resumed and continued throughout the day without rest, men crunching parched corn and raw bacon as they trudged along. They bivouacked for the night near Appomatox Courthouse and formed line-of-battle near the outskirts of the village on Sunday morning. Passing along the lines, wagons dropped off boxes of cartridges; Martin clearly remembered men rushing to break them open, filling pockets with cartridges and saying grimly, "If we'se going out, we'se going out with a bang, not a whisper!"

Cries of 'Forward!' set them moving, with officers continually shrieking, 'Close-up men! Close-up! Don't lag ... close-up!' They pushed through a thick wood to emerge into a large open area. Skirmishers deployed into another large wood to their front, moved quietly until brought up short by a strong line of enemy picquets. Screeching wildly, firing as they ran, the skirmishers scattered the startled enemy. Martin Early remembered it for the rest of his life, as it was the last time he had heard the fearsome Rebel Yell in battle. Coming to the far edge of the wood, everyone halted and sucked in their breath at the sight before them.

Like an all enveloping blue cloud, stretched out on a series of ridges to far horizons, lay the entire Federal Army - regiments, brigades, divisions, cavalry squadrons, artillery batteries, all unnaturally still and quiet, awaiting the signal to remorselessly roll forward. As though disdaining to loose the horde on such small fry, minor orders caused ripples of movement on the fringes of the host as the cavalry jingled forward to cover the retreat of the discomforted picquets. Layers peeled off from formed infantry regiments and skirmish lines began to move steadily down the slopes towards them.

Tearing his eyes from the panorama, Martin Early looked around to see that everyone except his own little group from the 13th had fallen back into the woods. Reluctant to go, they began firing as fast as possible, not bothering to aim but blazing off the cartridges that weighed down their pockets. When the advancing enemy was close enough for individual faces to be picked out, and with others moving round their flanks, the Captain called,

"Don't let them see you runnin' boys!" Slowly and stubbornly they fell back, exchanging shot for shot with the enemy who came on at the trot, cheering valiantly in their pursuit of half-a-dozen Johnny Rebs.

Dragging musket-butts behind them, loading as they went, turning, halting, firing, taking fire and returning it, doggedly they moved slowly back through the wood, until trees thinned and they came out into the open, where the main body of the Confederate Army were massed. The enemy skirmishers dropped back. Martin walked through the ranks and past a barn surrounded by torn and wounded soldiers laying on manure piles. To one side he saw numbers of guns and wagons parked together in a haphazard jumble and went over to investigate such carelessness in the face of the enemy. He asked a sergeant, sitting on the shafts of a wagon, what was happening. Slowly raising his head, the sergeant looked him straight in the eyes. 'General Lee has surrendered.'

Early recoiled. 'I don't believe it!' he whispered. 'You mustn't let anyone hear you say that ... it'll kill us stone dead!'

The sergeant rose wearily, like an old man and sadly shook his head as he walked away. Martin looked after him, then beyond him he saw the Federal cavalry walking their horses. He could hardly believe his eyes and was almost overcome with surprise, disgust and indignation. Moving back to his comrades, he tried to remember his last shot at the advancing skirmishers, as though fixing the final firing of the war was important. The rest of the skirmishers received the news incredulously. After some aimless wandering with rifles trailing by their sides, the men came upon a battalion in the woods near the road. Fires had been lit and some men were cooking what was left of the rations, others stared blankly into space, unable to take in the dreadful news. Federal cavalrymen, walking their horses up and down the road, called out awkwardly. "Hey, Johnny ... how are you?" Few men answered, except to nod an acknowledgement.

It seemed as though each Southerner had taken upon his shoulders personal blame for the surrender. Men sobbed and cried like children, in grief, mortification and humiliation. The skirmishers, still elated by their brief action and unable to arouse such deep feelings, tried to cover up by relating lurid and exaggerated descriptions of the way they had fought Grant's entire army. No-one was interested; fighting, shooting and killing were over and done with, things of the past. A few hotheads exploded indignantly, offering to resume the war, to escape or die in the attempt. Not a word of blame was uttered, nor any recriminations directed towards General Lee. Everyone sympathised and viewed him with great affection and understanding on that sad day.

Then, up the road came a file of Federal infantrymen, each carrying on his shoulder a box of hardtack biscuits. Taking up the rear was a black soldier driving a cow. Union troops, hearing of their famished condition, had contributed their days ration - a comradely act much appreciated by the dazed Southerners. Martin recalled how it went a long way towards lessening the immediate distress of their condition. As the day wore on, crowds of curious Feds strolled over to talk with them. Martin spoke to one who must have been in direct opposition at Antietam, perhaps killing his brother Matthew. He could find no animosity, no hatred for the conquerors; not a word of reproach or an insult was heard all day, not a fist raised nor any bad feelings shown.

The next day passed in a vacuum, a limbo of dazed Southern soldiers going through the motions of living as if the formula for it had been blanked from their brains, Martin Early was never able to recall that Monday. The next day, Tuesday 11th April, regiments paraded to receive paroles, printed on slips of paper like a bank cheque, with blank spaces for date, name, company, regiment and the signature of his Battalion or Company Commander. Later it was notable that these passes were as much respected by Union officers, picquets and patrols as though they bore the signature of General Ulysses S. Grant himself.

The voice of No. 3907 Private Martin 'Yank' Early, of the 5th Sub-Section, Left-Half 'C' Company, HM's 131st Regiment of Foot, died away. Men raised their heads to find out the reason as the American moved towards the rifle-rack, hands fumbling with a leather wallet. 'Here you are pardners ... come an' look at a beaten soldier's parole pass. May none o' ye ever have one pushed into your hands...'

Men only rose from their beds during the heat of the day, and with the utmost reluctance, when the call of the urine-tub or jakes could no longer be denied. Now they rose quickly and jostled each other to take a look at the only Confederate parole-pass in the whole of India. Obviously much handled, it was split at the creases and ragged-edged, the lettering was brown and faded. For three years it had lain in a wallet next to Martin Early's pulsating heart, which had not been broken by the fall of the Confederacy. The parole was a model of the magnanimity displayed by soldiers towards their beaten foe, not necessarily shared by civilians and politicians:

Appomattox Courthouse,
Virginia,
April the 10th 1865.

The bearer PRIVATE MARTIN EARLY of 13th VIRGINIA REGIMENT, WALKER'S BRIGADE, GORDON'S DIVISION, a paroled prisoner of the Army of Northern Virginia, has permission to go to his home and remain there undisturbed.

GEORGE CULLEN Capt.,
COMMANDING 13th VIRGINIA REGIMENT

Men looked at it as educated comrades read aloud. Some gazed thoughtfully and with compassion at their American comrade. In return, he regarded them impassively, thinking it was a long time since the parole had been removed from the wallet. In the days immediately following the surrender, sickened by humiliation and indignation, he had belligerently produced it when demanded. Slowly, it had become a sort of hall-mark, a certificate proclaiming his role in the glorious history of his country. It bestowed pride in him at being among the small, ill-equipped and starving armies who had held out and nearly beaten Northern Armies who had been superior in everything except courage. There came a time when it was displayed as proudly as a medal, but that was long ago and now it required a conscious effort of will to arouse the devotion and passion once he thought it deserved. After all, he had received nothing else, no other gesture of gratitude for giving up four precious years of youth and putting them on the line without any encouraging gambler's odds.

However, there was something else. Something all the more precious because it did not bear the stigma of ever having been touched by enemy hands; a symbol of victory rather than defeat. Carefully, almost reverently, from another pocket in his wallet Martin extracted a small square of folded paper and opened it, revealing two ragged oblong pieces of frayed silken thread, about the size of a postage stamp; each faded, one red the other blue. Men pressed forward to get a closer look at them as Martin spoke.

'At Appomattox ... at the surrender ceremony ... we had to hand in our Battle Flags. Afore that the Colour Bearer cut a strip from it and all the remaining men of the 13th Virginia Regiment were given a piece of it ... that there red mite is me bit of our Battle Flag.'

'What's the blue bit, Yank?'

'Ah yes ... 'cording to Reg'lations, Confederate infantry regiments carried only a Battle Flag ... but most of us also bore a State Colour ... that fer Virginny were a blue flag with a circle in the middle ... an' a pitcher of a man with a spear ... got 'is foot on another man a-lying on the ground ... and a Latin motto ... something about tyranny...'

'Sic Semper Tyrannus.'

Everyone gazed in awe at Private Saville who blushed and wished he had kept his mouth shut. Yank Early looked curiously at him. 'Well I'll be damned! Yeah ... that's jist wot it were ... how'd ye know that , Cap'tin?'

'I don't know really ... it's just a familiar Latin motto ... that's all ... can't recall where I heard it ... at school I suppose.'

'Wot's it mean Captain?'

'Oh ... Thus always with tyrants ... or Down with tyranny ... or tyrants.'

Speechless at such knowledge, men gazed admiringly at the young soldier. Yank Early nodded. 'Yeah ... I 'member hearing it thataway ... that's about right. Anyway, whin we heard colours had to be handed in it were bad enough to lose our Battle Flag ... but never ole Virginny's flag ... no sir! So the Captain took it off its shaft an' wound it round his waist ... had it there right through the surrender ceremony ... then we shared it out artewards ... that's my piece.'

Old soldiers exchanged knowing glances, remembering with feeling those occasions when man after man had fallen in their efforts to carry or save the Colours. No Regiment could hold up its head if it lost either its Regimental or Queen's Colour, and any soldier worth his salt would be prepared to give his life for them. Every veteran in the barrackroom could relate stories of incidents centred on the Colours ... at Ferozeshah, Sobraon, Chillianwallah and Gujerat, the last wars they had fought in where colours were carried. None of them had Crimean War service and colours weren't often carried in the Mutiny.

Yank Early had his memories too and he shared them with the men around him.

It was sunrise on the chill, grey morning of Wednesday 12th April 1865, when the Confederate Army broke camp for the last time, reluctantly as if an unwelcome duty. They had taken down their little shelter tents before slowly forming in ranks. The Union Army were already paraded along the principal street of Appomattox, from the bluff-bank of the stream to near the Courthouse on the left, waiting to face the final Confederate line-of-battle and receive their arms and colours. Then, in the old swinging route-step, they came forward in columns-of-march, at their head the National Colour of the Confederacy, the Stainless Standard, with its field of white and canton of star-strewn cross of blue on a field of red. Regimental Battle Flags - red with blue star-strewn cross - surmounted the column in a bright foliage so thick as to crown it with crimson.

The Federal forces, in the presence of their own countrymen and former enemies, still so proud in their moment of humiliation, were overcome with the desire to show compassion and wholehearted respect for the fighting ability of their late opponents. As the head of each Confederate Division came level with the Union Command Group, bugles blared and the entire Federal line in succession from right to left, regiment by regiment, smartly changed from Order Arms to the old Carry-in-the-Marching salute. General Gordon at the head of the Confederate column, riding with heavy head and downcast face, took in the situation and saluted by dropping the point of his sword to his boot-toe and called out orders for successive brigades to march-past in the same salute position. So honour responded to honour, without trumpets, drums, cheers, words or even whispers; not a sound nor sign of triumph or humiliation.

When each successive Confederate Division masked its Union counterpart it halted and turned inwards so that the formations faced each other across the road, twelve feet apart. Erstwhile enemies looked straight into each others eyes without any flicker of acknowledgement. Captains stepped forward to dress their lines and although ragged and weary and in the depths of misery along with their men, each strove to put on the best possible display for their Companies. Field and Staff Officers took a position at the end of Regiments, while Generals stood at the rear of their commands.

Then began the last round of orders. With the Union Army immobile witnesses, Confederate formations fixed bayonets, at least those who had them did. Next, lines of men filed forward to hesitantly stack arms and lay down cartridge boxes. Now came the worst moment of all as Colour-Bearers, some openly weeping, others biting their lips to hold back the emotion, stepped forward and reluctantly lowered the Battle-Flags, unseeingly fumbling to fold the worn, stained and torn flags, setting them on the ground with the same tenderness as laying an infant in a cradle. Stepping back, each bearer saluted his Colour, about-faced and returned to ranks, in the manner of men turning from the burial of a loved one. It was too much for the watching Confederate soldiers, more than they could bear; on all sides men broke from the ranks to rush forward and kneel over the bright heaps of coloured silk, no commanding voices being raised to stop them. Heads bowed, some ran loving hands over them, others clutched them to their breasts or lips, kissing the silk as their tears besprinkled the cherished emblems.

Private Early's voice died away, transported far from the heated confines of Hut 5, his eyes fixed unseeing on the wall. Seeking to bring him back among them, men manufactured coughs and belched. Hebdon, always lacking in sense of occasion, farted. Then there was Kinrade's rasping voice, barely concealing a cynical note. 'An' were ye one o' thim wot broke ranks an' kissed the Colours, Yank?'

Fiercely, the American nodded. 'Aye ... I were ... an' not 'shamed to admit it ... ye've not bin in long enuff, Dick, to know abart the Colours an' wot they mean ter yer. They keep yer goin' when things are hot ... you looks for 'em, yer rallied on 'em ... ye see, we'uns knew the Confederate flag wus nivver goin' ter fly again ... it were the end of our country ... from then on we wuz goin' ter 'ave ter live under the flag we'uns had fought since '61 ... fer nigh on five years.

Wright, Mort, Davies, the lance-corporal and the other veterans growled sympathetically, they understood how a man felt about the Colours - and that Dick Kinrade ... he'd never heard a shot fired in anger yet ... how the fucking hell would he know what it was all about?

Well, then it was all over, with paroles in their pockets men were dismissed and fell out for the last time. Standing in small groups they tried to find words for the comrades they had been talking to for years. Emotional men wept. Tears were rubbed quickly away with the backs of the hands. Men blew their noses and hard and firm hands on shoulders took the place of words. Many who had formed a Mess in the field agreed to leave together, as though to delay the parting. Groups of three and four resolutely turned their faces from the scene and sturdily strode off. Like water running down a hillside, these enforced civilians headed off to all points of the compass, without food or money and unarmed for the first time in years; plodding back to try and take up life again, the defeated in their own country. As a plague descends on the land, disbanded Confederate armies, without leaders or orders, roamed the country-side, hopeless, lawless, ragged, reckless and starving, making their way home as best they could.

Martin Early, always his own man, went off alone, marching in the old swinging route-step through the dusty Virginia by-ways. He slept under hedges or in barns when he was lucky enough to find a farmer willing to give a meal and a roof in return for chopping wood or some other task. Many were openly sympathetic, others guarded and embarrassed, a few antagonistic - encounters with them and their savage dogs made him yearn for the feel of the familiar Springfield rifle in his hands. Martin had a lot of time to think, there was nothing else to do and, as the days passed, he realised that the emotions of feeling lost were not so much due to the absence of his comrades and the sensation of being completely alone for the first time in years, but because he missed the high excitement of battle. The stirring of the blood and the quickening of the pulse brought on by the distant roar of guns and the whistle of missiles passing overhead. One night, awoken by a storm, his half-conscious mind took the thunder for guns and he leapt to his feet, feeling for his rifle and relaxing disappointedly when reality flooded him. Settling down again in the straw, Martin lay doubting his ability to ever become a peaceful farmer again.

He need not have worried, the decision was taken from his hands when familiar landscapes lent wings to his feet and he hurried up the last ridge. He stood gazing down at the homestead where he had been born but only saw a burned-out ruin surrounded by acres of neglected land that he never imagined his aching back turning. He searched through the long grass to find twin earthen humps covering his mother and father. He knew where his brothers were - Matthew in the mass grave at Antietam, and Wilbur similarly buried near Seminary Ridge at Gettysburg. Martin stayed only for a single night, beset by ghosts and memories that should have been fond yet served only to drive him away. Next day, without a backward glance, he adjusted his 'horse-collar' and set out, still at the old route-march pace, to find the action his soul craved.

It did not come quickly. It was a long-haul to St. Louis where a wagon-master welcomed this hardened, clear-eyed man who knew how to handle weapons; Martin again fondled a rifle and soon became accustomed to a pistol on the hip. Crossing the endless Plains was a slow, boring business, enlivened only by occasional brushes with Indians, whose bravery and inability to realise their day had ended touched familiar chords in his Confederate mind. Now that the War was over the Government were sending out West regiments of Regular soldiers - Federals of course, but with a sprinkling of restless Johnny Rebs - and they heard that General Sheridan had been given the task of taming the Indians. Martin toyed with the idea of joining but somehow could not bring himself to give oaths of allegiance to Northern leaders. Anyway, he did not particularly want to fight Indians, with whom he had a certain sympathy.

Meeting up on the trail with another wagon-train, he encountered a German who claimed to have served with the French Foreign Legion. Entranced, Martin listened to the man's guttural broken English, telling of his following Major Mangin up the slopes to take the Kabyle encampment at Ischeriden; of the colour-bearer, Schmidt ... or was it Leshefka, he couldn't recall ... at Magenta in Italy; and the bloody battle at Solferino. Martin liked the sound of men who fought in overcoats in blazing desert heat because they knew it would be stolen if they left it behind - desert nights were very cold - and it bore a certain affinity with the Confederate Army! Asked how he came to be in America, the German explained how in 1863, the Legion had been sent to Mexico to bolster up the Emperor Maximilian; in 1865 the 2nd Battalion came to Monterey, close to the border with the United States, and one day the German had slipped away, crossing the Rio Grande, dodging Indians to eventually reach a white settlement, then St. Louis and now ... in a wagon train. It all sounded reasonable to Martin Early, by now completely besotted after hearing of Captain Danjou and his Company's gallant stand at Camerone.

From that night on his mind was filled with an obsession to get to North Africa or Marseilles - the German had told him either would do, or even Paris - and become a legionnaire, join an army who were always fighting and never seemed to lose. He had had enough of being beaten. On finally arriving in San-Francisco, Martin signed on as a deck-hand on a cargo-boat going to Hawaii. Nine months later after jumping four ships in as many foreign parts, Martin Early found himself broke and hungry in Calcutta. Here he got into a fight with a bearded, kilted Highlander over the War of 1812. Afterwards, in drunken friendship, the battered Scotsman bought food and drink and regaled him with the glories of Her Majesty's British Army.

Next day, heavy-headed and with a mouth like a vulture's crotch, Martin found it difficult to remember why he was breaking his back trying to reach North Africa when, right here on his doorstep there was a fighting army who always won. Calcutta was full of time expired soldiers waiting to be trooped home, but the Army was reluctant to release fully-trained and experienced soldiers and made every effort to importune them to volunteer to continue service in India by signing-on for another corps, thus bringing regiments in India up to strength without having to ship men out from England. To do this, all discipline was suspended and drunkenness was both encouraged and connived at during the long boring weeks of waiting for a boat home. Many men were inveigled by these discreditable means into volunteering for other regiments, extending their overseas service without realising what they were doing. It was not really difficult with men already fearful of the enormity of exchanging their Regiment - their family and the only home they knew - for an unknown existence in civilian life.

In such confused conditions it was no trouble at all for an American seaman to become a British soldier. Almost without his feet touching the ground Martin Early found himself conducted to a cot in one of the splendid bomb-proof barrackrooms of Fort William. He spent a disturbed and noisy fortnight amid drunken men, some raving with delirium tremens, before being kitted out and sent up country to join HM's 131st Regiment of Foot. Over nostalgic through drink, he liked the idea of joining a unit whose number almost approximated to his old 13th Virginia Regiment; he had asked for HM's 13th of Foot, but had been told they recruited from Somerset in England, where the regiment was currently stationed.

'Yank ... you might 'ave bin one of the last to fire a shot in your War ... 'ave you thought of that?'

Early pondered, 'Why yeah ... you might just be right at that!'

Looking around to see that the American was not in earshot, Taffy Davies said to the lance-corporal, 'Ye know, Sam ... I've been thinking o' what Yank Early told us ... you know, about the surrender parade ... a-trying to put us ... the British Army ... in the same position ... of having to line up in front of them wots beaten us ... hand over our arms an' colours ... an' I can't see 'ow it could happen, like.'

Sam Mockford considered. 'I see what you mean Taff ... oo the 'ell ... inna whole wide world ... could there be lined up onna opposite side o' the street? I mean, oo could beat us?'

'That's right ... 'ave a job to find anyone. Couldn't be the bloody French, we always whip them. An' the Germans ... well, we got the measure o' them ... beat the Russians last time round ... an' the rest of 'em ... aint worth a light, are they?'

The lance-corporal pursed his lips. 'Tell yer wot, 'ave yer given a thought to the Yanks ... good fighters if Early's anything ter go by ... an' they're sort of English, aint they? Yes, if it could be anyone ... it might jist be them Yanks!'

Taff shook his head. 'No, I don't think so. Early's a bloody exception, man ... couldn't ye tell from 'is tale ... there were no bloody discipline ... none at all ... in them armies.'

The lance-corporal vigorously agreed. 'That's right! Can't win no bleedin' wars wivvout discipline ... must 'ave discipline!'

XI

Timing their entry to a few minutes before Lights-Out when the room was full and drunks had been dragged or carried to their charpoys, Privates Bell, Cox and Finnigan - members of the Big Gun Committee - burst in, escorting Private Alexander who was bowed under the weight of a huge rough log. Before this the group had apparently done little, now they had discovered a heavy tree-trunk that seemed ideal for shaping into a gun-barrel, it was dropped to the floor with a hut-shaking crash.

'Look what we brocht ... I ken ye'll nivver see a better topkhana barrel.'

Kinrade leapt off his bed. 'You lovely boys! Where'd you find it ... an' why didn't you sods tell me?'

'Round the back of the canteen ...' shouted Private Cox '... on'y seed it just now ... alright Sanny ... I'll tell 'em ... Big Sanny carried it all the way back by hisself!'

Private Alexander's gargoyle face creased into a beam of pride. 'Aye ... aye ... I carried it ... all the way ... by meself!'

Holmes the Pioneer stood over the trophy, a roughly hewn log some eight feet long and twelve inches in diameter. 'Yer bloody goojars ... you'll drop yerselves in the shit over this. It ain't buckshee ... ole Robbo had it moved there, I got to make a rustic table out of it ... to stand in front of the Sergeant's Mess.'

Kinrade took his arm, smiling down at the little fat carpenter. 'Holy me boy ... ye won't mind losing a job will ye? An' it'll be a sight easier shaping it into a gun-barrel than making a bloody table for them bastards an' their stuck up bibi's!'

Holmes dragged his arm free. 'Bugger off! I ain't having nothing to do wiv it!'

The log lay on the floor all night, being rolled under the bungalow next morning before tumbling out on to Parade, where everyone was unusually alert, moving briskly, the excitement barely suppressed as they all shared a secret that made the day different to others. The Sergeant marvelled at this, going through formal military manoeuvres pondering on the startling changes a sense of purpose will produce in the British soldier.

Jostling into the bungalow and hastily pushing down the hard grey rooti and watery coffee, everyone watched the Big Gun Committee bring in the log. Private Kinrade displayed a certain sense of occasion and transformed it into a military parade, standing stiffly with a cane under his right arm, barking orders at Privates Bell, Finnigan and Cox, and acting as escort to Private Alexander, who joyously dropped the heavy log onto the flagstone floor with a crash that shook dust from the beamed thatched roof. Onlookers cheered lustily, clapped their hands and patted their neighbours' backs in glee. Private Holmes remained aloof, whistling on his charpoy in studied nonchalance.

Now followed the inevitable shouting and snarling as the Committee discussed practical ways of transforming the shapeless log into a realistic imitation of a cannon barrel. Kinrade undeviatingly rejected all external advice and suggestions with impersonal finality. 'Piss-off! You're not on the fuckin' Committee!'

During the months it took to make the gun, this became a standard catch-phrase peculiar to the Bungalow and the 5th Sub-Section. Eventually the entire Committee sat around the log, enthusiastically hacking away with pocket-knives. The Sergeant, watching from the cubicle doorway, suspected this to be Kinrade's cunning method of stimulating Holmes' professional scorn, provoking the Pioneer to take over. It was not long before Holmes, who had been watching them with growing irritation, burst upon them like the demon in a pantomime.

'Git outa the bleedin' way! I've nivver seen such a bunch o' clumsy birks in all my life!' Fiercely, he swung on Kinrade' 'An' don't tell me ter piss-off ... 'cos I've been on the fuckin' Committee since the bleedin' start!'

With the Committee at the front, the entire Sub-Section sat around in a circle, watching with admiration as the Pioneer fussed with a folding rule and whistled tunelessly through his clenched teeth. He gazed heavenwards, silently mouthing measurements. Eyes followed his every movement as the Pioneer paced round the log, stepped over it and stared reflectively. 'Them soddin' wheels is goin' ter be the trouble.'

At last he went into action with axe and adze, chipping away purposefully as shavings ricocheted in all directions, When the men pressed nearer for a better view Holmes would straighten up and snarl at them. 'Git out uv it! Let the dog see the rabbit!'

Every so often Holmes brusquely ordered the Committee to move the log, presenting another surface for his axe or adze; Big Sanny was always foremost, pathetically eager to help while his fellow Committee men were happy to let him do the man-handling. At other times, the big ungainly man bustled around with a broom, sweeping the shavings into a growing pile, their disposal provoking a shouting match later in the day. Despite the undoubted soporific influence of the remorselessly chipping adze, the audience remained remarkably constant throughout the day, pausing but briefly at midday to shovel down boiled beef and carrots. Natives, trying to set up the trestles and boards for the meal, approached the theatre of operations and were roundly cursed, and forced to put up the tables so that a gap was left for the gun-making party. Kinrade's Committee officially warned the natives - employing solemn oaths - of dire fates that would befall them if they breathed a word of what they had seen in the bungalow.

By mid-afternoon, having shaped the log so that it roughly resembled a gun-barrel in that it tapered from the thick breech-end to the thinner muzzle, Holmes admitted that his knowledge of the finer points of artillery pieces stretched no further. Straightening up, he appealed to the watching Committee. 'Do you buggers know anything about guns? How's this barrel gotta look when it's finished?'

The Committee gazed at each other in silence before Kinrade took them off to the far end of the room for a meeting. Ears strained to catch the fragments from mutterings, oaths, outbursts and Kinrade's final harangue before he led his sheepish colleagues back to the centre of the room. He cleared his throat. 'Would there be a learned gentleman among ye who will volunteer for a vacancy on the Committee as Artillery Advisor?'

He glanced round appealingly.

From a charpoy at the bottom end of the room, Private Early called out. 'I know a bit about guns ... Yeah, I'll help you ... but I don't want to go on your goddamned Committee ... just call it a bit of international co-operation ... I know what the gun's for an' as a white gentleman from a Southern State, I don't have no love fer niggers either.'

Kinrade eyed him suspiciously. 'You never said nothing before about topkhana, Yank ... you was in a foot reg'mint.'

'We did a bit of everythin' in the Confederate Army ... I had a spell in Alexander's artillery ... it was our rifles at Gettysburg that supported Pickett's last charge up the Ridge.'

Seeking his lost limelight, Holmes the Pioneer counter-attacked. 'Them's bloody American guns, not British!'

'We had British field-rifles, Armstrong's and Whitworth's, but they were complicated ... you wanna make this simple ... like a muzzle-loading, smooth bore, bronze twelve-pounder Napoleon ... it'll look near enough British to fool most, including that son-of-a-bitch babu.'

The American rose from his charpoy in his singular, smooth way and sauntered over to the log. He squatted on his haunches and began chalking, with a soft pebble, on the flagstone floor, talking as he worked. 'Here's cascable and button ... with astragal an' neck ... fitted to base ring ... in front of it is the vent-field and vent itself ... a hole where you put the match to shoot it off ... here, in front of that is vent-field astragal and fillets ... then further on ... about here, you've got first re-inforce ring ... same distance on is the second re-inforce ring and ogee ... then the barrel really begins to taper to muzzle astragal and fillets ... leading up to muzzle mouldings ... you won't need to bother about a dispart patch ... that's the same as a foresight in our Sniders.'

The American looked up. 'You can handle that O.K., Holy, can't you ... only a matter o' cutting round an' leaving some o' the wood proud ... Oh, I forgot ... you'll need some stout trunnions here.' He marked a point on the barrel, level with its axis mid-way between the base ring and muzzle astragal. 'It'll have to be strong 'cos its got to take the weight of the barrel on its carriage.'

Holmes nodded. 'I'll bore right through and fit a length o' pole wiv enough sticking out each side to rest on the carriage.'

Came the time, towards the end of the afternoon, when Early's drawing had to be rubbed from the floor; Holmes protested that he could not work without it and would require a roughly scaled plan on paper.

This presented problems, because no-one admitted possessing paper or writing implements. Finally Private Saville played his part in building the Big Gun by donating a sheet of note-paper, a quill pen and a phial of black ink, thereby enabling the American to produce a much scaled down reproduction of his large floor drawing.

The Sergeant-Major's office was so situated in the Sergeant's Mess building that none could pass its tatty-curtained doorway without being seen, the impact of iron-tipped boots on a flagstone passage being a doorbell with many clappers. Few approached without trepidation or free from the awesome anticipation of the familiar booming voice ordering them to step inside. At five minutes to six o'clock in the evening, passing along the passage, the Sergeant received the unrefusable invitation and, asking not for whom the bell tolled because he knew it tolled for him, he stepped inside.

As always, the Sergeant-Major sat motionless, like a grim Buddha. Eyes cold and snake-like, fixed on the stiffly erect Sergeant for so long that the eventual movement of the right hand became the only confirmation of his continued existence. The hand held the familiar small blue-covered, gold-titled book.

'Read Section Eight ... aloud!'

Turning its pages, the Sergeant calculated - that's the section dealing with good order and discipline. 'Section Eight. Non-Commissioned Officers in charge of barrackrooms are responsible for maintaining good order and discipline in their rooms, and that all irregularities are immediately reported.' His mind raced, seeking which transgressions aroused this familiar ceremonial routine. The Sergeant-Major's impassive face and implacable stare gave no aid or comfort.

'Sergeant Oakley, do you understand what that means?'

'Yessir!'

'If you truly understand it ... why did you allow stolen Regimental property to be brought to your bungalow, hidden and wilfully defaced by the men of your Sub-Section?'

That bloody tree-trunk! Desperately, he played for time, seeking a reasonably truthful excuse that would keep him ... and the Sub-Section ... out of the shit.

'Regimental property, Sarn't-Major? Wilfully defaced? Sorry sir ... don't understand.'

The Sergeant-Major's face crimsoned and his voice escalated

into the well known Parade-Ground boom that made all men within a hundred yards wince. 'Don't play bloody games with me, Sergeant Oakley! You well know I am talking about my bloody tree-trunk!'

The Sergeant thought quickly - if Robbo had been sure, someone would have been charged long ago; no-one had been, so there was an element of doubt, probably a sort of habeus corpus in that the incriminating evidence had vanished.

'Sir, a large log of wood was brought into the bungalow last night, by men in drink. I ordered them to remove it, but they were prevented by Lights Out. It was removed at Reveille, I have no knowledge of where it was taken.'

'What about the cutting and sawing they did to it today ... in your bungalow?'

Again, if Robbo knew for sure, charges would have been laid already; fervently the Sergent prayed that Kinrade's dire threats had sufficiently cowed the natives to keep their mouths shut.

'Sir?'

'The Orderly Sergeant found shavings on the floor of your bungalow!'

Recalling the thorough way that Private Alexander had swept the shavings as they accumulated, the Sergeant was certain that there was precious little.

'Sir, I can only suggest that shavings must have been brought in stuck to someone's boots.'

The Sergeant-Major's voice rose to a crescendo. 'Stuck to boots! Bloody rubbish! Those bloody men of yours cut my log to pieces ... in your bungalow ... and you tell me you know nothing about it! When I find that log I'll have 'em inside so quickly their feet won't touch the ground!'

The Sergeant wondered where, in the wide-open Cantonment, his men had managed to hide the log after removing it from its obvious place under the bungalow. Still, the Sergeant-Major knew enough to make life unpleasant for him; sergeants were held in the palm of Robbo's hand, to make or break as he willed. Suddenly, the Sergeant-Major switched to another transgression - why had he permitted one of his men to be cobbed, instead of charging him in the proper manner?

'Sir, he had committed no recognised military offence ... it was a disagreement ... a misunderstanding ... between two mates

... they are files.'

'Then why didn't they settle it between themselves ... like men ... using their fists behind the bungalow?'

'Sir, the offended party was much older and physically weaker, he would possibly have taken an unfair beating that might have affected his military efficiency. I and the men in the barrackroom realised that, so it was felt best ... to everyone's advantage ... to make it a Sub-Section matter and punish the man accordingly.'

The Sergeant-Major stared steadily at the Sergeant, most other men giving him so much chat would have been classified in his book as bloody barrackroom lawyers, to be watched and despised. But this lad was fighting for his men, not for himself, he really believed that justifiable reasons and excuses existed outside the narrow bounds of military law. Of course he was wrong, but erring on the right side. He was weak, but his weakness carried a certain strength of character which, allied to other known qualities, made him a good man.

To his own astonishment, Sergeant-Major Robinson VC found himself launching into a lengthy, fatherly lecture on the role and duties of Non-Commissioned Officers, specifically slanted towards Sergeant Oakley's temperament and character. The Sergeant never understood Robbo's uncharacteristic leniency, even the Sergeant-Major himself found it puzzling. Yet there was a simple explanation.

The big Sergeant-Major, an early winner of the Victoria Cross, was a solid, unimaginative man who lived by the rule book; quite devoid of fear he prized courage in his fellow men above all other qualities. When he heard from his spy - one of a network of punkah-wallahs who joyfully kept an eye on the sahibs in return for a few pice - of activities in the bungalow, he remembered the night of 11th November 1863 on the Umbeyla when young Corporal Oakley had been by his side defending the Crag, a stone sangar on the high rocky hill. Only twelve defenders could crowd into it and they held off waves of fanatical tribesmen for six long hours of darkness. He had recommended the lad for the VC, but nothing had come of it. Now, almost unwittingly, he paid his personal tribute by offering advice rather than punishment.

Abruptly concluding, he curtly dismissed the Sergeant, who

turned on his heel.

'Are you a Catholic, Sergeant Oakley?'

'Catholic? No, Sir.'

'Then you'd be advised to keep a tighter check on those bloody Irish in your barrackroom. You know 'em ... call themselves the Pope's Boys ... always stirring up trouble!'

'Sir!'

XII

Traditionally taking it upon themselves to ensure that the fourteen year old Boy Farley did not too early acquire the bad habits they displayed, everyone in the room kept a keen eye on him, sharply checking lapses and squashing unwelcome traits before they got too far. The older soldiers were particularly zealous in this, playing heavy-handed father roles in a collective manner that allowed little to escape them.

Very little passed unnoticed in the barrackroom, it could hardly be otherwise when men spent most of their waking hours laying on beds a mere twelve inches apart. Actions, attitudes, demonstrations, every mood and nuance were noted and commented on, usually uncharitably with intentions of stirring it up, but sometimes with gruff kindness. Picking crumbs from blackened teeth with his cherished ivory tooth-pick, Private Wright had been observing Boy Farley, noting the black and sullen visage, the angry movements and the slamming down of his locker lid. He called over to Bandsman Mort. 'What's up wiv Boy Farley then?'

'Dunno ... 'spect 'e's 'ad trouble wiv the Trumpet-Major ... 'ere! ... Boy Farley! You upset the Trumpet-Major or somethin'?'

The lad tightened his lips and glowered at the feet stretching out in front of him on the charpoy. Mort looked enquiringly over at 'Mister' Wright. 'Wot's 'e say? Can't see the little bleeder through the rifle-rack.'

Wright sat up, glaring officiously up-room over the recumbent bodies of Privates Davies, Holmes and Hebdon. 'Boy Farley! Did'ju 'ear Bandsman Mort address a question to yer?'

Boy Farley nodded sullenly.

'Then bloody well answer him, yer cheeky little sod ... or you'll get a flea in yer ear 'ole!'

'Sorry Bandsman Mort ... it's just ... I'm all choked ... it ain't fair ... the Trumpet-Major ... 'e ...'

'Now, Boy Farley ... enuff o' that ... you know we can't listen to you criticising a superior officer!'

Bandsman Mort shook his head sadly. 'Don't know wot the world's a'comin' to ... the Trumpet-Major ain't a bad lad ... you ought to 'ave seen ole Henry Fowles ... I said you ought to 'ave been under Trumpet-Major Henry Fowles inna 50th o' Foot ... now 'e were a right bastard ...'

Staring into space, the larger than life image of the Trumpet-Major floated before his eyes, tall, thin and balding with bushy side-burns linked to his flowing moustache; fishy eyes that fixed you unsmilingly. When he attempted a watery smile that was the time to watch out.

'No ... Boy Farley, the Trumpet-Major ain't a patch on Henry Fowles. You ain't got nuffin to worry about wiv 'im. Why, in my days we ... the band rats ... lived tergether in the Boy's Hut wiv Henry inna cubicle at the end ... like the S'arn'ts down there.' Mort jerked his head down-room and let it rest reflectively on one side as he pictured that hut, twenty-five years back. 'My God, when I think on it ... it were all beating, buggery an' boredom ...'

The Boy's Hut was the Trumpet-Major's undisputed kingdom, ruled not with a rod of iron but bamboo-cane and birch. Groaning under his tyranny, the despot's subjects were fifteen boys ranging from 11 to 16 years of age, orphans of other ranks, work-house kids, unwanted stepsons and abandoned waifs, all sharing the common hallmark of being alone in the world with none to watch over them. They were military manikins, treated as soldiers in all respects, except that uniforms, equipment, food and pay were all in miniature, although their discipline and punishment was on a scale that would have caused mutiny among men in most regiments. A pious respecter of Army traditions, Henry Fowles regularly observed Black Monday, the day of the Feast of Triangles when, in the old hard flogging days, each regiment erected the upright triangular wooden frame to which men were strapped for lashing. Regularly each Monday morning, the Trumpet-Major flogged his boys, using birches of his own making. Formidable instruments with new, supple twigs laden with buds, the handle strongly tied so that they spread half open to a veritable bush.

In turn, each trembling victim lowered his trousers, clenching his chattering teeth on an india-rubber 'piggy' to make it more bearable and prevent him crying out. Four comrades - if there were not that number free then boys awaiting birching were pressed into service - pinioned the victim by his shoulders and ankles over a form. Knowing but for the Grace of God it would soon be their bare bums sticking up defencelessly into the air, they averted their eyes and held their breath as Henny went to work. Swishing through the air, the birch fell with a noise like a bucket of water splashing on naked buttocks. Over the years, Henny had perfected his technique by altering the position of the feet after each stroke, enabling him to progressively cover upper thighs, buttocks and the lower back with blows of maximum intensity.

Allowing for the exaggerations of passing years, Charlie Mort could not remember a single month when he had not been birched for some infringement of the myriad of minor rules devised by the Trumpet-Major.

Even this brutalising regime could not completely triumph over the natural exuberance of youth which struggled to surface during those few rare moments when, for the first and only time in the day, each boy became a singular entity in his own sagging cot. Then, before merciful sleep shrouded past memories and future fears, they whispered together as boys do, cautiously calling across the room and sometimes displaying Man's unconquerable spirit by even giggling or laughing. As they got older, Charlie and his mates came round to a way of thinking that Henry encouraged this by allowing it to proceed until it suited him to take action. Then, from his cubicle at the end of the room, he would bellow. 'Spats!'

The resulting pall of silence was broken only by a bed's spasmodic creaking as the Trumpet-Major, savouring every second of power, leisurely rose and came among the boys. An incongruous figure, the long shanks protruding beneath his shirt tails and looking as thin as the bamboo-cane swishing in his right hand. Padding from bed to bed, with rough eagerness he pulled back blankets to lash writhing bodies with the whistling rod. When all had received their whack, the stifled weeping and groaning that hung on the foetid air was effectively quelled by threats of a repeat performance.

At least twice a week, 'Spats' was routinely concluded by a selected boy being ordered by Henry to leave his bed and follow him to his cubicle for what was commonly known as ' a game of backgammon', beaten bottoms were further maltreated by being well-greased and buggered. Cocooned in their isolated male community, devoid of any influences that might have been exerted by mothers or sisters, the boys accepted the situation as normal, not taking any great exception to Henny's perversions and considering them in a way to be perks of the job. Most of them did it with their mates anyway, although if Henny caught them at it, or masturbating, he called them 'dirty little sods' and put them on his Monday list. The Trumpet-Major had his favourites who took on superior airs when frequently called, while the neglected ones fretted in sulky anticipation. Arousing ribald comment Charlie Mort indignantly rejected suggestions of being in either category.

If Trumpet-Major Fowles had his likes, he certainly had his dislikes, and to be in his bad books meant a wretched, friendless existence, ostracised by comrades for fear the association caused Henny to regard them with disfavour too. The current object of his contempt became the butt of the barrackroom, sadly cited by Henny as the one bringing punishment down on their heads, his persistent derision and ridicule encouraged toadies to persecute the unfortunate boy, in the hope of gaining esteem in their lord's eyes.

Willie Phipps, aged eleven and the youngest and smallest boy in the barrackroom, had reigned as the odd-man-out longer than most. But, just as with favourites, the despised went out of fashion and thankfully were allowed to climb a rung from the bottom of the ladder, immediately to become one of the most enthusiastic persecutors of the unfortunate who had taken their place. His father was killed in a frontier foray and, followed by his mother dying of a fever, it meant that the boy remembered no home other than the Henry Lawrence Asylum for Orphans of Other Ranks. When ten years old he was sent from its benevolent cloisters at Sabathu in the Hills to enter Boy Service with the Regiment. Scrawny and undersized, Willie did not possess a single quality capable of being militarily ground and polished. Pathetically inadequate at all he attempted, Boy Phipps was a scruffy soldier: on parade his stature and unmilitary appearance made him stand out like a sore thumb, infuriatingly spoiling the symmetry of the line. Guaranteed to turn the wrong way, and to be out of step when marching, his very being incensed the Trumpet-Major, who saw it as being personally detrimental in his superiors' eyes.

Although a good teacher who had turned out a generation of first-class trumpeters, Henny could make no headway at all with Willie. He feared as much when he had first run his meditative eyes over the timid child who shrank from the tall cadaverous man, all sucked-in cheeks and prolific moustache. The boy started at Henny's rapping voice.

'Give me a look at yer mouth!' The boy stared blankly at him. 'Yer mouth! ... open yer bloody mouth!'

Hesitantly Willie opened his mouth and revealed his gapped baby-teeth. The Trumpet-Major bent forward.

'Wider ... wider!' He thrust his rough thumbs between Willies lips. 'Hm ... you ain't got no embouchure at all ... none at all! Gonna 'ave trouble with you, I can see!'

Henny pushed a battered trumpet into Willie's hands, who stared at it in bewilderment. Impatiently Henny waved a hand at him. 'Blow into it ... blow ... you stupid little bugger! Make a bleedin' noise.'

Rounding his lips onto the mouthpiece, Willie swelled out his cheeks and blew until he was red in the face without a sound coming forth.

'Don' puff, yer silly little fool ... spit into it!'

At last the boy managed to produce a feeble blurting sound, the Trumpet-Major winced. 'Gawd! You ain't never going ter make a bugler as long as you've got a hole in yer arse! Ask the boys ter give yer some alum to rub on yer lips ... bugger orf outta me sight, you little rat!'

It was bound to happen sooner or later that Henny would summons Willie Phipps to his cubicle for a game of backgammon. Probably he did it out of curiosity, he did not really fancy the boy but thought it would be interesting to break-in the youngest in the room. He knew, even if he managed to get into him, all he'd get out of it would be a sore cock. Willie's screams of outrage, pain and terror kept the room awake and did nothing to endear him to them. His painful hobbling next day spoilt morning parade and brought punishment down on their heads, so they took it out of his hide in retribution. Although not particularly enjoyable, Henny found bottling little Willie a bit different and persisted in his efforts to teach the boy the game. If for Willie the coming of the night heralded the worst experience of his life, for discarded favourites it brought jealousy and anger to be vented on the unfortunate Willie the next day. Thus, torments and cruelties beyond his wildest nightmares plagued the boys waking moments, until every word and action was made muddled and incoherent by the pain and fear that consumed him.

Run-of-the-mill boy soldiers, Charlie Mort and his mates had resiliently fought their way up from being butts to bullies, untouched by qualms or conscience. But what was happening to Willie Phipps was too much to stomach and gradually they rejected and despised the bullying, jibes and ostentatious persecution - designed to curry favour with the Trumpet-Major - of the small boy's puny battered body. Strong and tough elders of the community, they could by example and force of fists, temper the conduct of their comrades to the point where it was noticed by Henny, who subsequently stepped up his personal vendetta on Boy Phipps. After days of discussion, they raised themselves to the most courageous step of their lives, of taking on the Trumpet-Major on Willie's behalf. Boy Mort rapped his knuckles on the wooden upright of the doorless opening to the cubicle. Without looking up, the Trumpet-Major, sitting at a table a mere two feet away in full line of vision, rasped in the familiar awesome, throaty voice. 'Who is it? Wad'yer want?'

'Sir ... Boy Mort and Boy Chivers ... permission to speak, Sir!'

Making every effort to avoid giving offence, both boys stood rigidly to attention with their heads up. In the room beyond all save Willie Phipps, who was hiding in the jakes, had their heads poised and ears strained so as not to miss a word of the unique confrontation.

'Permission granted ... what've yer got to say?'

Not daring to meet those bulbous eyes, Mort's gaze remained fixed on a small fissure high in the brickwork of the wall beyond.

'Sir ... we ... Boy Chivers an' me ... request the Trumpet-Major ease-up on Boy Phipps ... 'e won't take much more, Sir.'

'Yer what?'

'Request you ease-up on Boy Phipps , Sir.'

Beyond control, Mort's eyes slowly lowered to rest on the Trumpet-Major's face, a picture of incredulous indignation. 'You ... you cheeky little sod!' Henny reached out blindly for his book.

'You know what ... you're goin' on my Monday list ... that's wot's goin' ter 'appen ter you ... an' Boy Chivers ... on my Monday list, both of yer!'

'Sir ... we refuse your punishment ... want to go a charge of insolence afore the Company Commander ... for insolence.'

Like the Demon-King springing out of the stage trap-door in a pantomime, Henny was suddenly towering over them. From thigh level, his right arm came up in a wide swing to catch Mort a stinging open-handed slap on the side of the face, sending him reeling into Boy Chivers at his side. In rhythmic continuation of the movement his left arm swung up to take Chivers on the other side of the head, so that the boys were sent buffeting into each other. 'You'll take my punishment ... an' plenty of it, I guarantee yer!'

With his head swimming and eyes watering, Mort slowly regained his balance. 'Sir ... permission to go sick ...'

'Go sick? You're not bloody sick!'

'Sir ... goin' to show the Surgeon our arses ... tell 'im wot goes on 'ere!'

The Trumpet-Major stood stock still, staring at them both. The boys fought back an almost irresistible urge to turn and flee from his wrath. Then, to their astonishment, the fury slowly drained from his face and was replaced by a thin smile of sanctimonious sadness. 'Oh boys ... it really 'urts me to see such evil thinking ... such wickedness in boys as young as you ... an' directed at me ... me 'oo's bin yer Farver an' Muvver ... done me best fer you an' the rest, like a big family. Now jest 'cos I 'ave ter come down a bit 'eavy on the baby o' the family ... who's bin a bit naughty ... I find evil thoughts in me eldest ... 'oo oughta know better.' Sadly, he shook his head. 'I'm sorry about this ... very sorry ... an' it's goin' ter 'urt me more'n you ... 'cos I'm goin' ter 'ave ter beat the wickedness outa yer every Monday fer the rest of the year!' He placed a hand on each of their shoulders, causing Boy Chivers to involuntarily flinch. 'Don't worry about going sick, lads ... it's bin tried afore an' the Surgeon ordered me to give good whippin's to stop the buggering that was goin' on among yer!'

Twenty-four years had passed since that day but even now, a long-service soldier laying on his charpoy, Charlie Mort could recall the despair he felt when paternally dismissed by the

Sergeant-Major and marching blindly up the barrackroom to his bed. He remembered how Boy Chivers carried on out through the top door, to rush back within seconds, crying out. 'Willie Phipps ... 'e's gorn an' hung 'isself wiv 'is lanyard ... in the shithouse!'

Pushing through the crowd of boys gaping up at the eyes bulging from the thin purpled face of their late comrade, the Trumpet-Major lifted the light body with one hand by the scruff of the neck while loosing the noose with the other, at the same time ordering a boy to run for the Provost Sergeant.

Bandsman Mort pictured the lolling head and limp body. Thinking on it he realised if it had not happened then it would have been some other time. Willie would never have lasted another three or four years in the Boy's Hut, nor in the ranks as a private, come to that.

'Funny thing was ... that were the end of the Trumpet-Major too ... 'cos little Willie Phipps came back from the dead an' got 'im!'

'Wot d'y'mean? 'E 'aunted 'im ... like a ghost?'

'No ... nuffin' like that. About that time we got a new Surgeon ... out from England ... a real serious sorta bloke, an' 'e insisted on 'aving a post mortem ... you know, cutting a body open ter see what killed it. Anyway, it didn't take 'im long ter see what 'ad bin 'appening to Willie ... so 'e goes to the CO an' insists on an enquiry. It was said the CO 'ad ideas of wot 'ad bin goin' on but wanted a quiet life ... honour o' the Regiment an' all that. you know. Anyway, the Surgeon'd 'ave none of it ... 'e insisted and 'appened to mention 'is brother was a well known Member o' Parliament back 'ome. Well, they 'ad their enquiry an' everyone ... the Trumpet-Major an' all of us ... gave evidence ... an' we really dropped ole Henny in the shit, so's in the end 'e was shipped 'ome under escort for trial ... an' we 'eard months later 'e'd got ten years 'ard labour in civvy clink.'

Everyone lay thinking about it, then Cocksy spoke up. 'What about you, Mortie? Done any brown 'attin' since then?'

'I'll punch your fuckin' head, Private Cox ... I've never been partial to shit-stabbin' ... even if you 'ave!'

Mister Wright belched. 'Show me a brown-hatter an' I'll show you a bloke wot's done boy service.'

Boy Farley sat straight up in bed and glared across the room.

Wright shook his head.

' 'Cept Boy Farley o' course ... an' if I ever catch 'im at it I'll put a bayonet up 'is arse an' twist it!'

Staring up at the ceiling with his hands behind his head, Private Kinrade had the last word - as he so often did - morosely spitting out. 'Them poor little sods ... Christ, how I hate senior NCO's!'

XIII

There was a shrewd suspicion circulating around Bungalow No.5 that 'Mister' Wright was up to something. For more than a week he had kept his gob shut. On his charpoy in the far corner staring reflectively up at the lofty beamed ceiling, his mind was wrestling with matters of considerable importance. He ignored the spirited and provocative stirring, designed to get him going. He was in no trouble, he was an old enough soldier to know how to keep his nose clean. He had no bad news from home, he had not had a letter for more than three years to the best of recollections; a weekly visit to the Rag gave him all the nooky he wanted, and in the Wet Canteen he was supping his share along with the rest. So what was it?

Long-service soldiers, lips compressed as they sagely nodded, came to the conclusion that old Mister Wright was thinking of forming a boozing school! Heads together, they reviewed his past record. He had been treasurer to a couple of schools, schools with good reputations at Bannu in '63, and here in Mirzapur Cantonment a brace of years back. He had the know-how and could be trusted, for treasurers of boozing schools had to be men of rigid principles, devoted to serious drinking and capable of handling money and keeping accounts.

It was not hard to narrow down who was in it with him. Most of the younger soldiers had enough of Mister Wright's daily dogmatic ruling, without boozing with him at night. So it had to be the older soldiers, men whose length of service allowed them to understand his ways and attitudes, regular old cronies who had shared many a battlefield, bivouac and bungalow with him. It was generally reckoned the three men who would sit each night from opening time to stop-tap, at the same table in the Wet Canteen, sharing a quart-pot and taking it to the bar for refilling in turn, would most likely be Taffy, Sam Mockford and old Wrightie himself, with Mortie if they wanted a fourth - all men knocking on forty and with more years of service than they'd had hot dinners. They were not far out, Taffy Davies went in with Wright but everyone was surprised when they picked Polly Perkins as the third man. Of course, none knew if others had been approached and refused and it was generally believed that the lance-corporal had his nose put out of joint by not being invited. All agreed it was a promising school of good drinkers who could sup their ale and get heads down back at the bungalow without bothering anyone or causing trouble.

The gregarious drinking habits of the British soldier, and the excitement aroused by this variation in the monotony of daily life, stimulated everyone in the bungalow and keen interest was shown as the school prepared. Old soldiers who had been in such schools explained to the unenlightened the strict written rules controlling systematic drinking, telling how all pay was handed to the Treasurer who doled out a small sum for 'baccy and getting dirty water off the chest in a weekly visit to the Rag, or a bazaar brothel. Sadly they reflected on how all schools eventually ran into debt, when each member of the sold surplus kit and borrowed money for the general good of the school. Then came the time when the true character of the school was revealed, as all debts were scrupulously listed by the treasurer and borrowing halted when the limit of two hundred rupees was reached. That was the dreaded day when the school went 'on the tact', turning their faces from the Wet Canteen and becoming temporary tee-totallers. Pay would still be pooled and the minimal amounts set aside for 'baccy and the brothel, while they lived entirely on issue rations with no extra food or luxuries from the bazaar.

Every listener was stirred by this heart-rending situation, already feeling weeks in advance the pain and distress they would share with their unfortunate comrades during those wretched days when the school would devote themselves just as enthusiastically to raising money as they had to drinking. All genuine boozing schools made every attempt to repay their debts and, with every confidence in their mates, the Sub-Section was already pondering on how much they would be able to lend them. Even Private Saville, who was a non-drinker, felt carried away by enthusiasm for these exciting and quite incredible customs, hearing with great interest of the money-making efforts of the school on the tact. Apparently, for the group's general good, every latent talent was plumbed to the depths as jaded ex-drinkers laboriously carved little figures, painted pathetic pictures, drew portraits of their mates and turned out framed regimental badges. If without such talents they fell back on the inveterate standby of burning inspiring messages into slabs of wood with hot pokers, all of which were hawked round and bought by sympathetic comrades. Although he knew he would never be in a boozing-school, Saville found comfort in knowing his artistic abilities would stand him in good stead were he so placed.

Knowing exactly what they were embarking upon, the three exalted members of the school kept aloof from such conversations and discussions, time enough later to consider the tortures of the tact. No school worried about it until the time came, so none of the three gave a thought to how they would eventually distract themselves from the temptations of the Canteen and bazaar by going for long walks and endlessly discussing optimistic schemes for raising money.

For more than a week, Lance-Corporal Mockford, Pat Coughlin and Charlie Mort had a field-day regaling wide-eyed younger soldiers with the more lurid details of boozing schools. Private Holmes, the taciturn Pioneer Carpenter, who had been in a few such groups and knew a thing or two about them, could not be bothered to chat about it. For once, Private Kinrade listened, having nothing to say as he had never been in a school. At first he gave thought to organising a rival group of his own, before realising it was not his style to drink himself into situations beyond his control. He heard how schools paid off debts in a comparatively short time, then the treasurer was bound to call a special meeting to discuss whether to carry on. If it was decided to do so, they continued on the tact earning money to buy as much spare kit as possible, so that when hard times again afflicted the school, they had plenty to sell. Also they needed to amass a working capital of two hundred rupees. All this took about six months, half a years tee-total privation before systematic boozing began again. The dark brooding Irishman marvelled at so much will-power being shown for such foolish ends. Give him enough Paddies with the same sense of purpose and he'd have the English out of Ireland within a year.

Like an old war-horse made restless by the smell of powder,

all this talk aroused nostalgia in Lance-Corporal Sam Mockford. There came a morning when it seemed that all possible variations of the boozing-school theme had been played out and the unhappy room lay silent. Sam, a veteran of barrackroom chat, had been holding back what he knew to be a prime piece for just such a moment, from the corner bed-space his gruff measured tones reprieved the grateful room.

'Them three ...' His head motioned down-room. ' ... if they live to be a hundred will never have a boozing-school to come up to the one run by ole Joe Smales at Kohat in '51.'

In his cubicle the Sergeant had not missed any of the week-long chat about boozing-schools, being alternately amused, bored or irritated by it all. He had never personally been involved in one and, cloistered for eight years in Married Quarters, had seen little of them in action. At first he had thought it all a bit pointless, then realised that in a pathetic sort of way it provided what peace-time soldiering lacked - a sense of purpose. At the same time it revealed the close comradeship and mutual reliance that was the very life-blood of the British Army. Throughout, he had nursed a shrewd idea that one of the old soldiers was keeping a prize yarn up his sleeve, it was their way, they always did. When Mockford spoke out it pleased him for a number of reasons, it saved having to ask if anyone had a story to tell and while they were listening they could not be bickering. A good yarn always drew them together. He settled down to listen.

The room waited expectantly as the Lance-Corporal appeared to ponder on how best to begin his saga, although he had been rehearsing it in his mind for days. Kinrade stirred restlessly. 'Come on, Corp' ... if you're gonna give us a tale ...let's be 'avin' it!' he said.

Mockford's attempt to fix him with a baleful eye was intercepted by the bulky rifle-rack in the middle of the room, towering above recumbent men on their low charpoys.

' 'Ave a bit of respect for rank, Private Kinrade ... or none o' yer'll 'ear anythin'!'

'Oh come on, Corporal ... don't take no notice o' that bleeder'

'Please ... Corp'l ... tell us abart Joe Smiles ... '

'Smales. It were Joe Smales. The best damned treasurer the British Army's ever seen ... an' 'e were in a school along with Wally Grice an' MacAlpine ... '

It had been a damned good school, notable for the amount of ale they regularly pushed back at night, more than their exchequer could stand week after week. Now they had sold every mortal thing they could lay their hands on. Wally had even put his father's watch into the kitty but they had reached the two hundred rupees limit and going on the tact loomed before them. It was sad, but they had had a good run, better than Joe Smales had expected because it was a bit of an assorted school that could have fallen on its face early on. He and Wally Grice were old hands and had been in many a school together, he wouldn't fancy being in one without old Wally backing him up. They had taken a bit of a chance letting young MacAlpine in with them, they could both give him at least fifteen years in age and length of service, but he'd begged and sworn he could booze with the best of them. Well, he'd been right ... a really pissy-arse he turned out to be, a natural boozer, it was a talent you had to be born with, you couldn't learn it. The lad had stayed with them sup after sup, never welching, always up steady as a rock when his turn came to take the bowl to the bar. He never gave no trouble in the barrackroom, put himself to bed quietly and once or twice was even able to help with old Wally. Fights took up good drinking time, so were avoided whenever possible; MacAlpine never started fights but always pulled his weight when belts, boots, buckles and fists started flying. He was the odd man out alright, compared with the lean, raw, scarred and cropped old soldiers Grice and Smales, being stocky, round-faced with rosy-apple cheeks, soft brown eyes and silky fair hair - mind you, after a month or so his face was pasty and puffed, and covered with yellow headed spots, his eyes always bloodshot and sore-looking.

All good things must come to an end and the three agreed that they had had a glorious time and would do it again as soon as was possible, first they had to clear off debts and get a bit of money behind them. It was nothing new to Joe and Wally who could not make up their minds whether it got easier or harder to withstand the lip-licking pangs of being without a drink. Of craving a sup of ale more then they had ever wanted anything in their lives, when, like a mirage, they had day and night visions of translucent amber liquid swirling around a froth edged bowl. Both knew how the other was feeling so neither spoke of it but became increasingly fed-up with MacAlpine's continual blathering-on about how bloody awful he felt, how he wanted a drink, and how long would it be before he stopped wanting one. Blunt men who had never given a sod for man nor beast, they told him to put a sock in it and get on with whatever he could do to make money for the school.

And that was the nub of it. Joe and Wally settled down industriously to pursue the familiar handicrafts they favoured on such occasions, but MacAlpine was simply useless with his hands. In the end, after a succession of unsaleable failures, he went round offering to whiten equipment, clean boots and polish brasses, but the natives did it so much cheaper and better that even sympathy brought him few customers. In a boozing school it is one for all and all for one; if a man is a good mate to drink with then you stick with him when times get hard in other directions. So Joe and Wally assured him companionably that it did not matter, they could earn enough for the three of them, but it was not good enough for MacAlpine, who slouched around looking miserable and feeling guilty. Neither of his mates bemoaned about it, not to each other and particularly not in public. Both knew the way the game went and were ready to labour on, knowing in the long run they could make enough for all three to get by.

For about a week they did not see much of MacAlpine, except at night in the bungalow when he came rushing in just before Lights Out and got his head down quickly. They thought he was off on some new money-making tack, in fact, he told Joe he'd soon have some brass to put in the kitty. Wally asked if Joe had noticed how blokes stopped talking when they came near, looking at them with half-smiles on their faces. Not going near the Wet Canteen meant they missed most of the gup because it was there, over ale, that rumours and gossip circulated. Then Joe had to punch a bloke's head because he asked a stupid question about 'Miss' MacAlpine. The aggrieved victim called his mate to back him up and the whole story came out. It seems that they hadn't seen much of MacAlpine because he had taken up with the Company Quartermaster and spent all his time in the stores with him. The punched bloke said you could never get a shirt changed nor a pair of socks because they'd always got the door locked, getting up to things among the shelves.

Finally, running MacAlpine down, Joe asked him straight if he was the QM's fancy-boy. At first he denied it, but not very firmly, so they kept on at him until he admitted it, saying the QM had been after him for a long time, offering presents and money. MacAlpine said he did it for the good of the school, there was no way he could earn money, not being clever with his hands like them ... now he could get as much kit from the stores as they wanted ... and he had money too. He pulled out a handful of rupees and offered them to Joe, who knocked them out of his hand saying they didn't want brown-hatter's money.

Walking away and leaving MacAlpine staring after them, Joe said they would have to find someone to take his place, because they'd soon have enough behind them to come off the tact and start over again. Wally did not answer, having a bit of trouble with his words, muttered he was thinking of going on the skin. He had been thinking about it for some time ... he had less than twelve months to go before time expired ... it would be a good idea to save every rupee and pice and have the booze-up of a lifetime when he landed in England. He did not say he had got to like waking up in the morning clear-headed and without a mouth like a desert dried sock. He liked getting through the day better and being sharper at his duties, not landing himself in any trouble that might delay his going home. After the first surprise, Joe was annoyed, but not for long because Wally was an old mate and Joe had to admit that what he was doing was sensible, although a bloody sight harder than starting-up again. They parted good friends and passed the time of day when they met.

So the school broke up, the three of them going their own ways - and mighty different ways they turned out to be! On the skin more than anyone had ever seen, Wally soldiered on, denying himself just about everything that made a man's life worthwhile, not even taking an occasional drink or smoking 'baccy. He even gave his clays away and never once went to the Rag from that day on. Except for duty, he never left the barrackroom and sat on his bed with his head bent over his knitting like an old grandma, turning out socks, cardigans and body-belts like a damned machine. Blokes came from all over the Cantonment to see him, standing watching him like he was a fakir sitting on a bed of nails. When he cursed and told them to sod off they bought something and walked away, marvelling at his strength of purpose.

MacAlpine took his rejection hard, cursing sulking and showing off so that the QM had to jolly him round as though he were a woman. He got him interesting fatigues to take his mind off his troubles, such as working in Officers' Married Quarters' bungalows. One day, dragging things out as long as possible, he looked at a copy of a woman's journal belonging to an officer's wife. Quickly he passed over what had been the latest London fashions in hats and clothes a year ago, but took great interest in an illustrated article describing how to embroider with coloured silks on sacking stretched over a wooden frame, so carefully explained it did not look too difficult. Tearing the pages out, carefully he folded and tucked them inside his shirt, studying them in the privacy of the jakes. Later he was surprised to find he could buy everything he needed in the bazaar, apparently India had been doing it for centuries. After a bit of practice he could turn out creditable tapestries of English castles and rural scenes traced onto the sacking from pictures, later he embroidered coloured regimental badges. They sold as quickly as he could make them. As the money piled up he reflected that had he possessed this talent a few weeks ago he could have carried on happily drinking himself to death, instead of being a wealthy outcast.

Shattered at the rapid dissolution of the boozing-school, and the manner of it, Joe Smales mooned around for a week or so, wallowing in self-pity. He then pulled himself together to wholeheartedly throw his big frame and iron constitution into combat against strong drink in all its most virulent forms. Consorting with the dregs of the Regiment, men not fit to lace his boots whose disgusting drinking habits and unstable aggressions were too much, even for men who had boozed and brawled in the Crimea, China, Persia and most Indian stations. Forsaking his mates in the Wet Canteen, with its ales, porter, stout and grog, he lurched around the worst of the sleazy drinking parlours in the bazaar, knocking-back vast quantities of rot-gut, Billy Stink and other native-brewed alcoholic poisons.

The Regiment followed his progress. Men lost their names craning from the ranks during Regimental Parades to see what Joe Smales was doing, but he disappointed every curious eye by being as steady as a rock in everything he did. However, it could not go on. No-one, not even the Lord himself, could tear down his constitution like this without it showing or taking effect. Every other-rank reluctantly lived in anticipation of the end of this incredible soldier who had become a legend in his own lifetime; knowing it could only be convulsions, cramps, coma, blindness and death. Betting men made books on how long he would last. There were few lower-ranks who had not named a date and backed their judgement with some rupees. Men from other companies went out of their way to lurk behind bungalows, keenly scrutinising his face, seeking signs of deterioration.

The unequal contest noticeably began to take its toll of even Joe Smale's steel and whipcord frame, and men who had plumped for later rather than early dates lay awake counting their expected winnings. Meanwhile, up on the Frontier a fanatical fakir fermented rebellion. At short notice, after two hours of joyous bustling, the Regiment marched-out, every painful step taking Joe further away from his self-imposed sentence. In a few short days he had worked his way through the bottles secreted in his pack, its lessened weight hardly compensated for the agonies of drying-out that persisted for part of the three months hard marching and precious little fighting in the harsh Black Mountains. When the Regiment straightened-up to swing through the gates of Kohat cantonment, having lost two men to Afridi snipers and ten to sickness, upright in their midst marched Private Joe Smales, once again the hard, clear-eyed soldier of former days.

Packs slid off backs, rifles locked in racks and bedding was drawn from the stores, then everyone surged in a body to the Wet Canteen to fulfil the cherished dreams of slaking Black Mountain dust from their throats. Lowering empty pots, breathless men looked around for Joe Smales. He was nowhere to be seen and the word excitedly spread around that Joe had taken up where he had left off.

They were wrong. Joe was in the Temperance Canteen, knocking back ginger-ale and lemonade with the same enthusiasm as he had tackled the strong stuff that, but for the Frontier fakir, would have done for him.

Unable to keep a wistful note from his voice, Lance-Corporal Mockford spoke out. 'Yeah, ole Joe took the Pledge ... became one o' the fiercest bun-punchers in the cantonment ... won medals for it an' he wore 'em as proudly as his campaign medals ... them wot he'd risked his life fer ... but I s'pose he'd put his life onna line for them Temperance medals too, innaway.'

Gazing speculatively at 5th Sub-Section's boozing-school, none could cast Privates Wright, Davies or Perkins in Smales', Grimes', or MacAlpine's roles so they settled back to observe their progress. Anything the slightest bit different brightened up life at Mirzapur.

XIV

That morning the talk got round to bravery; to larger than life stories of comrades mostly long since dead, with everyone searching for examples of courage to cap what had already been said. Thoughts winged back to dusty, smoke-obscured battlefields, mercifully blurred by the passing of years so that men forgot the terrors of hissing roundshot and crackling musketry, the fearful cries, curses, shouts and screams. Plodding forward in ordered lines with heads bowed as though advancing into a rainstorm, the infantryman knew nothing of the general battle. His small, fearful world was bordered by the men around him, constantly changing as torn and twisted bodies were left behind and the lines re-formed. So although the soldiers in Bungalow 5 could claim battle honours painting a canvas of British Mid-Victorian colonial history - with Martin Early's American Civil War thrown in for good measure - their recollections of those battles were limited to memorable acts by individual soldiers.

Men whose bones had long been dust were re-incarnated to go forward in their familiar role of living and healthy soldiers. Their exploits, both real and legendary, serving as a sole epitaph, few of them had known graves. Remember Big Jim Reilly of 'C' Company ... he who brought down the chain-mailed Sikh Goorchurra at Ferozeshah ... my God, that's twenty years ago! And Paddy Smirke at Lucknow in '57 ... holding the breach in the wall of the Kaisarbagh 'til we got up ... why, there were ten dead Pandies in front of that hole and Paddy's bayonet was all bent and twisted! What about little Tommy Huggett ... remember how he fought all night in the Crag at the Umbeyla?

Listening in his cubicle, the Sergeant noted the sudden hush and guessed that the men were nodding and gesticulating in his direction. They knew he too had been in that rocky sangar, along with Robbo and Private Huggett and a score or so more. Only room for a dozen defenders, men crawled in to take the place of the dragged out dead and wounded. The Sergeant remembered

Huggett, a cheerful little Geordie who had been at most of John Company's wars without getting a scratch. He got a splinter of wood down his thumbnail and died of lockjaw.

The musical Welsh lilt of Private Owen Davies hung on the heavy air. 'Look ... bravery isn't always on the battlefield ... men can be brave without fighting.'

'You mean like when old Buck Ryan kept going wiv a bloody great lump in his guts, all yellow an' thin as a rake ...never gave up tho'!'

'Yes, something like that ... but I'm thinking of ... he weren't fighting to live ... had nothing wrong with him ... he was fighting. With no weapons 'cos it were all he had to hang on to.'

'You mean religious or something?'

'No ... it were like this. The Reg'ment was stationed in some grimy town in the North ... can't remember where it was now ... anyway, we'd been crowded in a mouldy old castle for nigh on five years ... walls six foot thick, streaming with water, freezin' cold in winter and summer ... shit-house was holes in the floor an' ablutions a tap in the wall. We had a hard bunch o' lads, all old soldiers with lots of service in, could drink an alehouse dry an' when they ran short of locals to fight, beat the hell out of each other. Well, one of 'em died ... consumption or some chest trouble I think it were ... he was a good lad and a favourite with everyone, so the boys didn't take too kindly to Josh Baker when he was drafted in to take his place.'

Nineteen years old, under-sized and spotty-faced, Josh Baker was a draper's assistant in Hertford when he was caught with his hand in the petty-cash box. To avoid arrest he fled to London and joined the Army. An exasperatingly inadequate recruit, he was hustled from the Depot as quickly as possible and pitchforked, like a foreigner from another country, into the midst of thirty-six foul-mouthed, drink-sodden soldiers. Crowded together with their beds almost touching, they existed in a dank lofty chamber, ill lit by two small windows set high in thick stone walls.

Exhausting and monotonous drill-parades, where screaming NCO's badgered and bullied, combined with communal cruelties and baiting in the barrackrooms, made life a tormented hell. Night after night, when drunken persecutors were eventually silenced by fatigue or stupor, repeatedly Josh's fevered brain raced over of ways to escape. Denied any other nebulous luxury of hope, desertion seemed the sole route to freedom. But his flesh cringed at the grim memories of apprehended deserters, pinioned to rings in the rough stone wall, their backs battered to a bloody pulp by the lash's nine hissing tails.

During a rare off-duty period, aimlessly wandering among the stalls of a street market, by accident Josh discovered something that might fractionally soften his intolerable existence. All year round, freezing winter and hot summer, the entire Company of more than a hundred men carried out daily ablutions in the yard, three flights of stone steps below, washing and shaving while crowded around a single brass water tap that jutted out from the brick wall. At night, or in the dark chill of the early morning, jostling and pushing in the perennial slush of the muddy area around the tap, men attempted to attain a degree of cleanliness sufficient to pass muster on parade. Significantly smaller and less militant than his comrades, Josh Baker invariably fared badly on these occasions, so, when on an ironmonger's stall he saw a small tin basin, he felt that expending slightly less than a whole week's pay was justified if it improved what seemed to be the sole alterable situation in his miserable life.

Men could not believe their eyes when, having jostled to fill the bowl under the cascading tap, Josh took himself to the other side of the yard, balanced the bowl on a low wall and commenced washing in a completely different way to everyone else. To a man they were enraged that a young soldier should consider himself too superior to wash in the time-honoured manner of generations of men, better men than he by far. The very sight of that bowl aroused instincts in his fellow men worse even than those previously displayed towards him. When he managed to fight his way to the tap, the bowl was tipped and its few inches of water lost. When he got it to the wall, men brushed past and knocked it over. It was confidently expected he would give up after a few days of this, but he displayed dogged, if tremulous, tenacity in his objectionable aim of being different. Efforts to deter him intensified and besides the vigorous demonstrations around the muddy tap the campaign continued in the barrackroom. The bowl vanished and when found was battered and crushed, painfully he straightened it. On finding it brimming with shit and piss, he would clean it and somehow he managed to repair the gash when it was savagely pierced with a bayonet. Although adding to the constant on and off duty harassment, the torments only strengthened his resolve. It was as if he was hanging onto a rusting iron ring in a jetty wall to prevent being washed away by the buffeting waves.

For ten days he desperately guarded the precious bowl against a variety of onslaughts. Of course, it would have been easy for the others to have taken it from him by force, or during the night, but they discovered it was more fun to have it around as a means of getting at him. Anyway, it saved men the trouble of going out onto the landing in the cold of night to use the urine-tub. There were few mornings when the bowl was not standing in solitary squalor in the middle of the room, brimming over with shit, piss and vomit.

One day the section, clattering back into the barrackroom after last parade, were highly amused to find an off-duty man had pissed in Josh's bowl to save going down three flights of stairs to the latrines. Laughing and jeering, men removed their boots and equipment and settled down on their beds while Josh plodded wearily downstairs to empty the bowl.

Some time later an outburst of cat-calls and jeering broke out at the sight of him standing in the doorway, bowl in hand, but he looked different, his head was unusually erect with his eyes meeting theirs in a steady gaze. The outcry faltered and died away, this was not his usual cringing manner. Staring in anticipation and curiosity, men awaited the next cue for uproar. Like a man with nothing to lose who has made up his mind on a course of action, Josh's eyes swept them all and the shrill, youthful voice, louder and more assertive than they had known, echoed round the lofty chamber. 'Listen! All of you! I'm beyond caring whether I live or die. Nothing can frighten me any more. I don't care what trouble it gets me into but if you don't leave me ... and my bowl ... alone ... I'm going to kill one of you!'

Men looked at each other, then back at Josh, before bursting into waves of uncontrollable laughter that rode high on an air that was heavy with odours of sweat, and rifle oil. Face expressionless, the young soldier stood unmoved until the noise died away.

'I know I'm not big enough or strong enough to kill any of you in a fight ... but you've got to sleep sometime ... and that's when I'll creep to one of your beds and cut your throat with my razor.'

From a breast pocket, slowly and dramatically Josh drew a black and silver razor. He flicked it open so that the keen blade gleamed in the fading light of the late afternoon. In utter silence the men stirred uneasily, licking their lips and looking at each other for assurance, then, collecting themselves, a hubbub of voices fractured the air.

'You're fuckin' mad!'

' 'E wouldn't do it ... ain't got the guts!'

'You ain't got wot it takes ter kill pussy!'

With every eye upon him, Josh Baker slowly walked to his bed-space and sat down on his made up bed. 'You'll see! Remember what I've said when you can't keep your eyes open any longer and you go to sleep!'

That evening the barrackroom was unusually quiet. Men polished their boots and cleaned their equipment, thoughtfully eyeing Josh who lay on his bed, fingering the razor. His bowl rested by his side on the dusty blanket. It was the first night since entering the room that Josh was allowed to go to bed and rest undisturbed. Even the drunks reeling in just before Lights Out ignored him, contenting themselves with muttering abuse in his direction but not directly at him. Distant bugles sounded, the Orderly Sergeant came in and turned out the batswing gas burner. Men settled down uneasily and unsuccessfully fought off drowsiness until the room came alive with the night noises of sleeping men. In the small hours, Private Sam Harker, a light sleeper, was woken by someone brushing the foot of his bed. Raising his head he peered through the darkness to see who it was weaving an unsteady path to the urine-tub. His eyes becoming accustomed to the half-light, he saw it was no full-bladdered drunk but Private Josh Baker, dressed in his shirt and trousers, methodically pacing the narrow aisle between the beds. The open razor was held chest high before him.

His startled shout awoke the room, men struggled back to consciousness and wrested themselves upright, glaring desperately around until they focused on the solitary standing figure. Every man in the room could hear his low voice in the stillness of the night.

'I wanted you all to see how easy it is for me to cut the throat of any one of you ... you can go back to sleep 'cos I'm going to bed. You have my word I'll do nothing tonight.'

The next day the men drew up a roster, each man taking it in turn to remain awake to do an hour's stag, as if on Guard. But it could not go on, barrackroom life was completely disrupted and none knew peace of mind. Gradually it became clear both to Josh and the men in the barrackroom that there was a limit to the length of time his threat could hang over their heads, that sooner or later they would call his bluff - Josh along with the rest being hedged by uncertainty as to whether it was bluff or not. However, both shared the common knowledge that in making the ultimate threat he had posed a problem with only one possible answer.

The solution came swift and sure. At Reveille, a sleep-drugged boy trumpeter, went into the yard below to sound Rise and Shine. In the gloom of the early morning he stumbled over Josh Baker's body. So Josh Baker finally found rest, mired in the mud around the ablutions tap. In his hand was a blood-fouled open razor, and his throat gaped over his own tin bowl, into which he had bled like a slaughtered pig.

Private Taffy Davies sighed. 'Official-like, it was called suicide ... but I never thought Josh had guts enough to harm himself ... although it took guts to stand-off some of them blokes in that barrackroom. They were bloody hard-nuts ... always thought he were very brave to do that!'

XV

In time, the Sergeant realised that if he was ploughing a lonely furrow, Private Saville, in his solitary bed-space at the cubicle end of the bungalow, was a man apart. Far beyond the comprehension of his comrades he was cruelly mimicked whenever he ventured to speak, other than that he was generally ignored, excepting the times when he became the butt of cruel jokes and piss-taking. Possessing but a single book, the youngster lay for hours staring into space, thinking about God knows what. If he had been a drinking man he would have been better off as even drunks have something in common, but evenings in the Canteen held no attraction for him. Nor was he the sort of soldier who skulked in sleazy bazaar alleys, digging premature graves with native drink and diseased sand-rats. He had no friends and had shied away from relationships after venturing on a walk with a reasonably spoken older soldier who had made repulsive suggestions and tried to handle him.

One morning the Sergeant noted a change in pattern as Saville began to take advantage of his solitary bed-space. With his back to the room, on his charpoy, he toiled with something on a rough piece of wood balanced across his knees. Nothing goes unobserved in a barrackroom, even furtive below-blanket activities soon earn a man the reputation of being a wanker. Saville's unusual preoccupation was being scouted by Hebdon and Cox, noiselessly advancing with obvious destructive inclinations only to be thwarted when the Sergeant appeared in the cubicle doorway. Oblivious, Saville's eyes remained down until the Sergeant's legs appeared in his line of vision. Guiltily he leaned protectively forward, then, in a gesture of hopeless inevitability, he straightened up to reveal that he was modelling a miniature animal in clay. Involuntarily, the Sergeant reached forward, Saville extended protective hands over the model.

'Please, Sarn't! Don't touch it! It's still soft ... got to be hardened by baking in the sun!'

'D'ye mean to tell me you made that elephant ... from a lump of clay?'

Saville flushed. 'Er ... yes ... I was rather good at modelling when I was a boy ... and I saw this clay near the ablutions ... and I thought ...'

Cox and Hebdon gaped down at the model. 'Bloody hell! 'Ere ... come an' look wot the Capt'in's made!'

Any break in the morning's monotony could not be ignored; laboriously everyone levered themselves from their heat-damped charpoys to straggle down the room. The entire Sub-Section tightly grouped around the seated Saville. Cursing, men elbowed, craned and pushed to get a glimpse of whatever it was that had so suddenly brought the Captain into prominence. Their eyes widened and mouths opened in astonishment as one man after another expressed admiration. The Sergeant noted the universal approbation, offered effusively as though men felt relief that at last this odd man out was displaying a talent to satisfy the innate and proud cohesiveness of the Sub-Section. Probably they had not meant to be cruel, to callously isolate the boy, they simply did not know how to communicate with this stranger who irritatingly possessed traits and manners common to officers, from who they were separated by the widest of gulfs.

Boy Farley wriggled through the press, gasping for a closer view: 'Coo ... it's bleedin' wonderful! Capt'in ... can I hold it when it's dry?'

Saville smiled at the gawky boy, only seven years younger than himself yet generations ahead in barrackroom know-how.

'You can have it ... I'll give it to you!'

'Give ... give it to me ... to keep ... for nothing?'

Saville nodded and the men smiled and nudged each other, patting Farley and Saville as though to seal the bargain. Big Sanny Alexander, his fingers clasping and unclasping covetously. looked towards Ding Dong Bell for a nod of approval.

'Capt'in ... Capt'in ... will you make an elephant for me?'

'Yes, I'll make you an animal, but we don't want too many elephants in the bungalow, do we? How about a lion ... or a tiger ... or a horse?'

'Horse! Yes ... I'd like a horse ... like the Colonel rides!'

Within seven days a menagerie of wild and domestic animals appeared on every bed-shelf; the dourest of old soldiers gruffly requested models after hours of brain-wracking over what it should be. Even Kinrade finally condescended to ask. 'Make me a model of an English politician ... or the RSM ... an' I'll stick pins in it like the old bogey-wimmin do in the villages!'

Eventually his temperament and sardonic sense of humour was satisfied by a bushy-tailed fox.

In the interests of discipline the Sergeant remained aloof. Nevertheless, he was gratified and proud to find on his bamboo table a six-inch statuette of an infantry sergeant in No.1 dress, bearing a definite resemblance to himself.

Tightly-knit groups cherish even the smallest talent as collective pride. By revealing that he could do something beyond the abilities of his comrades, Private Saville paid his entry fee and became a fully-fledged member of the Sub-Section, entitled to expect, or even demand, from every man in the room, advice, support, help and, above all, protection.

The Sergeant and his second-in-command, Lance-Corporal Mockford, had said all there was to say on Sub-Section matters, and still dinner was two-and-a-half hours away. Meals were milestones that measured the torrid hours of enforced banishment without contacts, conversation or argument. Although the thin matting walls blanked out nothing, often the Sergeant had to close his ears to the onslaughts of puerility and repetition. Then as a stream pursues a relentless downhill course, his mind filled with nostalgia and wistful memories, until he was wallowing in emotional solitude. Routine interruptions and even fleeting needless discussions provided a welcome break, hence he asked. 'How did the Section get on last year when the Regiment went out with General Wilde's force to the Black Mountains?'

Lance-Corporal Mockford's face creased in a grimace of distaste. 'Now that were a right bastard, weren't it? Out three months in the Hot Season, did nigh on 500 miles ... much of it forced marches ... only lost old Dick Roberts in three weeks hard fighting in horrible mountainous country, but we had a score down with the heat and two died.'

The Sergeant remembered the sheer fatigue more easily than the fighting, it would not be any different if they went out now - probably worse. All this laying around on beds destroyed men and made them worse soldiers; less able to withstand hard physical graft day after day; less likely to fight efficiently against hard-as-nails hill-men on their own patch. It seemed so obvious, he could not understand why nothing was done about it. Why some form of military training could not be devised for the long hours wasted in the bungalows, it was not like the Army to miss a chance to get their pound of flesh out of the men. His mind kept coming back to it until one day, appreciatively eyeing the little statuette of himself sculpted by Saville, he had an idea.

A few days later, after breakfast, when the table-boards were being cleaned of their crumbs and coffee puddles before being stacked, the Sergeant mystified the duty-men by ordering the tables to be left standing. The entire room ground to a halt and men looked apprehensively at each other, well aware that even the slightest break in routine usually spelt trouble for the men in the ranks. Some drew on reserves of energy to pad lethargically up the room, uniting to form a mystified group around the bare tables. The more worldly men - Kinrade, Early, Mister Wright and the Lance-Corporal - remained on their beds, knowing they would be told soon enough what they were in for. From his cubicle came the Sergeant, his arms full of folded clothing, rugs and blankets. He dumped the lot on the table.

'Is it a new way of laying kit, Sergeant?'

He shook his head.' 'Wait and see lad ... wait and see.'

Aided by Private Saville who tried hard not to show pleasure and self-importance from the role thrust upon him, the Sergeant laid out on the table-top some folded towels, shirts, socks and other items of clothing in an irregularly spaced pattern. He and Saville carefully covered them with dusty grey blankets, the ends hanging down all round. Bewildered men gaped alternately at the table-top and then each other as the Sergeant dived into a small sack to produce pieces of rock, pebbles, dried grass and feathery fronds of vegetation. He arranged them on the bare blanket, then stood back, his head on one side to see if it looked anything like the wild, barren North West Frontier it was supposed to represent. Big Sanny clapped his hands. 'Ding Dong! Look! The Sergeant's made a wee glen.'

Kinrade and the others sat up on their beds, craning to see what it was all about, reluctantly rising when the Sergeant ordered the entire Sub-Section to group around the table. When all were assembled Private Saville fetched from the cubicle a flat, towel covered tray and laid it with care on an adjoining table. All eyes were on the mysterious package as the Sergeant, with theatrical flourish, whipped away the concealing towel to reveal a miniature panorama of two-inch tall model soldiers, formed-up precisely as the men did each morning in the lines outside.

'Och! Wee so'jers!'

'It's ... it's a Sub-Section ... is it us Sergeant?'

' 'Ere! That's the Sergeant ... an' there's Boy Farley ... an Birchy ... an' the Corporal ... can tell it's you Corp', 'cos it's shorter an' fatter!'

Lance-Corporal Mockford drew himself up. 'Watch yer tongue Private Hebdon ... yer'll git yer name taken that way!'

'That's enough! Quieten down! Yes, it's the Sub-Section ... and there's a figure for every one of you ... including meself! Don't touch 'em! Not for the minute anyway ... you'll have plenty of time to get to know yourself! Oh, and if you want to know where they came from ... Private Saville made 'em.'

'Good ole Captain!'

'What are they for, Sergeant? Are you going to drill us ... on the table?'

The Sergeant laughed. 'Drill? No ... we get enough drill now. Private Savillc has made some old friends of ours ... we are going to renew acquaintance with them ... on this terrain ... on the table.'

Removing another covering towel, Saville exposed a group of white-robed Pathans, hill-men in their characteristic prone position with long jezails - made from spent lucifers - thrust threateningly before them. They received only cursory glances, everyone was far more concerned with picking out their own image and derisively indicating those of their mates. Most were impressed with the Captain's handiwork, but not all agreed with his personal interpretation of their physical attributes.

Cutting into the ribaldry, the Sergeant called them to order before patiently explaining that he intended setting-up a series of real-life situations, the sort of petty skirmishing actions regularly encountered on the Frontier. The figures representing the enemy - the hill-men - would be characteristically hidden among the rocks and bushes, to be winkled out by the scaled down clay models of the 5th Sub-Section, under his command. Each man would move 'himself' - the little figure representing him - a specified distance on Private Holmes' carpenter's rule, under the

Sergeant's direction, based on a movement-chart scaled to terrain size, so that they moved varying distances depending upon whether marching, doubling or crawling. Casualties and action when coming under fire were determined by the throw of dice, purchased in the bazaar.

Fascinated, the Sub-Section crowded around the table and watched the Sergeant set up an ambush by concealing Pathans in a gorge. It took a bit of doing, persuading men like Big Sanny and Private Birch that, although the little 'enemy' figures were in full view on the table-top terrain, that they were actually invisible, only revealed when the Sub-Section had collectively thrown three sixes. Until then they would take fire, two dice being thrown for each firing hill-man who needed a total score of ten or more for a hit. Then the unfortunate victim had to await further dice throws before knowing the extent of his injuries - a score of four, five or six indicating only a minor wound, allowing him to carry on; two or three meant being a serious casualty, knocked off his feet and left behind with a mate in attendance; the dreaded score of one spelled death.

In the initial flurry of fire, Lance-Corporal Mockford, Privates Bell and Perkins were hit, but with commendable dice-luck were only slightly wounded. Big Sanny displayed embarrassing agitation over his mate Bell's wound, insisting on knowing where it was and offering to rub it! Then, in the individual dice-throwing to locate the hidden enemy, unbelievable suspense reigned until the last two to throw - Mockford and the Sergeant - both produced sixes, impressively indicating the superior powers of those upon whom Authority had bestowed stripes. The Sergeant had strong suspicions that Private Kinrade threw twice, taking an early turn then slipping in another near the end.

Aware of the enemy's position, everyone was eager to charge forward up the hill, bayonets gleaming in the sun, but the Sergeant would have none of it.

'My God! If that's how the 131st fight their battles its a wonder any of us stay alive! Coughlin, Birch, Davies, Wright ... and you Early ... you've all seen more action than you've had hot dinners ... what would you do ... coming under fire like that?'

Supported by emphatic nods, Early answered for all. 'Get me goddamned head down!'

'Yes ... that's right ... you'd go to ground and keep them occupied while your commanders made a plan ... now, Corp'l Mockford ... you and I ... we're behind this bloody great rock ... how are we going to get the Sub-Section out of this mess?'

Before the Lance-Corporal could answer, 'Mister' Wright asked permission to speak. 'Sergeant ... it ain't the same, is it? If it were real like ... with bullets flying around ... we'd be shitting ourselves ... beggin' pardon ... but here ... with no real danger ... what's to stop one of us having a gamble like on a good dice score ... an' rushing up the hill?' He smiled thinly around.

'May I ask if Private Saville has any little clay VC's?' Ignoring the soldier's characteristic tilt, the Sergeant considered. 'Yes ... I'll give you that it don't have no fear ... and that's about the biggest factor in battle ... but we got to carry-on as though we ... them little clay men are afeared.' He paused and looked into Wright's eyes. 'Tell you what, Private Wright ... go on ... do what you like ... win one of them clay VC's you mentioned!'

Taken aback, the bearded lugubrious veteran looked first at him, then down at the table. 'You mean ... I can move me own figure ... do what I like?'

'Yes ... that's right ... have a go on your own!'

Private Wright glanced from face to face, licked his lips and braced himself for his dashing solo effort. Leaning forward, Holmes' rule in his hand, he carefully measured-out the six-inch 'charge-move' the chart decreed. The Sergeant nodded. 'Right! Now you're out in the open ... on your own ... them Pathans are going to turn all their fire on you ... that's fair enough, ain't it Wright ... everyone?'

All nodded vigorously, Private Wright slowly following suit.

'Well then ... that means there's a dozen jezails pointing in your direction and ... before you measure another move, they can fire back at you ... tell you what ... I'll be generous ... I'll throw a dice for each of them hill-men and for every 'one' that comes up, we'll say his jezail has jammed.'

Twelve bone dice rattled on the table-top, everyone craned forward to see three ones show amid a welter of dotted numbers.

'There you are ... that's nine left to fire at you ... an' remember ... scores of two or three mean you're on the deck ... while one's you've had your chips ... let's see what' happened to you!'

Again the dice rattled, once more all eyes stared downwards.

Uproarious laughter echoed round the high room as men slapped each other's backs and poked fingers into the ribs of Wright who was staring incredulously at two 2's, a 3 ... and a 1!

'Sorry, Private Wright ... 'fraid you're a gonner ... the lads will miss you!'

The thin face twisted. 'I were unlucky ... if I 'ave another go I'll be alright!'

'Ah ... but you don't get another go in war, do you? Now, you might be dead ... on the table ... but you ain't been scared, have you? It don't mean anything to you does it?'

Hesitantly, Wright nodded. The Sergeant nodded back. 'We'll have to make it so's you ... and the others ... ain't so keen on having a go ... and losing their lives needlessly.' He bent forward and picked up the two-inch effigy of Private Wright; the man's eyes anxiously followed the movement. 'In real life ... when you're dead, you've gone ... haven't you? An' soon you're dust ... well, now it's more sooner than later ... 'cos if you're dead 'ere, then you're dust straightaway!'

Opening his hand, the Sergeant let the little clay Private Wright drop to the floor, immediately grinding it under his heel, lifting his foot to reveal a smear of pale-brown dust on the flagstone floor. The old soldier's mouth dropped open, his hands out supplicatingly, he stared down at the crushed clay that had once been Private Wright.

'Sergeant! Ye din't have to do that ... what am I going to do now ... won't be able to fight no more!'

The Sergeant pursed his lips. 'Now do you see what I mean? Lucky for you them jezails were firing dud bullets.'

Raising a clenched hand, the Sergeant slowly opened his fingers to reveal a small clay figure which he replaced on the table, at the same time hoping no-one would count the Pathans scattered around amid rocks, pebbles and dried grass. Flickering sideways, Private Early's eyes caught those of Private Kinrade, each mirroring a certain guarded respect for the surprising guile displayed by their sergeant.

'Right! We've got over that problem ... now Corp'l Mockford an' I will make a plan!'

Lasting most of the morning, the action steadily progressed, with the Lance-Corporal and three men sliding out to a flank in a diversionary movement, covered by the fire of five men sheltered in the rocks, while the Sergeant took the other half of the Sub-Section up the hill in bounds, from one bit of cover to another. Covertly eyeing his men, the Sergeant was amazed at their complete preoccupation. It was an aspect he had never previously seen or indeed thought possible, although their reactions seemed to him to truly reflect the qualities he had assessed in each of them. When fluctuations of fortune decreed that a figure was pinned down by enemy fire, the man represented by that figure chafed and sulked until again able to move; dire dice scores, indicating a man wounded and out of action for the rest of the exercise, resulted in the soldier represented by the figure suddenly becoming quiet and saddened, occasionally even fractious. When Private Finnigan was deemed to have been killed, his depression stayed with him until dispersed by ale in the Canteen that evening.

Brought to an enforced conclusion by the arrival of dinner, the morning had obviously been an immense success, despite the Sub-Section's table-top manoeuvres failing to achieve their objective, with Finnigan killed and Coughlin and Davies wounded. Overlooking the undue familiarity aroused by euphoria, the Sergeant promised that they would do it again soon. Reasoning that too much of a good thing lessened its value, the Sergeant, hearing over the top of the cubicle's matting wall enough enthusiasm to encourage the effort, set up the terrains twice weekly. Even if others were unaware, he knew when life monotonously creeps along the bottom of the deepest valleys that any diversion represents a peak, even more so when it includes stimulating personal involvement.

As days passed the tactical exercise became more complex, partly through the need to convince men they were interesting games and not routine military training, which would have immediately produced a dogged loss of interest and innate resistance. So he posed situations where he was down and the Lance-Corporal took over, then he fell and the men took it in turns to assume command of the Sub-Section. Understandably, Private Early performed in a most competent, professional manner; Private Saville surprised everyone - including himself; while Private Kinrade revealed an impressive degree of control.

Although he did not fully understand what was going on, Private Alexander enjoyed playing with the little soldiers, taking great care of his personal model and invariably ensuring that it stayed close to that of Ding Dong Dell, just as he was his shadow in real life. Then the Sergeant began changing the way the game was played, making out that he had been killed and the Lance-Corporal was in charge; when he got killed, a Private soldier took over. Big Sanny did not mind taking orders from Yank Early, who sometimes made him laugh, nor from Captain Saville, who was a gentleman, but he hated being made fun of by Dick Kinrade. His struggling brain became obsessed with the dread possibility that his turn would come and he would be ordered to take over the little soldiers on the table and order them about. He knew he'd do it wrong, that they'd all go the wrong way, perhaps he'd even get Ding Dong Dell's little soldier killed! In a blind unreasoning panic he babbled out his fears to Ding Dong, adding yet another dread of being asked to tell a story; he didn't want to ... he couldn't do that! He liked listening to them, watching Ding Dong and laughing when he did; sometimes he understood them, but he did not know any stories to tell.

Big Sanny wondered why the Sergeant had changed things so they couldn't have a kip in the mornings like they used to, perhaps he was getting like Sergeant Digges and the other NCO's, they all had a down on him, picking on him all the time. If he had to order the little soldiers about, or tell a story, they'd shout at him, maybe take his name and put it in the book. The big Scotsman became restless and agitated at the thought of going in front of the Company Commander or, much worse, the Commanding Officer. Perhaps they'd tie him up and whip him like before!

Private Bell listened sympathetically, calmed him down and promised to have a word with Sergeant Oakley; he was a bonny man, not like Sergeant Digges, he'd see Sanny alright. Diffidently, he appeared in the cubicle doorway and asked permission to speak. The Sergeant turned his ear to the unfamiliar Scot's accent as the soldier launched into a disjointed discourse about his mucker, Private Alexander, who could not speak for himself ... he was'na very good at talking ... in fact, he was'na very good at anything! His brain was damaged when he was born and he'd never really grown up ... people didn't understand ... NCO's thought he was trying it on or being insolent, so they shouted at him and Big Sanny got frightened ...

did silly things so they crimed him.

'Are you asking me to go easy on him?' The Sergeant was curious.

Bell reddened. 'No, nothing like that ... Sanny's me mate and I'll keep him in line. Private Alexander is just very worried about the game with the little soldiers, in case he's order'd to take command one morning. And he's feared in case he has to tell a story.'

The Sergeant's lips flickered at thoughts of the likelihood of him ordering Private Alexander to take a leading role in the tactical exercises.

'Don't worry lad. I'll not put your mate in that position. Nor will I ask him to tell a story ... that has to be a voluntary affair ... I can't order men to do anything outside the line of duty. Different matter with the tactical exercises 'cos they're in the interests of the Service ... an' I can order who I want to take over ... might even set you up soon.'

Bell flushed with pride. 'Thank you, Sergeant. I'll do my best.' He brought his heels together in dismissal; the Sergeant raised a hand.

'What has Alexander been crimed for?'

'On early Parade, Sergeant Digges shouted and frightened him ... being on Parade I couldn't help Sanny ... he ran off and hid in the bungalow ... then, next time, the Sergeant-Major said he was sloppy and pushed him. Sanny pushed him back.'

The Sergeant winced, the lad could have been charged with striking a superior officer, under certain circumstances that carried the death penalty.

'Was he court-martialled? What did he get?'

'No, the CO had him flogged, twenty-five lashes first time and fifty the second.'

It was bad enough, but the poor sod had got off lightly. The Commanding Officer must have realised he was puggled and kept him away from a court-martial that might have awarded a couple of hundred lashes for laying hands on a superior officer.

'I'm a fair man an' I'll not be hard on him ... he'll get no favours tho'! For Christ's sake keep him in line and out of trouble.'

Something so stimulatingly different could not be permanently concealed, and Bungalow 5's war-games became a prime topic of conversation in the Canteen, where puffed-up privates demonstrated tactical manoeuvres with mugs or tracings in beer on the bare table-tops. It was not always harmonious. Derisive taunts about playing with toy soldiers caused brawls and increased numbers paraded with bruised faces. The Sergeant's Mess deemed it below their dignity to discuss it, although there was sufficient talk for the Sergeant to fear it would attract unwelcome attention from higher up. He was not surprised to receive an eventual summons to the Sergeant-Major's office, where the stern bearded giant sadly shook his head, at this Sergeant who, for some obscure reason, seemed to want to rock the boat.

'Sergeant Oakley ... it will not do ... it will not do at all ... and you know why!'

'Sir?'

'You know what I am talking about ... this business of playing with toy soldiers in the barrackroom.' He raised a restraining hand. 'No, you listen to me. I'll give you permission to speak later. Now, I am not a fool, I am aware of what stinking in huts throughout the Hot Season can do to a soldier ... I can see what you are trying to do, and in many ways it is worthy ... BUT, those who Her Majesty has seen fit to place over us are not fools, and if they thought what you are doing was necessary then they would order it to be done! Every single one of Her Majesty's Regiments in India ... Horse, Foot and Guns ... stays in barracks throughout the Hot Season and it ain't caused us to lose a war yet!'

'Sir.' Sergeant Oakley felt he needed some defence. 'The men get no tactical training at all. and them hill-men are the best Light Infantry in the world ... surely anything we can do to handle them better is worthwhile?'

The Sergeant-Major snorted in exasperation. 'Sergeant Oakley! The man don't need no tactical training, as you call it ... they ain't paid to think ... their officers do it for them! If private soldiers took it into their heads to start taking tactical decisions of their own, where would we be? Why, they might not obey lawful orders given by their superior officers because they fancied some scheme of their own!' He touched the bronze cross with the deep red ribbon on his chest. 'I won this at the Alma, but d'ye think I, or any of the others, would have gone up that hill if our officers hadn't ordered us? Of course we wouldn't! Private soldiers must not be encouraged to think for themselves ... it would never do!'

'Excuse me, Sarn't Major, but weren't you at Inkerman ... the Soldier's Battle?'

The Sergeant-Major looked up sharply, this man was bright as well as brave.

'That was a different kettle of fish ... we were surprised ... outnumbered ... it was not so much a question of thinking ... more of taking on groups of Russians as they loomed out of the fog ... fighting for our very lives. You must understand that when I say soldier's must not think, I'm allowing for the British having something the others haven't got that makes them natural born soldiers ... they don't need to think!'

'Sir, with respect, that may be, although I would like you to see what doing something purposeful has done for my men ... they're not half asleep any more ... they're alive and alert. Sir, will you come over to the barrackroom tomorrow and see for yourself?'

'No, I certainly won't! The Reg'mental Sarn't-Major can't have anything to do with unauthorised practices! What you are doing is causing discontent and disturbance among both NCO's and the men ... sergeants are coming in here complaining that their men want something similar ... can't have everyone going off on their own tack doing whatever they bloody well like! The other sergeants aren't feeling kindly towards you, Sarn't Oakley, because you are making their job hard! Why aren't you like the other sergeants? Why won't you conform?'

The Sergeant stood non-plussed, what was there to say?

'Your bloody tactical exercises are causing bad feeling among the lower ranks ... I'm told of fights in the Canteen over it, so that on parade your Sub-Section look more like prize-fighters than soldiers! It'll have to stop forthwith, Sarn't Oakley ... can't have the life of the Regiment upset like this! Don't let me hear of any more games with toy soldiers in your barrackroom ... and no fraternising with lower ranks either!'

Next day, in a studied non-committal manner, the Sergeant announced there would be no more war-games, the news was received with habitual lower rank stoic apathy; men returned to lolling on their beds. Another day of sweating boredom.

XVI

Barrackroom life had its rough edges smoothed by a system of unwritten rules and customs. High among them an awareness shared by the bungalow NCO and his men, that in his flimsy cubicle at the end of the room he could hear everything said outside in the hut. The Sergeant knew this, the men knew it, and both knew the other knew. Within carefully defined bounds, men availed themselves of this unofficial line of communication by audibly 'having their moan', airing grievances that put the room NCO in the picture, sometimes acquainting him with facts he had not other way of discovering. It had to be done carefully, without getting personal or too near the bone and thereby transgressing against good order and military discipline. Then, as the sole arbiter, the room NCO could clamp down hard on the offender, losing the room's respect if he did not.

As the Sergeant and his men in the 5th Sub-Section got to know each other, the system was much used. Sergeant Oakley's task being eased through old soldiers judiciously passing information via the open-ended grapevine. He always knew when it was going to be done, being signalled by voices stilling, until there existed that unique barrackroom phenomena of complete silence; it had all the strident warning of an alarm bell. Then, halting whatever he was doing, he would stand motionless, his head cocked to one side so's he wouldn't miss a word. Today it was the assertive voice of Private Wright.

'See Private Bell's on Guard again tonight ... that's the second time in ten days ... Ding Dong, you must've upset the Company Clerk in the Wet Canteen when you told 'im not to come acid with Big Sanny ... someone oughta tell S'arn't-Major 'is boy is abusin' 'is position.'

The message ended and the silence immediately shattered. Private Bell did not do Guard that night.

Sometimes, to avoid hearing too much the Sergeant felt it diplomatic to take a walk round the Lines or go to the Mess. In their turn, his rough unlettered men developed a highly sensitive compassion, never audibly discussing any subject that might hurt or be distasteful. Thus, he was absent on duty next morning when the talk centred around wives. Soldiers' wives, officers' wives and Sergeant Oakley's late wife. All knew his story, commonplace in India, but adopted by the 5th Sub-Section as a personal tragedy because it affected their Sergeant, whom they liked and respected. Only one soldier in the room could recall meeting her, yet every man had his personal vision of Amy Oakley, transmogrifying her into the epitome of the saintly wives and mothers all men deluded themselves they had once possessed. Respectful silence was always guaranteed when Private Perkins, one of a fatigue-party long-since detailed to repair storm damage to her Married Quarters bungalow, rhapsodised on their Sergeant's late wife. 'Can see her now ... small, well-formed, pretty face with a small, turned-up nose ... 'er little girl were spittin' image on 'er ... she 'ad a sort of sweet way wiv her, made you want to do things for 'er ...always friendly, talked to us like equals ... 'an always gave us coffee an' scones ... lovely Lady were Mrs Oakley.'

Chastened into melancholy, the room brooded in silence, their eyes tactfully averted from Private Alexander, gently blubbering at the vision of the gentle mother he might have had. Sam Mockford coughed discreetly, feeling, as the Junior NCO in the room, it was his duty to dispel sentimental yearnings that although cherished, were embarrassing. 'Course, all Army wives ain't like that ... S'arnt Oakley were lucky to 'ave her and damned unlucky to lose 'er ... but when I think o' some of 'em he could've 'ad ... Gawd Almighty!' He shook his head knowingly. 'Mister Wright ... Taffy ... Roomy ... Pat ... Paddy ... Charlie ... Holmesy ... you recall them wives inna Mutiny? Slogged our guts out gettin' 'em from Lucknow an' other cities ... yet I can think o' times when our columns marched into places an' they wouldn't even give us a chatty o' water, let alone do a bit o' dhobi-ing or mendin' for the lads!'

Mutiny veterans nodded, the flood-taps of memory were turned on and voices poured out.

'Orficers' wives ... in rags an' tatters ... using their late husbands' ranks to get privileges!'

'Wot abart them wimmin as lost their husbands ... other ranks

I mean ... poor sods just in the ground an' not yet cold ... chasin around seeking new husbands ... in case they got sent 'ome! Right ole bags some of 'em, wiv faces like busted boots!'

'Course, it weren't onny Military Wives ... wot about them wimmin on Delhi Ridge durin' siege ... bloody civilian refugees ... wives o' Company Officials ... they were a bloody nuisance, takin' tents an' blankets, rations an' water wot were needed for so'jers!'

'Christ! Yes, I remember them! Airs an' bloody graces ... never showed no gratitude 'cos they was 'customed to bein' waited on 'and an' foot. Resented even sharing tents wiv each other ... an' you ought to 'ave 'eard 'em moan about sleeping on 'ard ground ... an' queuing for beef-stew an' bread!'

'Mind you, it weren't always like that ... there were them ... orficers' ladies an' other ranks' wimmin bivouackin' tergither through necessity. They were mighty surprised to discover how alike they was ... that same things made 'em all smell an' feel uncomfortable ... weren't long afore both found out small comforts were the same luxury.'

'Yeah ... no-one ain't ever taught lice to respect Army rank!'

Private Perkins waited until the laughter died down. 'All this chat 'as brought to me mind a sad tale wot 'ad an orficer's wife at the bottom of the trouble ... not that she ever knew an' it weren't 'er fault 'cos she were only wot she were ... an orficer's wife ... but it had unfortunate results fer a lad in my Company ... were the death of 'im in fact.'

The secret of capturing and holding an audience owes much to a compelling start, and in fourteen years of barrackroom life Polly Perkins had learned the importance of an introduction that hit the lads right between the eyes, so when he talked of the death of a private soldier being in some way connected with an officer's wife, he could not go wrong. After stirring restlessly in anticipation, the room settled down to listen.

'It were an unusual situation an' a dangerous one ... 'cos 'ere you 'ad the Company Commander's wife ... fresh out from England an' newly married ... an' a private soldier in the same company oo' knew each other afore they joined the Reg'ment ... an' not onny that ... they both travelled out from England on the same boat. 'Er in First Class o'corse, an' 'im wiv a draft from the Depot. Don' get the wrong idea tho', there weren't nothin' between 'em an' it were sheer chance both ended up on the same boat an' in the same Reg'ment.'

For eighteen years, Jeremy Willis' life ran smoothly and uneventfully amid the warm security of Allington Court, where his father had charge of the stables. After a sparse period of schooling, he became a stable-boy at eleven, perpetuating the eternal ammonia and hay odours he had known since his birth when he had lived in the dark beamed attics above the stables. The Master, an impoverished landowner, had five daughters; Amelia, the youngest, being born in the big house at much the same time as Jeremy saw the light of day down at the stables. Despite the social differences, the children played together, although both being made much aware of their respective levels. In his early 'teens, Jeremy groomed Miss Amelia's pony; and the hand-holding and seemingly accidental physical contacts that occurred when aiding her to mount and dismount gave the boy many sleepless hours. She missed him when suddenly he vanished. The new lad was not half so good with Chuckles. Jeremy missed her, missed his mother and father, and all the other wonderfully serene things he had taken for granted, now tossed beyond recall for the sake of a few moments of excitement. Left by some wily mates on his very first poaching expedition and he had been taken red-handed by the Head Gamekeeper and disowned by the Master, enraged at his disloyalty. Faced with the crusty JP's alternative of prison or the Army, Jeremy had hastily chosen to enlist in the County Regiment.

A year later, chivvied up the gangplank at Southampton docks and formed-up with the draft on deck awaiting allocation to the deepest hold below, Jeremy's bewildered stare had fallen upon Miss Amelia who was peering curiously at the soldiers from beneath a parasol. During the tedious three month voyage he saw her often and tortured himself wondering whether she recognised him. They never spoke so he could only guess that she was visiting friends in India. He found it hard to believe what he discovered on joining the Regiment - that she had come out to marry an officer, the son of a local squire to whom she had been promised five years earlier. Jeremy consoled himself with the knowledge that, of all the places in this vast country, she had come to the same one as himself, so he would at least see her occasionally. A further vague sense of kinship arose from her marrying his Company Commander, whom he vaguely remembered as an arrogant overbearing youth he had jealously hated to see riding with Miss Amelia.

These youthful traits of Gervase Barnes had been immediately magnified and multiplied by his purchased commission and the captain's marks of rank he now bore. If fleeting contacts had upset Jeremy Willis in past years, now he was to find his whole life governed by the whims and temper of a tyrant whom he came to loathe and despise.

He was not alone in this, Private Perkins along with every other man in the Company, shared his feelings. 'Bully Barnes was a pig ... a real bastard 'oo couldn't do 'is job an' blamed everyone else when things went wrong ... drunk most o' the time an' always likely ter drop the Company inna shit when the bullets started flyin'!'

Amelia was shocked when, after a gap of five years, she again saw the man she had travelled halfway round the world to marry. She wondered what had transformed the big, shock-headed, amusing youngster she had flirted with into this obese man with a jowled face, piggy-eyes set deep in flabby cheeks, all beneath thinning hair with a lank moustache straggled over his wet mouth. She was not to know then that India gave many fascinating things to British officers, but insidiously extracted payment through heat and boredom which led to drink, laziness and readily available native women. It never occurred to her to break the contract; in the manner of women of her class and period she resignedly accepted her lot. It had been acknowledged for years that she and Squire Barnes' son would marry. Papa and Mama would be furious if she didn't and anyway, she was such a long way from home and had no money to pay for the journey back.

So the Regiment had its wedding, and Captain Barnes' Company were docked a day's pay to buy a present - besides providing the Guard of Honour outside the Garrison Church, taking up their free time with hours of cleaning and polishing, in no way repaid by the gratuitous glass of grog afterwards. Sourly,

Private Perkins recalled how he was on that Guard; Private Jeremy Willis, newly arrived, thanked God he was not detailed as he could not have borne it.

Occasionally Jeremy saw her, in a carriage on the Maidan when a punctilious salute would be acknowledged by a slight inclination of a flower-hatted head under the parasol while her boorish husband ungraciously flicked up a grudging hand - yet woe betide the man who failed to salute. Then came the day when she spoke to him, when her beautiful face was only inches from his own through her charming way of inclining her face towards one, as though seeking a certain degree of intimacy; who was to know it came about through extreme short-sightedness, and a vanity that rejected spectacles.

Perkins recalled the occasion. 'It 'appened on the Queen's Birthday ... when the Reg'ment 'ad a 'oliday an' celebrated ... in our Company we 'ad Sports Day wiv runnin' races, jumping, throwing the cricket ball and all manner of things. Jeremy, who were naturally a very good runner, 'eard the Comp'ny Commander's wife presented the prizes, so 'e trained as 'ard as 'ell an' won both the hundred and the two twenty yard races, so as to get 'imself up in front of 'er twice.'

For weeks Jeremy had had dreamed of just such things, imagining her little smile of pleasure when she recognised him, her childhood friend and pony Chuckles' groom. In whose hand she had let hers tantalisingly linger on so many occasions when being aided to mount or dismount. However, both times she peered into his face, whispered 'Congratulations ... well run' and presented him with a winner's certificate, a packet of 'baccy and a clay pipe, before resuming her seat. The second time around it was the same thing and it seemed she had not realised it was the same man up for both events. Turning it over in his mind later, Jeremy realised she had to pretend not to recognise him because of the Captain - her husband - sitting next to her. He suffered agonies of remorse for placing her in such an awkward predicament. Most treasured of all were those two brief moments when her small cool fingers rested in a congratulatory handshake within his callused grasp. Wildly he wondered if she recalled past occasions when their hands had touched.

'Up to now none of us 'ad tumbled to 'ow Jeremy felt about Mrs. Barnes ... the lad 'ad never said nothing an' I don't blame 'im 'cos no man wants the name of a woman he respects bawled around the barrackroom ... 'e never smoked so give the 'baccy an' pipes away - I recall 'e gave me one lot - but he treasured them ole certificates ... an' they were only bits o' cardboard printed by the Company Clerk. But yer know 'ow it is inna Section ... can't keep nothin' from 'em ... an' the smarter lads began ter tumble to 'is secret. But Jeremy kept 'is 'ead down an' din't let 'em get a rise outta 'im ... not 'til Smudger Smith went a bit too far ... can't remember now wot 'e said but it weren't much ... just jokin' ... nothin' really nasty yer unnerstan' ... but it were enough ter bring young Jeremy off 'is bed an' drag 'is ole lunger out of its sheath onna wall an' before Smudger knew wot was 'appenin' Jeremy were standin' over 'im wiv seventeen inches o' cold steel at 'is throat. Ole Smudger were frit ter death 'cos for a moment we all feared 'e were goin' ter use it ... but 'e warned Smudger an' all the others ...'

These were the days when County Regiments really did consist of men from the particular County, even the Irish and Scots became sort of honorary Hampshire Hogs and Lincolnshire Poachers. So, with literally dozens of men familiar with the country around Allington Court - some actually having worked there along with Jeremy's father - who knew, or knew of, the Master and Squire Barnes and their families, it was not hard to work out the story. Jeremy was too big and strong, too nice a lad to become an object of pity or ridicule. Combined with the Company's united hatred of Captain Barnes, this served to touch sentimental hearts into deep concern for the romantic aspects of a private soldier and his Company Commander's wife languishing after each other. Out of his hearing, the incredible situation was deeply discussed and ways sought of stopping him making a fool of himself, or getting into deep trouble.

Jeremy himself was no help to them in these aims. On Sundays in church he bribed men to let him sit where he had a clear, uninterrupted view of Amelia, singing, praying and calling responses so loudly to catch her ear that even the Commanding Officer looked round at him. Orderly Corporals making up fatigue-parties came to know, in time, that there was always a packet of 'baccy or a quart of ale in it if Private Willis were put down for parties tidying gardens in the Officers' Married Quarters; further bribes usually brought him round to Captain Barnes' bungalow. At nights, he took to standing outside the bungalow in the dark, staring in the direction of the Officers' Quarters, torturing himself with visions of his beloved, swooning with fear and horror when drunken Bully Barnes asserted his right to crush her delicate, shrinking frame with his fat, sweating body. The next morning, convulsed with hate, Private Jeremy Willis in the front rank on Parade, fixed his eyes on the Company Commander and hurtled belligerent challenging glares in his direction. All knew that sooner or later Bully would notice this and order his name to be taken, for Dumb Insolence, which could only end in Jeremy being spread-eagled on the triangle for fifty lashes.

Jeremy had long since given up any hope of her recognising or acknowledging him, sheltering behind the conviction that she did not want to get him into trouble by doing so. Nor did he ever aspire to do more than look at her, to cast glances of admiration and devotion in her direction - it was all very laudable, noble and touching. It was also very frustrating; this fact provided his mates with their very first chance of giving a helping hand. When a man felt low, had received bad news from home or got on the wrong side of the sergeant-major, it was usual to drown sorrows by getting roaring-drunk, then fighting or reeling off to a brothel. Up to now Jeremy had done none of these things, perhaps because he was too inexperienced to know where to start. But he was a man, and everyone knew it was not good for a bloke to go too long without a woman. His mates were ready and willing to help get him started and never set off for the Wet Canteen or Bazaar without making attempts to persuade him to go with them. Invariably he thanked them and said that he would rather stay in the bungalow and lay on his charpoy ... thinking things out.

This particular night he seemed worse than usual. They did not know he had had a particularly trying day, spending about six hours of it tending flower beds within six-feet of Mrs Barnes, lolling in a hammock on the verandah. Frequently he caught a tantalising glimpse of her slim, silken-sheathed ankles, and once she had bent forward, revealing the cleft where her small breasts began - he had to turn swiftly away for fear she would notice the physical effect it had upon him. Back in the barrackroom he was so restless and fidgety that knowing blokes whispered he needed to get some dirty water off his chest. When, as usual, he refused to go out with his mates they were really worried in case, later in the evening his desperation got the better of him and took him off to the Bazaar. There inexperience might cause him real harm by drinking Billy Stink or rot-gut and ending up in a dark, shadowy alley with a sand-rat. To go with one was a crude form of suicide, either from syphilis or a knife in the back. They knew the inexperienced Jeremy, drunk and caring about nothing, was just the sort of berk to stagger off into the night with one of the small boys parroting "jig ... jiggy-jig Sahib?" for an unseen ravaged-faced sand-rat.

In relays, mates talked hard and long, cajoling, exhorting, persuading and even bullying, until Jeremy showed signs of weakening. Then they redoubled their efforts till at last, rising to his feet he was beset by a host of clumsy valets, dressing him in clean clobber for a night out. Surrounded by an escort of noisy men, all laughing and shouting at once, he was borne to the Wet, quickly coming to grips with the unfamiliar environment and declaring they sold nothing that came up to the old Scrumpy back home. He was well away by half past seven when the party staggered out into the night for the final act of the evening's entertainment. Singing lustily, arms around shoulders, they lurched companionably down the dusty Mall to the Bazaar, where Jeremy's nostrils twitched at unaccustomed odours of spice, excrement, urine, bad meat and feebly flickering oil-lamps. There was no need to search or seek, knowledgeable feet stumbled straight to their destination - a shuttered house identical to its neighbours, save for one on the other side of the street bearing Hindustani lettering above the door. As Jabez Parker went to push through the bead curtain, Jeremy caught his arm.

'Wassat written over the door?'

'Dunno ... but yer can't go there ... that's for bleedin' orficers only.'

In the small, dimly-lit entrance hall, the Bazaar's reek was defeated by heavy perfume hanging on the air. From nowhere appeared a plump, middle-aged native woman, resplendent in her multi-coloured sari, her pock-marked face adorned with a glittering nostril-jewel and her hands heavily ringed. Palms together, she smiled benevolently at Jabez. 'Parker Sahib!'

Jabez put his arms around her shoulders, obviously they were old friends. ' 'Allo Mum ... brought along an ole mate ... wanna get 'im started ... is Lalla 'andy? She'll do 'im a treat! Wan' 'im ter 'ave the best of everythin'.' Clearing his throat, he inclined his head towards her ear: 'Hum pica dada hi ... malum?'

The Madam nodded.

Sweeny Todd nodded admiringly. 'Ole Jabez can really sling the bat, can't 'e?'

Jeremy's head was swimming and he found it difficult to focus his eyes. Suddenly he tired of standing there like a spare prick while Jabez chatted-up the old cow, pushing forward he shouted. 'They 'avin' a bobbery? Wot's she keep sayin' 'Yoti' for ... wot's it mean?'

'Yoti? Cunt ... its the tart's cunt see? She's praisin' up the tart your're goin' ter 'ave ... she's a nice piece ... an' clean too ... you'll get on famous.'

Pushed into a dim room, he found himself face-to-face with a small girl, standing compactly submissive with her palms together. Far from feeling lustful his immediate muddled reaction was to forcefully reject this little, rounded, dusky female. He compared her oiled, jet-black hair, dark shadowed eyes and Eastern appearance with Miss Amelia's tall, slim, English freshness and pale powdered face. The pulled back blonde hair, escaping in elusive wisps over her moist forehead. Without a word, the native girl slithered from her filmy sari. He had no comparisons as under such circumstances he found it revolting to even begin to think of a naked Amelia. He was aware from village girls that women had soft, squeezable breast with little raspberry-like tips that hardened and grew under the fingers. At their loins there was a 'v'-shaped patch of tangled hair, much the same colour as that on their heads, and below that a slimy, wet, odorous entrance to their bodies. But until tonight he had never actually seen it all, and here it was at his disposal without fear of being found out and punished.

The stimulation of strong drink and natural yearning left him little alternative but to unconditionally surrender. Miss Amelia ... Mrs Barnes ... vanished from his mind as insidiously the soft satiny girl guided the sweating young Feringhee from his unpractised roughness to an innocent tenderness that even she found surprisingly enjoyable. Naturally it did not all happen at once, needing weekly visits agonisingly intervalled with sham and pushed aside when the time drew near to go to the Bazaar. After the first occasion, when he had sobered up and come down from these new clouds, Jeremy found it hard to live with the sense of deceit arising from his betrayal. For a few days he was unable to make the usual attempts to be within sight of Amelia until, back on gardening fatigue, he gazed numbly at her, silently mouthing words of contrition, asking her forgiveness and understanding. Choosing to interpret her every unwitting expression or gesture as a form of pardon, he felt with increasing certainty that she accepted the position that put their relationship on new footing. His mates certainly noticed a difference in him, sagely remarking that the regular visits to the 'Angel-house' had worked wonders. They certainly had, but not in the way they thought.

Over the months of seemingly being ignored and rejected, Jeremy tormented himself wondering whether Miss Amelia was aware of his feelings for her, whether she shared and restrained them because of the sheer impossibility of the situation, or whether she even knew he existed? Now, Lalla was a woman who welcomed and was pleased to see him. She was doting and submissive instead of being proud and haughty. She pandered to his every whim and tried to please him with every ounce of her being. She made him feel like a master instead of a humble serf. Of course, she was a native, different in every possible way to Miss Amelia but, when laying with her in the dim room, he shut his eyes to try and make himself believe her heavy perfume was lavender toilet-water, that the smooth coloured skin was blanched white and dusted with freckles; that her rounded limbs and full breasts was the slim and small body of an English Squire's daughter.

He never really managed to transform the Indian prostitute into a surrogate Amelia, such vain hopes were quite dispelled by Lalla's peculiarly Eastern ability to tantalise him with a choice of the twenty-five positions of intercourse. In his wildest dreams he could not imagine Miss Amelia being familiar with the 'Rainbow arch', 'Somersault', 'Turn-about', or the 'Ram', and especially not 'auparishtaka'!

Private Polly Perkins paused, the story had ground to a standstill with interest momentarily waning while the audience gloatingly reflected on the varied merits of those positions of love, musing on their favourites or resolving to try a change when next visiting the Rag. He gave them a few moments before resuming.

'Then the Afridis got tergether an' almost wiped out a party o' sappers a'workin' on the Kohat Pass road an' a force were ordered out. The Commander-in-Chief himself were in Pesh'or at the time an' went out wiv us. I recall we took fourteen days rations an' were tole afore we went there'd be no reprisals an' any men caught lootin' would be 'ung or flogged. Besides us there were the 60th Rifles, 98th Foot an' 'Orse Artillery wiv twenty-five an' a 'arf inch mortars carried on elephants ... an' native infantry an' cavalry ... it were a goodly sized force ... they were determined to make an example of them Afridis.'

The villages of Akhor and Zhargun Khel in the Pass were shelled and destroyed, the enemy hidden behind the stone breastwork were strongly resisting and had to be driven out at bayonet-point. Jeremy had expected to be nervous when it came to action but, apart from a faint sinking feeling in the pit of his stomach, felt good when he was going forward with his mates on either side of him. He had worried about killing a man, especially at close-quarters with cold steel, but had told himself he'd imagine it was Bully Barnes and then it would come easy. In the event it all happened so suddenly that it was over before he realised. Boots thudding on the rocky ground, they rushed the last few yards to the low stone sangars and vaulted over. Landing heavily, as he struggled to regain his balance, a bundle of dirty white rags rose from the ground at his feet. He saw a dark, bearded face, white teeth in an open mouth and blazing eyes topped by a black skull-cap. Most clearly of all he saw a long jezail pointing threateningly at him. Lunging forward Jeremy felt a slight soft resistance as the bayonet effortlessly pierced a path through the rags, flesh and muscle before jarring on the tribesman's backbone. There were others, but he got most satisfaction from the first one.

All night they were kept awake by desultory fire on the camp, and were glad when the march continued the next day through the narrow difficult Pass, commanded by tribesmen on surrounding heights, which had to be stormed on the left by the 1st Punjab Native Infantry, while a detachment including Jeremy and Polly Perkins went up the slopes on the right, supported by Guides under Lieutenant Lumsden. Throughout the day the rearguard was under constant attack by large bodies of enemy and, when settling down for the night, Jeremy's Company under Captain Barnes were detailed to hold heights to the rear of the camp, beating off two attacks and under fire all night.

Perkins terse description had flesh put on its bones by most men in the room, who well knew such situations; indeed, Birch had to be told to shut his gob when trying to break in with a similar story of his own. Glaring sternly at him, Polly Perkins got on with it. 'I tell yer ... we were bloody glad ter see daylight ... an' none more pleased than Bully Barnes hisself ... 'e weren't actually a coward ... 'e were a windy sod 'oo took no bleedin' risks an' 'e wanted ter git darn off them heights as quickly as possible ... so 'e kept lookin' fer the relief an' cursin' when they didn't arrive ... we weren't ter know they'd taken the wrong path. Any road, arter a while ... when the firin' got 'ot an' it looked as though we were in for another attack ... Bully decided to take matters inter 'is own 'ands an' go down.'

In the room old soldiers hissed between their teeth in apprehension, knowing the one thing you never did was to retreat from a position before the surrounding heights had been crowned by troops whose fire covered your withdrawal. Private Wright acidly inquire. 'This Bully Barnes bloke ... were 'e fuckin' mad or summat?'

'No ... jist bleedin' windy ... an' 'e wanted 'is breakfast I s'pose.'

The sergeant-major got a bollocking for arguing with Bully about it, so he was bawling and shouting, getting men to their feet and detailing rearguard sections because the whole Company could not get down the narrow path at once. Before he had finished, Captain Barnes gave the order to move-out and was off in the lead down the steep rocky track so fast that, after only a few yards, he trod on a loose rock and fell heavily, injuring his leg. He lay there, bellowing to men pushing past to help him, to get him on his feet and down the slope. But this was the moment everyone had been dreaming of and some rushed past without a glance. Others cursed him and spat on him, one man - who was to regret it later - kicked him in passing.

Last to leave, with nimble-footed tribesmen fast looming, Private Perkins and Willis jumped feet first out of the rock-piled breastwork to immediately be confronted with the prone figure of their Company Commander, his fear-wracked face staring up at them. In the way the drowning man is said to see an entire lifetime flashing by in his remaining seconds, Jeremy sat in judgement on Bully Barnes, reviewing the reasons for and against stopping to aid him.

With her husband dead, his way was cleared to Amelia, but was it? ... Did he, a common soldier, have any chance with an officer's widow? She'd probably marry another officer and maybe leave the Cantonment .. or go home ... either way she'd be out of his sight, although never out of his mind. On the other hand, did she even know he existed? He pictured her pretty pale face, slack with shock and red-eyed with crying; he saw her in ugly, black widow's weeds; perhaps he'd been wrong, perhaps she did love her husband. Then Polly Perkins' breathless voice broke the spell.

'I don' recall wot I actually said ... summat about not leavin' a man to them murderin' devils ... not even Bully Barnes ... an' Jeremy nodded and turned to face 'em while I got Bully on 'is feet.'

The words brought into Jeremy's mind a sudden vision of the hate-twisted face and fierce eyes of the Afridi tribesman he had bayoneted the day before. God, you couldn't leave even a dog to the mercy of men like that! He swung round, steel-tipped Minie rifle presented towards the enemy. 'Git 'im up an' down the track ... I'll 'old 'em orf ... an' foller yer!'

He was never able to. The leading tribesman had no intention of getting within reach of that long shining bayonet and when he was twelve feet away his bazaar-made rifle smashed Jeremy's shoulder with a soft lead-slug, it splattered on hitting his bone to leave a melon sized hole in his back.

Struggling upwards to surface through the waves of raging pain, Jeremy's eyes slowly opened then closed quickly against the sky's glare above. A second attempt brought success, for between him and the bright light stood a figure, shimmering in a red haze of pain. Drowsily, his eyes focused and registered a native girl, bending down as though to whisper endearments in his ear - he recognised Lalla in the dark sari he liked so much. He tried to say her name, to ask what she was doing here, but his mouth locked rigid, he could not form the words. His arms were unwilling to stretch out towards her nor could he rise to be by her side. He had recollections of being hurt, that was why he could not move or speak; he resigned himself to laying back and watching her, bleary and without interest he watched her lift her sari to reveal the dark, triangular patch of hair at the loins, above her smooth rounded thighs. Haltingly eyes left the woman to slip into a form telling him it was all a dream, a nightmare that would soon be broken by raucous barrackroom noises or the Orderly Corporal's stick pounding Reveille on the flagstone floor.

Far from being the lovely, lissom Lalla, she had now become a witch, an old, bent woman from whose scrawny frame filthy, sweat-stiff rags hung in tatters. Her face, framed by lank grey hair, was pock-marked and wrinkled, dirt ingrained in every crease. The loose, wet lips of her cackling mouth curled open, exposing her gapped and blackened teeth. Painfully twisting his head to shut out the apparition Jeremy could see lurking behind her a coven of similar crones, cackling and jabbering in a foreign tongue.

Desperate efforts to rid himself of this fantasy mercilessly restored him to consciousness - and the terrifying realisation that he could not move his arms and legs because he was staked out by his wrists and ankles, spread-eagled on the dusty, hard-beaten earth amid a cluster of native mud huts. He could only gurgle and grunt like an animal because his jaws were locked open by a forked stick forced between his teeth.

Now that the soldier, awake and aware, was ready for them, the village women keened excitedly. Glancing wolfishly around, the crone bent lower, squatting with her scrawny bare buttocks poised over Jeremy's face. His head twisted and turned desperately, his nose wrinkling against the assault of the foul and odorous loins. Grunts, wrenched deep from his dry throat, were stifled and turned into a choking gurgle as hot stinking urine cascaded over him. His locked and open mouth was filled with a foul and bitter liquid. Steaming and straw-coloured it ran over his face and neck, dripping down to make a quickly disappearing dark patch on the dusty ground beneath. Cackling hysterically, the old woman strained and shook, not wishing to waste a single drop of her contribution to the carnival. She reluctantly straightened-up, to be pushed aside by the next eager performer.

Their minds full of the spine-chilling affair men lay shocked and silent on their beds. Polly Perkins looked around and said slowly, 'An' them fuckin' black cows a'pissed in the lads mouth until 'e drownded.'

Men wondered how Private Perkins knew so much about what had happened in that native village. Private Kinrade, who had yet to see action and did not fancy what he heard, asked in somewhat hopeful disbelief. 'Polly ... 'ow d'ye know that was the way of it?'

'Later that day the mountain-artillery brought up their little guns an' shelled the village, then we went forward an' took it ... no-one was there ... bleedin' wimmin an' kids all gorn ... lucky for them. But they'd left 'im behind ... the lad ... still staked-out ... stinking o' wimmin's piss ... an' that weren't all the bastards 'ad done. They'd sliced orf 'is privates an' stuffed 'em in 's mouth, slit up his belly ... pulled out 'is bowels an' walked away from 'm ... draggin' them out as they went. Stretched twenty feet or so across the square.'

Private Saville was laying on his charpoy, cringing with horror. In a moment of sympathy for this young man's fear, Polly addressed him quietly. 'Don't ever get taken alive. Roll over on you rifle an' put a bullet through your own head.'

Perkin's tale set many a train of thought in motion, the subject of brothels, prostitutes and fornication being far too interesting to be dismissed by a boiled beef and potato dinner. No sooner had the tables been cleared and the men settled down after visiting the jakes or urinal-tub, than Bandsman Mort called over. 'That Angel House the lad went to ... were it in Meerut? 'Cos there were an 'ouse in Meerut wiv a Hindustani word over the door ... Kamaledhiplava it were ... means somethin' abart a ship on a sea of love ... never really unnerstood that ... no bloody ships or sea within miles o' Meerut.'

Roomy Birch recalled Agra. '...where the bleedin' Rag were on the opposite side o' the road to the Protestant Church ... on Sunday nights the preacher 'ad ter shout 'is sermon to be 'eard over the noise o' kids a'touting fer the wimmin!'

Many of them knew it well, recalling it as a high-class place, with high-class prices to match. The proprietor tried hard to give it a touch of 'home'. Heavy European bedsteads and mattresses, marble-topped wash-stands, basket-chairs and brassware colluded in a quaint and pathetic English appearance, only spoilt by the drab Indian carpet and curtains.

Pat Coughlin voiced what was in all their minds. ' 'Ow could yer 'ave a decent fuck wiv a bloody great picture of the Queen ... Gawd bless 'er ... a'starin' down atcher from over the bed?'

Mirzapur was much the same as any other military station in India, its fifteen hundred or so troops being catered for by thirty or forty native girls, aged from twelve upwards. Less prized than boys, Indian girls ten to twelve years of age, were sold to rich men for private pleasure or to brothel keepers, who taught them the trade and provided food, clothing and a roof over their heads. In return they kept most of the money they earned, although it was rumoured that some girls in the Rag regularly sent money home to their families. The girls fatalistically accepted their lot but had little choice even if they hated it, there was nowhere to escape to. All came to the same end, riddled with disease and driven out to become sand-rats until dying in their early twenties. Indian girls matured early and most prostitutes were only thirteen to fifteen years old. They were examined by the Regimental Surgeon two or three times a week and any found to be diseased were immediately removed to the native Lock Hospital; few men caught VD in the Rag where everything possible was done to avoid contagion.

'One station we were in never 'ad no Rag ... all the girls 'ad their own little shack ... made o' plaster an' mud ... wiv just a charpoy. No bleedin' bedclothes nor nuffin ... an' o' corse, the usual earthenware water pitcher an' hand-bowl.'

'That were ... wait a minit ... Dinapur ... that's where it was ... I remember it 'cos of them bleedin' little boys a'shoutin' atcher while yer were onna job.'

'Wot were that then, Roomy?'

'Well them bloody shacks were 'ot as 'ell so you give one of the kids a pice ter pull onna rope and work the punkah over the bed. The rope went through a little 'ole in the door an' the kid put 'is eye to it and watched yer ... calling out ... Jiggy-jig Johnny ... jildi ... jildi ... arsty ... arsty ... aggy chel Johnny ... an' all manner o' things ... cheeky little sods!'

Dick Kinrade shook his head sadly. 'I'll be tellin' yer, me lads ... I'll not go with that bloody bibi Fat Emma in the Rag no more ... why, she's so soddin' idle the best bit's when she washes yer at the end.'

XVII

Lying in his shirt and drawers and gazing up at the half-obliterated ceiling stain, immortalising his predecessor, the Sergeant considered that rarely did anyone sing in the barrackroom. Officially out of order during the day, the dragging hours between eight a.m. and five p.m. constituted a Parade and nor were voices often raised in off-duty hours, not even in perpetuation of maudlin ditties after returning from the Canteen. He recalled how they had sung carols on 'Christmas Day', organised by the 5th Sub-Section as a private and personal function on July 5th. He smiled at the memory, remembering with warmth that it was an occasion when his men indicated that they regarded him as being more than just the man who ordered them about.

It began one dinner-time, when querulous complaints about the food were being aired, Roomy Birch wistfully offering a week's pay for an English 'banger', a good meaty sausage. 'Mister' Wright belched.

'Taff, d'ye remember in the Depot at Christmas, County Sheriff 'd send in a furlong ... two hundred an' twenty yards ... of prime Cambridge sausages to be dished up along with his dozen of prime Norfolk turkeys?'

Picking the last slivers of meat from between his blackened teeth, Private Davies smiled reflectively. 'Indeed I remember ... an' I recall how retired orficers and local gentry sent in hampers ... game, barons o' beef, ripe Stiltons an' the like ... Gawd, Christmases were wonderful in them days!'

Lance-Corporal Mockford joined in. 'An' local tradesmen ... them what had contracts to supply Regimental Messes ... they presented bottles o' wine, fruit and nuts ... 'member one grocer always provided stuff for a punch, enough for the whole Company.'

Veterans sat back, starry-eyed in blissful recollection. All waited expectantly, so far this was 'old soldier's chat', presumptuous for any but long-service men to join in for fear of breaking the spell and therefore forfeiting a flood of colourful reminiscences to wile away the long tedious afternoon.

Well qualified by his length of service, Charlie Mort, fearing this fascinating topic would peter-out, looked from one to another. 'I've heard tell o' Christmas at the Depot ... how'd you go about it?' He shook his head apologetically. 'Ye know, I ain't never served in England ... never even bin there.'

Old comrades nodded understandingly, there could be no better reason for telling of the hearty Victorian Christmases back home, even if the thermometer was touching well over a hundred.

'Well, we didn't leave nothing to chance when it came to organising traditional ceremonies, we 'ad a regular routine ... never changed from year to year, beginning in early December when each barrackroom elected a committee, with the Room-Corporal as Chairman ... on Christmas Day he had the power to look at each plateful and, if a man thought he hadn't got enough and appealed, then the Corporal passed judgement.'

Mister Wright shook his head. 'I never held with that ... if the first bugger appealed an' the Corporal was soft, then all the others shouted their bleedin' heads orf. Afore you knew it, dinner was cold.'

'Next we had a vote like ... to elect them as had official positions on the Day ... them what guarded barrels of beer, broaching an' drawing it ... an' them what uncorked wine and served it out ... special experienced blokes for carving, an' others for serving out veg.'

'Yes, an' you always had a sub-committee who got a pass to town to hire tablecloths, plates, dishes an' glasses from some pub or restaurant ... had to do the job proper on the day, didn't ye? Needed to keep an eye on that lot! Sam, remember when Lofty Short an' his sub-committee got pissed an' forgot to arrange for fancy things? Never had no cloth, no posh plates nor nothing that year ... we always checked on sub-committees after that.'

Struggling to picture it, Charlie Mort broke in. ' 'Ow did ye pay for it ... on seven pence 'apenny a day - after stoppages?'

'Each man invested three days pay, given by the pay-clerk in advance ... then officers chipped in ... they gave a one gallon cask o' beer to each Mess too ... Reg'ment made a grant of half-a-crown a man ... mostly went on booze ... an' extra food was bought from surplus Canteen profits ... generously surrendered by the Guv'ment.'

By now, everyone had given themselves over to a mid-summer Christmas, laying back and picturing barrackrooms donning festive garb, every spare minute of the three days before the 25th was spent in traditional decorating. Men made bunches and wreaths of holly and laurel and pasted paper-chains. Scholars cut large paper letters to form seasonal greetings and others made cardboard shields, emblazoned with Regimental Crests and mottoes, names of famous generals, popular Regimental commanders and battle honours. Eventually the big gaunt room was transformed into a bower of barbaric colour and greenery, with strings of paper chains running in a room-darkening profusion from the walls to the centre gasolier.

On Christmas morning the men were drunk and sick from the night before, but they struggled back to consciousness, momentarily bewildered by the unfamiliar surroundings, not wanting to miss a minute of this precious day. Struggling from their blankets they could have rested another hour, as on a Sunday. The chill colourful room was alive with men, wearing only the shirts they slept in, clasping hands and exchanging greetings before limbering up their beds - with no grumbling and swearing as on normal mornings. Shaving overnight, few used the ablutions before setting off with bottles of spirits to surge in and out of barrackrooms, exchanging toasts with old friends and comrades of many battle fields. Hardened drinkers knocked back a couple of mugs of gin, brandy, rum or whisky before sitting down to breakfast.

Jangling tin-pails competed with the raucous greetings as orderlies clattered past each other on the stairs to the kitchens; bursting vociferously into the barrackrooms with bread and coffee. The distant peaceful ringing of early church-bells was dramatically chased away by the Regimental Band beating out 'The British Grenadiers' in the barrack-yard below. Every window was flung up and hundreds of heads poked out, hoarse voices split the cold morning air, roaring out "Cheer boys, Cheer!" then setting up repeated 'Hiphip Hurrahs' until the whole barrack rung and echoed.

'So's to encourage peace an' goodwill, cells were cleared an' all punishments remitted. There were no drills nor duties on Christmas Day or Boxing Day. Guards an' picquets made up o' Jocks who got a holiday on New Years Day, all sitting down to dinner together.'

'Indeed, that were when I wished I was a Sawnie 'stead of from Wales! They done alright out of it, getting same Christmas fare brought to 'em in guardroom ... 'sides getting presents of liquor an' 'baccy from mates who felt sorry for 'em. One year when there weren't enough Sawnies to do duties, they used recently joined recruits ... an' I were a Welsh Scotsman that Christmas.'

'I recall Jock Weir one year when three of his mates each took him in a dinner ... he had three plates piled high with beef, goose, ham. pork an' veg ... two halves of plum duff an' a bloody great jelly ... 'bout four quarts of ale, two packets of 'baccy ... an' a bran' new clay-pipe!'

The room sighed appreciatively and Mister Wright pursed his lips in recollection. 'Yes, Ole Jock did alright that year ... but it didn't do him no good ... within the year he was dead of the fever ... within three weeks of landing in India.'

'Remember Church Parade on Christmas Day? Smaller'n usual with some men on leaf, but all orficers were there ... they got pissed-up later. Only C of E's paraded ... other denominations marched by NCO's to chapels or wherever they went. Wore No. 1 Dress with side-arms ... didn't have to take bundooks like out here ... lotta lads were in a right mess with tunics unfastened and hats on the back of their heads ... more'n half of 'em 'ad one too many ... an' most NCO's were as bad ... it were overlooked on account of it bein' Christmas, but if a man could hardly stand he were escorted back to barracks to sleep it off ... with lads shouting after him.'

Everyone could picture the Parade being called to order, then the Band striking up the familiar 'Church Call' with its stimulating chiming bells. The Commanding Officer crying, "Form Fours", and officers falling in besides their Companies. Before the admiring gaze of the usual assembly of nursemaids and children, on the word of command, the Regiment untidily stepped-off to march to Church. Inside the decorated building,

NCO's and men file in to the galleries, their boots clattering on the boards. Then the officers and their families elegantly strolled in to sit below them. Men craned forward, commenting audibly in criticising and admiring neatly dressed wives and children. Familiar carols were sung with gusto and the Service seemed far more stimulating than on normal Sundays.

Dismissed, the parade dissolved in all directions, men rushing off to lay tables, take up an appointed role or to seek old drinking-mates to fill time until half past one and the best meal of the year. Beer-casks, man-handled up to the barrackrooms and closely guarded by dependable men, would not be broached a minute before the appointed time. Warmed by a blazing fire in a well-blacked grate, decorated rooms bore a more homely atmosphere than on any other day of the year, yet still presenting a semblance of military order through the extra special nature of the Day, guaranteeing that cots and folded bedding were immaculately tidy and lined up regularly upon each other, pipe-clayed knapsacks and pouch-belts on shelves and polished rifles in racks vied with florid decorations. On the nearest bed to the door, centred exactly on the uncreased blanket, a polished tray held a bottle of sherry and glasses in readiness for the time-honoured ceremonies of providing refreshment for visiting officers.

Few listeners failed to remember how slowly the minutes ticked by while they awaited Christmas dinner. Here and there men querulously suggested that the bloody cooks had " ... gorn on fucking leaf", or "... p'raps the sodding bugler is too pissed to blow the dinner call?" Both Charlie Mort in the Band and bugler Boy Farley were aware that the Christmas Dinner call was difficult to sound. They pictured the bugler, remaining sober and nervously licking his dry lips before raising the bugle, to send lilting notes soaring skywards, penetrating the chill misty air and galvanising the entire Regiment into feverish activity and anticipation.

In the passage outside the kitchens, orderlies and a host of volunteer scullions jostled and jockeyed for position, surging forward in an irresistible tide as the doors opened on the first note of the Dinner Call. Soon, bent under iron baking dishes heaped high with beef, turkey, goose, sausage, roast potatoes and vegetables, and other delicacies such as huge holly-crowned puddings, larger and rounder than cannonballs and piles of mince-pies, orderlies passed in triumphal procession through cordons of flushed and excited men, cheering loudly at the delectable sight. Back in the barrackroom puddings and mince-pies were set by the fire to keep warm until they were required. Basins of oranges, apples and nuts were carelessly dropped onto cots for later eating.

Importantly, dishers-out stepped forward as the Corporal, frequently halting to curse hungry men jostling his elbows, began to hack at the rapidly cooling meat and poultry. Men greedily compared plates, piled high with succulent morsels, their lips smacking and eyes glistening with anticipation. Then hearts fell at the crashing cadence of iron-tipped boots on the stone floor corridor beyond. The door crashed open and the Regimental Sergeant-Major's familiar bellow fell upon them like a bombshell.

'Commanding Officer! Attention!'

Some faster and steadier than others, all crashed rigidly to attention as, swords clanking, the Colonel, the Company Commander, the Adjutant and other senior officers stalked through the door, their faces masked with seasonal military affability. Requesting them to Stand Easy, the Colonel's compliments of the season were reciprocated by mumbles rippling round the room. The Corporal cleared his throat and stepped forward, thanking his lucky stars he had the foresight to hide those men drunk enough, by an incautious or insolent remark, to precipitate an unsavoury incident that could become a permanent handicap to both himself and the barrackroom. Heels smartly clicking together, he requested permission to drink the health of the Colonel and his officers who, having already drunk nine glasses of cheap sherry in previously visited barrackrooms, graciously affected surprise. Ensuring that all held a filled glass, the Corporal delivered the customary carefully prepared and rehearsed speech, glasses were raised and toasts exchanged. The Colonel moved around, spoke a few words to men whose faces he recognised, said the decorations were quite the best he had seen, and the cortege departed on it rounds.

Door shutting was a signal for the banishment of good order and military discipline. Grabbing their cold, congealed plates, men rushed to the immaculately laid tables for the noisiest and most friendly meal of the year. Trying to talk loudly at the same time as they shovelled great forkfuls of food into gaping mouths, revellers spluttered and choked. Strong ale and cheap Spanish wine allied themselves to the spirits knocked back during the morning, arousing shouted conversations, raucous jokes and wild, uproarious laughter. Like a blanket, the smell of sweat, food and drink lay heavy on the hot air; the blazing fire made the room like a bake-house, crimsoning the faces of heavily breathing men so that they discarded jackets and unbuttoned their shirts to the waist. Rising ponderously, men weaved unsteady paths across the room to wrestle with the windows, flinging them up to admit blasts of cold air the plaintive complaints of draughts being answered with snarled abuse.

When the last overloaded stomach had refused the final morsel, men lurched from the table to fall heavily on their beds, or lay on the floor where they had fallen, snoring and snuffling in uncaring oblivion. Veterans of many such occasions, the real old soldiers, flushed and savage to behold in their shirt sleeves, remained steady at their posts, swilling down beer and smoking stubby clay pipes, glassy eyes pensively staring at nothing in particular. Intermittently, one or other of them would start from his trance to bawl a military soliloquy into the ear of the nearest comrade, wordily recounting with his gleaming eyes and waving hands, his victorious leading role in some lurid encounter, or confess happily to appalling crimes escaped scot-free. This hardened bunch kept drinking until either collapsing or the last drop was drained from the beer casks. If the latter then they staggered to their beds for bottles of spirits tucked away in the bedding, shared them around with ceremony and solemnity until empty. Survivors of this shakily buckled their belts and tottered away to "... 'ave a wet inna pub."

Throughout the afternoon, those unable to hold their drink were guided to the door by hardier comrades until a regular procession of white-faced men, hair sweat-plastered to their foreheads, crawled and supported themselves on walls to the landing outside, adding to the vomit and urine bespeckling the normally spotless flagstones.

Twilight of the short winter day mercifully misted a grotesque military carnival of dishevelled soldiers tottering aimlessly about the Barrack lines, mindlessly muttering and roaring out songs and belligerent challenges. On that single day of the year when disorder reigned, the gravelled parade-ground and barrack yards were dotted with unconscious men, shapeless mounds discoloured with vomit or blood from fights and falls. In irregular rings, crowds of drink-maddened men surrounded their fighting comrades and stridently encouraged grim and relentless combats that should have been halted by NCO's, among the spectators or lolling against the walls, too drunk to care.

Mister Wright shook his head sadly. 'It were always the same ... year after bloody year ... we all knew Christmas Day was a different day, when larks were winked at .... but rules are rules and them what went too far mostly carried can for lot on us. By Boxing Day about fifty percent of the Regiment were crimed. The cells in the Guard Room and the prisoners ward in the hospital were full, an' the nearest military prison took overflow. We weren't no different to any other Line Reg'ment ... they all had about fifty blokes on serious charges ... drunkenness an' going large a bit ... you know, rioting in streets, assaulting picquets or refusing to accompany them back to barracks, breaking leaf ... that's sleeping outta barracks without permission ... there were plenty up for insubordination an' for striking or insulting NCO's ... stupid buggers got drunk on Guard and finished up inna cells, along with them what got arrested for being drunk an' incapable on sentry-go. Oh yes, I forgot .... about another dozen up for fighting in barracks.'

His voice ebbed mournfully, allowing Taffy Davies to take up the recital. 'Yes, man ... an' don't forget just as many cases were overlooked ... had a blind eye turned on them ... an' to be fair to lads ... a lotta defaulters were young soldiers an' recruits not used to discipline ... nor strong drink.'

Fascinated by this incongruous saga of unbelievable discipline, Private Saville called out from his charpoy at the far end of the room. 'What happened to them ... were they punished?'

'Were they punished? I'll say they were! On the 27th, day after Boxing Day, they set up on the Square ... on parade-ground mark you ... half a dozen court-martials ... six lots of trestle-tables covered with blankets from the stores ... an' three officers sitting behind each, dishing out summary Army justice as fast as they could ... 'twas easy 'cos just about every case was proven ...

the evidence weren't challenged by the prisoner ... most on 'em were deadbeat, downhearted an' too dry to open their bleedin' mouths ... even if Sarn't-Major let 'em. Most on 'em got fourteen days confined ... but on them what were charged with crimes against an NCO or while on Guard ... they were remanded for District Court Martial ... an' they really gave 'em stick there. Hey, Wrightie, d'ye remember that Christmas when Sarn't Smithers ... you know, 'im at Sobraon who 'ad two Sixes spiked on 'is lunger at the same time ... 'anging one on the Company Commander ... Christ, they really gave it to 'im, din' they?'

'Yeah I recall him ... tall lad with a good head o' ginger hair ... never knowed 'im pissed afore that Christmas ... there was them what reckoned he'd 'ad summat slipped in 'is ale ... by a bloke he'd crimed.'

'What'd he get?" asked Charlie Mort'

'Well, he'd nearly done his twenty-one an' were going out with a pension in the New Year ... 'stead o' that ... he was stripped of his stripes an' got six months in Colchester Jail ... lost 'is pension an dishonourably discharged ... don't know what 'appened to 'im after that.'

'I 'eard 'e re-enlisted in the 86th Royal Irish Rifles an' made corporal again ... died o' cholera in Jhansi in '58.'

'Did he now? I never knew that.'

Laying in his cubicle, the Sergeant recalled many similar Army Christmases where all the eager anticipation and simple, sincere preparations ended just as ruefully and sadly. It was a pitiful conclusion to the only day in the entire year when soldiers could lift a corner of the otherwise rigid curtains that separated then from the British public, when they could briefly enjoy seasonal pleasures accepted by civilians as a right but granted only as a privilege to soldiers. Always they came back for more the next year, and always it went the same way.

His reverie gave way to awareness of a spirited discussion reverberating from the far side of the symbolic matting wall separating him from his Sub-Section. He recognised Private Alexander's accent, deep and mature male tones laboriously forming guileless childish phrases.

'Ding Dong, I like Christmas ... can we no have Christmas now?'

'Och, fer Chrissake Sanny. Ye dinna have Christmas in June

... ye canna have it when ye choose. Christmas comes on December twenty-fifth.'

Over the laughter rose the compelling steel-edged voice of Private Kinrade. 'Will ye wait a minute now ...?'

Noting their leader wished to address them, the Pope's Boys - Finnigan, Cox and Coughlin - quickly hushed the room into silence. His gaze fixed on the punkah waving lazily overhead, Kinrade said thoughtfully. 'An' why should we not have Christmas now ... today ... if we want to ... who the bloody hell says that Hut Five can't have its own private Christmas, whenever it wants?'

This stopped everyone dead in their tracks. The Pope's Boys anxiously stared at Kinrade, others stifled spontaneous sniggers and derision. There were those - the Sergeant, Privates Early and Saville - seeing it as another of the unpredictable Irishman's tilts at the established order of things. Slowly Kinrade lowered his gaze, raised himself onto his elbows and looked steadily around the room. 'Everyone likes Christmas ... we all agree its the best day o' the year ... so why ration it to one single fucking day out of three hundred an' sixty five?'

Out of sight in his cubicle, the Sergeant instinctively sensed trouble in the rocking of the boat and raised himself up from his charpoy, his head tilted to catch every word.

'Why don't we ... just us in this room ... organise our own Christmas Day ... do all them things that the Corp'ral an' Mister Wright an' Taffy old us about ... decorate the place, club together an' have a slap-up dinner an' all?'

Big Sanny Alexander clapped his hands excitedly. 'Ay! An' we can give each other presents ... an' ... an' sing carols ... I know some carols.'

The Sergeant grimly reflected upon features of Christmas in Summer that no one had mentioned. The long hours from 8 a.m. to 5 p.m. constitute a Parade, and no liquor - save an authorised pint of ale or porter at dinnertime - could be brought into the barrackrooms. On the other hand, he doubted if a day passed in a single bungalow in India when someone did not smuggle in a bottle of grog, arrack or even some bazaar rot-gut, tuppenny bottles of bhang, darro and Billy Stink that sent you blind. He imagined the RSM's reactions to decorated barrackrooms occupied by blind-drunk men in the middle of the day. If they got their Christmas Day organised, there'd be no going on the shout before Canteen time.

So far, unable to countenance such unorthodoxy, old soldiers had remained aloof, now Charlie Mort, he who had found such wistful fascination in English Army Christmases, gave it his blessing.

'If we have our own Christmas, what day will we have it on?'

Men looked at each other, none wishing to take responsibility for such a momentous decision. Then the American, Private Martin Early, a half-smile creasing his face, called out. 'How about the fourth of July?'

'Fourth of July? Why the fourth of July?'

' 'Cos its Independence Day an' I'll have me own celebration too!'

Private Thomas Saville, looking up sharply at Early's impassive face and catching a quick wink of his eye, was the only man in the room to appreciate the subtlety of British soldiers celebrating - if only in passing - the 92nd anniversary of the American colony's forcible breaking away from the Mother Country.

However, the fourth of July was a Saturday, when the Commanding Officer held his weekly Parade and Inspection, so it could not be then. Sunday seemed a good day, being free after Church Parade and fitting in with traditional Christmas morning procedure. So, Sunday 5th July 1868 was chosen as the 5th Sub-Section's Personal and Private Christmas Day; Private Early graciously assured anxious enquirers that was swell, thanks.

The customary committee was formed. Lance-Corporal Mockford, by reason of rank, was Chairman, members were Privates Davies, Early and Mort. The vastly experienced Private Wright was unable to completely reconcile himself with Christmas in July but agreed to be available for co-option if required. The first official act of the Committee was to approach the Sergeant for permission to hold the Christmas Day; he agreed, subject to a tight degree of control by the Committee, who guaranteed the only liquor brought into the bungalow would be the dinner-time beer ration. Well aware of pitfalls, the Sergeant did not find it an easy decision, anticipating the RSM's inevitable disapproval. However, after listening to the nostalgic preamble he could not bring himself to dampen such pleasure and enthusiasm. Weary of his running fight with authority over every barrackroom reform, he shrugged his shoulders. 'To hell with them! Might as well be hung for a sheep as a lamb!'

Charlie Mort's Sub-Committee, himself and Taffy Davies, explored the possibilities of hiring - or otherwise acquiring - such refinements as tablecloths, cutlery, china and glassware. Mort's well known influential connections with the Regiment were put to good use when, as anticipated, no local sources could be found. One of his mates, who happened to be an Officer's Mess Corporal, loaned them everything - free of charge - in a Cinderella and Slipper arrangement of everything being returned clean in time for the Officer's evening meal.

The Committee's major deliberations revolved around how to pay for this supplementary Festive Season. After surprisingly little argument it was decided that each man should contribute four rupees; Boy Farley on lower pay, one rupee. As, after stoppages, this was more than a week's pay, it caused a two week economy crisis with the Sub-Section staying away from the Canteen and the Rag, replacing those delights by extending day-time charpoy lolling to the evenings. For a single night, the absence of the entire Sub-Section from their habitual places of entertainment did not escape notice. The curiosity of men with little to occupy their minds was thoroughly aroused when the absence extended over two, three, four and more nights. Eventually the entire other-rank strength of the Regiment were trying to find out what the 5th Sub-Section were up to.

Although not asked, the Sergeant donated ten rupees - not without agonising as to whether he was buying their esteem, but it was received by Lance-Corporal Mockford with dignity. He told the Sergeant they reckoned on having about seventy-five rupees to spend and that the Committee were meeting that morning to decide what to buy. Huddled around a table, erected with permission in the trestle and board storage area outside the cubicle, the Committee argued for hours over what could be considered adequate quantities of food and drink per head. Every man in the room strained his ears to catch odd words of the delectable deliberations. Just before noon, the meeting broke up. The entranced audience licked their lips as they listened to the shopping list, read out by Lance-Corporal Mockford who was pleased to say that most of the money would be spent on food and drink as Private Mort's mate, in the Officer's Mess, had saved them the cost of hiring tablecloths, cutlery and glasses etc. There would be dropsy for the contractor's cooks preparing the food - under the control and direction of Private Mort - leaving enough to buy 20 chickens at 3 annas each; 20lbs of prime beef and 20lbs of mutton at 1 anna per lb; 20lbs of pork at 2 annas per lb and 12 rabbits at 1 rupee a dozen. There would be 120 eggs at 1 rupee; potatoes and other vegetables; flour for the Christmas pudding and Yorkshire pudding; dried fruit and spices; imported cheeses including a 6lb tin of Stilton for £1. Finally cigars, tobacco, clay pipes, casks of ale and porter, a bottle of Grog (Bengal Brandy) and nuts and fruit. With insufficient money to buy such imported spirits as whisky, gin and brandy, four rupees were put aside for a bottle of good sherry to be drunk by the Commanding Officer's representative making the traditional visit, exchanging toasts and compliments. In response to an official request, Private Wright graciously agreed to co-option on the committee and supervised the Room Decorations. He produced a systematic decorative scheme which prevented personal whims and fancies.

Now began a blissful period of almost complete sobriety and industrious good comradeship, every man in the room devoting all his waking hours to working for the common good. Committee men importantly bustled hither and thither; Private Wright detailed patrols to scour the surrounding areas for specified decorative materials, rejecting with politeness - tinged by minimal scorn - items not reaching his rigid specifications. Kinrade and Cox returned from a bazaar-bashing expedition, their tunics bulging with crumpled sheets of brightly coloured paper, darkly hinting of the dangers of stealing from a native religious building. Mister Wright immediately organised paper-chain making parties, cutting with scissors borrowed from the Regimental Tailor and sticking them with a paste of flour and water, courtesy of another of Charlie Mort's mates in the Officer's Mess kitchen.

Riding high above all this was an air of furtive secrecy as men, their lives not blessed with a single second of personal privacy, fumbled in corners or, diplomatically not remarked upon, sat with their backs to the room, industriously making Christmas presents for their mates. The Sergeant, remembering the pride bestowed by such an artefact in another regiment, asked Private Saville to make a large model out of clay, as his personal present to the Sub-Section. The young soldier, proud to be singled out, reluctantly agreed to accept a fee that included the privacy of the cubicle while making the model and his own presents.

Christmas, even when on a Sunday in July, is preceded by Christmas Eve, unfortunately coinciding with the Commanding Officer's Inspection of Barrackrooms, compelling the hiding of all traces of the impending festivities. Private Wright, aware from the first that he would not have the usual three or four days for decorating the room, had all the decorations carefully wrapped in old newspapers and, risking ants and other voracious insects, had hidden them beneath the bungalow. They were extracted and put up by a detailed party immediately after the Commanding Officer's inspection on Saturday, with excited and good-natured industry.

Proposed by Private Wright, seconded by Private Davies, the Committee considered a proposition that Christmas really began on Christmas Eve, that it would not be right without the customary piss-up on the night before the Day - "Everyone went to bed drunk as a fart on Christmas Eve" recalled Private Wright; the Lance-Corporal, Private Davies and the other veterans nodded in confirmation. The problem was that there was barely enough money in the entire Sub-Section to send even one man to bed pissed. This was not a bad thing, the Lance-Corporal sagely pointed out, otherwise some stupid sod might shout the odds and blow the gaff so that other Sections would want to help celebrate their personal and private Christmas. Disdaining general discussion and advice, the Committee retired to a corner, mumbled together, and returned to rule that all existing cash go into a General Kitty; the Sub-Section to proceed to the Canteen in a body, stick together drinking rounds until the money ran out, then, still in a group, return to the barrackroom - "...for an early night, so's we'll all be fit for tomorrow."

It went as planned, marching to the Canteen in a body, ignoring the ribald welcome and raucous piss-taking, sitting together in a smug tight group, suppressing the jubilant knowledge that they had something going that the others didn't know about. The kitty lasted two rounds, supped slowly to make it last. Then, standing up as one, surrounded by an incredulous silence, they marched out a full hour before stop-tap. Thirty minutes before Lights Out, every man had his head down and eyes tightly screwed up, like children fearful that being awake might frighten away a visiting Santa Claus.

The Great Day dawned. For once, the Sergeant did not have to laboriously rouse them, in fact, long before Reveille he was awakened by exchanges of greetings. Some claimed not to have slept a wink without the soporific aid of a skin-full, others admitting to being too excited to sleep. None took advantage of the extra hour's lie-in because it was Sunday. Men moved around the room shaking hands and wishing compliments of the Season; in a unique atmosphere of fellowship and happiness even the notorious early morning grumblers chatted happily with their neighbours. Surveying the happy scene, the Sergeant realised there was no swearing, no coarse or ribald shouts, that this morning was different from any other since he had arrived at the barrackroom. Rousing choruses of popular songs so alarmed the native breakfast-bearers that they entered gingerly. Quickly catching the spirit they began salaaming. grinning nervously as unpredictable Feringhees slapped their backs and shook their hands, sympathetic towards these poor heathens who did not have a Christmas.

Goodwill towards natives was soon dissipated by the punkah-wallahs whose narrow world was soon turned upside down when, after breakfast, they were violently assailed for actually pulling on ropes. In the middle of the room by the rifle-rack, stood a ceiling high Christmas Tree, made of sun-dried feathery palm fronds, rising in splayed tiers from a stout wooden base made by carpenter Holmes. Symmetrically arranged on its fronds were fifty small coloured candles, brought at the bazaar. Ceremoniously lit when the breakfast litter was cleared, they were blown out by the light breeze generated by waving punkahs. Immediately, cursing men rushed to the verandah, kicking the astounded punkah-wallahs into inactivity. At once, the dim shuttered room was miraculously transformed into a shadowy, seasonal cavern, so reminiscent of England and home that all were reduced to silence. Tears trickled down leathery cheeks and heads were averted to conceal emotions as Private Cox, with his pleasant untutored Irish singing-voice, softly rendered 'While Shepherds Watched their Flocks ...' However, tears were soon overtaken by sweat dripping from every pore, the myriad, motionless candle flames hanging on the heavy foetid air made the room intolerably hot: a second foray of forceful kicking galvanised drowsy punkah-boys into action. The punkahs creaked again and the candles blew out.

The Tree played its traditional gift bearing role. Men had surreptitiously hung small newspaper wrapped packages onto its drooping branches, to be given out before the men tumbled into the Lines for Church Parade. In a dignified official manner, the Committee waited upon the Sergeant in his cubicle, offering the compliments of the Season and courteously requested him to present the first gift from the Tree. Escorted up the room, diffidently wishing all a Merry Christmas, he picked a little package from the middle of the Tree. Reading the inscription aloud, written by Private Saville who had written on behalf of many in the room who couldn't write, it said, "To my old mate Roomy from his file, Pat."

Enthusiastic hand-claps sent Birch sheepishly shambling forward, his awkward fumbling with the string made men growl with impatience until the paper fell away, revealing the little shiny sovereign purse that had earned him a cobbing when taken from Coughlin a few weeks earlier. Not a whit embarrassed, Birch cheerfully thanked his Irish file. The Committee took over with the Lance-Corporal becoming Father Christmas and handing out small packages, enthusiastically unwrapped until the floor was littered with paper and just as enthusiastically gathered up by Big Sanny. Everyone got something; mostly men exchanged gifts with their files although other friends were not forgotten. Shaving brushes, cakes of soap, packets of 'baccy, clay pipes and boxes of lucifers seemed the limit of inspiration. Saville's talent in painting small water-colours on cardboard, depicting men's bed-spaces, the bungalow and other familiar scenes, was much admired. Polly Perkins fell back on poker-work, an old boozing school fund-raiser that entailed burning into slabs of wood with the tip of a heated ram-rod such sentiments as the Regimental Motto 'Quis Separabit', For Queen and Country and, in unconscious irony, Bless Our Home.

Watching, the Sergeant fell into a nostalgic reverie that was broken by Boy Farley marching noisily up the room, coming smartly to attention before him.

'Sarn't, Committee's compliments an' would the Sergeant do them the honour of coming to the Christmas Tree?'

Stepping forward from the Committee's solemn ranks, Lance-Corporal Mockford, on behalf of the Sub-Section, ceremoniously presented a small package. Displaying appropriate surprise, the Sergeant tore off the wrapping paper to reveal a brass whistle. Not knowing whether to laugh or cry, he thanked them. His own whistle had mysteriously vanished two days before, ensuring a need for the gift while answering the problem of what to give a man who already has everything. Later, ashamed of his suspicions, he closely examined the whistle and confirmed it was not his original property.

Dispersal was halted by the Sergeant sending Farley to the cubicle to fetch a wooden box from the table. Holding it in both hands and deliberately stoking up the curiosity to bursting point, the Sergeant said. 'We, this Sub-Section, need all the luck we can get. It might be a good idea to have a mascot to bring us some. Don't want a live one ... like the monkey in my story ... so I got Private Saville to make us a very suitable mascot, an' I'm giving it as my ... er ... Christmas present to you all.' Opening the box with a flourish, he took out a fine model of a pugnacious bull-dog, about half life-size and mounted on a wooden plinth. He let the gasps and intakes of breath die away. 'This is Bully, mascot of the 5th Sub-Section. He'll watch over us from the shelves above the beds. Each man will have him on his own shelf for a day ... in turn ... beginning with Private Saville, then Private Early an' so on ... 'cept when there's an inspection, of course. An' now ... pull yourselves together ... got five minutes to get ready for Church Parade.'

The men tumbled out into the searing heat of the Lines, in their best dress and bearing rifles - always carried since the Mutiny eleven years earlier when rebellious sepoys timed their actions to catch the British troops unarmed in Church. Private Early, the Lance-Corporal, Bell and Alexander, who were 'Other Denominations', took a chance on the lesser supervision of their Parade to absent themselves and, along with Bandsman Mort who had providentially developed a sore on his lip that prevented his playing, remained in the barrackroom to prepare for dinner - and ward off inquisitive intruders.

After singing their hearts out in joyous and conspicuous abandon, an exuberant group bundled back into the bungalow, halting in awe at the scene before them. The room presented a truly festive picture, immaculately tidy with decorations softening the military symmetry and gaunt, high ceiling. Stretching along the centre of the room was a spotlessly white-clothed table set with gleaming glasses, cutlery and crockery, triumphantly topped by the new mascot, Bully Bulldog. The beaming helpers were patted and praised as the men divested themselves of sweaty uniforms and carefully tucked them out of sight on this day of days. The Sergeant remained in No.1's, having been asked to stand in for the Commanding Officer's traditional Christmas Day visit.

He waited in the cubicle while a cask of porter was broached and each man filled his glass.Then Private Mort, senior Private soldier by two months over Private Davies, escorted the Sergeant to the centre of the room where Lance-Corporal Mockford called them to Attention, graciously amended to a Stand-Easy by the surrogate CO who accepted a brimming schooner of sherry. Nervously stepping forward, the Lance-Corporal haltingly declaimed the usual seasonal speech, sibilantly chivvied and prompted by those who helped write it. Then, wishing the Sergeant/C.O. compliments of the Season, all drank a hearty toast. The Sergeant responded with a laboriously written and rehearsed response, further toasts were drunk, compliments offered on the room decorations and he retired to his cubicle. With the Regimental Sergeant-Major in mind he had asked to be excused from officiating at the table-head. Partaking of his meal alone but within hearing of the festivities, he was royally waited on by Privates Early and Davies, plied with surfeit of wondrous victuals. Inevitably he found difficulty in blanking from his mind the saddening seasonal nostalgia, despite the sobering knowledge that this was Christmas in July.

At two o'clock, Private Wright belched and heavily remarked. 'Never would a' though I could enjoy Christmas Dinner so much wivout a skinful o' booze.'

Everyone nodded, too full to attempt greater physical effort. The meal had been all and more than they hoped. Well-prepared - thanks to Mort's unflagging bullying of the native cooks - plenty of everything, 'seconds' and 'thirds' on request, they all sat back, repleted. Languidly tables were cleared and stacked. The cloths, china, cutlery and glass was rushed out to waiting dhobi-wallahs, well paid to have them back to the Officer's Mess in pristine condition for dinner that evening. Now followed an hour filled only with heavy breathing, snoring, farting and belching as everyone fought desperately to be fit and conscious for the next part of the programme at three o'clock when the Committee had organised a Smoking Concert, chaired by Private Kinrade, to take the place of the traditional after dinner boozing - and fill in the hours until Canteen-time.

The unique occasion, sailing on waves of benevolence and goodwill, ensured that every pathetic effort at entertainment was rapturously received. Kinrade ranted and bullied shy comrades into public feats beyond their wildest dreams, in a demonstration of morale-raising fellowship that delighted the marvelling Sergeant, principal guest sitting on the only chair in the bungalow. All settled down to make sure that the Smoking Concert lived up to its name, dirty, chipped clay pipes competed with the new ones to overlay the heavy air with a thickening miasma of tobacco smoke. Battling violently against it, Saville and Cox brought tears to eyes with their sentimental songs. Wright's confident Midland loquacity extended to comic monologues. Birch's Cockney slang embellished an account of a military review in Hyde Park. Perhaps the only true artistry came from Boy Farley's trumpet and Charlie Mort's trombone, the sore lip having miraculously cleared up. Yank Early had just launched into a story of a turkey-shoot in Virginia when, without warning, came the unparalleled occurrence of the Orderly Officer visiting a barrackroom on an off-duty Sunday afternoon. The accompanying Orderly Sergeant's barked entry brought everyone all up to attention, the Sergeant ruefully thinking that news and noise spreads quickly. The young Lieutenant gazed around in wonder:

'My God! Whatever is going on here?'

The Sergeant clicked his heels together. 'Sir! Celebrating the 4th of July ... American Independence Day ... Private Early here is an American, Sir!'

'Fourth of July! It looks like Christmas to me!'

Men nudged each other in delight. The Lieutenant turned to the Orderly Sergeant. 'Sergeant, is there any Regulation forbidding the celebration of the National Day of a friendly power?'

'Can't think of one, Sir.'

'Well, they're not breaking any Regulation, causing or inciting an uproar, not doing anything contrary to good order and discipline, not damaging Government property, nor planning a mutiny. Carry on, Sergeant!'

The Sergeant clicked his heels. 'Thank you, Sir.'

The Officer and his Sergeant turned to leave the bungalow, unaware that in the bowels of the shadowy room Kinrade and Finnigan, flattened on the floor, were restraining Private Hebdon, belligerently drunk after continually swigging from a bottle of native darro secreted in his bedding. As the officer passed from sight the drunk soldier broke away to lurch swiftly down the room after him. Nearest to him and seeing no other way of stopping what would undoubtedly ruin the day, the Sergeant spontaneously lashed out, catching Hebdon on the side of the jaw, felling him to the floor. Immediately he realised what he had done, appalled at the enormity of hitting a lower rank before numerous witnesses, a court-martial and reduction to ranks flashed before his eyes. The drunk soldier dazedly rolled over, fingering his jaw. Without hesitation, Private Early pounded a full-blooded punch into the rough wooden door-frame; his face distorted with pain he nursed the wounded fist in his other hand.

Hebdon sat up, glaring accusingly at the Sergeant. 'You hit me ... now you're for it ... everyone saw you!'

Private Early leaned over him, pushing his bleeding knuckles under Hebdon's nose. 'The Sergeant didn't thump you ... I did! Look at me paw ... did that on your goddamned jaw!'

Hebdon shook his head. 'No, he hit me!'

Early appealed to the room. 'Come on you guys ... you saw it ... tell the son-of-a-bitch who hit him.'

The Sergeant held his breath, waiting. Private Kinrade leant forward. 'You bastard Hebdon ...you broke the Committee's rules 'bout drinkin' ... you coulda spoilt our fucking Christmas ... if Yank 'ere hadn't hit you ... I'd 've done it meself!'

The Sergeant retired to his cubicle, wondering whether it was him they were trying to save, or their Christmas. He had a warm feeling Early had put him first.

The Smoking Concert came to its dramatic end about an hour

before the Wet Canteen's recognised opening hour or, in the context of the 5th Sub-Section's personal Christmas Day, the moment when they could safely start knocking back the considerable amounts of booze that were stacked safely under Committee-men's charpoys. Time hung heavily, despite languid visits to the jakes, with a thorough wash and shave in the ablutions so as to look presentable for Christmas night; all hoped to have too much of a jag on at reveille to feel like bothering.

Well aware that not being in the Wet Canteen, coupled with the noise of a 'Christmas night' party in the bungalow, would attract unwelcome visitors, the Committee ruled that each man could invite a mate from another section if he put two rupees in the kitty. Shrewdly they reasoned that doubling the garrison's strength would be invaluable when gate-crashing began, so visitors were quietly requested to bring personal weapons with them - anything short of side-arms - to supplement the Sub-Section's armoury of clubs, belts, knuckle-dusters and other weapons. There were also certain tactical plans devised by the Committee and communicated to the Sub-Section and guests.

Knowing this, the Sergeant was certain that Sunday 5th July - Christmas night - was a most appropriate occasion to linger over supper and a few beers in the Sergeant's Mess. He might be able to occupy the RSM., the bungalow was too far from the Mess for the noise of the festivities to be heard.

Everything went much as expected. Despite strenuous efforts the booze did not run out, yet neither was any member of the Sub-Section too paralytic to take his place in the ranks when, immediately after the Canteen called stop-tap, the rest of 'C' Company marched noisily over to drink up what was left of the Christmas booze. They were met and held at the front verandah by Lance-Corporal Mockford and fifteen well-armed men while Privates Early and Kinrade led the remainder round to come up silently in the invader's rear. Although fewer, but better equipped than the invader's fists, boots, buckles and belts, the garrison completely routed them.

The Sergeant returned from the Mess just after this stirring event in time to be impressed by the relentless style of the Committee insisting that all take a hand in removing the decorations - there would be no time between reveille and first parade. Everyone worked with a will, never before in a barrackroom had the Sergeant seen such amiability, good comradeship and high morale. It was still in evidence a week later, proving the benefits of occasional breaks in the boring routine of army life.

By now every Other Rank in the Regiment knew of Christmas in July. It became fashionable to organise private Christmases, but they were not a great success. Certainly none approached that of the 5th Sub-Section, whose Committee was strong enough to prevent abuses and infractions of discipline and good order that eventually led to an official ban. The Sub-Section lay low, comforted by the knowledge that nothing had been said about banning American Independence Day.

XVIII

That morning both Company Commander and Sergeant-Major had livers and vied with each other in being harsh and dissatisfied so Drill was even more exhausting than usual. After breakfast, charpoys got a real bashing as everyone sank down to wage drowsy campaigns against marauding insects. By mid-morning the hush began to cause concern among the gregarious men unaccustomed to solitude, so men raised their heads and looked around, fearful of having been left behind. Private John Wright's flat nasal voice broke the silence, confirming that all was well.

'My Gawd ... I jist 'ad an 'orrible dream ... a bloody nightmare ... I dreamt of ole muvver Snaggs ... Corp'ral Snaggs missis back in the ole 16th ... ' Wright lay back, musing on previous service in the cavalry. 'She were a real cow ... put me right orf gittin' wed she did ... '

From the next bed, Taff Davies languidly threw him a lifeline. 'Married Corner ... behind the blanket, were she?'

'Yeah ... 'ad two nippers ... boy an' a gal ... wot was 'er name? ... Ain't though of 'er fer years ... yet she caused all the trouble ... Amy ... no ... it were Arabella ... that's it ... Arabella!'

Old soldiers enlisting before the Crimean War of 1854 had lived in barrackrooms where the four corners were screened by a bedraggled and holed blanket, hanging unevenly on a rope stretched from wall to wall. Behind it married soldiers carried on matrimonial life and brought up families. In return for the sparse accommodation wives sometimes cooked for the room, washed clothing and carried out other household tasks, for which they got a meagre pittance stopped from the men's pay.

Considered to uplift barrackroom morals by checking profanity, it was a hard existence not permitting much outward display of womanly feelings. It was even worse for those living their young lives behind the flimsy screen, beginning when cursing men were kept awake by the anguish of childbirth coming from behind the blanket. Knowing no other world than the barrackroom, children were treated as pets by the men in the room, encouraged to gulp down draughts of ale, pull on foul pipes and repeat lurid curses. Growing daughters had to crowd in to sleep behind the screen, boys took up the beds of men who were on guard or in hospital.

Old soldiers, Sam Mockford and Charlie Mort joined Davies and Wright in recalling the bad old days. But their musings were disturbed when Mister Wright suddenly abandoned the subject under discussion to plunge off into a favourite barrackroom amusement, Birch baiting.

'Hey Roomy, yer quiet these days ... don' 'ear a word outta yer ... cat got yer tongue?'

Laying on his charpoy and moodily staring up at the spasmodic movements of the punkah, Private Birch did not rise to the bait. Without turning his head he sullenly growled. 'Reckon I got a right to be quiet ... don' reckon it's anyfing to do wiv any of yer ... I'll not feergit yer gave me a cobbin' ... I'll git me own back, you wait ... you sods.'

Wright laughed hollowly. 'Believe that whin I sees it ... don' know wot yer fussin' abart ... a bleedin' cobbin' ain't nuffin ter wot used to go on in the old army!'

'Sod off! Bet yer nivver went around beating 'ell outta yer mates!'

Mister Wright cackled. 'Birchy ... yer don't know wot yer talkin' abart ... Christ, I were in a barrackroom when they cut a bloke's cock orf.'

It was a waking call that could not be denied, bringing men struggling back to consciousness.

'Cut a bloke's cock orf? That the troof Wrightie ... yer ain't 'avin' us on?'

'Corse it's the bloody troof. 'Appened at 'Ounslow ... on Christmas Eve ... in ... lemme see ... it were '47 ... after the 16th Lancers had got back from the war with the Sixes. I were nineteen at the time ... a bit of a lad and knocking orf this pusher ... an 'ousemaid she were. Like I said, it were Christmas Eve and she din't want me to rush fings 'til I got late and knew I'd 'ave to git over the wall.'

Set down in a gorse strewn waste, ideal for cavalry and artillery activities, Hounslow was a raw-looking half rural, half urban oasis of gaunt rectangular barrack buildings, in a bright red brick that was too recent to be mellowed or weathered, and set amid a small town of mean grey houses and beershops. The night was crisp, snow flurries had ceased and frost gilded the countryside and rooftops. Moonlight forced Private John Wright of the 16th the Queens Lancers to keep to the shadowed side of the road as, eyes peeled for the provost picquets, he crept back to the barracks. He was cautiously skirting the naptha-flare garishness of the 'Gay Hussar' when, through its open doors lurched a big man wearing the tall, flat-topped lance-cap and gilt-rayed front plate of the 16th Lancers. At once Wright saw it was Paddy Riley from his Troop who slept four beds down.. Drunk as a lord Paddy had stained and torn his scarlet jacket. He was blue faced with a slashed flap on his sleeves. Mud covered the blue, double-striped overalls, and his scuffed boots would need hours of boning to regain polished perfection.

'Paddy! For Christ's sake ... yer in a bloody awful mess!'

The Irishman shook off his hand.

'Le' me 'lone ... got a Chrissmuss prisint for li'l Arabella ... lorst me money but got a prisint ... li'l 'Bella ... used to set 'er on me knee whin she wor a bibby ... why din't I 'ave a kid like 'er?' He was quietly blubbering.

'Come on, Paddy ... I'll git yer back to barracks ... but fer Gawd's sake keep quiet!'

Wright supported him, Paddy's feet dragging in the muddy pot-holes of the shadowy side-streets and alleys. The drunken Irishman continued to mumble about Arabella, and Wright realised he would have to work hard to make himself presentable for tomorrow morning's Church Parade.

'I got a prisint fer li'l Arabell ... no money ... but me most precious possession ... goin' ter give 'er me most precious possession!'

They were stumbling along towards the foot of the iron staircase up to the barrackroom above the stable when suddenly Wright lost him. Wright unsuccessfully searched the area before tip-toeing onto the iron balcony running around the building. Then he jumped at bumping into a white-shifted girl, one of the married families children going to the urine-tub at the end of the balcony. Recognising her as the Snaggs' girl he wondered what Paddy was going to give her for a present.

Creeping into the low ceilinged room his nostrils wrinkled at the stench of sweat and dirty clothes, the pervading smell of generations of steaming meals blending with the penetrating acrid reek from the stable below. His eyes adjusted to the utter blackness and he peered unavailingy around for Paddy before sidling over to his iron-slatted cot and canvas covered, straw palliasse.

Over the subdued night noises young John Wright became aware of a disturbance on the balcony outside; a man's gruff insistent mumbling and a shrill child's voice, punctuated by a stifled scream. Christ, Paddy's bumped into the girl in the shift, he thought. The noise became a summons triumphing over sleep. Heavy heads lifted from hard pillows and querulous voices enquired what the fucking-hell was going on? A lucifer scratched to provide a momentary flare followed by a universal glow from a tallow-dip. White blob-faces peered and strained through the gloom and shadows flickered over the walls and ceiling.

' 'Oo screamed? I 'eard a scream!'

Then the shrill sleep-drugged wail of a woman rose high in the air. 'Bella! Where are yer? Arfer ... Arabella's gorn ... she ain't in 'er bed!'

Blobs of light flickered and danced as men wearily left their beds to funnel towards the door. Taking advantage of being dressed and not having to surface from sleep, John Wright darted ahead of the crowd. At the far end of the balcony by the urine-tub, the moonlight revealed Paddy Riley, overall-front gaping open to expose his flaccid penis. Pinned against the wall, cringed the pathetically skinny body of Arabella Snaggs, the expression on her pinched face, framed by lank hair, indicated surprise more than fear. Transfixed by the sight, a half-circle of open mouthed soldiers piled up behind Wright. On becoming aware of them, Paddy froze, flickering his dull eyes over them.

The tableau was brought to life by a bedraggled woman in a tattered shift, grubby fingers holding it primly together at the neck. In her wake fussed a small soldier wearing only a shirt, thinning hair and pallid bow-legs projecting at either end. From the woman's thin lined face circled by matted mouse-coloured hair, her lustreless eyes stared wildly at the scene.

'Arabella! Yer dirty li'l bitch ... wot yer doin' wiv that drunken sod?'

The girl's eyes rolled helplessly upward. 'Nuffin Ma ... I were goin' ter the tub whin 'e grabbed me ... said 'e wanted ter give me a Chistmus present ...'

'I know the sort o' bleedin' present 'e wanted ter give yer ... the filthy berk!' Her face pushed close to the girl's. 'Did 'e git up yer ... tell me the troof now?'

'No, Ma! Nuffin' like that! 'E din't touch me ... said 'e wanted to give me a present ... all 'e 'ad ... 'is most precious possession.'

Mrs Snaggs flung her hands into the air and screamed. 'O me pore child ... me poor darlin'. Yer dirty great bleeder Paddy Riley ... git away from me child! Go on ... git away!'

She showered blows onto the drunken Irishman. Dazedly he shielded his face with one arm, trying to fend her off. Only John Wright heard, or understood, his throaty mumbling.

'No ... no ... wanted ter give little Arabella a prisint ... got no money ... nuffin ter give ... onny me most precious possession ... couldn't really give it to 'er ... jist wanted 'er to see .. an know wot I were givin' 'er!'

A great light dawned on John Wright, he swung round to the indignant parents. 'Corp'ral ... Mrs Snaggs ... don't yer see? Paddy din't want ter hurt her ... but 'e wanted ter give 'er a Christmas present ... onny 'e didn't 'ave nuffin' ... so he wanted 'er to know 'e'd offered his most precious possession ... 'is ... 'is ... well, you know what I mean.'

Corporal Snaggs drew himself up. 'You shut yer filthy mouf, Private Wright ... in the presence o' ladies.' He screeched at the gaping men. 'Come on ... don' jist stand there ... get 'im orf 'er!'

Men surged forward, scrambling and getting in each other's way to grasp the big Irishman. Dazed by events he offered little resistance. Held up by four men, legs buckling under him and his head lolling forward, still he mumbled on the same theme. Rushing forward, Mrs Snaggs vigorously enfolded her daughter in her arms, affecting the girl more than what had gone before. She struggled to free herself.

' 'Old 'ard, Ma! I'm orlright ... lemme go, Ma! Pa, git Ma orf me.'

Releasing her daughter, the woman glared balefully at Paddy, being dragged into the barrackroom, then she followed, away from the cold night. Arabella sidled off, out of sight behind the blanket. Inside the dark shadowy room, Mrs Snaggs swung round on her husband fiercely, waving a demanding arm at the pinioned man.

'Wot you goin' ter do abart 'im? Let 'im go to bed an' sleep it orf 'cos 'e's one o' yer mates? There ain't a woman safe in the room wiv 'im around ...say 'e 'ad a go at li'l Missis Roberts down at the other end ... she's eight months gorn ... summats gotta be done.'

Corporal Snaggs puffed out his cheeks. 'I'll put 'im on a charge ... that's wot I'll do ... first thing inna mornin'.'

He recoiled at his wife's scornful screech.

'Onna charge! That ain't goin' to stop 'im ... decent wimmin won't be safe whenever 'e gets a skinful ... it's gotta be more'n that.' She stared thoughtfully at Paddy Riley, the her sallow face blazed with inspiration. 'Cut it orf! That's the bleedin' answer ... if 'e ain't got one then 'e can't give no trouble ... cut it orf I say.'

For a moment no one tumbled to what she meant, her husband stared at her in bewilderment.

'Cut wot orf, me dear?'

'Wot d'ye think, yer stupid berk? 'Is pecker o' course.'

' 'Is pecker! Cut orf 'is pecker? Yer can't do that to a bloke!'

Mrs Snaggs exploded into a fit of hysteria, crying screaming and cursing. Her eyes blazing and arms waving in the flickering light reminded John Wright of a picture of a witch he had once seen. He flooded over in a great wave of sympathy for Corporal Snaggs. He felt sorry for Paddy Riley too. Men looked around uneasily.

'Corp'l ... few Gawd's sake keep 'er quiet ... we'll 'ave 'arf the Rig'mint 'ere inna minit!'

Wailing and screaming, the woman lurched around the room, pulling at beds and lifting locker lids.

'Where's a knife ... give me a bloody knife an' I'll do it meself ... if ye're all too bloody scared ... not men enuff ter pertect yer wimmin ... where's a knife?'

The Corporal gazed helplessly at men uneasily shuffling their feet, looking from one to another, everywhere except at Paddy Riley, each blanching as he put himself in the prisoner's shoes. Suddenly, to everyone's astonishment, the big Irishman spoke, louder and more coherently than at any time. The lolling head rose and his slitted eyes opened to flit from face to face, nodding at mates as he recognised them.

'Charlie ... Tom ... Mick ... I bin silly ... wint abart it the wrong way ... she ... ole Muvver Snaggs ... is roight ... it's gotta come orf 'cos uvverwise I can't give it ter li'l Arabella, can I? Can't give a prisint an' keep it too ... can yer? Cut it orf I say!'

Mrs Snaggs roared triumphantly. 'There! Yer see! Even 'im ... filthy bleeder as 'e is ... even 'e knows it's the best fing ter do.'

Private John Wright raised his hand in protest.

'No! That ain't wot 'e means at all. 'E's too far gorn to talk sense ... but orl 'e wanted to do was to give Arabella a Christmas present ... an' 'e didn't 'ave nuffin' o' value ... nuffin that is 'cept the only fing 'e got any pleasure out of ... 'is bloody pecker ... an' now 'e thinks 'e can give it like a proper present.' He swung round on the Corporal's wife. 'Wot yer goin' ter do wiv it ... pack it in a little decorated box an' give it ter yer daughter? Talk sense. Let the poor sod sleep it orf and we'll talk about it in the morning when we're all more sensible.'

Transfixed in fascination on their charpoys, the entire Sub-Section were squeamishly contemplating the crude surgical operation, wondering how you went about it and afterwards. 'Mister' Wright's voice rose. 'An do ye know wot 'appened then ... the bloody woman attacked me ... scratchin' an' bitin' ... knocked me back right across the room ... like I said ... that cow put me right orf ever gettin' wed!'

After her explosion of fury, Mrs Snaggs darted away behind the blanket. On her return she brandished a open cut-throat razor. The wild swipes of the gleaming blade that men hastily recoiled from were absorbingly followed by the eyes of Paddy Riley. The woman advanced on the Irishman. Loosely held by two men he tried to pull his arms free, hands moving down towards his trouser front. From her small tight mouth, she muttered persuasively. 'Come on now Paddy ... it's the best thing ... ye know it is.'

Coming to their senses, repelled men protested on all sides in a chorus that brought Mrs Snaggs to a halt. The Corporal pushed forward, shaking his head. 'I ain't 'aving me wife doin' fings like this ... if its got to be done ... then I'll do it meself.'

'Ye can't do that Corp'ral ... 'e'll bleed ter bloody death ... yer'll find yerself on an 'anging parade!'

Corporal Snaggs pondered then jerked his head decisively. 'Adams! Go down to the stables an' see if the forge-fire can be worked up ... then put one o' them irons for firing 'orses in it ... the rest o' ye ... tie 'is 'ands behind 'im ... an' tie 'is feet while yer abart it .... 'e's a strong bleeder an' no mistake.'

Paddy looked round unsteadily then began to struggle. 'I'll not be branded ... yer can't burn me yer bastards ... jist 'cos I want ter give the gal a Christmas prisint! Yer aren't goin' ter brand ole Paddy Riley, are ye lads?'

Struggling violently, he threw himself and the men holding him back and forth cross the room, falling on a cot that collapsed under their weight and causing its owner to curse in protest. It was an uneven contest and soon he was under control with ropes on his wrists and ankles. He ceased to struggle and lay back, now and then raising his head to talk to the men around him. Astonishingly he was back on urging his own pecker to be cut off, apparently forgetting the cauterising to follow. The Corporal, now in full stride, was issuing orders as though for some military operation.

'Listen lads! Git 'im over 'ere ... to the table ... an' 'old 'im tight! When Adams gits back wiv the firing-iron I'll do wot 'as to be done ... and then we'll cort'rize it wiv the hot iron ... ter stop the bleedin'. Private Pegler ... git a blanket and lay it on the table ... don' want blood all over the place, do we? A,' Wright ... git some rags ... summat we can use fer bandages!

Wright shook his head. 'Sorry, Corporal ... you can't order me on this ... do yer own dirty work.'

Another man nodded. ' 'E's right Corp ... ye might kill 'im ... an' we'll orl be in the shit wiv ye.'

'Say 'e bleeds ter death Corp'ral?'

Snaggs shook his head impatiently. 'Corse 'e won't bleed ter death ... 'ere ... do any of yer recall Burrows at Aliwal ... 'e 'ad 'is pecker shot orf by a bloody Sikh wiv a blunderbuss full o' nails ... we got that stopped ... an' 'e were orlright arterwards, weren't 'e?'

' 'Cept that 'e did fer 'isself wiv a rope in the jakes nine months later!'

'Well ... 'e were a different sorta bloke to Paddy 'ere ... 'e'll be orlright ... in a few days.'

Feet clattered up the iron steps outside and Private Adams burst in waving a glowing, white-hot firing-iron, men in his path hastily moved away. Carefully taking the open razor from his wife's unresisting hands, Snaggs pushed her aside. 'Go on woman ... get away from 'ere ... go an' see if 'Bella's orlright.'

Reluctantly she moved aside, men elbowing her away none too gently. The Corporal moved forward. 'Come on now ... git 'im over 'ere ... afore the bleedin' iron gits cold.'

On seeing the hot iron, Paddy began struggling again, cursing and shouting, but was dragged by sheer brute force to the board erected on its trestles in the centre of the room. Men crowded around, some standing on cots to see over the shoulders of those in front. Others made no attempt to see what was happening, sitting on their beds with their heads turned away and their eyes closed; one man put his fingers in his ears. The struggling ceased and everyone tensed, then Paddy shouted, his bull roar echoing round the low room.

'Go on ... do it ... an' give it ter li'l Arabella! Ahhhhh! Fer the love o' God! AHhhhAhha! Christ!'

Tendrils of smoke slowly wafted upwards and the sweet sickly smell of singed flesh hung on the air. Pent up breath was released in a blustering explosion; heads turned away and retching men pushed blindly through the crowd.

'Come on! Where's them bandages? Git 'em on 'im!'

Half-conscious and moaning, Paddy was lowered onto his cot on his back, blankets were laid gently over him. Mrs Snaggs, emerging from behind the blanket, her face flushed with virtue and triumph, led her husband back to their curtained-off home in the corner of the barrackroom. Awakened by Paddy's screams, Arabella and her young brother were roughly told to go to sleep.

The victim tossed and turned and moaned and groaned for the night, until his comrades, silent with awe and shame at their own daring, shouted at him.

'For Gawd's sake ... shuddup!'

'Paddy ... will ye let us git some kip?'

'Wish we'd cut 'is bleedin' throat ... 'e wouldn't make so much noise!'

At the conclusion of 'Mister' Wright's tale, the room lay silent, savouring the event and conjuring up visions of the aftermath, which had to be learned. The story could not be left as there were vital facts which the men wanted to know.

'Wot 'appened to 'im afterwards, Wrightie?'

' Oo' ... Paddy Riley? Well, next morning 'e got 'is breakfust in bed ... the lads brought it in to 'im. Corse, 'e weren't fit to go on Church Parade but ... being one o' your lot Kinrade, it were a smaller parade an' the lads covered for 'im. As I recall it, 'e ate a decent Christmas Dinner but mornin' after the Corporal made 'im go sick.'

'Wot the 'ell did he tell the Surgeon?'

'Funny that ... 'cos when Paddy woke up, sober on Christmas morning ... 'e din't remember nuffin wot 'ad 'appened! Seeing this ... Corp'ral Snaggs an' the lads ... me 'specially ... come up with the story that Paddy 'ad stumbled inter the barrackroom night afore ... wiv 'is pecker gorn ... an' we saved 'is bloomin' life by cort'rizing it wiv the firing-iron. We all felt right bastards I kin tell yer.'

So Paddy told the Surgeon that when he was spark out drunk some of the town lads, with whom a long-running feud existed, had chopped him up. The Surgeon told the Commanding Officer, who told the Garrison Commander, and an official complaint was made to the Mayor of Hounslow. They had the Peelers chasing round for weeks trying to find the men who had cut up one of Her Majesty's soldiers.

'Wot abart Paddy? How did 'e git on abart shaggin'?'

'Mister' Wright laughed. 'It were a queer old business orl round. 'Parently Corp'ral Snaggs didn't do a very good job ... onny took the top orf ... and in a few weeks Paddy were as good as new ... in fact, reckoned shaggin' were better wiv 'is new pecker ... certainly different anyroad.'

True to form, Birch asked what everyone was wondering. 'Wot 'appened to it ... the bit they cut orf? ... Didn't give it ter the girl did they?'

'Christ no! It gort lost ... they couldn't find it ... searched high an' low ... thank Gawd none on 'em saw me push it wiv me toe ... down a rat hole in the floor.'

Big Sanny, who had thoroughly enjoyed the yarn, whispered to his mucker. 'Ding Dong ... what di' they gi' big Paddy for a Christmas present?'

'A new pecker, ye ken.'

'Whit are ye gi'ing me for Christmas Ding Dong?'

'Och ... gi' away wi' ye ... we onny jist 'ad a Christmas.'

Everyone lay back satisfied, aware of a certain sense of relief that this most dreaded of wounds was not always the end of everything. Private Saville put in the final question. ' 'Mister' ... what happened to the girl ... Arabella?'

'Oh ... her ... she died following year o' typhoid.'

XIX

All in the 5th Sub-Section in hut 5 Aliwal Lines had seen active service save three - Privates Hebdon, Kinrade and Saville - who had arrived with the last draft in the previous year, too late to go out when the Regiment was part of General Wilde's column in the Black Mountain expedition of 1867. The Sergeant had no worries over the old soldiers, who had not missed much in the way of Indian Wars over the past twenty years, hearing bullets whistle past their ears and marching until one foot could hardly be placed in front of the other, they'd be alright. He was more concerned with the three who knew none of this, wondering whether they would be reliable under fire or break and endanger the rest of the lads. Private Kinrade, at 27 the oldest of the three, a mature and highly intelligent, smouldering trouble-maker was obviously only in the British Army to dodge something worse. He might well be crafty and courageous when it came to looking after himself but how much would he do to benefit his comrades or the Regiment? He'd need watching. Private Saville, twenty-one, and, bar Boy Farley, the youngest man in the room, was well educated and intelligent. The Sergeant had known many officers resembling him, with pride, tradition and breeding to keep them up to scratch. However, this lad was wretchedly unhappy and nursing a mighty sense of grievance; his sensitive unsuitability for the role of a private soldier made him inadequate in a military sense. It was finely balanced whether in action he would degenerate into a cringing coward or bravely do his duty. The Sergeant had his doubts, he hoped he was wrong.

He was no surer of the third young soldier, twenty-three year old Private Hebdon, encountered on his very first night in charge of the hut when he reeled into the Sergeant's life as a drunken trouble-maker. A pleasant looking, open-faced country lad, it was difficult to know whether he was one of the guileless sheep or the half-crazy fox lurking around the fringe of the flock. Usually these cottage background boys, brought up strictly by principled parents, made good dependable obedient soldiers, stolid under fire and always ready to do their duty, however unpleasant it might be. But, with the passing of time, the Sergeant began to look askance at the irresponsible, easily led young man. His Puckish sense of humour coupled with a total inability to hold his drink frequently landed him in trouble. Then he heard of an incredible 5th Sub-Section 'domestic' affair in the previous year, a drunken escapade leading to a court-martial had landed Private Hebdon 100 lashes ... laid-on, twenty-five strokes each, as hard as can be at full length of the arm ... by four stalwart young drummers.

A sickened onlooker and never a wretched victim, the Sergeant well knew how these affairs went, having seen enough of them in his time. The entire Regiment, including all officers, the Commanding Officer, the Adjutant and the Regimental Surgeon, were ordered on to ceremonial parade to witness the punishment, forming a three-sided, hollow square facing the brick wall of a barrack building. After interminable minutes standing rigid and staring at nothing, the silence of the hot morning was broken by the the marching feet of a party of rifle-bearing soldiers in parade uniform, led by the Regimental Sergeant-Major who carried a drawn sword. In the midst of this party marched the prisoner, wearing trousers and boots, naked from the waist up, his sun-blackened arms and neck contrasting strangely with his pallid body. In the rear marched four drummers, without drums or bugles. One carrying the many thonged lash with which he would administer the first twenty-five strokes before handing over to a fresher man. Deceptively flimsy in appearance, the lash weighed only three and an eighth ounces. It had a nineteen and a quarter inches stock and its nine thongs, each twenty-four and a half inches in length and knotted nine times, were capable of tearing flesh in ribbons from a man's back.

The escort and the prisoner came smartly up to attention in the centre of the open space. The Commanding Officer nodded to the Adjutant who stepped forward and read out the sentence of the Court. A brief pause, then the harsh, clipped bellow of the Sergeant-Major ordered the party forward to the wall, where the prisoners wrists were lashed to a pair of iron rings high in the brickwork. The escort turned and marched away, leaving the prisoner spread-eagled, his bare back starkly contrasting with the rough red bricks. On the ground by his side was a pail of water and a folded towel.

The first drummer stepped forward, holding the lash's stock in his right hand with the thongs laying lightly across his left palm. He set himself and waited. There was no sound save the distant cawing of birds as the audience and performers of the grim tableau stood tense and motionless, their hearts racing within them. Then, despite knowing what would come next, all were startled by the harsh staccato call that fractured the stillness.

'One!'

There was a hissing blast of wind and, as the thongs landed across the prisoner's back, a slapping thud echoed hollowly from the walls of the surrounding buildings. The prisoner let out an explosive grunt, broken by the need to gulp in air. His bare-backed writhing body pressed hard against the rough stone wall, cringing from the blow he knew was to follow.

'Two!'

The drummer's shirt-sleeved arm slowly rose, then flashed down. Again, a hiss and a spongy slap as the lash bit home. Again the prisoner grunted and gasped, dragging on his bound wrists. Mercilessly and monotonously the RSM called the number of strokes, the lash falling in time with the calls. After the first three or four lashes, weals began to score the soft flesh in an irregular scarlet pattern, until it resembled a map of red ridges.

Picturing the scene caused the Sergeant to involuntarily flex his shoulders and the skin crawled across his back. Usually he managed to tear his eyes from the scene, turning them on dusty ground at his feet. But he could not block his ears.

In the guardroom, sympathetic Regimental Police had told the prisoner it was a point of honour not to cry out under the lash, and they had given him a 'piggy' - a small oblong of leather that looked as though a dog had chewed on it.

'This 'ere's a piggy ... yer grips it between yer teeth ... 'ard ... an' yer won't cry out. Won't bite yer tongue neither ... ole Josh Budd bit 'is tongue clean in 'arf ... an' spat it out onna floor ... din'e?'

The twenty-fifth stroke was called and, after a momentary torturing break, the fresh arm of the second young drummer began plying the lash. There was no question of easing up. Any noticeable lack of effort could result in a later beating from the drum-major, or hours of pack-drill. So the drummers laid into the task with all their strength, faces free of any signs of lust or emotion as they performed their duty to the best of their ability, using the skill and rhythm of a practised butcher handling a carcass on the block. The prisoner's back was turning the colour of raw liver, and on the twenty-sixth stroke he was unable to choke back a shriek. The piggy flew from his mouth and he twisted frantically on his bound wrists. Now the calls and strokes were more widely spaced as the drummer had to run the thongs through a rag after each stroke to prevent them sticking together.

Going into the second fifty strokes, the prisoner seemed to have lost consciousness, his body was hanging limply from the rings and swaying from the force of the blows as his feet weakly gyrated. He resembled one of the straw dummies they used for bayonet practice. Suddenly the surgeon stepped forward and threw his hand in the air. The third drummer paused with the lash uplifted over his shoulder. After listening to the prisoner's heart through a trumpet stethoscope and fumbling at the bound wrists in search of a pulse, the surgeon stood back and nodded to the drummer. When a prisoner showed signs of collapse he was examined and, if necessary, brought to with restoratives. Then the punishment was either resumed or stopped according to the judgement of the surgeon. The Sergeant could only recall one case where the punishment was halted but, in fairness to the surgeons, it had to be said that they allowed the punishment to carry on rather than subject the victim to the horror of being brought out a second time, when his back had partially healed, for the remainder of the sentence to be inflicted.

The drummer ran his tongue over his lips and brought the thongs down again. The grim sight, the sound of the lash landing on the pulped flesh, the sickly smell of blood pervading the still, hot air, all brought a tight feeling to the Sergeant's chest. Along with the majority of the watching men, subconsciously he was identifying himself with the prisoner in an uncomfortable blend of discomfort and, as each blow landed, relief at not being the victim. There had been occasions when he had felt choked, as though his breath was building up inside and would cause him to burst. He had never retched and been told by nearby NCO's to be quiet, nor had he slumped to the ground like weaker men who would later be charged and punished for being 'Idle on Parade'. The first time had been the worst when, as a young soldier he had been standing in the second rank trying to avoid the appalling sight by fixing his gaze on the carbuncle-spotted neck of the man in front. But he could not shut out the sounds and, on beginning to sway he heard as if a long way away, the muttered growl of the man on his right. 'Look at yer feet ... only ten more.'

Also he remembered the last time, when the prisoner was a popular man whom his comrades felt was being unjustly treated, given too severe a punishment for a minor jape committed when in drink. As the punishment proceeded an audible low whispering arose from across the rigid ranks, a murmured protest through clenched teeth and unopened lips. Despite a certain sympathy that his rank should have prevented, he quickly jumped on his Sub-Section, brusquely ordering them to be quiet.

He had never actually noted how long - in minutes or hours - a flogging took to run its course. Usually it seemed timeless, despite the mutual yearnings of nearly a thousand men for it to end as quickly as possible. Five ... four ... three ... two ... the last stroke of the hundred, or however many it was, fell upon the dangling puppet. One of the drummers stepped forward and flung the pail of tepid water on the prisoner's bloody back. Another cut him down and the two of them caught him under the arm-pits to take his dead weight. Not all men collapsed in this way, some took the punishment stoically, straightening up painfully when released, gingerly flexing their backs and then marching with a certain defiant jauntiness to the hospital. The Sergeant imagined somehow that Private Kinrade would be of this type, if and when he found himself tied to the rings.

With the moral lesson concluded, the Commanding Officer stepped forward, his husky, aristocratic bellow unemotionally filled the air. 'Her Majesty's Hundred and Thirty First Regiment of Foot ... form.'

His commands were taken up in chorus by Company Commanders, Half-Company Commanders, Section and Sub-Section NCO's. The hollow square broke up and the Regiment wheeled into a column to march briskly past the limp body, lying in the dust at the foot of the flogging rings. The officers sauntered off to do justice to the eggs, chops and kidneys awaiting them in silver chafing dishes on the long Mess sideboard. In the barrackrooms the men were hurried through their sparse breakfast, then jollied into full marching order before being chased out into the Lines for the Route-march - always ordered to take men's minds of a flogging. With a full band at the head lustily beating out 'The Dandy 'O!" , the Regiment set off on a march so exhausting as to completely achieve its object of purging fretting minds of the events of the morning.

The Sergeant hated the lash. He strongly objected to such corporal punishment, for not only did it smash a man's body but also his self-respect. The lash was awarded on a grossly exaggerated scale for relatively trivial misdemeanours and varied considerably according to the character and whim of the Commanding Officer or Officers forming the Court. He knew he was in a minority in this, most NCO's and the majority of soldiers accepted that their right to award corporal punishment was the symbol of traditional authority, and in the Army tradition reigned supreme. One night in the Mess he had reinforced the Sergeant-Major's opinion that Sergeant Oakley had a soft streak by his assertion that what might kill the officer had to be lightly borne by the man in the ranks. It was forcefully rejected by 'Robbo' Robinson VC, who echoed the words of his hero, the Duke of Wellington.

' ... no great effect ... produced on British soldiers by anything but the fear of immediate corporal punishment ...' He then added ' ... nothing but the lash can bring the British soldier to heel ... he is of course clay ... he understands it ... he accepts it.'

The Sergeant wondered if Robbo had ever felt the bite of knotted thongs across his huge muscular back. Perhaps he had got to the rank by keeping his nose clean, or maybe an early taste of the lash had turned him into what he was. Still, it seemed odd that in 1836 - about the same time as the slave trade was outlawed in the British Empire - a Royal Commission should only feel able to rule that the soldiers who defended the Empire be limited to a sentence of two hundred lashes by a General Court and one hundred by a Regimental Court. The Sergeant was not to know it would be another thirteen years, in 1881, before Parliament felt able to abolish the right to flog the British soldier.

Harsh discipline and barrackroom squalor had long ago transformed Private Ted Hebdon from the happy-go-lucky country lad, trapped into the Army at a Norwich fair two years earlier, his ordeal on the ring had set the seal on his metamorphosis. He looked no different, only those he lived amongst noticed the harder eyes and the twist of the mouth, marking the commonplace shrewd and shifty soldier. With his shirt off, Hebdon was hall-marked by the web of scar-tissue he would carry to the grave. Young and strong, his body healed quickly, but his mind had been taken over by a burning, deep-seated desire for vengeance. Not at those who charged, tried and sentenced him, but on the four young drummers who so effectively wielded the lash. With simple barrackroom logic he reasoned that by standards of military justice he had a fair trial, by officers whom he could not bash up anyway. Someone had to pay for the hundred shattering blows he had received, who more suitable than those who actually laid them on.

As the Sergeant heard it, the affair began in a commonplace sort of way when a drummer was found, badly beaten with his right - and whip-yielding - hand mangled, as though repeatedly stamped on by a heavy boot. Found amid the filth of a bazaar alley where he should not have been anyway. Not an unusual occurrence, it provoked the customary reprisal when a gang of his mates descended on the area and savagely exacted revenge by beating up the first natives they encountered and wrecking a few shop fronts. Then a second drummer was attacked on the outskirts of the cantonment, his skull battered and the fingers of his right hand pulped by a bloody rock left lying by his side.

Another vengeful mob was gathering to descend on the bazaar when it dawned on cooler heads that there was a similarity too coincidental to blame upon the natives; before hospital records brought official action they decided to do some detective work of their own. It did not need a Bow Street Runner's training or experience to see such significant features as two men of a flogging party having their flogging hands mutilated, who more likely to do such a thing than one who had suffered at those hands? Narrowed down dramatically, the finger of suspicion pointed at one or more of half a dozen men flogged during the past three months. Drummers wielded the lash by rota and records showed both the injured to have officiated at the punishment of three of the six men. That left Private O'Cassidy of 'A' Company, Private Loosely of 'G' Company and Private Hebdon of 'C' Company, all flogged by the two men assaulted plus any two other drummers from the four. So, an attack on a third drummer would reveal three-quarters of the party and almost certainly pinpoint which man they had flogged.

The denizens of the 5th Sub-Section's bungalow did not need to tax their brains on anything like the same scale to find the culprit, in fact they were two moves ahead of the avengers in knowing who it was. As Mister Wright so aptly put it, "... it was that gormless sod Hebdon ... who's going to drop us all in the shit and give the sub-section a bad name." It was not that they had sympathy or held any brief for the bloody drummers. No one was happy about those cheeky young sods laying stripes on the shoulders of men who had got service in before the had a hole in their arse. In fact, there were those who could hardly wait to see what happened when a drummer got himself a sentence to a lashing and his mates had to lay it on.

Anyway, Hebdon blandly denied all knowledge of the attacks, claiming an alibi for each occasion. But he lacked the guile to conceal from shrewd, cynical customers like Wright and Kinrade, his smug self-satisfaction. A special meeting was held in the jakes, where Hebdon, long since shorn of sympathy, was warned of the dire consequences of his reckless actions by comrades who could think of no way to stop him yet could not give him away.

Immediately the bugle sounded, Hebdon rushed from the bungalow, without cleaning up or putting on freshly dhobied clothing for the Canteen. Then Boy Farley saw him prowling out towards the nullah at the back of the camp, pick-handle in hand. Heads shook and voices prophesied trouble. They were not to be disappointed. Just before Lights Out a sweat-blackened, blood bespeckled and exhausted Hebdon burst through the top tatty-curtain. He had laid in wait for the drummer and managed to belt him across the swede with the pick-handle, only to be pursued by a big escort of the boy's mates who had followed close behind. He had made a run for it but they might have recognised him.

Save for Sergeant Digges, luckily still in the Mess, everyone was back in the room and most of them felt he deserved anything he got; what would happen to military justice if everyone carried on like this after a flogging? However, something had to be done, they couldn't let the drummers and their mates crow over the 5th Sub-Section. Early dragged off his shirt, Boy Farley rushed out to the ablutions and soaked it in water while Hebdon's soiled clothes were spirited away. Shivering in the wet shirt, Hebdon was pushed down onto his charpoy and covered with a pile of rugs hastily picked up from the surrounding beds. Yank Early leaned over him. 'Shiver, you son of a bitch ... and save your lousy skin!'

Pursuers clattered over the wooden verandah and burst into the room, halting in a glowering body and swinging clubs and staves. Men rose from their beds to repel the invasion as their leader gruffly asked for the bloke what had been flogged last month. Taking his time and putting on a tunic to show the NCO's stripe, Lance-Corporal Mockford padded down the room to face the intruders, men forming behind him in a compact body. He nodded his head at the middle bed behind the rifle-rack.

'There 'e is ... in bed ... bin there all day ... since comin' off parade ... shiverin' 'isself away with a fever.'

Astonished, the invaders looked at each other. Their leader asked permission to go to the bed, permission was granted and everyone moved up the room to crowd into the area which now resembled a glade in a forest of tall trees. The low charpoy and its humped blankets were pulsating with such real and simulated shivering that Yank Early feared he was over-doing it. Pulling back the blankets the lance-corporal revealed a sweat-beaded face with tightly closed eyes and tremulously quivering lips. Not entirely convinced, the baffled mob reluctantly drifted down the room and out into the night. There they had the bright idea of looking up the second of the lately flogged men and, finding him in Company Lines sitting on verandah steps, vomiting and showing signs of wear after a Canteen brawl, they gave him a good hiding. Thus, almost everyone went to bed happy.

Back in bungalow 5 Aliwal Lines, Hebdon was hauled from his bed and solemnly warned that he would be given the worst cobbing in military history if there was any more trouble. Then, in the same ingenious spirit which had invented his fever, it was decided to cure him of it. Working in shifts throughout the night everyone in the room took turns at soaking Hebdon with water, beating him with bundles of twigs, forcing nauseating purgatives down his throat and walking him up and down until he was exhausted. No more drummers were attacked and in a few days everyone had forgotten the whole business: that is except Private Hebdon who, for the rest of his life, involuntarily shuddered whenever he touched his scarred shoulders or saw his back in a mirror.

XX

In Victorian India, death by battle or disease perpetually dogged the heels of the British soldier. And the soldier failed to accept that fact simply because, throughout the ages, soldiers have always been aware of death lurking near at hand but invariably believed the bony finger would point at the man beside them, in the rear rank, in the next bed, never in their direction.

When Private Wright recounted the stirring legend of his old Regiment the 16th Lancers at the Battle of Aliwal in 1846, he was talking vain-gloriously of the way of men at war, their passing being incidental. It was a colourful story of a scarlet jacketed Lancer regiment, red and white pennons fluttering on lowered lances as they charged a battery of Sikh guns, going through them into formed squares of crack Regular Infantry. On a great grey charger, close behind Major Rowland Smythe, the Commanding Officer, rode handsome Sergeant Harry Newsome. With a ringing shout of "Hullo boys! Here goes for death or a commission!" he forced his horse right over the front rank of kneeling men, bayonets bristling above them like quills on a porcupines back. Spurring the reluctant horse forward, Newsome leaned down and grabbed an enemy standard before being pierced by nineteen blades. Falling within the square, he was immediately despatched by razor sharp tulwars. Then others pushed into the gap he had made and desperate fighting broke the Sikh formation, sending them streaming away in disorder. Close by, the gigantic Lance-Corporal Mowbray, the best lancer and swordsman in the Regiment, fought to the death surrounded by the enemy. He was found after the battle lying on blood-soaked ground amid a circle of dead Sikhs, his splintered lance and broken sword by his side.

Growls of respect echoed round the room. As foot soldiers they appreciated the magnitude of cavalry breaking formed squares of steady Regular Infantry, even if they weren't white - although they knew the Sikhs to be the best native soldiers in the country. It was comforting to believe, as every man did, that even the 16th Lancers would not be able to break HM's Regiment of Foot.

Private Owen Davies, who had fought in both Sikh Wars, mused aloud. 'Corse, no-one wants to die, but if your name an' number come up then it's best it happens like that ... it don't always! I remember we had this lad join us straight out from England ... he were the only man I ever met who enlisted for fighting an' glory ... talked of nothing else ... always asking old soldiers what battles were like ... spent hours on his own practising bayonet fighting ... couldn't wait to get into action and smell powder. Perfectly happy to die gloriously!'

'What happened to him Taff?'

'Oh, he died alright ... in the Regimental hospital, with nary a ball, bayonet, bullet, spear nor sword within a mile. Took 'im about fourteen hours to snuff it ... on a bed awash with sick, shit an' sweat ... convulsed with cramps, half-conscious an' wasting away before yer very eyes!'

Men lay silent, digesting this all too familiar story. In his cubicle the Sergeant winced in recollection of watching his wife and child dying under similar conditions.

'Funny really ... I though about 'im a lot afterwards ... don't usually think o' mates much after they've gone, do yer?'

Another old soldier, Bandsman Charlie Mort, recalled.

'A bloke inna 29th ... Ezra Stevens ... see 'im clear as tho' it were yesterday ... had been a schoolmaster afore he got into trouble an' 'listed. At that time ... it were '49 ... I know that 'cos he were killed at Chillianwallah ... there were only two blokes in our barrackroom that could read an' he were one of 'em. He had a book of his own ... Pickwick Papers it were called ... by Charles Dickens ... an' every chance 'e got 'e'd read it to us ... in barrackrooms an' by light of campfires. Lads loved it, 'cos it were different ... in them days there was only about twenty-eight books allowed into barracks, all approved by a bench of bishops so you can guess wot they were like! Anyway, Ezra hurt his foot an' fell behind the Reg'mint when it went forward ... an' he got cut up by Ghoorchurras ... bleedin' Sikh Irregular cavalry ... when we found 'im they'd looted his knapsack an' ... Gawd knows why ... the stupid sods had taken Pickwick Papers. We looked everywhere for that bloody book ... never found it ... so we heard no more of ole Pickwick an' his mates, that Fat Boy ... and the Christmas party at Dingley Dell ... recall it all well ... and recall ole Ezra ... silly bugger for taking the book into action.'

Private Valentine Finnigan stirred restlessly. 'Sure, an' we 'ad a bloke inna 98th oo saw 'is mate killed ... an' wouldn't believe it ... kept a'talkin' to a bleedin' bit wot ad gotten chopped orf ... calling it Micky!'

'Tell us about it Paddy ... ain't 'ad a tale from you yet.'

However, it was time to set up the tables for dinner so Private Finnigan, who wished he'd kept his mouth shut, reluctantly promised to tell his tale the next morning. Not one of your talkative men, he sweated on it the rest of the day and all night, hoping they'd forget. But they didn't, and the next morning, with breakfast cleared away, they all settled down to temporarily replace the stifling heat, voracious insects and current miseries with another nostalgic existence as colourful as the tellers articulacy allowed.

'Well, there were these two mates, see ... Sean Donovan an' Micky Flanagan.'

Born in Dundalk, Sean and Micky fought and scavenged their way into their teens before the potato blight drove them - along with thousands of their countrymen - into the British Army. Inseparable, they boozed, fought and whored together in England and India where, on a bazaar stall, Sean saw an ornate ring he fancied enough to buy instead of spending the money on a native prostitute. Deeply superstitious, he called it his lucky charm and certainly it seemed to protect him in many a tight corner over the years.

In April 1858, the 98th, along with the 31st Foot and some guns, went out with General Sir Sydney Cotton on a Frontier operation against the Khudu Khels. On returning, the force was closely harried as they withdrew, with sections 'crowning heights' - holding commanding ground while others pulled out then withdrawing themselves, similarly covered. Posted on the extreme right of a rocky ridge, sheltering behind a hastily built stone sangar, lay Sean and Micky, their bayonet-capped and newly issued Enfields projecting forward.

It was quiet, nothing seemed to be happening and the hot sun made them careless. Sean was fiddling with his ring. He had taken it off and was rolling it between his thumb and forefinger. Carefully he placed it on a rock to swat a fly feeding on his arm and when he looked back, the ring had gone from the rock. Micky Flanagan was ostentatiously slipping it on his finger.

'Will yer give me the ring ... take it off yer silly sod!'

Micky grinned and pulled his hand out of Sean's reach. 'Sure an' it looks mighty good on me, don't it?'

'Will ye be giving me the bloody ring!'

His imperative outstretched hand froze in mid-air as stones rattled to their front. Their heads jerked forward to see two white robed tribesmen rushing towards their position. The leading man was a gigantic, skull-capped native wielding a huge curved sword. Grabbing his rifle, Sean leapt to his feet and set himself to receive the attack. Taken by surprise, Micky frantically scrambled up, endeavouring to present his bayoneted rifle. But the sword-bearing giant was upon him and the upraised weapon cut fiercely down onto Micky's shoulder. In disbelief, the Irishman stared down at his own left arm laying in the dusty ground at his feet. With blood cascading from his shoulder cavity and his rifle held in the remaining hand, Micky tried to fend off his assailant but the big man side-stepped. He firmly planted his feet, leaned back and, slashing sideways in a great gleaming arc, lopped Micky's head from his shoulders.

With his Enfield held hip high, Sean allowed his native opponent within a yard before pulling the trigger; the short range impact blasted the turbaned tribesman from his feet. Having seen enough men die to recognise the flaccid transmutation from living being to bundle of dusty rags, Sean wasted no time but swung round in time to see Micky's arm hit the ground and gently bounce before settling in the dust, the precious ring standing out, beacon like, on the convulsively moving fingers of the hand protruding from the khaki sleeve.

Sean's wild banshee screech echoing round the barren hills seemed to transform what followed into a dream, everything happening in a deliberate, dispassionate manner, immeasurably slower than real life. The native sword timelessly completed its graceful arc and Micky's head leapt from his shoulders to bounce away down the hill, his forage cap incongruously remaining on the close cropped poll. The body folded at the knees and hips and slowly slumped, blood gushing from the truncated neck.

The huge tribesman struggled to regain his balance as Sean postured forward ... one ... two ... three paces. The bayonet languidly thrust forwards and upwards to bury itself to the hilt under the native's rib-cage and was pulled out before the weight of the falling body dragged the rifle from Sean's grasp. The sequence ended with the gleaming blade in a strangely rhythmic frenzy, plunging again and again into the humped carcass.

Wild eyed, Sean bent over the lonely arm and spoke softly as if waking a man from sleep. 'Come on, Mick, give us the ring ... come on, you berk, give me the bloody ring.'

Impatiently he struggled to remove it but, lacking an anchorage, the arm assumed its own animation and rejected his advances. Cursing and cajoling, he pulled and tugged until warned by the clattering of stones of more tribesmen approaching the stone sangar. 'Come on Micky me ole mate ... its time we got outta this ... ye can give me the ring later.'

Swooping down, he grabbed the arm and took off on a wild promenade in a lonely barren world, inhabited only by his alien self and three nimble tribesmen skipping lithely over their own rocky terrain. Hindered by his heavy ammunition boots and the surprisingly heavy human arm, he bounded down the khud-side, falling, bouncing, rolling, tumbling in a tumultuous race. Handicapped by his refusal to relinquish either arm or rifle only madness bestowed him the strength to remain the front-runner. Throughout he maintained a breathless disjointed chatter. 'Come on Mick! Not much further ... we'll come up with the lads soon ... they'll see them sods off ... you should'na taken me ring ... it's me lucky piece, ye knows that ... look at the bleedin' trouble you got us in ... now, Mick ... take it easy ... nearly fell then didn't ye ... they'll have ye if ye fall ... come on, keep going ... '

Then other inhabitants of the lonely world bestirred themselves and the sharp rattle of musketry bounced back from the sheer hillsides and brought down two tribesmen like stricken rabbits. Slithering to a standstill, the remaining Afridi vanished wraith-like among the rock cluster. Unaware of this Sean maintained his wing-heeled flight, bursting through prone skirmish lines of startled men until, rounding a huge rock, he skidded up to a halt before the Commanding Officer and his satellites. The sudden injection into their midst of a dusty, ragged, hatless and blood-soaked apparition, nursing a human arm startled the group of officers, who quickly regained their composure when it drew itself up, gasping and gulping, to breathlessly jerk out. 'Sir! Privates Donovan an' Flanagan ... reportin' for duty , Sir!'

Revealing an unexpected sense of drama, story teller Private Finnigan lay back in silence, his Irish brogue replaced by the sempiternal buzz of insects and the creak of punkahs.

'Well, go on ... wot 'appened arter that Paddy?'

Finnigan deliberated. 'Well ... in the correct military order o' things ... the CO stood them ... 'im ... at ease an' asked what 'ad 'appened. Speakin' fer the pair of 'em, an' sayin' nothin' about the ring, Sean reported they'd been attacked by superior numbers an' 'ad run fer it ... the CO an' 'is orficers kept a'lookin' fer the second bloke afore they realised Private Flanagan were only there in spirit as it were. Anyway, they let Sean get the ring orf his finger before taking the arm away from 'im ... said Micky were wounded an' goin' to hospital ... later Sean were told Micky 'ad died o' wounds ... an' 'e went to the funeral ... with bugler, firing party an' all.'

'Were 'e alright after that?'

'Yes, right as rain ... but if ole Sean had been a crafty bugger 'e could've kept it up an' maybe worked 'is ticket ... if 'e'd played 'is cards right! Still, 'is ring certainly were lucky ... 'e nivver got a scratch fer the rest o' his service ... an' were trooped 'ome a couple o' years later.'

XXI

Living a violent, brutalised existence, it was not surprising that soldiers, particularly when in drink, were sometimes driven to lose control and strike-out at the object of their annoyance. When he who received the blow was an officer or non-commissioned officer, a serious crime against military discipline and good order had been committed, and the striker was in grave trouble. Soon after Sergeant Oakley rejoined the Regiment, a spate of such crimes occurred and General Orders of Commander-in-Chief-in-India repeatedly published warnings, cautioning men that striking a superior officer was an offence punishable by death and that he - the Commander-in-Chief - would be compelled to change the current lenient policy of allowing sentences of transportation for life if the incidence of crime did not cease. On his Saturday morning Parade, Lieutenant-Colonel Pearse-Frodsham, the Commanding Officer, uniquely changed formalised patterns by ordering the Regiment to form a huge hollow square. Riding into the centre on his charger, he earnestly addressed them, doing everything in his power to impress upon their minds that the full power of the law would be evoked. If men did not control themselves someone would die for a momentary loss of temper.

To no avail. On the very next day a private in 'A' Company struck his Section Sergeant in the face with his cap. Duly court-martialled for striking a superior officer, he was sentenced to the mandatory punishment of death and confined for two months awaiting promulgation by the governor-general and Council, the only authority in India authorised to sanction the judicial execution of a British soldier. The delay in confirmation indicated the heart-searching involved in depriving a man of his life for a spontaneous action in the heat of the moment. The prisoner was shocked by the verdict, weeping bitterly as he buoyed himself up with the belief that at worst he would be transported. While confined he witnessed two other men being shot for murder, all prisoners had to be marched to the place of execution to witness the punishment.

Designed to deter, there were few occasions more solemn or impressive than punishment-parades, and a military execution was the most awe-inspiring of all. After an early Reveille, the Regiment paraded before daybreak. Muted men sleepily arrayed themselves before reluctantly drifting out into night shadowed Lines. Marched to the place of execution, the eight companies formed up on three sides of a square, one side being left open for balls to pass through when the firing party carried out their duty. To occupy the men's minds there was much manoeuvring, dressing and 'as-you-were's', then all stood awaiting the morn's dawning, so silent and thoughtful that a pin might be heard to fall.

Meanwhile, an escort formed of a Section commanded by an officer went to the cells and returned with the prisoner. Dressed in a clean white shirt with a black kerchief at his neck, fatigue khaki-drill trousers, jacket and cap. His arms were behind his body and corded above the elbows so that his hands enjoyed a little freedom. Awaiting daylight, they fell-in on the left of the square, next to the prisoner's Company.

The interminable delay caused some of the more imaginative men to faint, crashing to the ground and being assisted away by comrades. Varied emotions plagued the motionless ranks. Some, involuntarily shivering, identified themselves with the luckless prisoner then found the greatest relief that it was not so. Others cursed him for so stupidly throwing away his life and placing them in the unpleasant position of having to watch him die. Others blanked their minds and thought ravenously of breakfast, five hours away.

Dawn came as day skirmished briefly with night's retreating rearguard before light took over the field. It was a signal for all heads covertly to turn towards where the prisoner and escort stood, before being called to order to play their part as witnesses in the grim and inexorable proceedings. The procession formed-up. First, the provost with reversed arms; then the band and drummers playing 'Dead March', the drums muffled with black material; next, the firing-party with arms reversed. Finally, four men bearing the coffin, ahead of the prisoner, with a praying padre on his right and chosen friend on the left. They were flanked on each side by an armed man while the remainder of the escort took up the rear.

The sultry warmth of the early morning did nothing to prevent the blood chilling to the band's solemn dirge when they started off from the left, in slow-time. Through habit and pride, the prisoner kept step as smartly as anyone in the procession, despite his bound arms and the minister's hand clutching him above the elbow. Under the sympathetic gaze of comrades of his own Company, only a few averted their eyes, the prisoner broke down and began to weep, then tried to speak through his gulps. The minister whispered in his ear, evidently counselling him to continue praying. Shaking his arm free the prisoner pulled himself together and, in a loud clear voice, bade his comrades farewell, telling them to let him be a warning to keep from the strong drink, which had led him to this.

Unable to lift his arm in salute, the doomed man smartly gave 'Eyes Right' to his Company Commander and Section Officer, both returning the salute punctiliously. The pale face half-turned towards the serried ranks, he glided rigidly past, searching each visage as though to memorise the appearance should ages pass before they met again. Several men found this unbearable and fell-out to the rear. Approaching the Commanding Officer and the Colours, his steps perceptibly stiffened and, as on a Saturday's CO's Parade, he smartly turned his eyes right, maintaining the salute for the correct number of paces before sharply swivelling his head to the front.

On reaching the end of the third arm of the square, the procession slowly moved to the middle of the open side and halted. The coffin was lowered to the ground and the band ceased grinding out their lamentable dirge and filed to the rear of the Regiment. The escort fell-back and the firing-party took up their distance, leaving the prisoner alone with his guard and the minister. The Adjutant stepped forward to read out the charge and sentence, doing it slowly and loudly so that all on the parade could hear. Awkwardly, the prisoner knelt on his coffin and was blindfolded by the Provost who then drew back. The minister read the funeral service then he and the prisoner prayed together. After which the Minster hastily moved to a position at the side and rear of the firing-party.

Wasting no time, the officer in command of the firing-party gave his commands in a clear ringing voice, running them together so that the final 'FIRE' came more quickly than anyone expected. The sudden loud rifle reports, rending the still morning air, caused the entire Regiment to start nervously. Then came the hissing inhalation of a thousand breaths. The blindfolded prisoner jerked convulsively at the impact of the heavy .577 iron-tipped Snider bullets, his body folded in the middle and he slumped forwards so that his head and upper part of the body rested on the sandy ground while his legs remained stretched across the coffin. Later they heard he had two bullets in the head and two in the body, the rest missed. The surgeon stepped forward and examined the body, then nodded to the officer commanding the firing-party, indicating that the man was dead. Had he been alive the officer would have had to come forward and put a pistol bullet into the head, behind the ear.

Now the air was full of staccato orders, restoring men to reality as they marched forward in column sections, getting the words 'Eyes Left' as they passed the recumbent body. As the last section cleared the area, leaving the unfortunate soldier to eternal seclusion, the band stuck up a lively quick-step and the Regiment, mounted colonel at its head, set out into the country on the route march that traditionally followed punishment-parade.

Three and a half hours, and ten miles later, a dust encrusted, sweat-soaked 5th Sub-Section filed wearily into the bungalow. They slowly stripped down to their grey issue-shirts and aggressively fought their way into the latrines and ablutions before ravenously re-invigorating themselves with a coffee and bread breakfast. Now life took on its customary ordered routine as all settled down for a day's charpoy bashing.

Despite being attuned to violence and death, with mourning even for a close comrade a brief transitory affair, emotions aroused by the execution were now dispelled by resentment towards the dead soldier for sending them on an exhausting route march. Conversation centred around firing squads and hangmen's ropes, the men lolled on their charpoys and searched their minds for macabre memories. None could cap the astonishing facts purveyed by a smugly knowledgeable Private Birch whose father, acquainted with Calcraft, the London City Executioner, had actually assisted at a Newgate topping. For an entrancing hour, Birch regaled them with details of the varied length of drop for persons of different weights; how the rope was three and a quarter inch, five strand Italian hemp, thirteen feet long with a one inch brass ring worked into one end and a leather washer to prevent the noose slipping; how pinion straps consisted of a broad leather body belt, with attached elbow and wrist straps and a two inch strap for pinioning the legs below the knees.

Then Birchy got around to the scaffold, started telling them how it was built. He was cut short in mid-sentence by Private Pioneer Carpenter Holmes, astonishing because Holy Holmes was renowned for rarely speaking from one week's end to another.

'It ain't like that at all! You're talkin' cock, Birchy!'

Private Birch glared indignantly at him. 'How the bleedin' hell do you know?... Were your dad a mate o' Calcrafts?'

'No, nor were I ... but at Jhansi in '58 I were ordered to build a gallows 'cording to instructions sent up from Provost Department at Fort William ... an' it weren't like yourn!'

Birch blustered belligerently, but he had lost centre stage. Kinrade authoritatively called out. 'Shut yer gob Birchy! Holmesy, tell us about this bleedin' gallows you built.'

'Well, it were like this ... Sir Hugh Rose had ended campaign an' some of us were garrisoning Jhansi. Some wounded lads were in hospital and one an 'em had a bag under his pillow with his savings in. This tempted a hospital orderly who tried to take it during the night, but the bloke woke up an' began shoutin', so lad put a pillow over 'is head an' suffocated 'im to death. Any road, they caught 'im and sent 'im back for court-martial.'

Neither prisoner not defending officer made much attempt to deny the crime, relying on a plea of mitigation. It had no chance. His abject attitude was obviously of a soldier undeniably guilty of a heinous military crime, not only stealing from a comrade but killing him in the process. The officers forming the Court, their Victorian sense of retribution strongly stimulated, sought punishment even more severe than the mandatory death penalty. So they sentenced the wretched man to be hanged as his crime was considered to be so disgraceful a nature that he was to be denied the less humiliating fate which a firing-party would have afforded him. This presented difficulties as there were no gallows, nor experienced hangmen, in the area. Neither did anyone have the slightest idea of procedure. An urgent dispatch was sent to the Provost Department at Fort William in Calcutta, asking for construction details so that Pioneer Carpenter could build a scaffold. They also requested the services of an experienced executioner.

During the weeks it took for messages to pass to and from Calcutta, and the Commander-in-Chief to confirm the sentence, the prisoner was confined in a small, tin-roofed prison cell. It resembled a bakers oven during the fierce heat of day and was very little better during the night hours. When, eventually, the construction details arrived, Pioneer Carpenter Holmes confirmed what he had already surmised, that the cross beam from which the rope was suspended had to be supported on two strong, upright posts, or by the walls of the room wherein it was erected. He would have to make the trap-doors and the mechanism that released them when the executioner pulled a lever, letting the prisoner drop through into a deep pit below. He thought hard on how to avoid digging such a pit in the iron-hard earth, with temperatures touching a hundred and twenty degrees.

His problems were solved when, prowling restlessly around the Royal Palace at Jhansi, he discovered a small, but high, basement chamber with a ledge running right round some five feet from the ground. On this ledge he laid stout planks to form a false floor. A sweating, cursing, fatigue party man-handled the ends of a heavy eight-by-four inch cross-beam into notches cut in the wall, ten feet up. Two large hooks were bolted right through the beam to take the rope. Two thirds of the false floor consisted of the trap, a pair of massive doors hung on strong hinges and were set in a frame of three inch planks. When the trap was set, the ends of the long hinges rested on a one and a quarter inch iron draw-bar that slid in solid iron staples, forged with three spaced 'U' notches, allowing the doors to fall open downwards. It had to be constructed accurately so that both doors fell at exactly the same moment, even without a man standing on them their weight causing them to drop very suddenly.

'It took me nigh on a month to make that scaffold, working from instructions ... an' tho' I say it mesself I did a right good job ... I were very proud on it ... reckon it were one o' me best pieces o' work! D'ye know. I even heightened the doorway an' made steps up to the false floor, so that the doctor could pass through bottom part o' door, go under floor and certify the man dead arter he were dropped. An' that's what a real fuckin' scaffold's like, Birch ... nuffin' like bloody rubbish you was talkin'!'

Knowing when defeated, Birch mumbled. 'Well, me dad knew Calcraft ... an' that's wot 'e tole me.'

Disdainfully, Holmes carried on with his tale. 'Well, now they'd got best gallows in bloody country ... but no hangman to use 'em.'

It seemed that there were no experienced hangmen in India. Calcutta informed that the last one had died of cholera and his replacement had yet to arrive from England. Volunteers were asked for but none came forward. Then certain inducement produced a single, indifferent, drunken, unwilling soldier, prepared to despatch one of his comrades in return for a free discharge, a passage to England and a sum of money. The Provost-Marshall, Private Holmes and the volunteer hangman repeatedly tested the gallows, using a net full of cannon-balls weighing ten stone odd, same as the prisoner. The volunteer performed so indifferently and with such growing reluctance that Holmes began taking bets that he would never go though with it.

He won his bets. Troubled by his conscience and shame and taunted by his comrades, the volunteer drank so heavily that on the night before the execution he was unconscious and unlikely to be fit to perform such a duty.

Required to provide a substitute, the Provost-Marshall peremptorily ordered the Duty Provost-Corporal to take over the role. Unemotionally and without dissembling, the Corporal said "Yes, Sir!", saluted and marched off to find Private Holmes. A quiet and efficient soldier trained to believe orders to be orders, he arbitrarily appointed the Pioneer Carpenter to be his assistant next morning. Holmes, fearing his handiwork might function inadequately in the hands of an inexperienced man, reluctantly agreed to be there.

Next morning, at the appointed hour, both were in their places on the scaffold when the procession entered the chamber - prisoner, escort, Minister, Provost-Marshal, Garrison-Commander, Commanding-Officer and all. Promptly and efficiently the two men pinioned the prisoner, fitted the white cap and positioned and adjusted the rope. The CO raised his hand and the Corporal pulled firmly on the lever. With a great crash the ponderous trap-doors fell open and the prisoner disappeared, leaving the rope taut and strumming. Over a welcome glass of grog, the Corporal confided that hanging one of his comrades was the last bit of work he would ever have voluntarily undertaken, but he was on top of the roster and obeyed orders.

'Garrison-Commander were very happy with the way things went an' presented me and the Corporal with a couple o' guineas apiece ... Corporal said 'e wouldn't do it again for ten ... an' at the time I thought the same.'

Proud at owning perhaps the only working scaffold in the entire country, the Garrison-Commander felt twinges of regret at having no more victims to despatch on its trap. As he told the Adjutant, there were unlikely to be any more singular occasions when soldiers could be executed by means other than the firing-party. Fortuitously at this very time, mutinous sepoys began to be captured and brought in for trial. This provided excellent fodder for the new gallows, besides saving valuable gunpowder blowing them from gun muzzles.

Lying on his charpoy and gazing reflectively into space, Holmes chuckled. 'Corse they came along to me an' Corporal to do our stuff again ... at a guinea a head as they were niggers ... an' as it weren't the same as hanging a white man ... we both did quite well out of it for a few months ... until Regiment marched out. Garrison-Commander offered to make me up to Corporal if I'd stay but I were getting tired on it and wanted to stick wiv the lads.'

XXII

Many men in the 5th Sub-Section could speak from personal experience of having lain helpless for hours under the blazing sun, praying to be found by searching comrades or bhisti and brought in on a nightmare journey in an unpadded dhooli borne by untrained Indian bearers. If the battle was lost a wounded man could expect nothing but murder and mutilation from savage foes, or, worst of all, to be handed over to the women.

At Moodkee in 1845, Taffy Davies had his left shoulder smashed by a Sikh soft-lead bullet, .68in calibre and weighing almost an ounce. Making a small hole on entry it had spread on impact with the bone, producing a huge cavity when emerging and partially exposing the shoulder blade.

'Bloody wound were still open twelve months later, muck an' shit coming out of it, me shoulder stiff an' arm nearly useless ... but I 'ad a mate who'd worked with horses an' he massaged it, made me move me arm an' use it ... slow but sure I got well enough to return to duty.'

'Mister' Wright nodded sympathetically. 'Still hurts now an' then, don't it Taff? I seed yer moving it painful-like only the other day. Being wounded ain't so bad if you gets picked up quick ... at first the shock numbs an' you feel no pain, then your thirsty an' its hot ... that takes yer mind off the wound. But if yer left out all night like I were at Chillianwallah, then pain an' thirst an' cold begins ter get yer, an' even the bravest start to cry out.'

Like most soldiers, Private Wright's limited vocabulary prevented him painting the picture in all its stark, forbidding colours. He could recall but could not describe, how the misty field of pain replaced the field of battle. How men, brave in the light of day when buoyed up by comradeship and discipline, reverted in the lonely darkness to being little boys crying for their mothers, for water, for help, for death, for God. Until the battlefield was eerily alive with a seething under-current of low pain-pitched voices, gradually silenced as the cold night caused men to die and quickly stiffen.

It was a meaty subject, listened to in apprehension and with professional interest. Taffy Davies spoke with feeling.

'Them bleedin' surgeons! When you finds yerself in a field hospital yer can reckon to be in fer worst time of yer life. They love ter amputate ... don't matter whether its a flesh wound or a broken bone ... they'll 'ave yer bloody arm or leg orf. If its mortal ... like a bullet inna guts ... then they'll waste no more time.'

The most vivid memories in the minds of Lance-Corporal Mockford and Privates Davies, Wright, Coughlin and Charlie Mort, were when they had been taken in charge by bare-armed surgeons, fearful in their blood-stained aprons with spare knives held between their teeth. Laid out on a board trestle operating table, kindly but rough orderlies had pushed and pulled them into position, their teeth grating to avoid crying out. With one orderly holding down the shoulders and another grasping the wrists, a rum induced haze masked the realisation that the high-pitched screaming, and the accompanying exquisite agony, was all part of your body into which the surgeon was probing deeply and remorselessly.

The passing of the years brought a merciful blurring of the pain and anguish, so they probably forgot that even when the terrible ordeal ended they remained where it had been staged, the operating theatre was merely an unscreened part of the ward. With rough tenderness they were laid a few feet away from the place of pain, on a dirty blanket with straw beneath, covered by a greatcoat stiff with blood and filth, their boots serving as a pillow.

Private Wright, lugubrious as always, set the mood for dinner. 'An' that ain't the end of it ... if a man's lucky an' strong he might come through losing only a leg or an arm ... but lots can go wrong ... I seen a simple gunshot wound, not much larger than the bullet what made it ... get larger an' larger until you couldn't cover it wiv yer hand ... an' going down into body so's you could put half yer fist into 'orrible wet wound. Sometimes blokes are going along nice, wounds discharging muck, then suddenly they dries up an' bloke gets feverish and full o' pain. Next thing yer 'ear he's got blood poisoning ... an' that's a bleedin' death sentence ... only 'bout three in a hundred don't snuff it.'

Without sustaining a scratch, Private Martin Early fought for the Confederacy in most major battles of the War Between the States, yet he knew that all he was hearing, and more, was true. At Antietam, from dawn to dusk on 17th September 1862, the bloodiest single day of the War, the 13th Virginia Regiment of Early's Brigade in Ewell's Division had fought alongside J.E.B. Stuart's artillery by the North Woods on the extreme left of the Confederate battle-line. With the terrible fighting finished, the two armies of Americans had drawn apart to ponder on whether it had been worthwhile, to lick their wounds and once more become individual personalities. Laying in a shallow shelter, scraped in the hard earth behind a rail fence, Martin Early felt the usual fears for his twin Matthew and elder brother Wilbur, serving in different companies. This time Providence was not to show mercy and, in a dreadful moment he was never to forget, Wilbur came up to stand above him. One look at his face made unnecessary the words he uttered.

'Martin ... Matthew's missing ... I can't find him anywhere ... we've got to look for him!'

Except for the odd musket-shots and the occasional boom of cannon, as though men were reluctant to let the fighting finish, the noise of battle had ceased, replaced with what sounded like the buzzing of a host of bees but was, in reality, cries, groans and sobs, choked death rattles and monotonous curses, prayers and pleas for help. They picked their way through a vast jumble sale of death. Trampling upon a litter of abandoned muskets, hats, canteens, cartridge boxes, cannon balls and clothing; shoes, torn packs and haversacks, pitiful contents trampled into a bloody slush; papers, letters and personal belongings all defiled by dirt and gore. In shapeless mounds the wounded, dead and dying littered the field in a characteristic , haphazard mingling of friend and foe, officer and private, all punctiliously sharing the blood-soaked acres. Their barrels dejectedly drooping or tilted over on smashed wheels, guns formed little islands, their limbers standing where the horses lay dead on the pole.

With the other searchers they moved slowly across the field, fumbling hands desperately grasping their feet and legs. Their ears rang with the ebb and flow of monotonous mumbling, voices that spoke directly to none yet addressed everyone, said nothing yet said everything.

'Water! For Christ's sake ... water!'

'Help me ... help ... you sons o' bitches ... can't you hear me?'

'Hey ... you there ... get this body off me ... its crushing me!'

'Did we win? Good! If you see a doctor send him this-away.'

They gave men water until their canteens ran out, then, realising there was little they could do to relieve the wounded they hardened their hearts and closed their ears; stopping only to turn over and examine men who, at first heart-stopping glance, looked like Matthew.

In the face of mounting exhaustion and lassitude, dejected beyond belief now that the fever of battle had fled from his blood, Martin Early struggled on, intensely affected by all he saw around him and horrified at the ghostly similarity to actual battle. As though their world had actually come to end, combatants were frozen in postures of mutual belligerence, their glassy, sightless eyes peering down musket-barrels that were gripped by hands convulsed in death. Some, in their agonies, had buried their faces in loose soil and filled their mouths with earth, their hands twisting the leaves and grass as though seeking to retain a hold on the natural things they knew so well.

Sweat-channelled faces, black with burnt powder and nigger-minstrel mouths circled through biting cartridges, they came up to the shattered buildings of a farm, dark against the distant hills turning purple before the sultry sunset as shadows of approaching night lengthened over the land. From a distance the forlorn buildings seemed steeped in solitude, if the truth were known, since the first bricks were laid that house and its barns had never known such a press of humanity, so much irrevocable coming and going.

On the bare ground and on doors wrenched from their hinges, crowded close together in an untidy queue, wounded soldiers lay prone along the packed and battered walls that separated them from the surgeons within. The surgeons that relentlessly cut, sewed and probed on unanaesthetised tissue. Painstakingly they searched among the stricken multitude, finding some from the 13th Virginia but never their brother, and none seemed to remember seeing him. Peering into countless pain-wracked faces, lifting bloody blankets and greatcoats from torn bodies and gently replacing them when the heavily breathing man was not the man they sought, Martin and Wilbur tremulously passed into the house. They entered a dim, candle-lit purgatory, vibrant with pain and redolent with suffering. Elongated shadows played upon the bare brick walls, resembling torturers in a medieval castle dungeon. A heavy stench lay on the still air, sickening them. Wearily straightening up a surgeon angrily called. 'Hey you! Don't stand there staring ... get a goddamned bucket and give them a drink ... some have had no water since this morning!'

Carefully they picked their way through the litter of closely packed bodies, now and then stopping to gingerly lift heads and press a tin cup of water to cracked lips that never failed to haltingly whisper their gratitude for such small mercies. Increasingly anxious, their search progressed among the ranks of the helpless host. Laying on stained blankets, overcoats, straw or bare earth, reddened rags were their badge of suffering. Most were grotesquely torn, gouged or mutilated, others had limbs torn off by bounding round-shot or whistling canisters. There were clean shaven boys in their first and last battle and bearded veterans, not for the first time ending up in a field hospital.

Patiently, all awaited their turn to briefly visit hell, few making any fuss save for suppressed groans or unavoidable screams when they were lifted onto the operating table for a brief and perfunctory examination. Those with torn intestines or obviously mortal wounds, for whom there was no hope, were removed without treatment to join others at the far end of the building. Smashed limbs were invariably amputated, without anaesthetics - save rum straight from the bottle forced between clenched teeth.

Hardened as he was to war and its attendant horrors, Martin Early could prevent himself retching only by diligently fussing and concentrating on the simple task of serving out water. Desperately he feigned deafness when a surgeon brusquely ordered him to come and give a hand.

'Me, Sir?'

'Yes, you! Come over here!'

Leaden footed and apprehensive, he sidled across to the board-and-trestle table. Reluctantly lowering his eyes to the huddled figure laying there, he looked upon the pain drawn face of his twin brother, Matthew. Wincing, tightly he clasped his hands together.

'You know this man?'

Martin's eyes travelled fearfully down to where the leg ended above the knee in a bloody stump, with the white bone protruding.

'He's my brother, Sir.'

'Well, you'll want to help him, won't you? A twelve pound ball from a Napoleon did this ... got to tidy it up ... he'll probably be as right as rain in time ... so pull yourself together and hold him while I work.'

As he talked, the surgeon methodically wiped his hands and crusted knife on his soiled apron, eyes calculatingly fixed on Matthew's leg. An upraised finger brought the orderly, bearing a bottle.

'Fill the poor devil with rum.'

Weakly and with his eyes watering, Matthew gulped down the rum, coughing and retching, trying to avert his head when persistently the orderly pressed the bottle to his mouth, causing liquid to dribble from its corners. Studiously looking anywhere but into their brother's eyes, Martin and Wilbur pinioned his limbs and body. As the blunt teeth of the surgeon's saw grated into the bone, Matthew shrieked, causing Wilbur to release his hold. Without looking up the surgeon snarled. 'God rot your soul, man! Keep hold! Hope to Christ you never have any surgery!'

Where was there that Wilbur could have run to hide, had baleful Fate revealed to him that ten months later his own life would ebb away in a similar manner at Gettysburg? Unknowing, he muttered through clenched teeth. 'By God, so do I! I'd rather be killed stone dead!'

Within sixty seconds it was over. Tenderly the unconscious Matthew was lifted from the table, bumping into another wounded man being lifted into his place. They laid him on a blanket, Martin peeled off his jacket and rolled it up to make a pillow for the sweat-dewed head. Looking down, he found it difficult to recognise this man as his twin, with whom he had played, fought and laughed for twenty-two years. Why, he looked eighty years old at that moment. Helplessly they stood gazing down. Noticing the surgeon looking around for helpers they hastily turned and, to a fanfare of blood-curdling shrieks from the man on the table, left without a backward glance.

Incapable of speech, they stared at each other, gratefully taking deep breaths of cool night air. Then, struggling against almost overpowering exhaustion, weary steps took them away from the hateful place. A few yards from the building they came upon a heap of recently amputated feet, hands, legs and arms, then rows of blanket covered bodies. A burial detail were slowly working with pick and shovel, their sergeant, sitting on a log, removed the corn-pipe from his mouth and shouted. 'That's enough single graves for the officers ... now we need a big pit over there ... a mass grave for enlisted men!'

The 13th Virginia Infantry Regiment marched out the next day. They never saw their brother again, later hearing he had died of wounds and was buried at Antietam, probably in the big mass grave they saw being dug.

XXIII

For nigh on a month, in uncharacteristic silence, Private Kinrade had listened to his comrades tell tales. He was increasingly restless at not entering the fray, realising that as leader of the Pope's Boys, and among the strongest characters in the barrackroom, he was losing face by remaining silent. He wanted to tell a tale but could not conceive of one of the quality he knew would be expected of him. He had a recurring vision of the room admiringly hanging on to every compelling word, praising his strong yarn and its clever ending. In his heart he knew the only admiration he craved was from the Sergeant, Yank Early and maybe 'Captain' Saville - he didn't care a shit for the rest of them.

It had to be a good story and he racked his brains to think of one. He knew plenty of interesting things from back home in Ireland; plots and activities against landlords, the police and the soldiers, but that was all done with and he was no longer part of it. He though of doing a rip-roaring tale that took the piss out of C of E's, then surprised himself by not wanting to stir up any trouble that might make the Sergeant's job any harder. Suddenly he was surprised to realise that since Sergeant Oakley had come into the barrackroom he had been more at peace with himself and the British Army than at any time since enlisting.

While his silence set men muttering behind their hands he sought a yarn not featuring himself yet reflecting his own guile and superior intellect, as it had earned the unqualified admiration of the few he respected.

One evening as the Regiment were let loose from the bungalows, a wizened and white bearded Indian fakir appeared in the Lines and began to perform very clever, fascinating tricks. He attracted a large crowd of gaping soldiers who quickly vanished when the collection was made. The few who remained had asked the old man to do the Indian Rope trick but he had declined, saying that only the highest grade fakirs had the power to do it. Much of the talk in the Canteen that night centred on these men and their tricks. Afterwards Kinrade lay awake for hours, thinking on it.

With breakfast cleared and the room settled down, Kinrade steered the conversation round to fakirs and their tricks, encouraging the old soldiers to relate unbelievable tricks and stunts they had seen these men do.

'Sure, an' that's fine ... but have ye actually seen the Rope trick ... before your very eyes?'

Mister Wright pontificated on an occasion he had heard about but did not personally see. Lance-Corporal Mockford recalled a similar happening.

'What wid ye say if I told ye I knew of a swaddy who could do it?'

'If you believe that you'll believe anything Dick Kinrade.'

'Bollocks Wrightie ... I'll be tellin' yer I know of a lad ... a British soldier not a Paddy I regret ter say ... who found out how thim black buggers do the Rope Trick.'

'Well, let's be 'avin' yer then ... but it'll have ter be a good 'un 'cos I'll not believe a word otherwise.'

'Oh, it's a good 'un alright! There were these two mates, see ... in the same section ... names o' Dick Roberts an' Billy Bates ... 'e were the one who learned the trick.'

Privates Dick Roberts and Billy Bates had been files for five years and, like the Sergeant's Bricky Tate and Jockey Rix, were close mates. They did everything together, pooling pay and sharing equally. Now they were coming to the end of the road, breaking up because Dick was brassed off with Billy losing their money on hare-brained gambling, betting on anything, even on a fly crawling up a window. Billy was very upset on pay parade when Dick refused to hand over his pay as usual. He offered to let him hold the kitty but Dick had no head for figures and knew he would make a mess of it. They agreed to go their own ways, at least, Dick insisted they did and that night was off with a bunch of the lads to the Wet. Billy sat supping ale by himself on a bench in the corner, sourly glancing across at Dick while he racked his brains for some way to get back on the old footing. The next night, not fancying watching his mate laughing and joking while he felt miserable, as soon as the parades ended Billy set off on a long walk out of camp, to think things out. His feet scuffed up the dust and his narrowed eyes stared grimly ahead as he thought over what had gone wrong. Wallowing in self-pity, he reflected how everyone was against him, all because of a few silly bets. How was he to know Jake Mills had specially trained that bloody beetle for the race? Or that one bottle of grog would put Mike Dennis on his back - normally he knocked back two or three. He squirmed at recollections of the dog-fight fiasco, they'd lost a packet on that. Couldn't blame old Dick for taking it amiss, still, at the time every one of them seemed a certainty.

If only he could think of something ... something that really was a certainty ... that couldn't go wrong ... something they could build up so's everyone in the whole bloody camp'd put their shirts on it ... and be cleaned out! Licking his lips and rubbing his hands at the delicious dreams, Billy was dizzy at the though of how much they could make. If only he could think of something really big ... the Indian Rope trick for instance. Ah, now! That was really something. My God, if he could do that they'd end up millionaires. Of course, he'd never seen it done ... nor had anyone else he knew ... suppose it could be done else there wouldn't be so much chat about it. Perhaps he'd find an old black bugger who'd sell him the secret ... no, they never let on ... kept their secrets those blokes.

With his head on one side, staring up into the cloudless sky at a circling bird, Billy pondered. Just make a length of rope stand up stiff and straight in the air, then send a nipper climbing up it to disappear at the top and reappear somewhere else. No doubt about it ... t'was the greatest trick of all. If only he knew how to get that bloody rope to stand up in the sky ... stand up ... in the ... wait a minute. If you ... and if the rope ... then the boy would ... Was that the way it was done? It might be! No, it couldn't be ... it was too easy!

He stopped walking and, standing motionless he gazed around. Perhaps he'd been dreaming? No, he was wide awake. He felt sick with excitement then, pulling himself together he marshalled his thoughts. Yes ... it could be ... it might be the way ... he'd got to test it ... find out if he had discovered how to do the famous Indian Rope trick. Turning, he hurried back, doubling until his dripping brow and breathlessness forced him to slacken the pace. Keeping well clear of the Wet Canteen, distinguishable by the rowdy singing and shouting pouring out of the open doors and windows, he roamed the empty Lines, desperately searching for some rope. Finally he found a twelve foot length in a rubbish dump behind the 'D' Company stores.

He shook a fist in the direction of the distant Canteen. He'd show those sods, they'd have no money left for booze when he'd finished with 'em. With a dry mouth and his shirt black with sweat Billy forced his weary legs to plough through the dust, passing nullah after nullah until he came to a dried up watercourse deep in the middle of the maze. His fumbling fingers coiled the rope on the parched, cracked mud making it look like a dirty, dormant snake. Staring irresolutely at the inert coil, his confidence ebbed away and despondency swept over him. Could he do it? Dare he try? Shaking himself he took a deep breath and tried to remember what he had to do. With his eyes fixed on the rope he concentrated hard.

For a moment nothing happened, then, incredulously ... the rope stirred. The movement increased, reluctantly it writhed and sibilantly began to uncoil. Gathering speed, frighteningly it fed itself steadily upwards until the earth bound coil had become an erect and quivering rod. Billy stared at it, overcome with awe, his right hand tightly squeezing his left wrist to convince himself he was awake. The vibrations ceased and he took a halting step forward and extended a tremulous hand, timidly touching the taut rope. He closed his hand around it and, like a prisoner testing the bars of his cell, tried to shake it. The rope was iron hard and immovable.

Time and time again in the next hour, Billy similarly tested its tautness because, although he knew how to send the rope up he was ignorant of how to get it down. Eventually he gave up, pacing impatiently back and forth, eyeing the bloody rope and wondering what he would do if it was still up when distant trumpets blew Lights Out. He was looking up into the sky at the myriad twinkling stars when, with a rustling hiss, the rope dramatically dropped. Swinging round he just caught its last trembling motion as it settled into an untidy coil. Swooping down he gathered up the soft, pliant hempen strands and scurried back to the camp; getting into the bungalow by the top door and covering the furtive concealment of the rope in his locker, just as the drunks poured in at the other end.

Keeping his head down, Billy carried out his duties the next day in a frenzy of suppressed excitement, causing Dick to stare curiously more than once. On being given 'Dismiss', immediately after turning right and momentarily halting, Billy caught Dick by the arm.

'Dick, old mate ... I wanna talk to you ... I've got something to tell yer ... somethin' so bloody big I can 'ardly believe it meself!'

Dick shook his arm free. 'Christ! You still at it? Wotcher got this time ... an unbeatable racing mouse? I got no time fer yer wild schemes ... its best we go our own ways.'

'Dick, mate ... yer've gotta listen ... I got somethin'll make us millionaires ... the richest bloody swaddies in the British Army!'

Fiercely compellingly, Billy Bates low-voiced his secret and its financial implications before standing back, his eyes fixed pleadingly on Dick's face.

'Billy! Fer Gawd's sake ... this is another one of them times like when you was pissed up an' gave a bloke in the bazaar ten rupees ... five of 'em mine ... to teach you 'ow to make a body float in the air.'

But Billy would not be denied and half an hour later, taking a scrawny fourteen year old Band-Rat Boy Saunders - with them, they set off for the nullah where Billy coiled the rope - on exactly the same spot as before in case that had something to do with it. He took a deep breath and sent the rope up into the air,. Sighing with relief he turned to Dick. 'There! Wot'd I tell yer?'

Staring in disbelief, Dick fingered the taut rope, shaking his head. 'Don't know 'ow you do it ... but it ain't right ... there's somethin' wrong with it that'll lose us our money!'

Billy shook with rage and frustration. 'Wot d'yer mean ... somethin' wrong? Yer got eyes ... yer can see the bloody rope can't yer?'

Slowly, Dick continued to shake his head. Billy swung round on Boy Saunders who was open mouthed and goggle-eyed. 'Up yer go! Go on, shin up the bloody rope ... an' I'll give yer a whole rupee fer yerself!'

Cringing, the boy hung back. In no mood for juvenile reluctance, Billy clutched the pipe-stem arm in a vice-like grip and pushed him forward.

'Go on ... you little rat! Git up that bleedin' rope.'

Timidly, the boy touched the firm, unyielding fibres, cast a pleading glance at Billy and was rewarded by a shove that pushed his face against the rope. Putting out both his hands he took a firm grip and began pulling himself up, ascending awkwardly. When his dusty boots were a yard from the ground Billy, dancing with excitement, screamed hoarsely. 'Hurry, hurry! Go on ... up ter top!'

Laboriously the boy struggled up the rope until his hands reached the top. Haltingly he looked first at the void above the abruptly ending hempen pillar and then at Billy below. His thin, youthful voice drifted down. 'Wad do I do now, Mr Bates ... there ain't no more rope! Wot do I 'ang onto?'

'Go on! You'll find somethin'! Put yer 'ands 'igher!'

Cautiously and timorously the boy extended his right arm which disappeared inch by inch into the open sky above the rope's end. Mesmerised, his pinched face a mirror of bewildered concentration, Boy Sanders carried on. Arms, head and shoulders, all vanished, disappearing piecemeal. Then his body and legs. Soon only the rope remained, erect and untenanted.

Transfixed, both men gazed stolidly upwards, Billy's heart singing within him. Then, ten feet away, like a sudden image projected by a magic lantern, the dazed boy suddenly reappeared.

' 'Ere! Wot's the lark? 'Ow'd I git 'ere?'

Billy comfortingly took his arm. 'There. Din' 'urt, did it? Nuffin to it was there? 'Ere ... wot was it ... wot was it like ... up there?'

'I dunno ... cold ... chilly like.'

Billy swung round triumphantly. 'Now Dick ... wot d'yer think o' that?'

Mechanically, like a clockwork doll, Dick continued to shake his head. Billy resisted the impulse to belt him one, that would spoil everything.

'Well!'

'It's no good Billy ... don' know 'ow yer do it ... but it's a bloody fake ... I know it is!'

Billy Bates cursed. The bloody fool ... didn't know how he did it but was sure it was a fake! Seething with frustration, bitterly recalling stories of soldiers dying of thirst with a pocketful of looted diamonds, he looked wildly around. He'd a gold-mine here, for both of them, if only Dick'd recognise the fact. Calming himself, he reasoned with his mate, explaining the idea ... everything but how it was done. When Dick asked him that, somehow he could not bring himself to answer. He couldn't share his secret with anyone, not even an old mate like Dick. The old mate continued stupidly to shake his head, finally driving Billy into paroxysms of fury. Dramatically he indicated the rope, still extending stiffly skyward.

'You wunna know if it's genuine? Well, there's the bloody rope ... go on ... go up yerself ... go on!'

Decisively, Dick shook his head. Billy glared at him. 'Alright. I'll show yer ... if you won't go up the bleedin' rope ... then I will ... I'll show yer!'

He flung himself at the rope, clutching its stiff strands. Dick put a restraining hand on his arm.

'Careful Billy ... don' do nuffin yer'll regret later.'

Shaking the hand off, exhibiting an unusual agility born of fury and frustration, Billy began ascending the slender column until, on reaching the top, his hands disappeared as though cut off at the wrists. He paused, shuddering involuntarily. 'Christ! It's cold up here!'

He looked down at Dick's face, bearing the beginnings of grudging surprise. Billy continued to climb, jerkily vanishing until all that could be seen were the iron-studded soles of his ammunition boots; then they too disappeared. Dick Roberts and Boy Sanders looked at each other. Dick shook his head, this time in wonder. 'Blimey! He can do it! I'd never 'ave believed it.'

Eyes riveted on the spot where Boy Sanders reappeared, Dick waited impatiently, not wishing to miss a moment of Billy's triumphant reappearance. Then Dick would congratulate him and promise to go along wholeheartedly with the plans. Tired and hungry, Boy Sanders began to complain.

'Shut yer bloody row! Billy ... come on ... come down! Where are you? Come on!'

Nothing happened, the tableau of soldier, boy and rope remained the same. Thinking that Billy was trying to get his own back, Dick began to lose his temper. 'Come on, Billy! Come down ... its wonderful ... you're a bloody magician ... but come down ... an' let's get back to camp fer some scoff and a few beers!'

There was still no sign of the missing Private Bates. Dick and the Boy Sanders began searching; poking around the nullah, calling, cajoling and imploring. By now thoroughly alarmed,

Dick sent Boy Sanders back to camp for help. Dick continued with the search, extending it to nearby nullahs in case Billy's sense of direction was poor. Finally giving up, he stood alongside the still erect rope as it dawned on him that he might have a job getting anyone to believe the story. Thank goodness the rope was still up there to bear him out, he began praying that it would stay like it until some witnesses arrived.

Fortunately it was still there when Boy Sanders arrived with the Orderly Sergeant who stared at the rope, gingerly felt it and then got out his official notebook and wetted his pencil point in readiness for taking down statements. Looking increasingly sceptical he clearly did not fancy the tale very much. Just as Boy Sanders was haltingly telling of how he had reappeared there was a spine-chilling hiss as the rope sighed and crumpled lifelessly to the parched earth. The Orderly Sergeant nudged it with his boot toe, causing it to move in the manner of any ordinary rope.

Not standing to his bed at Lights Out, Private Bates was marked Absent Without Leave, being so notified for each of the statutory twenty one days when a Court of Inquiry had to be convened and he was declared a Deserter. It was the only possible course, once the Orderly Sergeant's confirmation of the stiff rope had convinced the Commanding Officer that his Regiment was not going to be shamed by having men accused of murdering their comrade and hiding the body.

'An' that's the truth of it ... Billy Bates was never seen again ... an' let that be a warnin' to any of ye thinkin' of learning the secrets of the Ancients from them old fakir men!'

Kinrade's voice died away, the last words hanging on the silent fetid air. Puzzled, Private Hebdon enquired. 'Ye mean ... he were nivver seen again? Well, where'd he go?'

Kinrade shook his head and smiled, amply rewarded by 'Yank' Early's appreciative guffaw and 'Captain' Saville's amused nod. 'Your guess is as good as me own!'

Mister Wright's sepulchral voice rose accusingly. 'Dick Kinrade ... I think you're 'aving us on ... I think your taking the piss.'

The dark, saturnine Irishman's unconvincing protestations were drowned in a welter of argument and accusation, the more discerning men laughed both at the tale and themselves. In the cubicle the Sergeant wonderingly shook his head.

XXIV

The Sergeant stepped out of his cubicle, advanced a few paces up the room and called for Corporall Mockford. Every man of the 5th Sub-Section, while seeming to carry on with whatever he was doing, pricked up his ears as, from his bed-space at the far end of the bungalow, the Lance-Corporal strode swiftly down the room and came up to attention.

'S'arnt!'

'Corporal ... the RSM has told me to keep eyes open for a large log o' wood ... if you see one anywhere near this bungalow ... let me know!'

'S'arnt!'

The Lance-Corporal clicked his heels and went back to his bed. The room breathed again and men exchanged knowing looks. The Sergeant never again set eyes on the log, nor the completed Big Gun. Neither was he witness nor party to any of the events arising from its construction. However, by devious means he learned of its progress, of a rota of men doing stints in Pioneer Holmes' Carpenter's shop until the log, painted with pitch and laboriously polished with boot-blacking, took on a remarkable resemblance to a real gun-barrel.

Incredulously he heard over the low matting wall which separated him from his men of the dramatic acquisition of a pair of wheels - the big stumbling block in making the gun. It seemed that Private Cox on Main Gate sentry duty halted a native tonga - a pony cart. He had turned out the Guard who marched the driver to the guardroom. Privates Davies and Perkins had then, in the middle of their two hours off period, removed the cart's wheels and concealed them under the guardroom verandah. The native driver, aided down the wooden steps by the toe of the Guard-Sergeant's boot, found his patient pony tethered to a wheel-less cart. Rifle butt and bayonet-point aided Cox in assuring the native that there were no wheels on his tonga when it came up to the post.

Pioneer Holmes found some timber for the carriage and trail.

Yank Early provided technical advice and Kinrade, touched by the devotion of non-Committee members, allowed them to aid in the carving, shaping and polishing. Once assembled the wooden gun looked so realistic that Davies and Mort agreed that it looked no less fearsome than the well-served pieces that had pounded them so severely at Moodkee, and other battles of the two Sikh Wars. The gun was dismantled and hidden away while careful plans were made for its use.

Aware that the gun was finished, and knowing its purpose, the Sergeant never gave any thought to taking steps to prevent the Babu being given a rough time. He considered him a cheeky bloody nigger who had got above himself; if you let 'em do that there was no knowing where it would end, probably in another damned mutiny.

The next day, breakfast tables cleared away, the men assembled at the top end of the room in a tight-knit, sweating group, all under the forceful chairmanship of Kinrade who harangued them whilst organising nominations and voting for specific roles in the scheme. The muttering, cursing and arguing, punctuated with outbursts of uproarious laughter, lasted throughout the day, broken only by dinner. In his cubicle the Sergeant heard none of their plans, and did not want to; the less he knew the better.

The QM's Babu, Ramjee Banerjee, was a sleek, plump, self-satisfied Parsee of early middle-age. He had risen from the ranks of the battalion-employed natives, controlled by the Quartermaster. Through a shrewd combination of guile, smarming-up and sheer industry he finally became the QM's personal Babu. Once established in the Stores, gifts of native arrack and a first class pimping service, coupled with his undoubted efficiency, influenced the fat and idle QM to increasingly shrug off more and more responsibility onto the Babu. Then the Babu's power began to drive the Company to distraction. Sergeant Oakley and the entire 5th Sub-Section had all suffered from the Babu's over zealous attitude, been infuriated by his high-handed dismissals of reasonable requests and thoroughly aggrieved by his attitude towards his white masters. Complaints to the senior NCO's, conveyed to the QM, produced no results; it was a waste of time telling the RSM as he and the QM were Crimean War cronies.

Something had to be done about Ramjee Banerjee. Night after night the Wet echoed to the wild drunken schemes of retribution. Vague plots to waylay him and administer a good cobbing were dismissed as being too obvious and thereby inviting punishment. All were agreed that he could not be punched in the face as that would show marks, a bash in the guts was the answer as Plains natives had enlarged spleens. A good punch in the stomach would be damned painful. Each man imagined himself doing it, getting great satisfaction out of mere thought. During this gup the 5th Sub-Section remained smugly aloof. Dick Kinrade had convinced them that their scheme was fool-proof. When the bleeding Babu complained about them threatening to shoot him from a gun everyone would think he had gone off his little swede - where would an infantry sub-section get a bloody great 12pdr field-piece from?

The last note of the five o'clock trumpet had hardly died away when Yank Early, Paddy Finnigan and Ted Hebdon dashed from the bungalow. They hared through the Lines and were hidden behind a hut when the Babu emerged from the Stores and minced off on his way home. Quietly coming up behind him, Yank and Paddy fell in step with the native, each taking an arm in a firm grip. Hebdon covered the rear. With his eyes rolling fearfully in the dark face, the naive's head turned from one side to the other. Licking his lips he tried to brazen it out. 'The sahibs should not hold my arms like that ... there will be plenty trouble if you do not let Ramjee free.'

Yank Early smiled reassuringly. 'Don't be frit matey ... we onny wanna have a little talk with you.'

Taking a circuitous route they reached the bungalow without seeing a soul or being seen themselves. When the Babu's eyes adjusted from the bright sunlight to the semi-darkness he saw he was in the middle of a circle of fully dressed and accoutred soldiers. Most were familiar faces and some, like Private Wright had names he knew. He opened his mouth to appeal to the old soldier but Private Wright's attention was focused downwards, nodding significantly at the Babu's feet which were neatly clad in a well-polished pair of ammunition boots. Before the native realised the ominous implications of that nod the men were upon him.

'Yer black-faced git ... doncher know bleedin' niggers ain't allowed in white men's buildings wiv boots on?'

'Boot the black soor aht!'

'Take 'is bloody boots orf an' chuck 'em away!'

' 'Old on a minnit ... they're a sight better than me own chaplis!'

Men pushed and jostled to land a kick on the plump native, propelling him out onto the verandah where he was forced down onto the wooden boards and relieved of the offending boots. Looking around anxiously, Kinrade called out. 'Get the sod back inside, quickly ... afore someone sees 'im!'

In the bungalow beds had been pulled back and the tables set out as for a court-martial, lockers serving as chairs. Enough men in the Sub-Section had been on the receiving end of the courts to be familiar with the layout. Privates Finnigan and Hebdon stood at his shoulders as Ramjee, sitting behind a table, faced the Court. It was a 'Hanging Court' alright, composed of Lance-Corporal Mockford as President and Privates Davies and Wright as Members - all were old soldiers steeped in the British Army traditions as to the right way to handle natives. Private Kinrade rather fancied himself as President but chose instead to be the Prosecuting Officer. It had been agreed that everything must be square and above board; Justice had to be done and therefore the accused must be given the services of a Soldier's Friend or Defending Officer. After careful consideration the role was bestowed upon Private Alexander. Big Sanny, not being very bright, did not understand at all so his mucker, Ding Dong Dell, was deputised to instruct him in his duties.

The accused was becoming increasingly disturbed, sweating profusely and looking desperately from side to side seeking some avenue of escape. So much so that his keepers roughly placed their restraining hands on his shoulders. The President called the Court to order. Not having a gavel he rapped on the blanket covered table-top with a knife handle and proceeded to read the charges - set out in proper military fashion by his mate in the Orderly Room in return for a few jars of ale. The Lance-Corporal was not a very good scholar and his halting delivery drove the impatient Kinrade into frequent corrections and urgings to get a bloody move on.

'The Accused, Ramjee Banerjee, Babu ... a follower of Her Majesty's Forces ... being subject to military law as a soldier under the provisions of the Mutiny Act and the Articles of War ... is charged with ...One ... behaving in a scandalous manner unbecoming the character of a Babu and a gentleman in that he did misapply the care and distribution of Regimental clothing and necessities ... Two ... conduct to the prejudice of good order and military discipline in that he, when serving as Babu in the Quartermaster's Stores of Her Majesty's 131st Regiment of Foot, did indulge in gross over-familiarity with his superiors, to wit, white British soldiers of said Regiment.'

Laying down the paper, the President looked at Ramjee. 'How do you plead ... guilty or not guilty?'

The Babu wrung his hands and rolled his eyes. Birch nudged his neighbour. ' 'E's goin' ter fuckin' cry!'

But the Babu disappointed them. Pulling himself together he began to speak in the dignified tones of a forbearing man prepared to overlook the whole affair if they let him go. It was so like his customary infuriating manner that it completely alienated any sympathy, even in the hearts of such softer men as Private Saville. Quite out of order, Kinrade shouted across at him. 'Shut yer gob, yer black soor ... you'll git yer chance ter address the Court later ... wot d'ye plead ... guilty or not guilty?'

The President glared at the Prosecutor. 'I'll ask yer to keep quiet and know yer place Private Kinrade! I 'ave ter ask 'im that!' He looked sternly at the Babu. 'Enuff o' that now ... come on ... are yer guilty or not guilty?'

Despairingly the Babu shook his head, realising he had no alternative but to go along with the Feringhee's peculiar sense of humour. 'Not guilty, Sahib.'

The President nodded. 'That's better! I call on the Prosecution to state its case! Now you can 'ave yer say, Kinrade.'

Stepping forward importantly, the Prosecutor called his first witness. 'Number 3899 Private Birch, E ...'

Smirking self-consciously, Roomy Birch stepped forward and took the oath. 'The evidence which I shall give before this Court shall be the truth, the whole truth and nothing but the truth, so help me God.'

Then, frequently prompted by the Prosecutor, Birch told a rambling tale of his repeated efforts to get an old shirt changed, dramatically producing the tattered garment as evidence.

There followed a succession of witnesses parading worn

boots, holed socks and frayed trousers and tunics. Each man displayed remarkable memories of verbatim statements made by the Accused when slighting and insulting his superiors, to wit, white British soldiers. As the case unrolled it was seen that every man in the Sub-Section, bar those actually employed as Court Officials, had been subpoenaed as Prosecution Witnesses. All save Private Bell, who had to tell the Defending Officer what to do, and Boy Farley who, for the sake of appearance, had been detailed as Witness for the Defence. So far as he was able, the Band Rat violently objected to his role, claiming on account of his years of being given a worse time than most by the Accused.

The Accused was given the opportunity of cross-examining each witness but, to everyone's disappointment he just shook his head and continued to sit with his eyes gazing downwards at the flagstone floor and his own bootless feet. In fact, the Babu's lack of spirit was taking the gilt off the gingerbread a bit, arousing fears that they were not going to get true value for the weeks of work on the Big Gun and trial planning.

Kinrade's last witness sat down and the President looked across at Private Alexander. 'Defending Officer ... are you ready?'

Startled by the sudden attention, Big Sanny gazed wildly around before being prodded to his feet by Ding Dong Dell. With his hands clasped nervously in front of him, Big Sanny stared with awe at the solemn triumvirate seated behind the table. 'Er ... er ... aye Corp'l ... aye ... we ... me an' Ding Dong ... we're riddy.'

The President nodded. 'Call your first witness.'

Sanny looked at Bell who hissed, "Boy Farley."

'Er ... er ... aye ... er Boy Farley!'

The President shook his head in exasperation. 'No ... no ... no ... give 'is name an' number!'

Private Bell stood up. 'Och ... Sanny canna read ... kin I read it for 'im?'

The President conferred with fellow members, then nodded. Bell spoke. 'Call the first witness ... Number 1815 Boy Farley!'

The slim, spotty-faced boy stood up, gazing expectantly at Big Sanny who turned a similar look in Bell's direction. Resignedly, Ding Dong again rose to his feet. 'Wi' the Court's permission ... '

He swore Boy Farley in and everyone waited with interest as the lad looked dubiously at the lifeless Babu. Farley racked his brains for something to say in favour of the Babu whereas he would dearly have loved to add to the chronicle of misdeed - but he daren't as Bandsman Mort would beat his arse raw for not doing as he had been told.

'Well ... well ... 'e ain't akcherly 'it me!'

Raucous laughter rolled and echoed around the high-beamed room and Boy Farley beamed in surprise at his success. Frowning, the President asked if that was all ... had he nothing else to say in the Accused's favour? Boy Farley shook his head.

'Then the Prosecutor can make his final address.'

This was the moment for which Kinrade had been impatiently waiting, having spent a great deal of pencil-licking time on his statement. As befitted perhaps the best barrackroom lawyer in 'C' Company, it was delivered with all his undoubted articulacy and conviction. When, after ten minutes he came to the end of the long catalogue of misdeeds and omissions, the admiring audience could be forgiven for thinking he had forgotten to say the Babu had also been responsible for starting the Mutiny of '57. Ramjee sat motionless throughout, with his head lowered and displaying a disappointing lack of emotion. He didn't even look up when the impassioned Prosecutor's voice died away.

The President looked at the Defending Officer. 'Now you make your final statement an' plea o' miti ... miti ... mitigation.'

Big Sanny stood up, dragging Bell with him. He felt he was beginning to understand what was required of him. ' 'Im ... yon laddie ... 'e would"na gi' me any socks ... an' 'e tole me ta git outa 'is store.'

Ding Dong pulled his sleeve. 'No, Sanny ... no ... ye s'posed ter say nice things about 'im ... you're 'is friend!'

Sanny glared indignantly at his mate. 'No ... no I'm not ... I dinna like 'im ... 'e would'na gi me any socks!'

Suddenly, to everyone's surprise, the Babu came to life, his Mission school voice contrasting strangely with the deep boom of the bewildered Scotsman.

'Sahibs ... I am a Christian ... like you ... made in God's image same as you ... I have a wife and children ... three ... two boys and a little girl ... Sahibs ... it is time to stop cursing and beating my race ... we are brothers ... but I am afraid of you ... and that is not right ... in the Lord's eyes.'

His voice died away and he looked round despairingly at the

sea of faces surrounding him. For a long moment there was silence. Gazing first at the Babu, then at each other, men sought through howls of rage to salve their conscience and paper over any sympathetic cracks that might have appeared in the purposeful walls of contempt and hatred.

'Cheeky bastard! Bruvvers ... 'e ain't my bruvver ...black bugger!'

' 'E may be a Christian ... but 'e ain't a good Catholic!'

'Stop cursin' an' beatin' why, that's orl that keeps them sods in line!'

The President beat frantically on the table-top. 'Order! Order in the Court!'

The hubbub died down. Ramjee again sank into his shell of apathy. Huddled on the locker sweat poured down his dark face that, a far as its colour would allow seemed to be taking on a grey hue. Lance-Corporal Mockford waited for complete silence.

'Well ... I s'pose that were the Accused's plea o' defence ... now we gotta consider our verdict.'

Sitting on either side, Privates Davies and Wright inclined themselves and the three soldiers briefly conferred. Straightening up, they stared solemnly to the front as Private Kinrade stepped up and placed a square of black material on the Lance-Corporal's head. That was his own idea; no one in the room had ever been on a court-martial where a death sentence was passed but they all knew this action to be routine in civil courts, and it seemed a neat touch to round off proceedings. Despite looking a bit silly, no one laughed or even thought it amusing. As Kinrade had surmised, that little piece of rag blackened with boot polish was awe-inspiring. It certainly seemed to affect the President of the Court as he cleared his throat nervously. 'The prisoner will rise and face the Court.'

The Babu had to be dragged to his feet by Finnigan and Hebdon. Weakly resisting he muttered. 'Sahibs ... let me go home ... I feel ill.'

'Babu Ramjee Banerjee ... the sentence of this Court is that you shall be taken to the place of execution and there be launched into Eternity by being fired from the mouth of a gun ... and may the Lord have mercy on your soul!'

The native shuddered, fighting wildly against the restraining hands of his escort. His voice rose in a wail. 'No ... no ... Sahibs

... no .... not that ... my wife ... my children ... what will become of them ... no no!'

Seeing him standing there, wailing, seemed to knock the stuffing out of some and Kinrade had to bustle around, bullying and urging. The Court shed its legal coat and donned the mantle of executioner, forming up in procession to escort the condemned man outside to where the Big Gun had been erected. Lance-Corporal Mockford called the Parade to order and everyone stiffened, staring straight to the front as though on a Saturday morning Commanding Officer's Parade.

'Execution Party! Execution Party ... by the lafe ... slow march!'

To the beat of Boy Farley's drum and the shrill pipe of Bandsman Mort's borrowed fife playing the 'Rogue's March', the party stepped off in a jerky, rhythmic ceremonial slow-march. The Babu's feet refused to move and he had to be supported and thrust forward by the two soldiers marching alongside. He looked into Finnigan's face. 'I am a Christian ... I must have a priest ... a priest.'

Staring straight to his front, Finnigan hissed from the corner of his mouth. 'Sorry mate ... 'fraid we ain't got one.'

Birch gave the same answer as the party came to the top of the wooden steps leading down from the verandah to the open space between the back of the bungalow and the jakes and ablutions. At that moment the Babu, set down on his feet after being carried down the steps, caught sight of the Big Gun, standing ominously solitary.

It looked tremendous. Black and menacing like a crouching monster about to roar and spit fire. It even caused the escort, who had personally spent so many weary weeks manufacturing it - to catch their breath. On seeing it, the Babu was galvanised into a frenzy, frothing at the mouth and contorting his body as though convulsed by pain. With difficulty, the men dragged him to the muzzle, lowered so as to press into his back just above the waist, and tightly tethered him into position. Then everyone stood back at Attention behind the gun on either side of the trail, leaving the struggling native alone at the muzzle. Rigidly, Lance-Corporal stood apart, his arms straight down by his side with his head back and his eyes staring unseeingly forward. Stretched down at the seam of his trousers, his fingers curled.

'Prepare to Fire!'

A brief pause ensued as everyone drew in a deep breath.

'Fire!'

'Bang!'

As loudly as they could possibly shout, every man roared out the word, fracturing the still evening air and scattering the birds from the distant trees. At the gun muzzle the Babu jerked violently, as a man under such circumstances would and, instead of disintegrating into a far-flung cloud of bloody flesh, bone and frizzing goblets of fat, he slumped lifelessly in his bonds.

'My Gawd ... weren't that the bleedin' limit!'

'D'jer see 'im jump ... as though 'ed 'ad the rough end of a pineapple stuck up his arse!'

'Christ! I ain't seen anythin' ter beat it since Piggy Mullins shit 'isself on C.O's Parade.'

Kinrade led Birch, Hebdon and Mister Wright to the front of the gun. 'Let's untie the poor bleeder ... kick 'is arse and send 'im 'ome to 'is wife and kids.'

Kinrade put his hand under the Babu's chin and lifted his head, slapping the sweat-dewed face with his other hand. 'Come on mate ... wake up ... it's all over ... teach yer to be a good boy ter yer superiors in future.'

The native's head sagged. Wright looked closely at him. 'Christ! I think the bugger's dead ... we've really done for 'im!'

They untied the Babu and lowered the body to the dusty ground. The Lance-Corporal knelt and put an ear to his chest.

' 'E's as dead as a bleedin' doornail! Must've frightened 'im ter death.'

Birch sneered. 'Soft as shit these bleedin' niggers.'

'Can't take a joke neither.' said Coughlin.

Later that evening the Sergeant heard how the Babu had been found dead on the steps of his Store, evidently collapsing with heart failure. Wondering if it had anything to do with his lot or whether Providence had taken a hand to waste all their efforts with the Big Gun, he reflected that the man was a Parsee; their bodies had to be put on a hill for the birds to peck. They'd have a job finding a suitable hill on this bloody great Plain.

XXV

That night Private Birch could not sleep. laying awake he reflected morbidly on wounds and death. Always a fearful soldier, he had providentially cringed his way through five campaigns without a single hurt, firmly believing that if he had to soldier he would as soon serve his time on a charpoy in the barrackrooms as anywhere else. With his eyes tightly shut in an effort to attract the elusive slumber he sensed a movement from the bed opposite occupied by his file, Pat Coughlin. Birch raised his head expecting to see the big Irishman stagger to his feet and pad to the urine-tub on the verandah. When no shadowy figure arose, Birch became curious and stared intently through the gloom. He was then struck by a thought that made him go rigid from head to toe, perhaps old Pat was going to get them diamonds out.

For ten long years Birch had nurtured the conviction that his mate Coughlin was hiding a hoard of precious stones, looted when they had stormed the Palace at Lucknow in 1858. In all those years, watching and waiting, he had never seen anything to confirm his belief. Hardly daring to breathe he gazed across the dim room to where Coughlin, supported on his right elbow, was ferreting around under the bed with his left hand, eventually to bring up a small package that cascaded a stream of small pebbles with a faint but audible tinkle. Incredulously, Birch watched the Irishman play with the pebbles, rolling them between his fingers and allowing them to drop, one by one, onto the dark blanket beneath. Finally Pat put them back in the bag and again secreted them beneath the bed.

For much of that night Birch lay awake, thinking of ways to get the precious stones and what to do with them, all the time trying to work out how much they were worth. Somehow he stumbled through his drills the next day. His mind was in a turmoil and full of feverish impatience for the hours to pass until the dismissal from Last Parade would empty the bungalow. To mates rushing off to the Wet Canteen he said he had a touch of the shits and would hang around near the jakes for a bit.

Alone in the room at last he roughly upturned Coughlin's rope-mesh charpoy and slowly ran his eyes over its under-surface, seeking some secret compartment in its bamboo frame or legs. He could see nothing, but with his fingers running along the smooth wood he soon found the edges of a small cavity with a wood plug 'door'. His trembling fingers brought out the little leather bag. He stuffed it securely in his trouser pocket, righted and tidied the bed and rushed from the bungalow, his scurrying feet not halting until he reached a quiet nullah on the outskirts of the cantonment. Breathing hard, Birch sat on the sandy ground and opened the little bag, tipping onto his palm a collection of various sized pebbles. With his forefinger he sorted them. There were four large, brilliant, cut-and-polished and ten smooth uncut stones. Birch remained there for an hour, gloating and playing with the diamonds and then he ambled back to the Canteen to smugly drink with his Irish file, thoughtfully eyeing him and wondering what he would do when he found the stones were gone.

Birch did not really expect anything to happen too quickly; surely Coughlin did not inspect the stones every night? In the event, some inner alarm must have prompted the Irishman to check as soon as the room settled down and Birch was visited sooner than he expected. He had tried to remain awake but, tired after the previous night and worn out by the tension of the day, Birch must have dozed off, suddenly being brought to life by a gentle but insistent shaking of the shoulder. Slowly opening his eyes he found Coughlin's face close to his own and, three inches from his throat, the dully gleaming point of a 17.5 inch Snider-Enfield bayonet.

'Birchy you bastard ... give me them fuckin' diamonds!'

'Diamonds? Wot diamonds?'

A sharp point pricked the loose flesh of Birch's neck.

'Don' ye be givin' me that! Ye know wot I'm talkin' of!'

'Pat ... calm down ... yer knows arf of 'em rightly belongs ter me ... gi' me yer word ter share an' share alike ... an' I'll give 'em ter yer.'

Coughlin stiffened. For a moment Birch was frightened, wondering if he had gone too far as the Irishman's voice grated in his ear. 'They're fuck all to do wiv ye. They're mine ... bought an' paid for wi' me own money ... at Lucknow ... bleedin' years ago ... give 'em to me ... or I'll fuckin' do for yer!'

The bayonet thrust threateningly forward, then both men started as Kinrade's grating voice broke the stillness. 'An' wot the 'ell is goin' on over there ... may I ask?'

Straightening up, Coughlin looked over his shoulder. Across the room Kinrade was sitting up and he could see Yank Early, always a light sleeper, rising on his elbows. Down the room men were stirring restlessly. Posed in a tableau, the minds of both Birch and Coughlin raced over their options, united only in their determination to keep the diamonds within the family.

'Ah ... it's you then Dick ... well ... nuffin really ... onny bit of trouble wiv Roomy 'ere.'

'Pat ... are ye sayin' that bloody Protestant's nickin' yer stuff agin?'

'Well ... yeah ... I s'pose so ... yeah ... that's it ... Roomy's nicked me ... me button-stick.'

With his long, black-haired legs protruding below his shirt, Kinrade roused the room as he came padding across. 'Wake up me lads ... come on the Pope's Boys ... we got trouble with them C of E's agin!'

The age old urgency of an appeal to religion brought Privates Cox and Finnigan to Kinrade's side before anyone else had left their beds. As he looked from one side to the other, Kinrade remembered that both the Sergeant and the Lance-Corporal , with Private Wright, were away from the bungalow on Main Gate Guard.

'Me lads ... Birchy's up to it agin ... he's gotter be broken o' them thievin' ways of 'is once an' fer all!' He looked around the sleep-drugged faces of men now crowding round the bed. 'Seems a cobbin' ain't enuff to teach 'im a leson ... 'e's got to be stopped from takin' honest Catholic lads belongings ... nuffin worse than a thief inna barrackroom ... Birchy ... if ye took Pat's button-stick then yer got to be taught a lesson ... did ye take it now?'

Frantically, Birch considered his position. Certainly he did not relish another cobbing but, after waiting eleven years neither did he wish to lose the diamonds. He reasoned: making a fuss might cause deeper searching into why he and Pat were arguing in the middle of the night, on the other hand, he was sure that Pat would not tell of he stones. Birch answered, with not altogether simulated indignation.

'Button-stick! I ain't got 'is bloody button-stick. 'Ere ... come an' search me bed-space ... you'll find no button-stick 'ere.'

And indeed that was found to be the case. But Kinrade was in no mood for such unimportant trivialities, button-stick or no button-stick, with the NCO's away from the room this was a real chance to get one over on the Protestants.

'Ye've hidden it somewheres, Birchy. I'll take the word of a good Mass-going Catholic ... if 'e says you've nicked his button-stick then so far as I'm concerned you 'ave ... and you got to be punished fer it.'

In any self-respecting military circle a man who stole from his mates, particularly items of kit whose loss could land the owner in trouble, had nothing much going for him. To tired men wanting to go back to bed but excited by the prospect of seeing rough justice, Private Kinrade's rabble-rousing oratory was pretty persuasive. Seeing that he had got them going, Kinrade inspiringly introduced a fanatical religious aspect, strongly supported by his Pope's Boys and accepted by the others out of sheer morbid curiosity.

'Me lads, cobbin's no use ... 'e's 'ad it once an' it didn' do the trick ... its gotta be somethin' Birchy'll remember all his life ... so's every time 'e looks at 'is thievin' hands he remembers it.'

Snatching the bayonet from Coughlin, he flourished it above his head. 'This is it! We'll put one o' these lungers through each o' Birchy's 'ands ... pin 'im ter the table-top ... crucify 'im ... like they did ter the good Lord.'

'Crucify 'im? Christ ... yer can't do that ... be all sorts o' trouble whin 'e can't 'old a rifle!'

'No. It won't do nothin' like that ... pushed 'tween the bones of the hand it'll onny make a small 'ole ... it'll heal up in no time. Come on lads, git 'im over 'ere.'

At his signal the three Pope's Boys flung themselves on the stupefied Birch, dragging him to his feet and across to where the table boards leaned upright against the wall. Men looked at each other, waiting for someone to protest. Private Wright, the one most likely to do so was out of the room on Guard, and Yank Early seemed lost in fascination at the primitive antics of his adopted comrades. Coughlin and Cox held the writhing Birch still while Finnigan grabbed his left wrist with both hands and, dragging the arm upwards, forced the back of his hand flat against the board. Kinrade stepped forward with his bayonet poised, only to leap back as one of Birch's lunging feet came near.

'Will ye be 'oldin' 'im still, yer berks!'

Holding the bayonet with both hands like a dagger, Kinrade carefully placed its point against the palm of Birch's hand and, leaning his full weight on it, slowly drove the slim, tapering blade through the skin and muscle between the metacarpal bones. It ended up in the wood behind. Ironically this was the table-top Birch was responsible for keeping clean and would later be required to scrape his own bloodstains from it.

Up until the moment he felt the point penetrate, Private Birch had not believed it was going to be done to him. Then, as it bit home, he took a deep breath that filled his lungs with air and let out an ear-splitting scream. Nocturnal shouts and screams were common in barracks: sleeping soldiers had nightmares of hissing scything canister in a host of battles, of gigantic native warriors about to disembowel or decapitate with razor-sharp spear or sword. However, shattering the silence of the night, this unnerving screech jolted some sanity back into the shocked men of the 5th Sub-Section and set them in motion. As Kinrade stepped away and reached for the nearest bayonet in its sheath on the wall behind Private Saville's bed-space, Martin Early blocked the way. 'Goddamn it! Haven't you done enough ... there'll be no more of this!'

'Giddout of me way Yank ... got no quarrel wiv you ... don' you wanna see justice done?'

Eyeball to eyeball, they confronted each other as men slid into opposing parties, determinedly facing up. Coughlin, Cox and Finnigan sprang to their leader's side, letting go their hold on Birch so that the weight of his slumping body fell agonisingly on his bayonet-speared hand, causing him to scream yet again. Hardly had the startled men recovered and the scream's echo died when a fully dressed and equipped Sergeant Oakley was among them. Bursting through the open doorway he stopped short at what he saw.

'Christ Almighty! What in God's name are you up to?'

For the past hour, in the Main Gate Guardroom he had been uneasy, made restless by a premonition that, with both NCO's away, there might be trouble in bungalow 5. Finally he had left Lance-Corporal Mockford in charge and come over, to prove an affinity had matured between him and the occupants of the hut that might have afforded gratification but for the horror it revealed. The Sergeant stepped over to the fainting Birch and gently and tenderly withdrew the bayonet from his hand. Slumping forward, Birch was caught by the Sergeant but not before a small leather bag dropped from his shirt pocket to fall on the flagstone floor; the stones scattered.

In the stupefied silence that followed, each man digested what he saw before him. All had repeatedly heard Birch's story of Coughlin's diamonds without really believing or disbelieving it, now they saw the proof before their eyes. Coughlin moved to collect them but was halted in his tracks by the Sergeant's glare. Birch, sitting with his head bowed on Saville's bed and nursing his injured hand, looked up and momentarily forgot his pain.

Haltingly, Coughlin explained how he and Birch, serving in John Company's 1st Bengal European Regiment at the storming of Lucknow, had got into the Palace too late to find any worthwhile plunder left behind by the British and native soldier-looters. Outside, a Sikh sergeant in charge of a party ordered to confiscate loot furtively offered Coughlin the little bag of diamonds. The Irishman, who had had money in his pocket for months with no chance of spending it, gave every penny he had for them. He had been hiding them ever since, ready for the time when he was trooped home to the old country. Plaintively, the Irish soldier appealed for justice, saying that the stones were his and Birch had no claim on them.

Pondering the situation, the Sergeant bent down and picked up the largest and most brilliant of the four faceted and polished stones. Turning it in his hand he noticed a minute hole drilled into it; Coughlin said that was where a chain went. Private Saville, by far the most educated soldier in the room, looked puzzled. He politely asked the Sergeant if he might view the stone more closely. Shrugging, the Sergeant handed it to him. Examining it intently, Saville held it up to the moonlight that was streaming through the high windows. He bit on it gingerly then handed the stone back to the Sergeant. The Sergeant looked enquiringly at Saville and, polite as always, 'Captain' Saville smiled gently. 'Sergeant ... I'm afraid they are not diamonds ...

real diamonds are among the hardest of known substances and could never be drilled like that ... I think ... I think they are pieces of glass ... probably from a chandelier.'

All eyes turned on Coughlin, then onto the stricken Birch. They returned to look at the Sergeant who was gazing down at the 'diamonds' scattered on the stone floor. Suddenly, in an impetuous gesture, the Sergeant raised his Snider rifle and crashed the iron-bound butt down onto the stones. Outraged, Coughlin flung himself protectively forward, only to find the 'diamond' that he sought to scoop up had become a small heap of powdered glass splinters. He gazed forlornly down amid an uproar of hooting and laughter. The Sergeant, encouraged by his men, pounded the rifle onto the pebbles until all of them were powdered and splintered.. The pent up tension of the nigh was released by men roaring with uncontrollable laughter and bringing tears to their eyes. It was a laughter so infectious that before it petered out even the principal actors, Birch and Coughlin, had managed to raise a weak guffaw.

XXVI

Creeping drearily onward, the days of the Hot Season formed a drab backcloth to the ritualistic soldiering, hated by all but better borne by some than others. All ranks, from commissioned officer to lowly private, laboured under a burden of life patterned as unalterably as the seasons. Change was only capable by little short of death - and that an irrevocable solution necessarily imposed by an outside agency or, when existence became intolerable, by one's own hand.

Perpetually balancing his position and privilege against the accompanying sense of isolation, the Sergeant floated along in a limbo of bad and better days, but no good days. Men in the ranks mostly had bad days but they were made vaguely tolerable by a sense of comradeship, rough as it might be. But, long solitary hours spent mulling over the dual afflictions of loneliness and sadness gradually aroused in the Sergeant the conviction that eventually he would succumb to the pressures weighing upon him.

He did not believe that Sergeant Digges' exit line was his solution, the very thought was as hard and chill as a Snider muzzle was to the teeth and lips. Anyway, if it was going to come to that he would have done it when Amy died.

Perhaps by another's hand? There were no signs of trouble up on the Frontier and it was unlikely that the Regiment would march-out in the middle of the Hot Season. The job would not be done for him by Afridi, Orakzai, Mohmand or any other tribesman.

One of his own side? Well, it had been known for a fellow soldier to go mad and run amok in a 'Hot Weather Shooting', Indian newspapers were full of such incidents.

The Sergeant shook his head. These were not the solutions for a life that had lost its savour. A month or so back he might have become pre-occupied with morbid introspection but of late he had found comfort, in the rough and awkward comradeship and gruff warmth of the men under him. It was an unbalanced relationship with men revealing in embarrassed, indirect ways, their awareness of his problems - as when Lance-Corporal quietly said. 'I were married once.'

'Were you? What happened?'

'Well S'arnt ... you know how it is ... only two wives per Company taken overseas ... drew lots ... she weren't lucky. Last saw 'er ... oh, twenty years ago ... she were standing crying wiv the kids clinging to 'er skirts ... as we drew away from Gosport Hard.'

The Sergeant pictured it happening to Amy. Christ, in some ways it was worse than dying. Well, he wasn't the only one who'd had troubles.

'You haven't heard of her since?'

'No ... neither of us can read or write.'

The fierce sun transformed the Cantonment into a pot simmering over a slow fire, boiling away until its tight lid blew off, but slowly ... like an avalanche beginning with loose stones until it got beyond its own control. The first rocks had rolled when the Sergeant introduced the telling of stories in the barrackroom, planting fears in Private Alexander's apprehensive mind that he would have to speak. The downhill movement picked up speed when the tactical exercises with model soldiers brought to the same soldier a nagging dread of being ordered to take command, leading to ridicule or even another flogging. The inexorable progress along the road to violence and destruction raced towards its climax on a Saturday morning in late July, when the Commanding Officer inspected his Regiment.

Keenly scrutinising each man he led his entourage down the ranks; Adjutant, Company Commander, Half-Company Commander, Regimental Sergeant-Major, Company Sergeant-Major and the non-commissioned Officer in charge of the section under inspection. Eventually they arrived at the 5th Sub-Section of No.3 Section of the Left Half of 'C' Company. The Commanding Officer returned the Sergeant's salute and the Sergeant tacked himself onto the end of the procession. Lieutenant-Colonel Walter John Howard Pearse-Frodsham gazed steadily at Private Birch, right-hand man of the Sub-Section. He slowly passed to Privates Saville and Kinrade before coming to a halt before Private Alexander's squat, unsoldierly figure. Stepping back a pace the Commanding Officer slowly and penetratingly eyed him from head to foot. The searching gaze of this terrifying officer who had twice ordered him flogged drove from the big man any chance of remaining impassive; he trembled, his face twitched and he blinked his eyes. Fearing an explosion the Sergeant fervently prayed that the man would hang together and not erupt in some incongruous unmilitary manner. He was alarmed at the sight of the Scotsman's knuckles whitening and his fingers tightening on the rifle barrel.

Affronted by this blot on his Regiment's smartness, the CO snorted. 'Keep still man ... keep still, I say! Take one pace forward ... march!'

The dreaded voice did nothing to freeze Big Sanny into immobility. It resurrected in his fevered brain the whistle of the cat-of-nine-tails, its impact searing through the flesh and muscle to the very heart. Such memories were beyond bearing and, working on the Scot's simple mind transformed him from a stiffly erect soldier into a cringing hulk, vainly seeking some sort of sanctuary and finding none save comrades tightly crowded around him. In his desperation, Private Alexander perpetrated the unique military enormity of turning without being ordered, presenting his sweat-blackened tunic shoulders to the purpling Colonel.

Appalled along with everyone else, the Sergeant's spine twitched as he involuntarily constricted his body, as though to vanish within the damp uniform. My God, the RSM would have plenty to say about this ... there would be blame, Army style, coming his way. Moving only his eyes, he looked into Private Bell's anguished face who was appealing to Sanny, to the Sergeant, to God ... to someone to do something to help his pathetic mate. The Sergeant's eyes moved back to Private Alexander and, glancing down, the big trembling frame seemed to be compulsively gripping its hand onto the rifle-butt; the beginnings of a full-bodied swing that would smash the CO's jaw. Incredibly flouting every military instinct ingrained by years of soldiering, the Sergeant jumped forward, pushing his way between the stiff ranks of the entourage. Forcing aside officers and sergeant-majors alike, the Sergeant forced his body up against that of the big Scot. Grabbing the rifle he cried loudly.

'Bell ... Kinrade! Fall-in! Arrest and escort Private Alexander to the Guardroom!'

As though on cue, the two men leapt forward, single sharp strides confining Big Sanny to the front and rear. The Sergeant crashed his heels together, drew himself up and slapped his rifle butt in salute.

'Sir! Permission to place Private Alexander under close arrest! Sir!'

Adjutant, Company Officers and Sergeant-Majors all stiffened in outraged incredulity. The Commanding Officer, looking directly into the Sergeant's eyes, did not speak for a moment then dryly observed, in a surprisingly mild tone.

'It seems you have already done so, Sergeant. Yes, march him away!'

Boy Farley was the Duty Drummer when Private Alexander and his escort halted on the Guardroom verandah. Open mouthed he stared at the big friendly bear before gathering himself to flash a furtive wink of comfort. The big Scotsman ignored him, oblivious to everything. His lumpy, squat body hunched forward as though drained of life and sweat dripped from his round face, his opaque eyes stared unseeingly at the ground. Private Bell was ordered to remove the prisoner's equipment, the Sergeant anticipating less chance of resistance if his mate did it. Bell also carried out the routine removal of boot-laces and braces that could be used for suicidal purposes. Knowing he had to confine this pathetic hulk of a man safely in a cell before he did something to bring a major punishment down on his head, the Sergeant began making out a charge sheet, worded in the mildest possible style.

'What's your number Alexander?'

No answer. Desperately, Private Bell unavailingly mouthed the number before gulping and blurting out. 'Four O Five One, S'arnt.'

Ignoring the breach of discipline, the Sergeant completed the charge-sheet.

'The accused, No. 4051 Private Alexander, William, HM's 131st Regiment of Foot, a soldier of the Regular Forces, is charged with - disobeying in such a manner as to show wilful defiance of authority, a lawful command given personally by his superior officer, in the execution of his office, in that he, at

Mirzapur Cantonment, on 3rd July 1868, when personally ordered by Lieutenant Colonel W.J.H.Pearse-Frodsham HM 131st Regiment of Foot, to step one pace forward did refuse by turning his back on said officer.' He handed it to the Guard-Commander. 'Go easy on him ...he's as puggled as they come.'

Studying the charge-sheet, the Guard-Commander raised his eyes heavenward. 'I'll say he is! Turning his back on the bleedin' CO! They'll throw the book at him for that.'

The Sergeant shrugged his shoulders and glanced at the Scotsman whose hooded eyes were open and glaring at him with burning malevolence. In the wake of the Guard-Commander, the prisoner shuffled out of sight in a graceless progress to a cell, his hands holding up his falling trousers and his laceless boots scuffing the ground. Drained and despondent, the Sergeant fell-in Privates Bell and Kinrade on the verandah and the three men struck out into the shimmering heat that bounced from the dusty ground like a missile. He thought of his arbitrary actions on Parade. They were punishable although he had a feeling the CO understood even if the rest didn't. He knew there would be plenty said by the Company Commander, the Half-Company Commander, the Regimental Sergeant-Major and his own Company Sergeant-Major. Private Bell, his cycs rigidly to the front, muttered. 'Sarn't ... what did you charge him with?'

'The least I could ... disobeying a lawful command.'

'What do you think he'll get? They won't flog him again will they?'

'I don't know ... I hope not. If I get a chance I'll say in evidence that he don't know what he's doing.'

Bell's step faltered, half turning he looked over his shoulder. 'Then they'll say he's fanti ...an' put him away!'

'Look to your front! What do you want? Something's got to be done for his own safety. He might have killed the CO out there ... then you'd have been on an execution parade you'd never forget.'

Tramping steadily forward, Private Kinrade spoke softly two empty spaces before him. 'Hope he's worth sticking yer neck out fer.'

'I think he is!' The Sergeant muttered.

Falling-out, the three pushed through the tatty-curtain into the stifling shadowy barrackroom. Momentarily halting the inevitable and untidy tableau of men divesting themselves of uniforms and equipment, the Sergeant studied their faces, seeking understanding. He was reassured by nods and fleeting smiles that bordered on undue familiarity and undiscipline. Still in need of human contact and disinclined to bury himself in his cubicle, the Sergeant walked slowly up the room in the narrow space between trestle-tables and beds. He felt overwhelmingly that he had to make contact with these men, fleetingly smiling as men's eyes caught his before turning away in confusion and embarrassment. Warmth flooded over him, a glow of goodwill at being one of them, of belonging. Suddenly happier than for months, the Sergeant had the strange feeling of coming home to a familiar niche where he was welcome. Wryly, he reflected that they were poor substitutes for a wife and family, but they were all he had.

Unresisting, Private Alexander allowed himself to be pushed along the passage and into the cell. The iron door gave a hollow crash and the key creaked in its lock. He stood with his head lowered and his chest heaving. From beneath his beetling brows his eyes glowered as the sweat trickled down his face to drip from the tip of his simian nose. He'd done wrong again, he knew he had. He could not remember what it was but he knew it was the Sergeant's fault. He'd always had it in for him. Wanting him to tell a story when he didn't know any and couldn't talk good. Then all them little soldiers what Captain made, one for each man, the Sergeant tried to make him look stupid, moving all them little clay men around on an old blanket, with bits of rocks and grass on it. Next time he wouldn't move them, even if the Sergeant ordered him to. He'd knock them on the floor and stamp on them. Tears filled Sanny's eyes and his heavy feet passionately pounded on the cell floor. The Sergeant had taken away his rifle ... on Parade! Then he'd ordered his own mate ... Ding Dong ... and Kinrade ... who always took the piss out of him ... to march him to the Guardroom! Everyone was laughing at him. There was nothing to laugh at 'cos Big Sanny was locked in this terrible hot cell again, and the Sergeant had charged him ... he'd marched him in front of the CO ... he'd turned his back on him ... he'd be 'raged against him ... have him flogged again. Oh God!

Cringing and whimpering at such fearful thoughts, Big Sanny hunched his shoulders, tightly wrapping his arms around his body like a man chilled. In the oven-hot cell Sanny stood thus for a while, then, lifting his head he shook himself like a dog emerging from water. He glared maniacally around the box's smooth, lime-washed walls and ceiling, at the well-scrubbed wooden platform stretching from wall to wall, rising at one end in a round log pillow. There was no furniture save a brass-bound, wooden urinal bucket in a corner. Little air came through the stubby bars of a small, high set and recessed glassless window. As the minutes passed it seemed as though the incandescent walls were relentlessly expanding and contracting, pumping out what little air there was.

The big Scot began gasping and fighting for breath. His brain felt like it was being compressed by his aching and pulsating head. Knuckled fists rubbed hard into the sockets to prevent the eyeballs popping out through the heat. Increasingly agitated at the thought of being left to suffocate, Sanny prowled the restrictive area; jumping on and off the bed platform, sobbing and growling, muttering in panic, pounding and kicking the iron door, arousing metallic reverberations on the still, sullen air. Nothing happened so he looked around for somcthing ... anything ... that could be used to free him from this intolerable confinement. He clutched the urine-tub with both hands, dementedly beating it against the iron door until the bucket splintered into wooden fragments.

Outside in the Guardroom, men glanced uneasily at each other. Those not on stag and resting fervently hoped that something would be done to quieten the noisy sod, and that they would not be the ones ordered to do it. The Guard-Commander, reluctant to employ a restraining detail for fear someone would be hurt in the rough-house, set an anxious eye to the door spy-hole. He saw enough to warrant sending in the lance-corporal, four men and a strait-jacket.

The assembly of the restraining party in the passage outside, followed by the squeal of the key in the lock, caused Sanny to move from the door and stand passively in the centre of the small room. This was a great relief to the restraining party as they grouped around him, awkwardly fitting him into the strait-jacket. Though an inadequate soldier, Private Alexander's current mental condition bestowed upon him a degree of tactical guile more than sufficient to outwit the nervous party fumbling around him. Their vulnerable nearness and the open door beyond detonated a startling explosion of berserk savagery, strewing dazed and broken men around the confines of the cell. Bursting through the doorway and out into the passage, he felled the Guard-Commander before lumbering on to erupt into the Guardroom beyond. Grimly familiar with Hot Weather madness and shootings, men tumbled over each other in their frantic efforts to get out of the way. No hands were raised to prevent a rifle being snatched from the rack or a handful of cartridges from a box on the table.

Boy Farley, knowing the Scotsman's strength, had expected him to break out and had positioned himself by the doorway, diving out the moment Sanny appeared from the passage. Scuttling to the nearest bungalow, Farley lurked breathlessly behind the verandah corner, his eyes fixed on the Guardroom's shimmering outline. The familiar squat figure duly appeared and lurched down the steps. With a rifle in one hand and his trousers held up with the other, Sanny shambled awkwardly along towards the Aliwal Lines, his flapping boots setting up small clouds of dust.

Running as fast as he could, Boy Farley darted between the bungalows of Moodki and Ferozeshur Lines, into Aliwal Lines to the 5th Sub-Section's barrackroom. Taking the steps in a single bound, he leapt across the verandah and, brushing aside the tatty, projected himself into the dark room where men, unaware of the fuse lit beneath them, pursued the grooved routine of the Hot Weather Season. Clarioning above their chatter, the shrill, breathless young voice rang out. 'Big Sanny's gorn mad ... broken outta the Guardroom ... just behind me ... wiv rifle an' ammunition!'

Paralysed men gaped as the boy scampered nimbly to the doubtful shelter of his charpoy, then the room exploded in a top-of-the-voice hubbub of apprehensive speculation. It was immediately settled by the clatter of iron-tipped boots coming up the steps ... one ... two ... three. Across the verandah ... four ... five. The tatty-curtain swished .... he was among them. Their comrade, Private Alexander ... Big Sanny ... a massive swaying shadow. Noisily gulping at the air his slitted eyes blinked, desperately trying to adjust from the searing sun to the soft shadows of the barrackroom. Benumbed, the men gaped at the sweat-dripping, hate twisted face. They noted the blackened shirt was torn to the waist and the trousers concertinaing onto the dusty, laceless boots. Above all they noted the Snider rifle.

Unable to discern the Sergeant standing among the men in the middle of the room, Big Sanny broke the spell by lurching forward to thrust the lowered rifle barrel through the cubicle doorway, galvanising the men into precipitate action. Privates Birch and Coughlin, in synchronous leaps, took-off from their beds to vanish through nearby doorways. Private Saville, nearest to the intruder, flung his hands to his face and shrunk fearfully against the wall. The American Early, carrying a six-foot wooden table-top, dropped behind it in the space between his and Coughlin's charpoys. Private Kinrade, boot in hand, sunk into a half-crouch in his bed space. Others, with the soldiers innate urge to seek cover, flung themselves behind the meagre protection of the flimsy beds. Private Bell, his ears belaboured by Farley's dramatic warning, sank helplessly down on his charpoy, stunned by the vision of another Execution Parade, this time with his mate being led down the ranks, and being able to do nothing about it. Then Sanny, backing out of the cubicle, was standing over him. Bell jumped up, his hands stretching imploringly forward.

'Sanny! Gi' me the rifle!'

Blank-eyed and without recognition, the burly Scot contemptuously pushed Bell away; Kinrade, taking advantage of the diversion, leapt up, calling loudly as he flung the boot. 'Saville! Go on ... get him!'

Crouched against the wall, Saville shook his head, averted his face and sank lower. 'No ... no! I can't ... I can't!'

Cursing between his clenched teeth, Kinrade threw himself forward, colliding violently with Early who was struggling to rid himself of the cumbersome table-top. Sanny swung round, bringing the weapon to bear up the room. In a single swift movement Kinrade and Early leapt apart so that if one was hit the other would be on Sanny before he could reload. Then the Sergeant's voice froze them. 'Keep still everyone! Leave him to me!'

Approving Kinrade's efforts and reflecting that Saville would never make an officer, the Sergeant walked slowly from mid-room, holding his hand out for the rifle. Calm, assured and with no feeling of fear, the Sergeant remembered the time his poor, dead, little Timmy took up a stick with which to hit his sisters; he handed it over to his father when asked. It would be the same now, Alexander would give him the rifle because they were just like a family ... he was their father ... and Alexander would never fire at him. Thinking on these things the Sergeant was unprepared for the sudden crack of thunder and the lightning flash that hurled him into a pitch-black bottomless pit.

Before the shot's echo had died away, Kinrade and Early were on Sanny. The other men, discovering their courage a little too late, flung themselves into the melee. Resisting fiercely the big Scot was borne to the ground and held until the Guard-Commander and his men came panting in. They dragged away a dazed and hand-cuffed Private Alexander.

Knocked from his feet by the impact of a .577 iron headed bullet, fired at a two yard range with a muzzle velocity of 1,200 feet per second, the Sergeant lay on his back before an area discoloured by blood, brains and gobbets of flesh sprayed out from the left side of his face. The bullet carried on to plough into Bully Bulldog, the Sub-Section mascot, this day on Private Kinrade's bed-shelf. The brittle, dry clay model was shattered into dusty fragments.

Private Kinrade crossed himself. 'The only NCO I've ever respected ... the on'y bleedin' Englishman come to that! He cared for us bastards in the barrackroom ... but we did for him in the end. Come on Yank, let's get the poor bugger on his bed ... then we'll get back to so'jering ... with every man for his fuckin' self again.'

Boy Farley flung himself face down on his charpoy. Boys were allowed to cry.

GLOSSARY

Aggy chel: go on!

Arsty: slow down

Auparishtaka: fellatio

Babu:a native clerk in European service

Bazaar gup: gossip

Beehive: knapsack

Bhisti: native water-carrier. Accompanying regiments into action they were highly thought of. Immortalized by Kipling's *Gunga Din.*

Bibi: a woman

Black-strap: sorghum syrup

Bobbery: a row, argument or disturbance (from Hindustani)

Brogans: shoes

Bullock-Dak: a bungalow, a staging post on a recognised route at which travellers would rest overnight.

Bundook, bandook: a rifle

Canteen medals: beer stains on tunic breast

Canteen rat: an old soldier hanging around the canteen in the hope of being stood a drink

Cinch: look lively! Get on with it!

Coffee-cooler: a straggler

Cootergoosht: bad food. Hindustani for 'dog meat'

Dhobi-wallah: washerman

Ek dum : at once!

Fanti: mad (from Hindustani)

File: two men, a front-rank man and his rear-rank man

Feringhees: Englishmen

Going large a bit: misbehaving in the streets

Going on the shunt: drinking

Goojars: professional thieves

Hokee-mutt: drunk

Hum pica dada hi: pidgin Hindustani meaning 'I will pay for it'

Hunky: fine, magnificent

Jakes: latrines

Jildi: faster, quickly

Lunger: name given by other ranks to the long, slim 17,, Snider bayonet

Malum: do you understand?

Marrow: to beat

No. 9: a British military standardised purgative pill

Nullah: a ravine or watercourse

Pandy: a mutineer. All mutineers, regardless of caste, were known to the British soldier as 'Pandies', arising from Mangal Pande, a sepoy of the 34th Native Infantry who, on Sunday 29th March 1857 shot down his adjutant and sergeant-major. The first named mutineer he was tried and hanged.

Peddle-lead: shoot too fast

Pice: a copper coin, quarter of an anna

Pugaree: a strip of cloth, binding hat or turban, and falling down over the neck as protection against the sun

Puggled: insane, mad

Punkah-wallah: native boys who sat on verandahs pulling ropes attached to grass matting suspended in a room, thereby creating a gentle breeze

Rooti: bread. From Urdu *roti*

Shell fever: nervous paralysis before action

Sinkers: hard-tack biscuits

Sixes: British soldier's euphimistic name for Sikhs

Skedaddle: run away

Slap-jacks: pancakes

Sling the bat: talk pidgin English/Hindustani

Soor: pig

Sow-belly: bacon

Swaddy: a private soldier; derived from 18th century swad, swad-kin or swad-gill

Sweeper: low caste native carrying out menial tasks such as emptying latrines

Tatty: a fibre and straw door over which a a tatty-wallah boy would spray water in order to keep the air in the relatively cool

Tank: a pond or waterhole, sometimes surrounded by an ornamental wall or balustrade; often presented by a wealthy or illustrious local man as a memorial

Tope: a grove or clump of trees

Topkhana: artillery

Tulwar: curved native sword

Yoti: vagina, female sex organs

H.M. 131st REGIMENT of FOOT

Commanding Officer - Lieutenant-Colonel PEARSE-FRODSHAM
Walter John Howard; b.1810
First Appointment 1826; Lieut.1832; Captain 1856; Major 1858;
Lieutenant -Colonel 1865

Adjutant - Lieutenant SPROULE
Christopher Julian; b.1836
First Appointment 1856; Lieut. 1856

Regimental Sergeant-Major No.971 - Sergeant-Major ROBINSON VC
Walter George; b.1823
Date of Enlistment 1841 Age at Enlistment 18 Embarked for India 1857

Active Service - *Campaigns against Boers and Kaffirs, South Africa 1843-1852;Crimean War 1854/5; Indian Mutiny 1857/8; NW Frontier 1858; 64; 67; Ambela 1863.*

'C' COMPANY Left-Half

Commander - Captain FAGAN
Aubrey Hallam Maurice; b.1825
First Appointment 1645; Lieut. 1845; Captain 1858

Left-Half Commander - Lieutenant LAYDEN-HILL
Courtney Percival Lloyd; b.1845
Firts Appointment 1866; Lieut. 1866

No.3 SECTION 5th Sub-Section

Regimental Number:

1303 Sergeant OAKLEY, Benjamin. Age 31.
Age at Enlistment: 16 (1853): Embarked for India 1857
Indian Mutiny 1857/8; Ambela 1863; NW Frontier 1858; 1864; 1867

2872 Lance-Corporal MOCKFORD, Samuel. Age 39.
Age at Enlistment: 18 (1848): Embarked for India 1847
2nd Sikh War 1848/9; 2nd Burma War 1852; Indian Mutiny 1857/8; Persian War 1856/7;Ambela 1863; NW Frontier 1858; 1864; 1867

4051 Private ALEXANDER, William. Age 26.
Age at Enlistment: 19 (1861): Embarked for India 1863
NW Frontier 1864; 1867; Ambela 1863

4052 Private BELL, Timothy. Age 25
Age at Enlistment 18 (1861): Embarked for India 1863
NW Frontier 1864; 1867; Ambela 1863

3899 Private BIRCH, Ellis. Age 33
Age at Enlistment: 20 (1855): Embarked for India 1857
Indian Mutiny 1857/8: NW Frontier 1858; 1864; 1867; Ambela 1863

4566 Private COUGHLIN, Patrick. Age 41
Age at Enlisment: 21 (1848): Embarked for India 1848
2nd Sikh War 1848/9; 2nd Burma War 1852; Indian Mutiny 1857/8; Persian War 1856/7;Ambela 1863; NW Frontier 1858; 1864; 1867

3181 Private COX, Michael. Age 25
Age at Enlistment: 18 (1861): Embarked for India 1863
NW Frontier 1864; 1868; Ambela 1863

4375 Private DAVIES, Owen. Age 44
Age at Enlisment: 17 (1841): Embarked for India 1843
1st Sikh War 1845/6; 2nd Sikh War 1848/9; 2nd Burma War 1852; Indian Mutiny 1857/8; Persian War 1856/7;Ambela 1863; NW Frontier 1858; 1864; 1867

3907 Private EARLY, Martin. Age 28
Age at Enlisment: 26 (1866): Embarked for India 1866
NW Frontier 1867. Gettysburg and numerous other battles of the American Civil War

3395 Private FINNIGAN, Valentine. Age 33
Age at Enlisment: 19 (1854): Embarked for India 1857
Indian Mutiny 1857/8; Ambela 1863; NW Frontier 1858; 1864; 1868

3704 Private HEBDON, Edward . Age 23
Age at Enlisment: 20 (1865): Embarked for India 1867
No active service

3785 Private KINRADE, Richard. Age 27
Age at Enlisment: 24 (1865): Embarked for India 1867
No active service

4085 Private PERKINS, William. Age 32
Age at Enlisment: 18 (1854): Embarked for India 1857
Indian Mutiny 1857/8; Ambela 1863; NW Frontier 1858; 1864; 1867

3768 Private SAVILLE, Thomas. Age 21
Age at Enlisment: 19 (1866): Embarked for India 1867
No active service

3596 Private wright, John. Age 40
Age at Enlisment: 18 (1846): Embarked for India 1848
2nd Sikh War 1848/9; 2nd Burma War1852; Persian War 1856/7; Indian Mutiny 1857/8; NW Frontier 1858; 1864; 1867; Ambela 1863

<u>Men Attached for Rations and Accomodation</u>

4567 Private MORT Charles (Bandsman). Age 38.
Age at Enlistment: 11 (1841): Born in Regiment
Boy service in India - *1st Sikh War 1845/6; 2nd Sikh War 1848/9; 2nd Burma War 1852 Indian Mutiny 1857/8; Persian War 1856/7;Ambela 1863; NW Frontier 1858; 1864; 1867*

4195 Private (Pioneer) HOLMES,James. Age 34.
Age at Enlistment: 18 (1852): Embarked for India 1857
Indian Mutiny 1857/8; Ambela 1863; NW Frontier 1858; 1864; 1867

1875 Boy (Drummer) FARLEY, Joshua. Age 14.
Age at Enlistment: 10 (1864): Born in Regiment
Boy service in India - *NW Frontier 1867*